HAUNTING MEMORIES

"The coroner's not ready to call it an accident. He doesn't like the idea that guns go off by themselves," Sheriff Truitt said.

Gale crossed her legs and studied her tennis shoe. He was waiting for her to say it, waiting for her to be the one to acknowledge what had really happened in that room. Well, why not, she thought bitterly. When you have a problem, call in an expert. And God knows, in matters such as this . . .

"You think it was suicide." Even to herself, her voice sounded flat.

Truitt jerked his head up. "Hell, no," he said. "I've known the man for twenty-five years. Martin had a problem, he solved it. He wasn't the suicidal type."

"The suicidal type." Her hands were so cold. The fingers were suddenly thinner and the skin drier, as they were in winter when their summer plumpness had gone away. Her wedding ring dropped easily to her knuckle. "So what you're saying . . ."

"Someone killed him."

"Teri Holbrook writes with grace and wit and with a keen eye for the small details that so enhance a story."
—Margaret Maron, Edgar Award winner

The Grass Widow

Teri Holbrook

BANTAM BOOKS
New York Toronto London Sydney Auckland

THE GRASS WIDOW
A Bantam Crime Line Book / December 1996

ISBN-0-553-56860-4
Published simultaneously in the United States and Canada

Bantam Books are published by Bantam Books, a division of Bantam
Doubleday Dell Publishing Group, Inc. Its trademark, consisting of
the words "Bantam Books" and the portrayal of a rooster, is Regis-
tered in U.S. Patent and Trademark Office and in other countries.
Marca Registrada. Bantam Books, 1540 Broadway, New York, New
York 10036.

PRINTED IN THE UNITED STATES OF AMERICA

RAD   10 9 8 7 6 5 4 3 2

To my father Gene
who wove the Not-Olly stories,
and my mother Jann
who carried me for nine months
beneath her heart,
reading like a hungry woman

Acknowledgments

If it takes a village to raise a child, it takes a village to write a novel as well. I wish to thank family and friends for their patience, insight and support. For technical assistance, I thank the following: Major Al Yarbrough of the Walton County, Georgia Sheriff's Office; Sergeant Teresa Race of the Conyers, Georgia Police Department; Mark Kopenen, M.D. and Jeffrey Smith, M.D. of the Fulton County Medical Examiner's Office. Thanks as well to Nancy Love for her unerring advice; Casey Blaine, who held the lamp and urged me forward; and the men of Embry Hills United Methodist Church, who spent the wee hours one morning demonstrating their method of authentic Southern barbecue. All mistakes and embellishments are my own.

The Grass Widow

Prologue

Malcolm Hinson saw it first, hanging from the tree like a piece of cotton cloth. He would have passed it by, too, figuring it for an old sheet whipped from somebody's porch rail and caught half-hidden in this tangle of pines, if it hadn't been for the tiny curve of black shoe that peeked from beneath the cloth's edge, pointing at him, blinking in the buckshot rays of the sun.

He ran the three quarters of a mile to Parrish's house. Together the two young men sprinted back through the field, the spikes of uncut fescue tearing at their legs. "Maybe we should bring the ladder, maybe we should," Malcolm panted. But Parrish kept running, his boots dread whispers in the tall, breaking stalks.

The stand of pines was a broad one, and when they reached it, Parrish raced along its front, frantically seeking white amid the shades of green and the dark plugs of bark and cone. He returned to Malcolm.

"Where is she, goddammit? Where is she, Malcolm?"

Malcolm stood with his head thrown back, his jaw jutting forward. "I swear to God, Parrish. I swear to God."

Parrish grabbed him by the coat, and Malcolm shut his eyes, waiting for his friend to pummel his face. Instead, Parrish slumped to the ground, his fist still coiled in Malcolm's collar, and the two men lay in a heap, breathing heavy and sobbing.

A week later it was a Eppie Falcon's turn. On the first sunny afternoon after three days of rain, she stripped her two babies of their pants, collected the colander from the cupboard, and snapped beans in the yard while the children played bare-bottomed in the mud. She kept her attention divided—one eye on the beans plinking into the colander and the other on the children—so at first she thought a neighbor stood by the side of her house, right on the corner, watching the children silently.

But the seconds grew, and finally Eppie turned her head to shout halloo. Later she would tell people she went all goose-pimply, that someone walked over her grave and she couldn't speak. But in truth she was fascinated. There by the blue-budded hydrangeas stood a round-and-round woman, feet planted in a deep mud puddle, her gaze trained on the babies. Eppie knew at once the woman wasn't real. It wasn't her face, so pale and unearthly; it wasn't her hair, all black and wild. It was the hem of her white nightie, floating in the red-brown water without even the beginnings of a stain.

After that there were many sightings—by the cotton mill, at the church, on the iron railroad tracks that bisected the town. Jeffrey Peterson saw her in the window of the tiny photography studio on the main road, posing with a lily held to her cheek. She looked downright peaceful, he told his mother. Not like in life, where Linnie Glynn Cane had been the angriest female he had ever seen. Suicide might be a sin, but it had at least given that woman some tranquility.

He didn't tell his mother this, but tranquility was a far cry from what had been on Linnie's features when he'd first found her dangling from the pecan tree. Her face had been purple and bulging, her tongue black, the skirt of her yellow dress darkened with urine. Jeffrey had vomited at her feet, his retching so violent that the brown leather shoes, swaying inches off the ground, tapped him on the forehead. He knew as he cut the rope from beneath her chin that her death had not been tranquil. Something wrathful had possessed Linnie Cane and made her slip that noose around her neck. Something raging had spurred her feet to kick and her limbs to quiver in death.

So if her afterlife wasn't exactly dormant, the whole damn town was grateful it was at least benign. As the sightings increased, attendance at the Statlers Cross Methodist Church surged. A Baptist church was constituted. Widowed women stayed at each other's houses; single women canceled their plans to move to the city. Marriages picked up and more babies were born. All in all, it was a good year for Statlers Cross.

Parrish Singleton drew into himself. He spent long hours in the fields or walked along the main road and stared into the gullies. He'd go home, caked in orange dirt, and sit at the kitchen table. His fingernails grew thick. His thoughts grew small. And he grieved.

I guess I know'd it was a person by the color of her hair, but I couldn't have told otherwise. She was layin' across the railroad tracks, all cut to pieces. I started hollerin', but when I got to the tracks, I noticed there weren't no blood—just a dress and some long brown hair, tossed on the tracks like a bag of cat bones. But then the wind blew, and her hair moved, and she looked up at me and smiled.

—Matthew Langley,
    Statlers Cross postal worker, 1927

1

STATLERS CROSS, GEORGIA
1996

The fish house sat approximately twenty feet from the edge of Martin Cane's pond, on a little incline of grass that would have delighted children with its downhill roll if in the end it didn't deposit them in a soup of scum and muddy water. Martin had built the fish house himself the summer he turned thirty, when the heat from the big house, combined with the squalls of his infant daughter, had caused him one day to lift the blender from the kitchen counter and drive it through the cabinet. His wife Cammy, the baby on her hip, had looked in silence at the splintered door. *Say something,* he had yelled. *You know damn well it was the baby I wanted to smash through a wall.* She had leveled her eyes at him. *Go away,* she had said evenly. *Go do something with your hands. And don't come back until you're in control.*

He left for two weeks, sleeping by the pond in a pup tent and working late into the night hammering two-by-fours until he had the frame of a small building. He wanted to be able to hose it clean, so he left a one-inch gap between the bottom of the wooden frame and the cement floor. And he wanted the structure airy to combat the searing Georgia summers, so instead of boards he stapled wire screen halfway up three sides. Five years later he added a sink, and ten years after that, electricity and a stove. But in the beginning, the fish house was nothing more than a handwrought sanctuary, his retreat from the world when he felt like putting his fist through somebody's face.

Martin stood in the fish house now and stared through the wire at the pond. To the left of the pond a pack of men in light cotton shirts and baggy jeans sweated over a barbecue pit and a pair of roasting pigs. Far to his right he could hear the grunts of men erecting tents on his land and detect the sweet odor of grass as it ripped beneath their shoes. But mainly he smelled cologne. He didn't need to turn around to recognize the man who had carried it into his sanctuary.

"Martin, are you prepared?"

The fragrance was spicy, like a woman's fingers when she baked. His daughter Sill had snide names for the man's cologne: the Preacher's Patchouli, the Savior's Sweet Scent. But Martin didn't put much stock in what his daughter said. Sill was an abnormal concoction. A lost soul.

"It's nearing time, Martin. People will start arriving soon. Are you ready?"

Martin listed forward, his nose inches from the

wire screen. He had built the barbecue pit following a
rage, too. It had always struck him as ironic that a project started in so much anger could result in so many
blessings. He watched as two men poked tongs into the
cinder block pit and lifted a small pig from its grate
above the embers. They carefully rested it atop a thick
wooden board anchored to the top of the pit. Through
the wire, Martin could discern the animal's parched
flesh. It looked strangely dressed with its ears and tail
wrapped in damp cotton strips. He had given the
roasting instructions himself. *Don't let the ears on the
little one burn. It'll look unnatural if you do. And put
rocks in its mouth and belly. Otherwise it'll wither up
and the women'll have a fit if it's too ugly for their vines
and fruit. People from all over the country come to this
shindig for the real McCoy, boys. Let's make 'em
believe they've found it.*

Now the pig, tipped in swaddling clothes, looked
unnatural anyway. It lay on the wooden board like a
crisped baby.

He heard impatient shuffling behind him. "Martin?
Where is your mind at? What in the world's wrong with
you?"

Martin turned and settled his eyes on the lanky
man in the doorway. "I'm gonna be honest with you,
Ryan. This sounded like a good idea when we planned
it. I'm just not sure about it anymore."

Ryan Teller gave a snort, not, Martin thought, a
particularly attractive act from a man of God.

"Of course it's a good idea, Martin. The best idea.
What's the key to any event? Crowds of people. And
they'll come. We've heightened the show. A little music,
a few games, a lot of religion. They'll be here, buddy,
'cause you're so damned good at what you do."

Teller moved to the side of the table, close enough
for Martin to catch the faint odor of his body beneath
the cologne. Despite the beat of the fan paddles overhead, beads of sweat plumped along his hairline. Teller
smiled, and his lips glided over his teeth like eels.

"Did I ever tell you about the first time I heard of Statlers Cross, Martin? Five years ago I was reading the *Atlanta Journal-Constitution*, and there it was, on the upper right-hand side, clear across the page: 'Praise the Lord, It's an All-Night Pig-Pickin'.' I punched my finger right through the middle of the paper, I got so excited. A town with enough sense to preserve an old-fashioned church barbecue and singing. What could be more perfect?"

Teller's face was suddenly grim. "Then I forgot all about it. I was too busy doing Man's work. But eventually the Lord found me and guided me here. He said, 'Ryan, give up your $150,000 advertising job in Atlanta, sell your expensive cars, become a minister. I'll find a way to get you to Statlers Cross.' And He did it. Why, Martin? 'Cause of you, brother."

From inside the main house, a phone jangled faintly. Martin's throat constricted. Silently, he counted to eight. If it was for him, it would take eight seconds or whoever answered to register the information, ask the caller to wait, walk to the back door, and call his name. A prayer might have been more effective, but he had learned that prayer was too close to panic. Better to focus and count.

At nine seconds he relaxed. He shoved his hands into the pockets of his jeans and sighed. "Don't think we're not grateful, Ryan. I'm just worn-out. We been working on those damn pigs for nineteen hours straight." He shrugged. "You're right, of course. It's perfect."

Ryan grinned. "There you go, buddy. The devil's wearing you out. But you keep pushing him away. Everything's in my car. After the gospel singers finish, we'll have our turn."

The preacher slipped from the fish house and headed to the western part of the lawn where members of the youth Sunday school class were rolling out barrels for the cold drinks. His cologne lingered. *Never trust a minister who smells prettier than your wife,*

Daddy. Sill had said it laughing, but her eyes had been like marble.

From the barbecue pit a man yelled. "Martin! Big one's done. Come take a look at her!"

Martin banged open the fish house door and strode toward the rising smoke. As he approached, the pack of men broke apart. Cooper Langley, one scrawny leg hiked onto the wall of the pit, grinned and slapped Martin on the shoulder.

"Whatcha say, Martin? Looks good this year, don't she?"

The pig weighed forty pounds—not enough to feed the hundreds of people expected but enough to keep the mystique of an authentic Southern ritual. Funny what a little good press could do for a place. Twenty-odd years ago candidate Jimmy Carter had stopped at a church pig-picking in a spit on the map called Statlers Cross, and the national press corp had gone wild. Every June since, the suburbanites and city dwellers had packed the fields, looking for the quaint and true. Never mind that most of the pork, 2000 pounds of it, had been cooked yesterday by a restaurant over in Walton County. Never mind that the homemade biscuits had been frozen for weeks. Anything for the work of the Lord. Martin smiled broadly and returned Langley's slap.

"She looks fine. Heck of a long day, fellas, but I'd say it was worth it." He gestured at the smaller pig. "Why don't you two younger boys carry the little one over to the food table? It'll work as a centerpiece. As for Mama here, let's get the show on the road."

On the ground lay a cloth feed sack. Martin reached inside and pulled out a single-bit axe.

"Wanna let her cool a bit?" Langley asked.

Martin shook his head. "It's getting near time and the women are waiting in the kitchen to pull the meat off. Besides, it'll be nightfall before the dang thing cools off out here, it's so damn hot."

Langley picked up a pair of cooking mitts and

pulled them on. "I'll hold her, Martin. The rest of you, stand back."

He pressed his hands into the large pig's haunches and carefully turned her on her side. With the mitts firm against the belly and spine, he nodded to Martin. "Go ahead."

Martin lifted the axe over his head and brought it down with such force the blade bit into the board. The pig's neck severed cleanly, the head sending up a shower of ash and embers as it rolled into the pit well. Langley bent down and grabbed it by the snout.

"My grandmother could've made a heck of a stew outta this," he said.

"Mine, too," said Martin. "But Ella doesn't like to look at it. Toss it back behind the pen for me, will you, Coop? I'll put it with the rest of the parings once the women finish. Right now I got a load of things to take care of. And if I could get a couple of you fellas to carry this swine into the kitchen . . ."

As the men trundled away with their load, Martin sucked in a breath thick as gauze. It was too damn hot. During the week, the thermometer had soared past ninety, reaching temperatures usually reserved for the dead of August. And it wasn't the type of heat that disappeared quickly—with evening coming, the air still wrapped around Martin as if to bury him. Maybe no one will come, he thought. Maybe they'll stay home in front of their air conditioners, and all of Ryan's plans will be for nothing. But the nausea in his belly told him he was a fool. Ryan would get his multitude. That's why God had called him. Ryan Teller was a bulldozer for the Lord.

Statlers Cross was a place of grass and roofs—this was what Gale Grayson decided when she was five years old. Atlanta, where she lived with her grandmother Ella, was woolly with ivy and had hard buildings. In Statlers Cross the country buildings sagged beneath her feet. The fields were blond and wide, and the orange gullies split like lips. But the queer part was a long grassy hump that cut the town in two, leaving only roofs visible on the other side.

At six Gale discovered the abandoned railroad track atop the hump. Ella's sister Nora walked her down the gravel drive of her house and up the slope until they stood on the tarry ties, dandelions knocking at their shoes. She led Gale to the end of the tracks where the hump ended abruptly, and she described how, many years ago, trains from the Southern Railway Company had wheezed to a stop in front of her house. The trains were like snakes, Nora said, fat from swallowing, the air around them hot as animals' breath. Gale thought the air in Statlers Cross was plenty hot without the trains, but she never said so to Nora. Nora had no children, and she tolerated her great-niece's summer visits on the condition the girl walk quietly, eat well, and not argue.

It wasn't until she was ten that Gale realized the track wasn't her aunt's personal property. After all, didn't Nora wear a hat and stockings every day, as if she were a lady at a train station? Didn't she wander through the echoey, brick house and check the clocks by her wristwatch? Didn't she, to be blunt, have the voice of a train whistle and hair as bulging and black as a puff of smoke? But the track had never been meant for her aunt, or for the generations of family preceding her. Instead the train had stopped for the cotton mill on the other side of the tracks, where it deposited unprocessed bolls and loaded up finished cloth before reversing its direction and heading back through the heart of Calwyn County.

Gale ran her hand over the brown and indigo coverlet airing on the grass. Now, at thirty, she knew Statlers Cross was more than its parts—more than the raised tracks, or the truncated buildings, or the mill, now stone ruins, hidden from view behind the grassy divide. It was more than the curious Alden house behind her, sitting like red origami in a field. Statlers Cross was home, and she, the returning warrior, had just fucked up royally.

Behind her she heard a growl.

"Mama," Katie Pru said. "I know what jag-wires eat."

Gale pressed her palm over a white blotch on the coverlet, the musty smell of old cloth combined with bleach huffing into the air. "Do you, ladybug? That's great. I'm proud of you."

The blotch on the coverlet wasn't small—when she stretched her palm to its fullest width, white veins crept past both sides. It had been a lark: She had glanced up at the coverlet hanging over the staircase, noticed the familiar dark spot and decided, why not? Somewhere she had read that bleach, salt, and a little liquid soap would take out any stain, and indeed it had. Not only was the dark spot gone, so was the aged dye beneath it.

"Mama, I said I know what jag-wires eat."

"I know, baby. That's wonderful."

To make matters worse, she wasn't supposed to be at home. She was supposed to be at Martin and Cammy's house helping with the barbecue, but she had delayed, postponing the heat, the bugs, and other more human irritants. She told herself she wouldn't be missed—after all, she had been gone for six years, too long to have retained the knack for slapping coleslaw on a paper plate.

She lifted her palm from the coverlet and grimaced. She could swear the bleach was slowly saturating the entire piece. By the time her grandmother Ella came home, the coverlet would be pure white and smelling like a bathroom stall. Gale groaned. Why wasn't the dye colorfast? More to the point, why hadn't she checked? She was a historian, for God's sake. How much stupider could she be?

"Mama, jag-wires—"

"I know, Katie Pru. Please. I need to decide what to do here. Just a second and you can tell me."

The stain had been made nineteen years earlier, when she and her cousin Sill had decided to use chocolate syrup to settle a preteen brouhaha. Ella had been furious.

"Your great-grandmother Linnie Cane spun the yarn for that coverlet herself, Miss Sill. She dyed it and wove it, too." She lifted the corner of the coverlet and yanked it at Sill. "See? She wove her 'L' in it. She was proud of her work. It's hung over those stairs for nearly fifty years and here you monsters go and ruin it."

The punishment had been deceptively lenient: The girls were to turn cotton balls into thread using Linnie's antique drop bobbin. But the thread was too thin and the bobbin too heavy—every time they dropped the bobbin into a spin, the strand broke. After an hour they were both in tears. Ella watched with satisfaction. "Maybe this will teach you a little respect for a woman's efforts," she had said.

Gale stared ruefully at the spot. God, what method would her grandmother devise to punish her for this?

"Jag-wires eat eye shadow and lipstick."

Gale twisted around. Katie Pru stared at her mother, her lips tucked in a pout. Next to her stood a life-size iron jaguar, his spots long since covered with black Rust-Oleum spray. An orange scarf was wrapped around his head like a turban, and from one ear drooped a strand of pink beads. Blobs of thick red goo spackled his teeth, and blue fingerprints dotted his face like liver spots. Scattered around Katie Pru's feet were half a dozen clotted lipstick tubes and empty compacts.

"Kathleen Prudence! Where in the world did you get all that?"

"The jag-wire got 'em."

"Katie Pru. Where did you get those?"

"He found them in Grandma Ella's drawer."

Gale closed her eyes. Terrific. Perhaps she could explain the coverlet as a well-intended error, but convincing Ella that it was mere oversight and not rampant irresponsibility that allowed a four-year-old to pilfer her makeup and feed it to a lawn ornament was beyond Gale's resources. This, she thought, is what you get, Gale Lynn, when you try to tell God you don't want to serve up His side dishes.

"All right, Katie Pru," she said wearily. "Go inside and wash your hands. Then get some paper towels from the kitchen. Let's clean this mess up before somebody thinks that jaguar's been out hunting Mary Kay ladies."

"Jag-wircs don't hunt merry gay ladies. They . . ."

The warning look Gale shot her must have made an impact, for Katie Pru dashed up the brick stairs and disappeared into the house. Gale collapsed on top of the coverlet and spread her arms; the rough wool scratched her skin.

"Please, God," she groaned. "We gotta get out of here."

The line was more cuss than prayer. When she and Katie Pru had first arrived from England, she had believed their stay with Ella would be for a couple of months, long enough for Gale to catch her breath, find a home, and start work on her third book, an examination of rural women's diaries. Realization had hit hard: On her writer's income alone, she could never afford a house *and* a babysitter *and* a car.

Rubber soles scrunched on the brick steps. A wad of paper towels landed on her face.

"Here, Mama," Katie Pru said. "You'll need these."

Gale laughed. "Oh, no, ma'am. *You'll* need those." She pulled herself up. "Tear off a couple of towels and start wiping up the goop. And Katie Pru, don't go into people's drawers without asking them first."

Katie Pru grabbed an armful of towels and turned away, but not before Gale heard her mumble something about "jag-wires" and "some 'spectable clothes." Gale shook her head. Ella's influence. If she wasn't careful, her grandmother would have the child wearing pageant dresses and Mary Janes.

"Jag-wires don't need hats," Katie Pru said, removing the jaguar's scarf. "Girls need hats."

Gale grinned. She slapped a mosquito on her bare arm, and a drop of crimson spurted onto her palm. Absently she reached forward and wiped her hand on Linnie's coverlet.

She stared at the new blotch in disbelief. Shit. The blood was spare, but visible.

She darted toward the jaguar and grabbed a paper towel from between his legs. Pressing it into the drop of blood, she sighed. The color lightened only minimally.

"Katie Pru," she said. "I believe this is a sign God wants us up to our elbows in coleslaw."

The phone rang and Martin started counting. At nine seconds he glanced at his watch. It was six-thirty P.M. He looked across the grounds, taking in the tents, the risers, the strings of lights with electrical cords that snaked through the air and curved over the windowsills of his house. No drink table, no dessert table. He started toward the food tent. Dammit all, they were behind schedule. People would start arriving within the hour. It was all too much. And it was all on him.

Five tables stretched end to end beneath the khaki tent. As he stepped up to the first table, his foot kicked an opened box of utensils, sending scores of plastic forks sliding across the grass. He slammed his fist onto the table. The metal safety catches on its legs clinked. The pig in the middle of the table shivered, the dried cloth strips on its ears swaying like curls. A teenager loitering by the tent gawked and took a step backward.

Martin managed a smile. "Sorry, son," he breathed. "It's all the pressure of this thing. You know, I'm thinking of turning it over to you young people next year." He wiped his hand across his mouth. "Don't let on you saw me lose my cool. Everyone might think this job's too much work and I'll never get rid of it."

The youth smiled uneasily, then turned and trotted off to his friends. Martin watched as the boy shoved his hands into his pockets and, talking, shrugged in his direction.

Jesus Christ. Martin opened his mouth to ask forgiveness for the sacrilege, but thought better of it. *It's not a sacrilege at all, Lord. It's an invocation. You've given me this burden. Now what the hell do you suggest I do with it?*

The phone rang. Taking a handkerchief from his pocket, he mopped his brow. One, two . . .

At nine the back door popped open. His cousin Ella stuck her head out.

"Martin! You've got a phone call."

Martin's mouth went dry. "Take a message," he hollered. "I'm busy out here."

"I tried. She says to tell you it's county business."

County business. Martin's laugh seared his lungs. *Push the devil away, Ryan? Not this time. He's come to ride my back, kicking my sides with his heels all the while.*

She's a darn fine dancer for a dead woman.
— Willy Peterson, at breakfast
with his wife, Elizabeth, 1931

2

Miss Linnie used to visit me at night, gliding down the
hallway, hair glowing like a lamppost. I was just a blur
of a girl, no more than six or seven, and it was years
later that I learned she was dark headed. To me, her
hair was a light, drawn in a puff around her face and
shining as if a socket sat on the top of her skull and
she'd screwed in a lightbulb and flicked it on. Of
course, that was before we had electricity here, but
when I think of it, that's how I remember her, like she
had turned on a lamp in her hair, so that all the strands
gleamed and her face was left in shadow.

She reminded me of Guinevere. I saw pictures in

my sister's book about King Arthur, and Miss Linnie looked to me like Guinevere dressed in a gown. I could see her through my bedroom door, sliding down the hall, pausing in front of my parents' room, then my sister's, then finally stopping to peer into mine. She'd twist her head from side to side, like she was trying to direct some of that light from her hair onto my bed. But no light ever shone in—it just stayed balled around her head as if the hood of her gown had turned to embers. She'd keep at it a while, the light bobbing in the black hall, until she finally stilled herself and disappeared into the back of the house. One time, I got up and followed her, but her feet, not having to touch the ground, were faster than mine.

I told my daddy about her once, and he just shook his head and told me to leave her alone. I said that she was kind, and a little sad, and he said, no, she was evil, ghosts were evil. I said, but she wanted to check on me, she twisted her head back and forth so that the light would shine into my room, and he just said, no, Zilah, she wasn't twisting her head to see you better. She was braying like an angry mule, trying to get that cursed rope from around her neck.

The corner of an unopened envelope slipped beneath Zilah Greene's fingernail, and she dropped it onto the kitchen counter. She recalled the ghost at the strangest times, such as when she thought of her daddy bent over his sawhorse, that dirty fedora pushed back on his head. Or when she spotted a scrap of fabric the pearly color of her own crib linens. Or now, as she stared out her kitchen window at the little Grayson girl, dressed in red and lolling on top of Ella Alden's ugly iron cat. All her life she had heard Miss Linnie ghost stories, but she never believed them. Having seen the ghost herself, she learned to recognize the lie.

She didn't know why she thought of the ghost now. Perhaps it was the orange scarf, so like a light, tied over the little girl's hair; or perhaps it was the child's dark eyes, from a distance set in her fair skin like bruises. She didn't try to guess. The images in her head jumbled around more and more lately, and it only confused her to try to sort her mind.

The envelope had landed in a drop of water. An ink drawing scribbled on the corner bled across the blue paper. She picked up the envelope and pressed the wet spot against her apron. Zilah had started watching the little girl six months earlier, when she and her mother had arrived in Statlers Cross. Zilah had been standing at the kitchen window when a car drove up Ella's gravel drive and deposited them on the paving-stone walkway, literally at the mouth of the growling cat. They had looked like two burnt shrubs, dressed in black and standing hand in hand in front of the huge red house. She had clicked her tongue. "Law, another Alden woman come to grief. I swear, I do think that family's cursed sometimes."

Barry had disagreed. *The Lord gave man free will, Zilah. That woman made her own decisions. She's got a helluva lot of gall coming back after what she's been party to.*

She's a poor widow, Barry. With a child.

Poor widow, my ass. You're being a foolish old woman, Zilah Mae. Her husband was a terrorist. He killed himself in a church sanctuary, for God's sakes. I hope she's not thinking she'll find forgiveness here. Nobody's likely to shrive a murderer's widow.

Where else can she go? Zilah had wondered. If we don't forgive her, who will? But Zilah had been silent. Barry hadn't understood the Aldens the way she did. He had always been too busy with his hardware store in the middle of town. He hadn't kept the vigil at the kitchen window.

Outside, Katie Pru looped her arms around the cat's neck and slid off his back until she dangled upside down. The scarf fell to the ground. Immediately she dropped to her feet and scooped it up. Glancing at Zilah, she wrapped it around her head again.

Zilah smiled and lifted her hand. Katie Pru, her arms pressed to her side, wriggled her fingers.

She supposed it was their secret, hers and the child's. Gale stood about ten feet from her daughter, her peculiar black-and-white hair swinging as she folded the coverlet. She never looked in Zilah's direction. And why should she? To her the little blue house on the other side of the wire fence was a workers' house. Zilah's own father had tended crops for the Alden family through the Depression and had overseen the maintenance on the ungainly Alden house until he died. She knew too well that such arrangements bred a lopsided fascination.

The water on the envelope had dried. Zilah could tell now that the drawing was a dinosaur, squares covering its belly like patches. She held the envelope close to her face and examined the foreign stamps. Queen Elizabeth—Gale Grayson had received a letter from England. The postal service had begun assigning numbered street addresses to everyone in Georgia, but Statlers Cross was still a rural route. Mail was delivered reliably as long as the regular mailman was on duty. She had noticed this morning, however, that a woman drove the truck. She lightly ran her fingertip over the dinosaur. Even it looked foreign. An American dinosaur would have looked more ferocious and less embarrassed. If the letter was for the mother, surely the drawing was for the child. Whoever this writer was, maybe he and Katie Pru also shared a secret.

A buzzer sounded and Zilah quickly grabbed a potholder. She lifted a hissing blackberry cobbler from the oven, crunching the letter against the hot bottom of the dish.

"Law," she whispered. "You truly are a foolish old woman, Zilah Greene." Oh well. She would tell Gale the woman in the mail truck had crammed it into her box. Neither one would ever know.

She slid the envelope into her apron pocket. Even though she would see Gale at the barbecue, she would wait and give her the letter at home. Any excuse to visit the Alden place. She loved that saucy old house with its curious colors and pointy top. Sometimes she felt she could stand at the kitchen window and stare at it forever. When Nora Alden was still alive, Zilah would walk next door and sit with her for hours listening to the tales—about how Nora and her sister Ella had married brothers who never spoke to each other past the age of sixteen, how the house had been built after the Civil War by Nora's grandfather, who wanted the bricks the color of blood and the roof the shape of lances to remind everyone of his brother killed at Chickamauga, how her grandfather had wanted to leave the house to a son. . . . Then, invariably, the stories would drift to Miss Linnie.

Zilah had told Nora about the ghost only once. The older woman had flushed with anger. Miss Linnie had been Nora and Ella's aunt, and Nora wouldn't tolerate any notions of ghosts.

"Zilah, you were just a child fed by too many hysterical old coots. Linnie hanged herself. Her body was cut down and buried in the family plot down Praterton Road. I'll take you there myself if you want to see it. You want to believe she's in purgatory or hell or wherever, it's fine with me. But one thing you can be sure of, Linnie Glynn Cane is not walking this earth."

No, *ma'am*, Zilah had thought. *She isn't walking the earth. Her feet don't come near to touching the ground.*

In the middle of the night, I heard squealing in the coop. I grabbed my hat and my shotgun and went out there, and what do you think I saw? It was her, all right. She was sitting on the roost, a dead hen in one hand and feathers flying from her mouth. She disappeared, but the chickens ain't been right since. They cluck all night, and their eggs are a funny color.

—Jim Jenkins, during a conversation at the Statlers Cross General Store, 1933

3

Gale grasped the handle of Katie Pru's plastic red wagon and, skirting the gully running alongside the road, navigated transport and child onto Martin's yard. It was a good thing the social took place in the evening—at seven-thirty, the heat was dissipating somewhat, and the walk, which under daytime conditions would have left Gale red faced and irritable, instead relaxed her. Whistling tunelessly, she pulled the wagon over the uneven ground, compelling Katie Pru to clutch the sides.

The retreating sun cast a peach tint over the outlying fields and the white clapboard of the two-story farm house. In front of the porch two badminton poles hoisted the message *Southern Gospel Singing and Barbecue, $4.99 a Plate.* A row of vehicles chugged past, stopping on the other side of the driveway to follow a yellow-vested Sunday school teacher's parking instructions. Families sauntered toward the tents. Well, well, thought Gale. God must be pleased. Once again Martin Cane lifts his eyes unto the hills and delivers the goods.

After depositing the wagon by the porch, she took Katie Pru by the hand, mounted the wooden steps and entered the house. Immediately, she grasped her daughter's shoulders and steered her to a corner. If any of the outside's summer lethargy had leaked through the clapboard, it had been duly trampled. Martin's house rumbled with activity. Females—brassieres and serving spoons fronting their chests like armor—genteelly shouldered one another into walls as they hurried from room to room. The aroma of maple syrup and vinegar filled the air, occasionally punctuated by an imprudent dose of Jean Naté.

Katie Pru tugged on Gale's hand. "No jag-wire's gonna hunt them," she whispered.

Gale laughed aloud. "I think you're right, punkin. What do you say we wait until the waters part before looking for Grandma Ella?"

If the waters didn't exactly part for Maralyn Nash, they certainly wobbled—a fitting enough obeisance to Ella Alden's oldest daughter. Maralyn emerged from the kitchen and loomed in the doorway, so tall her teased blond hair missed the frame by mere inches.

"Ladies!" She paused until the hum settled. "It's nearly seven-thirty and we've already got a hundred people waiting. I've given Myra instructions to start collecting the money, which means all those folks are going to be passing onto the grounds soon. Paper goods are out there, meat's on its way, but we need beans, slaw, and sauces in place, pronto. If that's your job, move into the kitchen, grab a bowl, and exit through the back door." She placed her hands on her hips. "And don't forget to keep checking the level of the bowls. Last year we had complaints about not replacing them fast enough. Now, ladies, let's go."

Maralyn pressed her six-foot frame against the jamb and let the line of women bob into the kitchen. For proper church barbecue attire, Maralyn had selected a safari walking-shorts set, complete with hiking boots and a necklace resembling an elephant rifle.

She reeled around and shouted over the retreating line of heads. "Oh, I just remembered one more thing, ladies. As always, there's a possibility the press will show up. *Please* turn on the charm."

As the last of the women passed into the kitchen, Maralyn strode down the hallway, making a show of checking her watch.

"An hour late. Not bad. Means Mother's asked where the hell you were only twenty times."

"I got tied up."

"Huh." Maralyn knelt and pulled Katie Pru to her in a bear hug. "And I bet the culprit wants to give Aunt Maralyn some sugar. Lord, Katie Pru, it seems like forever since I've seen you. I've got to get out of Atlanta and visit the home place more often." She grinned as the child squirmed free from her grasp, then looked up at Gale, her face serious. "Late or not, I'm glad you're here. I'm afraid we're going to see fireworks tonight."

"Why?"

Maralyn hauled herself to her feet. "Sill called Martin earlier. She's coming. With Faith."

Gale stared. "What? Has she lost her mind?"

"Says she wants Martin to accept them."

"Good for her," Gale said dryly. "But has anyone suggested that maybe a church barbecue is not the place to ask one's Bible-thumping father to accept one's alternate lifestyle?"

"I think that was the subtext of Martin's reply. But you know Sill."

Gale shook her head. "Jesus, Maralyn, she's twenty-nine years old."

"So? I'm fifty-six. Think I've stopped rebelling?"

Gale opened her mouth to answer when a voice, drawled and briery, sounded from the end of the hall.

"Gale. Where in the blessed hell have you been?"

If Wes Craven cast Barbara Bush in a film, Gale thought, this would be the result. In the kitchen doorway Ella Alden looked like a butcher about to conduct a home tour. Brown smears covered the apron protecting her blue linen suit, and globs of grease sat like beads on her well-coiffed white hair. Rubber gloves, coated in pig gunk, protected her arms to the elbows.

Gale pointed to her own upper lip as she and Katie Pru joined Ella in the kitchen. "Missed a piece," she said.

Ella wiped her arm across her mouth. "Don't be cute with me. I expected you at least an hour ago." She wagged her finger toward a diminutive, gray-haired woman scooping pork remnants from the sink into a galvanized can. "Cammy's been needing help and you're off God knows where."

Gale plucked a cloven hoof from the sink basin. Fragments of meat, still warm, clung to its severed top. "I just saw the Bosom Brigade head out the back door. I can't believe you really missed me." She tossed the foot into the can. "But I'm here now, Cammy. What do you need me to do?"

Cammy Cane didn't look up as she wiped a paper towel around the bottom of the sink. "I don't know, Gale. Let me think a minute." Her glasses slipped to the tip of her nose; she arched her wrist back and pushed them in place. "No, I think everything's fine. Everything's under control."

Maralyn raised her eyebrows at Gale and fiddled with the twist tie on a stack of paper cups. " 'Fine' and 'control' are careful words, Cammy," she said.

Cammy tilted her head, trying to look at Maralyn beneath her smudged glasses.

"That's right," she said coolly. "Everything's fine and under control. Now, Katie Pru, sweetheart, will you hold that door open for me so I can take this can outside?"

The screen door creaked as it swung open, creaked again as it slammed shut. Gale watched Cammy hike across the yard, the can knocking her leg with each step. She looked strangely anachronistic, a tiny woman in a navy cotton dress and sensible shoes, lugging her pig parings toward the pond amid tents and folding chairs.

Gale waited until Cammy had disappeared behind the fish house before turning to Ella. "She's frightened."

Ella picked up a sauce bowl, opened the refrigerator door, and wedged it next to a carton of milk. "Damn right she's frightened. Martin's been in a mood all day. He's usually under pressure at these barbecues, but it's different this time." She slammed the door shut with such force the bottles inside clanked. "Sill's a fool."

"Does anyone know if she and Faith are here yet?" Gale asked.

"Don't know," Maralyn answered. "They haven't come into the house if they are."

"Hmm." Gale glanced at Katie Pru, who was pressing her weight into the bulging screen door. "Okay, ladybug. What do you say we fix you something to eat and drink? Then I'll see what I can do to help out."

They stepped from the house and into the evening's warm air. The barbecue table sat at the western end of the mown lawn, beneath a green tent on loan from the smaller of the county's two funeral homes.

Gale scrutinized the festivities. No doubt Martin would win the King Christian title again this year. Already a line snaked from the barbecue tent. Across the lawn members of the gospel choir began to congregate. Before long paper plates would be empty, bellies full, and the tones of "Pow'r in the Blood" would roil through the close summer night. She had to give Martin credit—when it came to latter-day religious sacrifices, the man knew how to stage a hit.

Across the lawn a microphone screeched. Martin stood in the middle of a riser. In front of him another man manipulated the knobs on the sound equipment.

"Folks, if I could have your attention for just a minute." Martin waved his arm, the foam ball on the microphone pushed against his lips. "On behalf of the Statlers Cross United Methodist Church, I want to thank y'all for coming tonight to our twentieth annual Southern gospel singing and barbecue. Some of you I recognize from past years—a few of you have been coming since the beginning, so you've heard my spiel before. This is a gathering born of tradition. We are a people who believe in friendship and integrity and the love of the Lord."

He paused, perspiration dripping down his face. His plaid shirt was damp around the navel, the cloth pulling at his slight paunch. Martin was a sturdy man, and even Gale admitted that with his gray hair and square build, he cut an impressive evangelical picture.

He raised his hand into the air. "Now, many of you know me. You know me as a public servant, as a former county commissioner and an extension agent. You know me as a citizen of this town, as someone who loves this little community and has done my best to make it thrive. But those are all earthly things. I now want you to see me as I truly am, a humble member of God's flock. I want you to raise your hands with me and close your eyes. I want you to tell Jesus that you thank him for this bountiful feast. Jesus is it, folks, and we need to remember that for all the joy and singing and clapping and shouting that will be done tonight, Jesus is the one."

"That's right, Martin," said the man at the sound equipment. "Jesus is the one."

A smattering of hands waved in the air, accompanied by murmurs of assent. Most of the crowd stood still, arms crossed and smirks swallowed. Suburbanites didn't raise their hands, and they sure as hell didn't clap and shout. They came to be entertained.

A young woman with a camera stepped in front of Gale. Gale moved to one side, idly noticing the woman's long beige skirt and untucked cotton blouse. Holiness, Gale thought, and then quickly dismissed the idea as the woman bit down on a darkly painted red lip and lifted her camera to her face.

"Friends, bow your heads and let us pray. Dear Lord, you have given us so much. And being sinners, we take from your goodness, Lord, because we are so needy. But tonight we will lift up our voices for you. We will sing hallelujah for you. For you are our salvation, Lord. We humbly ask your blessing and forgiveness. In His name we pray, Amen."

The shutter clicked. The woman lowered her camera and drifted away.

"Just one quick announcement," Martin said. "It's hotter than Hades out here tonight. Let the older folks sit in the fish house underneath the fan. Now, eat, my friends. Y'all have a great time."

A taped recording of a fiddle spattered to life as Martin climbed down from the riser. He grinned and walked toward the fish house, pausing to slap backs and shake hands.

Gale nodded and smiled as he walked toward her. In answer he gripped her shoulder, winked, and kept going. When he reached the fish house, he slid his hand under the elbow of an elderly woman and guided her through the door. Martin wasn't exactly Gale's cup of tea, but he wasn't a bad sort. She certainly had known men equally fervent but less sincere.

A short distance away stretched a long, paper-lined table bordered with rows of chairs. Few of the chairs had been taken, and it was in this direction that Gale guided Katie Pru.

"Here, punkin," she said. "Why don't you sit and save us a seat while I go fix us some plates."

"I want big chunks."

"You got it. Now wait right here."

Katie Pru climbed into a chair as Gale took her place at the end of the barbecue line. From a glance she could tell that the women, for all their lock-step organization, were not ready for the hoopla to begin. The sauce bowls were in place but without spoons, forcing diners to pour lakes of sauce onto their collapsing plates. The broken head of a plastic fork protruded from a bowl of baked beans, and as Gale watched, a man dipped the edge of his plate into the goo shovel-style. Even the roasted pig, Cammy's prized centerpiece, wasn't completely decorated. Silk magnolia blossoms rested against its haunches, and a hard peach was wedged into its mouth, but the freshly woven honeysuckle vine wreath which Cammy took such care to prepare every year was absent from around its neck. Not that it mattered, Gale thought, as she moved past the pig. The woman would have enough on her hands today without playing Martha Stewart.

Above the chatter at the food table, she heard the door to the house slam. Good, she thought. If it's Ella, maybe she'll take over feeding Katie Pru while I round up some utensils.

Suddenly the fish house screen door flew open, banging against the side of the building with such force the thin walls shook.

"Get out of here, Sill. And take that girl with you!"

Martin burst from the fish house, followed by a tall slender woman dressed in white shorts. Sill's blond hair flicked in the air as she hurried after her father.

"Would you please just stop and listen to me?"

Martin whirled around, his face empurpled. His voice dropped to a whisper. "Listen to you? What are you talking about, 'listen to you'? This is a Christian gathering, Sill. Get out of here."

His eyes were wet as he stalked by Gale. Two steps past her he stopped. The woman in the long skirt moved beneath the food tent and steadied her camera at him. For a second Gale thought he was going to reach across the table and knock it from her hand. Instead he drove his fists into his pants pockets and hurried toward the back steps. Gale turned back to Sill. Patches of bright pink stained her cousin's cheeks as she picked at a silver cross pendant dangling against her chest.

A second woman, small and dark, appeared in the fish house door. "Come on, Sill. Let's go home."

"You go," Sill said.

She followed her father into the house. Around the yard, voices stilled, plates paused in midair. Gale crossed her arms in front of her, more from the expectation of a night chill than the possibility of it.

Katie Pru lifted one leg, then the other, listening to the sucking sound as her skin pulled loose from the metal chair. She enjoyed the feel of it, like the Velcro on her shoes when she ripped open the tabs. Only it wasn't Velcro holding her skin to the chair. It was sweat, and she liked the way it made octopus cups on her thighs.

Her mother moved slowly beneath the barbecue tent. Katie Pru knew she was sad. Yelling always made her mother sad, which was why Katie Pru yelled only when she had to. Sometimes, of course, she couldn't help it, like yesterday when Ella said she couldn't play the piano. She loved the piano—the *tink, tink, tink* of the highest keys. It sounded like caterpillar feet, and she wiggled her octopus legs in response.

Her mother disappeared in the line of people in front of the tent, but that was okay. Her mother would bring back food, and food was what Katie Pru wanted.

She looked around her. People walked back and forth across the grass. Some wore shorts like she did, others wore bright-colored dresses with flowers and stripes. One lady had on a skirt covered with big pink frogs. Katie Pru liked frogs. She watched the lady walk toward the drink tent and tried to imagine how it felt to be a frog hanging on to a lady's skirt. Like swinging on a curtain, she thought, and she swayed back and forth.

Glancing at the barbecue line, Katie Pru decided her mother was out of sight. She hopped from her chair and followed the frog skirt. It was so white and the frogs so pink that she didn't have any trouble keeping up. The lady walked from the drink tent with three cups in her hands and headed toward the fish house. Katie Pru jogged after her, watching the frogs swing from the lady's behind.

It was past the fish house that she caught a glimpse of the pen. The metal fence looked rusted. Beside it two boys were pointing and laughing, until their mother called and they ran away. Katie Pru knew about pens—the jag-wire had told her about them. They were horrible places with bad smells. Frogs and jag-wires hated them.

She glanced back at the pink frogs as the lady disappeared into the fish house. The jag-wire had warned her about pens—keep away, he had said. Still, jag-wires didn't know everything.

She crept up to the metal wire and peeked in, wanting to see what the boys had found so funny. Three dogs, all long-haired and covered in dirt, huddled in the middle of the pen, grunting furiously. They bit at the earth, their lips pulled back and their teeth flashing white. The ground seemed to move between them, back and forth, like a tug-of-war.

Katie Pru stepped closer. She curled her fingers around the rusted links and put her nose through one of the holes.

A few feet away from her, lolling on the ground, was a pig's head, its eyes squinted closed, its mouth clamped shut. The skin was deep brown, and its ears, which Katie Pru knew should have been as pink as the frogs, were black and crusty.

From the far end of the yard she heard a high peal, almost as soft as the *tink, tink, tink* of Ella's piano. She knew this sound—she had heard it coming through the church windows. The choir was getting ready.

On top of this an old, dry voice filtered through the mesh on the fish house.

"I remember one time, this boy wouldn't feed his family. Wife out stealin' food, children ain't had no clothes. So one night some fellers rode out there. . . ."

Katie Pru glanced at the fish house. Through the green mesh she made out the form of an old man seated in a chair poking a plastic fork above his head. All around him the chairs were full, and above him a fan stuttered in the air.

She turned back to the pen. The singers grew louder, their chorus smothering the grunts of the dogs, but not the old man's story.

"Another time, there was this colored boy. A no-good one, messin' with people. So one night a gang went out and took him."

"Katie Pru?" Her mother's call seemed far away. "Come here to me, please."

"Gawd, did he cry. But he was messin' with people, so they took him out to Baker Ridge and strung him up. Course, then they just got silly about it."

"Come here, Katie Pru. I'm not telling you again. You come over here and stand with me!"

"They started twistin' and twistin' that rope until it was knotted up at the branch like a muscle. One of the men held the boy's feet so he wouldn't take off too soon. Then, when the rope wouldn't twist no more, he let it fly. Legs and arms flappin' around like a damn black puppet. They came back to town fallin' all over themselves, laughin'."

The old man cackled. Katie Pru stood beside the pen, unable to move.

A shot cracked the air. The choir mumbled into silence. The people in their shorts stopped moving; the flowered and striped dresses swayed until motionless in the yard. At the fish house door the frogs clung to the woman's skirt, their shiny feet digging in for dear life.

And then, a scream. Katie Pru clutched the wire fence, the rust powdery on her palm. Mama, Mama, she thought desperately. And in a rush her mother was there. She snatched Katie Pru into her arms and ran with her toward the pond, until they could no longer hear the sobbing cries coming from the house.

*When she was alive, she never raised her voice
to that child. I never knew anyone to be so quiet
with a boy and still get him to act right. It's a
shame how they talk about her. They say she
was angry—I say sad. You could tell by the
roundness of her eyes when she prayed.*

> —Venice Perkins, talking with
> her daughter Maye, 1938

4

The problem with a man's head is it's not the side of a
buck. Blast into the side of a buck with a rifle and the
damn thing falls over, with the hole in the torso and
the shine of blood the sole evidence of what happened.
Blast into the front of a man's head and there is no
man, only a ball of pulp, chunks of skull and a halo of
gunk splattered on the wall.

Sheriff Alby Truitt stared first at the ceiling—scant
debris, just a sweep near the juncture with the wall—
before surveying the rest of the room. He had never
been in the Canes' bedroom before, but he knew
Cammy well enough to envision the space as she

intended—whitewashed walls, the clean line of a well-made bed, simple dark furniture inside a simple white house. If God was in the details, then the Canes worshipped a minimalist indeed. The caulk filling the spaces between the planks had discolored, so the walls looked like sheets of a child's writing paper. Only this God's child had a penchant for red.

A rifle, a .308 Remington, rested barrel-up against the bedroom doorjamb. Truitt had seen Martin shoot that gun dozens of times, eye steady at the sight, stock to his shoulder. *Damn it to hell, Martin. You've been hunting too long to be so stupid. What were you doing with your gun out during a church barbecue? How the hell did your brains get all over Cammy's goddamn white walls?*

Through the partially opened door he could hear crying. He had left an unsettling scene in the Canes' living room—four women clinging to each other on the sofa, blood streaked in their hair and discoloring their clothes, as though they had soaked themselves in it.

He looked around the room again—dashes from bloodied shoes on the light gray carpet, red handprints covering the blankets beneath Martin's body, smudges near the door of the master bath. On the wall beside the bed, finger smears interrupted the splattered tissue. A small gun cabinet, empty with its door open, stood in one corner. Not a typical accident scene. Not even a typical scene of a crime.

"What you been doing in here, Martin?" he asked softly. "You started teaching me about guns when I was sixteen years old. What was going on in that head of yours?"

Truitt turned to the bed. Martin Cane had been a proud man, and his women had seen to it that death didn't negate that. In addition to folding his hands neatly on his chest, they had evidently buttoned his shirt to the collar, the messy daubs around the buttons attesting to the postwound work. His head, or its remains, rested on a pillow. Truitt bent closer. Pieces of skull and brain tissue lay loose on top of the pulp. He studied the finger smears on the wall. Jesus Christ. Someone had scooped the tissue from the planks and tried to put the man's head back together.

The keening in the living room pitched higher as Cammy wailed. "Oh God," she cried. "Oh, please, God." Truitt's chest tightened. He'd seen hunting accidents before. But never so much blood on breathing women. Never so much red on a room's white walls.

Outside, the dusk had grown heavy, and a wind batted the branches of the oaks. Truitt lifted the edge of the frilly Cape Cod curtains and peered into the dark. On the grounds below, people huddled in clumps, illuminated by strings of lights that ran from the back of the house and disappeared into the leaves. Despite their bright summer clothes, they had the unmistakable look of mourners, all hunched backs and folded arms. Truitt checked his watch. Nine-thirty. Over an hour had passed since the sheriff's office in Praterton had received the call. But he knew this crowd wouldn't leave until ordered. At least here they could commiserate. From the living room Cammy's voice rose again in anguish.

Truitt let the curtain drop and slipped from the room. On the staircase two Georgia Bureau of Investigation crime scene techs were carefully laying plastic sheeting on the stairs.

"The sides are okay, Sheriff." The chief crime scene tech motioned him down. She held her arm out to steady him as he gingerly stepped over her. "Hell of a mess here. Shoe prints everywhere. Hope you minded your feet going up."

He sighed. "Don't worry. If I could have figured out a way to fly in through the window . . ."

Her smile was sympathetic. He wondered if his deputy had warned them when he made the routine request for assistance. *Watch what you say on this one, guys. The sheriff's old hunting buddy. More than that, really. You ever hear about the sheriff's daddy . . . ?"*

Truitt maneuvered his way to the bottom of the

staircase and wondered, not for the first time, about the placement of the stairs in the Canes' house—a series of lopsided and narrow steps hammered onto the back wall of the den. Martin had explained to him that at one time a front set of stairs had opened into the central hall, but in the 1960s he had torn them out to install a new furnace and the upstairs bathroom. "Hottest damn bathroom in Calwyn County," Martin had said, laughing. "Cammy's always ragging on me about getting a wood stove so she can have someplace warm to read in the winter. I tell her, 'Take a pillow and sit in the tub.' "

Truitt glanced around the den at the worn plaid sofa, the reclining chair, the console television with its nicked veneer. At the wooden gun cabinet he paused. Six rifles, all the slots filled. The key was in the lock. Turning away, he crossed the room and motioned to his sergeant standing by the living room door.

"Craig, go tell the guys outside that when they've taken down all the names and addresses, they need to get those folks to go home."

Sergeant Craig Haskell shook his head. "Nobody'll want to leave until the body does."

"I know. But I have no idea when Bingham's going to get here. Say I'm asking them to leave. Point out that it's about to storm."

"I'll try."

Truitt nodded toward the living room. "I'm about ready to separate them and let you get on with the questioning. What's it been like in there?"

Haskell's mahogany crinkled in a frown. "Pretty awful. They're just holding each other and crying and praying."

Truitt peered into the room. The four women were as he left them—Cammy on the sofa, Ella Alden and Maralyn Nash on either side of her, Sill on the floor. With their hands clasped together, they looked like a communal pietà. He sucked his upper lip thoughtfully. Something wasn't right. Martin would have been the first one to tell him to trust his instinct about what was natural.

He looked at Haskell. "The other witnesses still on the front porch?"

"Yep. Ruch's with them."

"Who claims to have been first through the bedroom door?"

Haskell whacked his notepad against the palm of his hand. "Well, there evidently was a pack of them pushing into the room all at once, but the nearest I can tell at this point, the preacher was at the front."

"What's his name again?"

Haskell referred to his notes. "Ryan Teller."

"Go on and get those folks outside to leave," Truitt said. "But first have Ruch take Reverend Teller to the kitchen. Tell him I have a few more questions."

Truitt waited until Haskell had disappeared through the front door before entering the living room. The women still huddled on the sofa, heads bent together. Only Sill looked up as he approached.

"How you holding up, Cammy?" Truitt asked gently.

Cammy's lips fluttered into her mouth as she breathed in to answer. Her blue eyes were negligible inside their swollen lids.

"God, Alby," she whispered. "How could it happen? Martin's such a careful man. You know he is. He'd never mess with a loaded gun. It just isn't possible."

Truitt crouched down beside her. "It happens sometimes, Cammy. A man's been careful all his life, but all it takes is one time."

"It was the gun, Cammy," said Maralyn. "I'm sure they're gonna look at it. Maybe it was faulty. Maybe it wasn't something Martin did at all."

For a second, Cammy's face cleared. "You're right, Maralyn. It had to have been the gun. My word, he's had it for years. It's his favorite. Something finally went wrong with it." She looked at Sill, her face suddenly silly with hope. "It just broke, honey. Your daddy's gun just broke on him."

Sill clutched her mother's hands tighter. "That's right, Mother. Daddy was too good a hunter for it to be anything else."

Truitt felt Ella Alden shift beside her. "And how about you, Miss Ella?" he asked. "How are you doing?"

"I'm fine," she said curtly. "But these children could use some water. Do you think one of your men could find the time to get them a glass?"

Truitt nodded. "Sergeant Haskell will be back in a second. He'll see to it." He hauled himself to his feet and stood staring down at the tops of the women's heads. He would have expected speckled tissue on anyone who had been in the vicinity of that gun blast. But he could detect no specks. The blood looked smoothed. Goddamn. *It's like they combed their hair with it.*

He left the room and made a quick turn to the left. Cammy's kitchen, like her bedroom, was simple, a nice balance between the house's demand for primitiveness and her own delicate tastes. Evidence of the barbecue was everywhere: bowls on the counter, balls of plastic wrap in the sink, shears and tendrils of cut honeysuckle trailing over a work table in the corner. Despite this the room maintained its sensibility. Yellow pot holders hung from a wrought-iron strip nailed to the wall, and a shade the color of pale butter topped the only window in the room. The cabinets were burnt orange, the original brown of the wood peeping through nicks in the paint. Truitt had spent many early Saturday mornings in this kitchen, sitting at the iron legged table and finishing one last cup of coffee before he and Martin headed for the woods north of town. They were companionable mornings, made all the more so by Cammy's discreet attentions—warm sticky buns in the oven, scalloped paper napkins beside their saucers, but never the woman herself, who Truitt always assumed had hurried upstairs in her robe when he drove up, her duties completed.

With a pinch of guilt he realized his sheriff's duties had kept him away from Martin and Statlers Cross for more than three years. Giving his deputy a dismissive nod, he straightened his tie and walked to the kitchen table. The man seated with his back to the door looked slightly older than Truitt, possibly just the other side of forty. He was well dressed in a pair of sand-colored linen pants and a navy knit shirt. His hair, a tousle of blond curls, had taken on a dull green tint, whether from the strength of the kitchen's competing yellows or too much time at the pool, Truitt couldn't guess. Drawing his notebook and pen from his pocket, the sheriff slid a chair from beneath the table and sat down.

"Reverend Teller . . ." he began.

Teller leaned forward, his face a mold of concern. "Martin Cane was a friend of mine, Sheriff. I am truly sorry about his death."

The minister's hair hung in damp curls around his forehead, and his cheeks looked flushed. Truitt let a smile touch his eyes. "He was a friend of mine, too, Reverend."

Teller waved his hand. "Please, call me Ryan," he said. "You know, I've been student pastor here at Statlers Cross for nearly a year now, and I've performed five funerals—lots of elderly members of the congregation, you understand. But this . . . I have to tell you, Sheriff, I'm not sure how to handle this myself."

"That's understandable, Ryan. I'd hope most preachers go through their entire careers without encountering a death like this." Truitt paused. "Where were you before you came to Statlers Cross?"

"Nowhere. Well, not at any church, anyway. I was a businessman in Atlanta. But the Lord called me. He sent me here."

"Ah." Truitt flicked open his notebook and glanced down at the first page. "I've always said it's a good thing some of us have excellent hearing."

Teller grinned. "The Lord can get your attention when He wants it."

"Is that a fact? Well, He certainly has my attention now. I'm trying to figure out what in the Lord's name happened in that room up there. My sergeant says you were one of the first people into the bedroom. Can you tell me about that?"

Teller squinted his eyes and tilted his head toward the ceiling. "Yes. I was in the yard by the back door, listening to our gospel singers warming up. I heard the shot. It was obvious it came from the house, so I ran inside. I heard screaming and crying from upstairs, so I hurried up there. The door to the bedroom was closed."

As the minister brought his folded hands to the top of the table, the light from the overhead lamp caught a shine on his fingernails. Buffed, Truitt thought. Curious. He wondered if Atlanta's urbanization had crept so far east that the few beauty salons in Calwyn County now offered manicures for men. He doubted it. More likely, the minister drove the hour to Athens, or, even more singularly, did his own.

Truitt tapped his pen lightly against the table. "Go on."

"Well, I tried to open the door, but it was locked. They were crying in there, Cammy was shouting out Martin's name, and I banged on the door, yelling at them to let me in, but they didn't. I guess they couldn't hear me."

"How did you know there was more than one person inside?"

"I heard them. Wailing. Screaming. Someone shouting, 'Oh God,' over and over, and then, 'Stop it, please stop it.' "

"Anything else?"

"I recognized Ella's voice. She kept telling everyone to calm down. 'Calm down, let's see what we can do.' "

"Those were her words?"

"Something like it. But mostly it was just Cammy, crying out Martin's name."

"Did you hear anything from Sill?"

Teller frowned. "I didn't know Sill was in the room until the door finally opened," he said. "But then, I've only met her once before. I'm not sure I would recognize her voice."

"Did you hear any other sounds?"

Teller shook his head. "Pounding, maybe. Thumps. I don't know. It was too indefinite. I just remember the crying. And feeling so helpless because I couldn't budge the door."

"So how did the door finally open?"

"Several people had come in from outside. And we were all banging on the door. Finally Ella opened it, but there was nothing anybody could do."

"How long before she let y'all in?"

Teller took in a long, deep breath. "Kinda long, actually. I know somebody said they were going to go get a screwdriver to take the knob off."

"Really? So how many minutes?"

"Could've been five minutes, could've been more. It certainly felt like forever."

"Is ten possible?"

"Maybe ten. Surely not any more."

"And what did you see once you got into the room?"

Teller closed his eyes. A muscle at the corner of his left lid spasmed. "Martin on the bed. Cammy and Sill leaning over him. Ella's daughter—Maralyn—holding the gun. Blood was everywhere."

"Maralyn was holding the gun?"

"Yes. I didn't know who she was at the time—I'd never met her before. She was covered in blood and she was just looking at the gun, like she was amazed."

"Did you see what she did with the gun?"

"No. I ran over to the bed and took a look at Martin and . . . well, Sheriff, you've been up there. There was no doubt he was dead. I just remember taking hold of Cammy and leading her from the room. She wouldn't go. She kept grabbing at Martin's shirt, trying to hold on to him." He looked at Truitt, his eyes widening. "I'd never seen anything like it. The man didn't have a head. His wife was trying to hold him, and he didn't even have a head."

Truitt sat in silence, slowly running his thumbnail across the edge of his notepad. "Tell me something, Reverend. How often did you see Martin?"

"Pretty often. Least twice a week. Sometimes daily, depending on what we were doing at church."

"And did you notice anything different about his behavior recently?"

Teller looked at him blankly. "Different?"

"Sure. Did he act like he normally did? Did he seem withdrawn or preoccupied with anything?"

"No, couldn't say that at all. Same old Martin— loved doing the Lord's work."

Truitt smoothed his eyebrow. "When you got to the women, did any of them say what happened?"

"Martin was cleaning his gun and it went off."

"And did they say why they thought he was cleaning his gun during a church barbecue?"

Teller winced. "I asked Ella that. I think she must have felt my timing was bad, or I was being insensitive, or something. You know, ministers are supposed to have a second sense about what to say during a crisis, but we don't always. At any rate, I think I made her angry."

"Why's that?"

Teller raised his hands palms up above the table, more an act of wonder than supplication. "When I asked her, she just looked me dead in the eye and said Martin always cleaned his gun when gospel singers were around."

Never trust a woman with blood on her teeth.
— Reb Falcon, during a conversation
while fishing in Meanlick Creek, 1941

5

In her sleep Katie Pru grumbled and kicked her legs. The night heat had dampened her hair, and as Gale leaned over the picnic table to give her daughter a kiss, she smelled the distinctly musty odor of a sweaty child. Outside the fish house the strings of electric lights lit the grounds like a midnight madness sale. Periodically, people passed, their retreating murmurs followed by the cough of a car's ignition. It had been two hours since the gunshot. Everyone was finally leaving.

Overhead, rain clattered like coins on the tin roof. Gale rested her hand on her daughter's head. From the moment the sound had cracked the air, she had recognized it as a gun blast. She was too familiar with the breed—had spent too many nights waking from the memory of it, with her heart pulsing and her skin burning—for misinterpretation. Her reaction had been instinctive. With Katie Pru in her arms she had pounded down the grassy slope from the fish house to the pond. At first she merely cradled Katie Pru, crouching with her at the water's edge and watching the people above her drift in uncertain circles. Then, as the crowd began to moan, Gale set her daughter down and took her hand. By the time the sheriff arrived, they were on the far side of the pond, pacing their steps around its red clay perimeter.

They walked around the pond three times before Gale led Katie Pru into the empty fish house. She plopped her down on top of the picnic table and made a show of cleaning her face. Katie Pru was quiet, but not unusually so. Gale kept smoothing her daughter's hair and asking, "Baby, how are you doing?" She didn't know what she expected, maybe for the dark eyes to turn mournfully to her and for Katie Pru to say *I know that noise. It scares me. Why have you never been good at keeping me safe?* But instead Katie Pru simply reached up and ran her hand gently down her mother's hair. Then she curled up on the table and fell asleep.

They had remained there now for over an hour. Through the wire screen, Gale watched the shaggy branches of an oak quiver in the rain. As a teen, Gale used to sit with Sill beneath that tree and tell ghost stories—about never-ending dinner parties and weeping cemetery statues and, of course, Linnie, who had long ago hung herself and then evidently changed her mind. There were many Linnie stories—Linnie in white robes riding a black horse, Linnie swooping into barns and eating chickens whole. Sill, skinny legs drawn up to her chest, would clasp her hands behind her head and squeeze her arms tightly against her ears. *Stop it, Gale, stop it. I don't want to hear any more.* Gale could not have told her then what she could now, that ghost stories always leak through. No amount of ear-clamping, night-screaming, or prayer-shouting can stop them.

Gale wiped a crumb from Katie Pru's cheek. Well, Sill's learning now. The recently deceased make the most demanding ghosts.

The fish house door opened without warning, and a deputy stepped inside. In one swooping glance he took in the empty folding chairs, the long, checkered-covered picnic table, and then leveled his muddy eyes on Gale.

"Ma'am," he said, "we're asking everybody to go on home. There's nothing more anyone can do for the family tonight. It'd be a better idea to check on them in the morning."

"My family's in the house. My grandmother, my aunt. I'm waiting for them."

The deputy studied her in silence. "I see. You been into the house tonight, ma'am?"

A hot flush started in Gale's cheeks. "Not since . . . I was inside earlier, before the barbecue started."

"You were on the grounds when the gun went off?"

"Yes."

"And we took your name down?"

Gale hesitated. "No."

"We didn't? You been in this hut all evening? How'd we overlook you?"

"I didn't stay once the gun went off. I took my daughter down to the pond."

The deputy swung the screen door open wider so that it smacked against the wall, and rested his shoulder against it.

"You heard a gun go off in a house full of relatives and you go hopping off to the pond? You must be quite an angler."

Gale's throat tightened. "That was uncalled for. I have a small child. Whatever happened in that house, she didn't need to be anywhere near it." She paused. "Not too difficult a concept, I would imagine."

The deputy pursed his lips. In the fish-house light

his black hair appeared algal. Large splats of water dappled his brown uniform. His eyes steady on hers, he rapped the back of his head against the screen door several times.

"I would imagine not," he said calmly. He tugged a notepad from his breast pocket and flapped it open. "What is your name, please?"

"Gale Grayson."

He stared at her, his fingers still fishing his pocket for a pen. His eyes started at her breasts, moved slowly up to her mouth, then down.

"I've heard about you," he said finally. "You're not what I pictured."

She could guess what he pictured. Someone huge and grinning with flaming red hair and black clothes— the irony of gossip mills was that they could build a victim into a mountain while grinding her into sand. She should have been fearsome, even mythical. Instead, the terrorist's widow cowered in a smelly shack, her face blanched green with light and her fingers plucking nervously at a child's limp shoelace.

She cleared her throat. "When can I talk with my grandmother? Is she still being questioned?"

The deputy shrugged. "That's not my job. Please come with me."

He remained motionless against the open screen door as Gale scooped the sleeping Katie Pru against her shoulder and exited the fish house. Heavy drops of rain slapped her skin as she walked briskly toward the beams of light obscuring the back porch. Discomfited, Katie Pru brushed at the water pelting her face.

"Stop it, Mama," she grumbled. "Stop squirting me with the hose."

"It's okay, baby. We'll be inside the house in just a second."

Following the vague stink of the fish house the kitchen, with its aroma of cooked meat and spices, felt comforting. After a second, however, Gale detected the scent of hot men in cotton uniforms, and a more intangible, unpleasant smell. She turned to the deputy entering the room behind her.

"I'm not staying here." She kept her voice even. "My daughter and I came here on foot, and I'm not going to walk home with her when it's dark and raining. I would appreciate it if you would find someone to take us home."

The deputy opened his mouth, then closed it. Pushing past her, he left the kitchen and disappeared down the small hallway that led to the front of the house.

Katie Pru jerked, her foot catching Gale's thigh. Grimacing, Gale swayed back and forth and sang softly. The walls of the house were made of hand-hewn pine logs, twelve inches thick and covered by milled planks which cramped the rooms and effectively muted sound. Gale dropped her song to a whisper, concentrating on the faint murmurs from the front of the house. She expected to hear crying, but instead detected only a low drone. The sound of men buzzing. A violent death occurs and men descend like bees, circling around, trying to salve with a steady hum.

"Hello, Gale."

She whirled around, her grasp around Katie Pru tightening. Alby Truitt hadn't grown into a large man, and as he approached her, the floorboards were silent. "It's been a long time," he said. His voice was raspy. "The customary thing to say would be 'I heard you were back and I've been meaning to call,' but the truth is I figured I'd eventually run into you. This isn't how I would've engineered it."

Gale nodded. The last time she had seen Alby Truitt, he was standing on the side of the pool in Calwyn County's only YWCA, blowing his whistle at her and yelling at her to open her eyes and stop swimming in circles. She had been seven and he in his late teens, a college student home for the summer, scrounging a few dollars as a swimming instructor. She had hopped out of the pool and run into the showers, her child's pride hurt by the image of her Busby Berkeley turn in the water. Every summer for years afterward Ella teased her about it. *Saw Alby Truitt down at the bank today, Gale. He said to tell you he saw an Esther Williams movie last night. . . .*

To a seven-year-old he had been a tower with wet legs and a tan back. In actuality he was compact, although he still topped her by a good eight inches. His brown hair, longish across the top, had grown lighter with the coming of gray. Long lines were beginning to form along the length of his cheeks, and a harder line topped his nose and separated his eyebrows. On the street Gale never would have connected the man with the teen, except for Truitt's mouth, which now, like then, had a boyish lift to it.

She shifted Katie Pru farther up her shoulder. "It's hard to know what to do. How is Cammy?"

"About what you'd expect. Your grandmother's going to take her and Sill home with her tonight. It's going to be a rough time, all around."

Gale shut her eyes. Jesus. Where else would they go except to Ella's? But the idea of those women, wailing away in closed rooms down the hall . . .

When she opened her eyes, Truitt was studying her.

"I'm sorry," she said. "I'm just thinking of Katie Pru. She doesn't need this." She paused. "I don't need it, either."

"I can understand that." Stretching forward, he pulled a yellow leatherette chair from beneath the table. "I'm sorry. I should have offered you a seat. She's a little thing, but she must be heavy."

Gale eased into the chair. Katie Pru's head fell into the dip between her breasts. Gale hadn't wanted to stay long. She had meant to demand that someone take her home. But now she felt reluctant to leave. She gazed around the room at the spent dishes and dirty cutlery. Someone will have to clean this up, she thought. Ella will have to get the Bosom Brigade back in here, armed with Brillo pads and dishwashing detergent, and instruct them to put this room back in order. Then they'll have to march themselves upstairs. . . .

Her voice caught in her throat. "Someone is going to have to clean upstairs," she said.

Truitt pulled out a second chair and sat down. "I'd suggest contacting a cleaning service," he said softly.

She nodded. What does one do with blood on the carpets, blood on the walls? Thank God Tom had died on an altar, where people were used to dealing with blood and bodies. A bubble of laughter caught in her throat. She swallowed hard and felt heat flush her lids.

She fought for control, focusing on the yellow fabric shade tied over the sink window. It was aging now—the outline of a brown stain ran in and out of the folds. She remembered the summer Cammy hung it. Gale had sat at the kitchen table eating peanut-butter-and-banana sandwiches and wiping the excess spread on a giggling Sill. Cammy sat across from them, sliding a crochet needle strung with yellow yarn through the top of a dish towel.

"I want something sunny," she said. She whipped the yarn from its skein and sent a yellow horseshoe into the air. "Your daddy, Sill, says we can't afford it, but this old kitchen hasn't been redone since my grand-mother put the plumbing in back in the 1950s, and I think it's about time. After all, your daddy doesn't have to spend half his day here, does he? I want it done all in white and yellow. What do you think, Sill? Reckon that'll look nice?"

Sill kicked Gale under the table and spit a piece of chewed banana onto her plate. "That sounds fine, Mama, if you like douche commercials."

Sill smiled with her mouth wide open. Remnants of sandwich clung from its roof. Cammy reached across the table and slapped her.

"You don't say such things in my house, Sillena Anne Cane." Cammy's eyes had been red, her thin mouth as small as a staple as she struck her daughter again. "Filth, that's all that is. Nasty stuff. I'll beat the tar out of you if you ever say something like that again."

Gale focused her gaze on Truitt. "Is Faith still here?"

His forehead wrinkled. "Faith?"

"Faith Baskins. She's a friend of Sill's." Gale hesitated. "Actually, they're lovers. This is going to be hard on Sill, and Faith ought to be with her."

Truitt shoved his hands into his pockets, scrutinizing her. Despite her efforts to keep calm, she felt her face color. "Did Martin know they were lovers?" he asked.

"Yes."

"Before today?"

"Yes."

"And he approved of them coming to the barbecue?"

"I didn't talk to him about it."

His eyes were gray flecked with amber and dark enough that when she looked away, she could still see them staring at her. "I'm told you were outside when the gun went off," he said.

"That's right. In the barbecue line. Katie Pru was over by the dog pen."

Truitt ran his finger along the edge of the table, then whacked the top abruptly. "You know, it's been three years since I've laid eyes on Martin—six months since I talked to him on the phone. Can't believe I let him get away like that. You reach a point where everything's work—all else just slips to the side." He paused. "You've been home for about six months, haven't you, Gale? Notice any changes in Martin during that time?"

"No. No changes."

"How about Cammy?"

Katie Pru's head was hot, and Gale felt a trickle of sweat inch down her side. She bit back her anger. She'd left all this, dammit. She didn't come back home to be subjected to questioning in a dowdy yellow kitchen under a glaring white light. She tried to remain calm, but she felt her face grow steely as she stared at Truitt.

"No."

"Do you talk to Sill much? Does she come home often?"

"You'll have to ask her."

He returned her stare for several seconds. Then he broke into a grin and tapped the table almost happily. "Got a copy of your book. Had to order it directly from England, but I figured, heck, I practically taught that girl to swim, might want to see what she turned out to be."

More likely, you wanted to see what the terrorist's widow was up to, Gale thought. "Really? How long ago did you read it?"

He smiled wryly. "About two years. Well before you returned, Gale. Although, yes, I'd be a damn poor lawman if I didn't read it again once I heard you were here. I bet you didn't know my minor in college was History. By and large I don't have much use for Southern history—too much like contemporary sociology, if you know what I mean—but I like your take on things. You see beneath the obvious. Which is why I'll want to talk to you again tomorrow."

Gale's mouth went dry. "Whatever for?"

Truitt shrugged. "To get your take on things."

Gale heard the pitch of her own voice rise. "What are you implying, Alby? It was an accident. Martin was forever messing around with those damn guns."

He reached over and gently lifted a strand of hair away from Katie Pru's face. "This little girl's a beauty, Gale. Looks just like her mama. Let me go get one of my men. You need to get this child to bed."

Zilah Greene had dressed lightly for bed—only a simple blue cotton nightie, no lace around the collar or cuffs to scratch her skin. She had taken to noticing such things lately, like how even the softest of her lace nightgowns left faint red scrapes on her arms and neck in the mornings. She didn't know if her skin was growing more sensitive, or if her nights were so restless that the fabric rubbed and chafed against her as she tossed in bed. Given the choice, she would take the latter. She preferred to think that her mind was going and not that her body, increasingly tired of late, was enduring yet another sign of elderly decay.

But tonight she couldn't sleep. The air was too heavy, the storm having settled down to stay. The pressure in her head created an intermittent stabbing over her right eye that retreated when she lay perfectly still. *If* she could lay perfectly still. Beneath her the mattress burned her calves and spine. *Our Heavenly Father,* she prayed. *Hear thy humble servant's request. . . .*

It was cooler in the living room. She walked back and forth on the beige carpet, its nubby surface soothing her bare feet. She lifted up her arms to see if the lace had rubbed marks onto her flesh and was surprised that there was no lace—in fact, there was no nightgown. She was buck naked. Her hair tickled her exposed shoulders, but when she tried to push it away, it circled her fingers in blond curls. She hadn't been blond in years, and she'd never been naked outside the bedroom and bath. She dragged her fingers down her torso, letting the chill follow their touch. Barry used to touch her like this. He used to slowly draw the tip of his nail along the length of her stomach, following the pinkish lines of her stretch marks. *I love my children,* he would whisper. *I love you for making them.* Then he would mount her, and a sweetness would fill her. After the darkness had rolled over her and away, she would fit her moist buttocks in the warm curve of his groin, and they would sleep.

"We would sleep so soundly, Miss Linnie," she said. "Barry wasn't one of those men who paid no mind to their wives. Barry wanted me happy, and I was."

It seemed so natural, Miss Linnie standing in the living room like she had wandered in from a stroll. And from the way she tilted her head, Zilah assumed she understood her words. It didn't seem quite right, Miss Linnie understanding happiness, given the way she'd wrapped that rope around her neck, but Zilah wasn't going to question. The light around Miss Linnie's head glowed too brightly to see any details, but Zilah thought she could detect a smile on the woman's face.

Zilah smiled back. It must have been the graciousness of that act, the caring invitation it implied, that caused Miss Linnie to push the light away from her face so that Zilah could see all her features. She was a lovely woman, after all.

Zilah walked toward her. She wanted to thank her for being there all those years, even during the decades when Zilah, through blindness or busyness, couldn't see her. She approached the woman slowly, smiling as brightly as she knew how.

Miss Linnie lifted her hand and pressed her thumb and forefinger to her lips. Then, gracefully, she pinched her fingers closed and ripped the lips from her face.

Zilah moved back in horror. Miss Linnie's eyes, still kind, fixed onto hers as her long, sculpted hands, like angry gulls, plucked at her own arms, breasts, thighs, gouging holes in both flesh and fabric. Blood streamed down her face. Her brown dress clung like a wet and reddened sheet to her legs.

When Zilah awoke, her bedclothes were soaking. The skin around her neck and on her arms was fiery red with scratches.

The old men were talking about Miss Linnie again. I swear, I wonder what we'd all be like if she had just died in her bed.

— Becky Lawrence, in a letter to her
   newlywed husband Clarence,
   received in France, 1944

6

It was eleven-thirty P.M. when the sheriff's patrol car glided past the shuttered row of storefronts and slowed in front of the cotton mill. Raindrops, lean and sharp, pecked at the car windows. The sky was starless—the only illuminations at this end of town were the beams of the patrol car's headlights and the lonesome blink of its turn signal.

Gale leaned heavily against the rear door. The crumbling walls of the cotton mill stretched past her, crow-black and distorted by rain. She didn't know what kind of roof the mill had once borne; the only existing photographs were of unsmiling people clumped around exterior doors, a facade of stone pressing into their backs like a posture device. The top wasn't visible in the photographs, just rough rock walls cropped to white at the paper borders. It was an incomplete picture, and from adolescence it had niggled at her. *It was a roof, Gale Lynn,* her aunt Nora had said, *a plain ol' cover-yer-head roof. What'cha worryin' about a roof for?*

Because I don't understand how you can live across the tracks from something your whole life and not remember it, she wanted to retort. It was a frustration that turned into a teenage fascination. Sometimes when Sill spent the night, they would slip down the stairs after dark and out the back door. On occasion, the moon was full, making it easy to find their way; other times they strained to make out the landmarks: the Greenes' wire fence, the iron jaguar, the pale gravel drive. They crossed the tracks and hurried through the open door of the mill, ignoring the vast, jagged space where the east and south walls lay in rubble. The mill was less shell than angle—two broken walls comprised of granite and the rare splint of a windowsill. Inside, the ground was a mix of weed and dirt, littered with hunks of stone and debris. The girls would huddle at the joint of the walls, Sill's eyes bright.

"Old Deak Motts says you can still hear the sound of the looms. He says sometimes the children cut by the spinning machines cry out in the night."

On the other side of the ruins, the lights from the mill village shone like distant fires. At the mill's heyday there were fifty houses—gnomish, whitewashed structures one room wide. The number had steadily dwindled even as the houses expanded, until the community solidified at twenty-one. Gale gazed at them until the lights blurred.

"Yes," she whispered. "I can hear them."

It was faint—the thunk of worn soles on wood, the suck of the spinning machines. She would close her eyes and hear a chair scrape, a thread break on a loom. "I can hear them, Sill. Just listen."

Every time, Sill would slap Gale's arm and laugh, the sound cracking against the rocks. "Goddammit, Gale. You're a crazy Atlanta bitch. You can't hear nothing." And she would squat on a broken stone and light a cigarette.

Sill had been right; she'd heard nothing. But the pull of the ruins had been enough to lure Gale to the loom. In England the spinning wheel had been her saving grace. Now her wheel lay dismantled and untouched in its packing crate. So much for comfort. As the patrol car turned to bump over the railroad track, the headlights swung away and the silhouette of the mill walls was gone.

Gravel rumbled beneath the tires as the vehicle crept up the drive to Ella's house. From the crook of her mother's arm, a dozing Katie Pru groused.

"That man's throwing rocks at the jag-wire, Mama. Make him stop."

Gale looked at the back of the officer's head, a roll of blond bristles bulging beneath his hat. "That's Deputy Ruch, ladybug. And he's not throwing rocks— it's the car. Grandma Ella's car does that, too."

"The jag-wire knows Grandma Ella's car. A policeman's car is gonna scare him."

Out of the mouths of babes, Gale thought dryly. "Well, I bet that jaguar won't be scared once he sees us. You need to wake up so we can go into the house."

"You need to carry me. Little girls don't walk at night."

Ruch stopped the car and turned to face them. He was younger than the deputies Gale had seen at Martin's house, his face pudgy, the hollows bordering his round nose made deeper by the night. He jerked the steering wheel nervously as he inclined his head toward the house.

"Awful dark looking, ma'am. I'll walk in with you."

Gale stared past him at the blackened outline of the house.

"I'll take you up on that," she said. "The thing is, all I have is a front door key, and when electricity was put into the house in the 1940s, my great-aunt didn't think to put a switch by the front door. I suppose she figured anybody who had business being in the house would come in through the back."

"How long before you earn a back door key?" he asked, smiling.

"I've put in my application. Anyway, would you mind waiting in the foyer while I run through to the back and turn on the lights?"

"No problem." He reached over, flipped open the glove compartment, and pulled out a flashlight. "If all I had to do was walk people to their doors, I'd be a happy man."

An oddly insouciant statement, Gale thought, given the circumstances. As she recalled, the year she left for England, Atlanta's annual murder toll had reached a dismal 250. Calwyn County's had been two. It was difficult to believe that in six years the malevolence of a rural province had increased to the point where country lawmen waxed nostalgic about a saunter to the porch.

She looked at Ruch's face as he opened the rear car door. He couldn't have been more than twenty-five. Gale scooted from the car and held out her hand for Katie Pru. She remembered the buzz in Martin's house, the peculiar smells. Perhaps there was more abandonment than bravado in this young man's words.

The rain slowed to strings of slack droplets. Ruch pulled Katie Pru's wagon from the trunk. With Katie Pru clutching Gale's hand, they hurried along the drive to the line of paving stones running along the front of the house. Ruch trudged beside them, the flashlight beam waggling in his hand.

"You know," he said, "I grew up across the county in Praterton, but even over there we heard about this place. Used to tell stories about it at Boy Scouts."

Gale glanced at him curiously. "Really?"

"Sure did. Well, when I say 'this place,' I really mean the people in this place. Or the ones who lived here long ago."

"Miss Linnie."

In the dark, Gale sensed his surprise. "Yeah. I guess you've heard the stories."

"Oh, yes," she said. "Miss Linnie and the cows, Miss Linnie in the tree . . ."

"My favorite was Miss Linnie and the locked outhouse." He chuckled. "We used to see who could make the loudest squealing noise, just like the old man trapped on the seat with her."

Gale lengthened her stride to reach the next paving stone and helped Katie Pru leap over the wet ground. "I missed that story," she said.

"It was a good one. See, it's in the middle of night and this old man hears the call of nature . . ."

The light bounced over the jaguar's face—to his credit, Ruch was only momentarily unsettled, the beam jolting sideways before it steadied on the growling mouth and then moved on. Behind the jaguar a massive pecan tree shivered, its tips rasping against the bricks.

"You know," Gale said suddenly, "she did it there."

The light stopped moving as Ruch roughly dropped the wagon. He aimed the beam at her torso. "Where?"

She pointed to the pecan tree. "The branch is gone. Her husband cut it down and burned it."

She squeezed Katie Pru's hand and continued toward the house, leaving Ruch and his beam searching the tree behind her.

At the stoop she halted. She didn't know why she had said it. It was an unspoken rule that the family could discuss Linnie among themselves, but never outside the cognate circle. If strangers wanted to find some magic in her death, that was fine. But strangers could not be allowed to own Linnie Glynn Cane. In the end it was all a family matter.

"Hey," Ruch yelled, "there's a chain around this tree. Seems to me I remember a story about this chain, but I can't recall it."

"Iron makes the tree strong."

"This was something else. Some story ... You know what I'm talking about?"

Gale didn't answer. She opened her purse and searched noisily for her keys.

The beam bobbed over the face of the house as Ruch jogged up to them.

"I never knew exactly where it happened." His voice took on a boyish pitch. "I guess I always figured she died in the house. I wish I'd've known that when I was in the Scouts. It would have made me one up on everybody else."

"Well, don't go spreading it around so that we've got a line of cars strung along here on Sunday afternoons. I don't think Alby Truitt will take too kindly to providing traffic duty."

"Aw, you know I won't do that. Besides, I think there're only a few of us who remember anymore. Thank you, ma'am. That was really cool."

He directed the flashlight at the knob as she wrestled with the key. She jabbed at the lock several times before the key slid in and she could turn the knob.

As soon as they stepped through the doorway, Ruch sucked in his breath. He swept the beam from wall to wall. "Godawmighty," he breathed. "What in the name of . . . ?"

"Calm down, Deputy," she said. "They're just dead fish."

The beam slowed. "Damn," he said, then immediately shot her an embarrassed glance. "Sorry, ma'am, but I've never seen anything like this."

"Then you haven't seen the rest of the house."

He gawked in the dimness. "There must be hundreds."

"Somewhere around five hundred and fifty. I used

to know the exact number. Summers could get very boring around here."

"Who in the world caught them all?"

"My grandfather."

"Je-sus Christ."

The light rolled around the foyer like a phantom marble. Beneath the plaques the walls were white—at one time, Gale thought, this entrance must have been a different kind of breathtaking, with its wide white planks and polished central staircase. Now the structure took second place to the accoutrements. The fish mounted on the walls had been caught over a period of thirty years; the oldest brass plate boasted a date of August 2, 1935. They had been hooked in streams, rivers, and lakes in every U.S. state and Canadian province. Some, no doubt, had been caught illegally; others were probably endangered even as Gerry Alden flicked his line into the water. All were painted and shellacked until their natural colors were mere basecoats to the final effect.

Gale turned to Katie Pru. "Baby, I'm going to go turn on the lights. You stay here with Deputy Ruch, okay?"

In the gloom, she saw Katie Pru's head move up and down. Gale hurried down the hallway to the kitchen. It only took a couple of seconds to feel her way around the table to the double switch by the back door.

A weak light leaked from the kitchen into the hallway. When she returned to the foyer, Ruch had pocketed his flashlight and stood reading the inscription below a stiff-tailed carp.

"Ely, Minnesota. July 22, 1956." He shook his head. "What on earth did your grandfather do for a living?"

"Stockbroker, or something like it. He wasn't a professional fisherman." She paused. "My grandmother wouldn't let him keep his trophies at the house in Atlanta. My aunt told him he could put them here."

"Lucky him. Most of us don't have an extra house

around—we have to eat what we catch." He looked at her in amazement. "And you say there's more in the rest of the house?"

"Not fish. Other creatures, though. My grandfather was quite a hunter."

"I reckon."

Gale walked to the open front door and gripped the knob. "Well, Deputy Ruch, thanks for walking us in."

"No problem. Need me to take a look through the rest of the house?"

"We're fine."

He nodded. "Thanks a lot, Miz Grayson."

At the top step he turned back to her. "You know, it's a good thing we didn't know about the inside of this place when I was in Scouts. It would've been too tempting. I'd probably be on the other side of the law by now if we had."

Alby Truitt stood on the far edge of the Canes' front porch and watched Ryan Teller dart beneath the string of bare lightbulbs and disappear into the shadows of the field. Only a handful of cars remained in the makeshift parking lot—Truitt suspected these had been temporarily abandoned by residents too unnerved to drive home alone.

From the far end of the field a car engine started. A few seconds later a blue sedan sputtered by the house. For nearly an hour Teller had pestered Truitt and his men, flitting from one to another like a mosquito trying to gain access to some juicy flesh. *I can't go home, Sheriff—those women in there are members of my flock. They need my comfort. I can lead them in prayer.*

Ella had looked at Truitt dully when he'd asked if they wanted to see the minister.

"Whatever can that man say to us, Alby? Tell him to go home and wait by the phone. There may be plenty of people in town who want his 'comfort,' but they aren't in this room."

For Truitt, Ella's dismissal made the proceedings less complicated. He returned to the minister with a politely phrased order: Go, Reverend, or be prepared to engage in a little jailhouse religion. Teller had reluctantly left, giving his horn a toot as he drove past.

The screen door whined and one of his deputies stepped onto the porch, holding the door open behind him.

"They're coming, sir."

Truitt nodded and slipped into the house. Dull clomps of rubber on wood sounded from the rear of the den. He didn't envy the mortuary crew its journey down those narrow steps.

John Bingham, the Calwyn County coroner, puffed into the hallway and grimaced at Truitt. He plucked a handkerchief from his trouser pocket and wiped a film of sweat from his corpulent face. "All I can say is, I hope you paid attention in sheriff school."

Truitt motioned Bingham to follow the body outside. As the gurney started down the porch steps, the crewmen on the bottom slipped on the damp wood. Truitt lunged forward, afraid the bagged parcel would snap free from its straps and loll gruesomely to the ground. The crewman swore and recovered his balance. Martin's body moved only a fraction beneath its tethers. Truitt's heart pounded as the crew pushed the gurney over the wet grass toward the waiting van.

He turned to Bingham. "Give me your theories."

Bingham shook his head. "I don't know what to tell you, Alby. I'll get the paperwork done so we can get the body down to the state crime lab tonight for tests."

Truitt regarded the coroner critically. "Let me rephrase it, then. Just what do you think I'm looking at here, Johnny?"

Bingham shrugged. "What I'm saying is, I can't offer you much with what I just saw. Listen, Alby, a rifle blast is no slit wrist or carbon-monoxide-filled garage. You blow a man's head off and a lot of your forensic data ends up all over the damn room. You add to that the damage to the evidence done in that room . . ." He gave a low whistle. "Now, we're sending the body over to the boys in Atlanta, but I'm telling you, don't hope for much. I can pretty much guess what they'll tell you—a .308 caliber bullet fired at close range to the front of the face, causing instant death and some serious mess. Did Martin pull the trigger or did someone else shoot him? Hell, it's going to take more than medical work to answer that. I checked for an indentation left on his finger by the trigger. None there, but that doesn't prove anything. You do a gunshot residue test on his hands?"

"Yeah. Negative, but that's no surprise with a rifle. Christ, Johnny, just how much of a difference forensically speaking is there between a man putting a rifle close to his own face and pulling the trigger and someone doing it for him?"

Bingham shook his huge head, dislodging the carefully combed rows of gray hair. "I will tell you one thing: No gun goes off by itself. Anybody tell you why he had that gun out?"

"Cammy said he was cleaning it—something he did when he was under a lot of stress."

"Huh. And I've got some swamp land . . ."

"Yeah, I know." Truitt eyed him critically. "So you wouldn't rule out suicide?"

"Nope."

"How about homicide?"

"I don't know many men who'd want to hold a rifle a couple of inches from their faces and stare down the barrel before pulling the trigger. Most suicides are going to press the gun against their heads where they can't see it, and off-hand I didn't see any evidence of a contact wound. And considering the condition of the room . . ." Bingham dragged the handkerchief across his forehead. "I noticed you haven't taken the women to the station for questioning."

"Doesn't seem necessary to drive them all that way. Ella's elderly, we can do it here." He stared at the porch floor for a long moment before sighing heavily. "Goddammit, Johnny, I don't mind telling you I hate this. Martin was a well-respected man in this county—extension agent for the Department of Agriculture, former commissioner, past president of the Chamber of Commerce. Not to mention his church work. This is bad business any way you slice it. But I've got four women, all related to him, covered head to toe with blood. Now, they may be the victims of a terrible accident. . . ."

"Then again, they may not be. I'm not here to tell you how to do your job, Alby, but if they're not victims, you're going to want their clothes. What about fingerprints on the gun?"

"Several." Truitt pushed his thumb into his palm until he felt a satisfying crack. "Basically I have three choices. I can treat this as a suicide and continue the questioning nice and gentle. I can treat this as a homicide and lock them all up for disturbing the evidence. Or I can treat this as an accident and send them home until tomorrow."

"Your predecessor would have been a gentleman and sent them home."

"Shit. My predecessor would have hit them up for a 'loan' and *then* sent them home."

"Life in the South, Alby. You knew when you ran for office that Andy Taylor was a myth—there's no such thing as a beloved sheriff in a world full of manners. Not if he's any good."

Bingham paused, a hangnail capturing his attention. When he spoke, his voice was soft. "Listen, buddy. You know, Haskell's a good man. He could take this one."

Truitt stiffened. "Why do you say that?"

"You know why I'm saying that, Alby. Martin Cane was your friend. Can you maintain objectivity?"

"I'm a better sheriff than that, Johnny."

"All right. Let me ask you this one. Ella Alden nursed your mother at home until she died. That wasn't more than, what, a year ago? How much of a debt does a man owe someone for doing something like that?"

Truitt's chest tightened. "I stand by my last statement, Coroner."

Bingham held up his hands. "Fine. Just be careful, that's all I'm saying. You were voted into office, Alby, because people were tired of the courthouse gang, and they wanted things shaken up. That's flimsy coinage, if you ask me. Folks in these parts have a skewed kind of loyalty to Ella Alden and her clan—she's peculiar and she's powerful, and they don't necessarily trust that. But she sits in that Methodist church pew every Sunday, and her lips move when she reads along with the Lesson. They're gonna trust her before they trust you."

"Why do you think I'm walking on eggshells?"

Bingham gripped Truitt's shoulder before lumbering down the steps. "Maybe the state boys can put a rush on things."

The coroner crammed his considerable weight behind the wheel of his Ford Escort and turned the ignition. As Truitt watched, the mortuary van rolled down the drive, with the minuscule car and its giant driver trundling after.

He turned back to the house and looked at his deputy, standing in the doorway.

"Get a hold of Ruch," Truitt said. "Tell him to go back to the Alden house and ask Mrs. Grayson for a change of clothes for her grandmother."

In the limp glow of the porch light, the edge of the living room curtain quivered, then stilled.

"I don't care if your lips do move during the Lesson, Miss Ella," Truitt said quietly. "Whatever you were doing up in that room, it sure as hell wasn't reading the Bible."

Gale retreated from her bedroom and pulled the door after her until the light fell to the side of the bed and cloaked Katie Pru in shadows. Normally, Katie Pru slept across the hall in the smallest of the spare rooms. Tonight, however, Gale anticipated other occupants. She glanced at the three remaining rooms—Ella's at the end of the hall and the two extra bedrooms across from her own. She only prayed, selfishly, that Ruch's request for clean clothes meant it would be morning before anyone else arrived.

Tightening her bathrobe sash, Gale slipped across the oak floors and down the staircase. Two hallways bordered the stairs: the one covered in fish, which led past the dining room and into the kitchen, and a narrow corridor, walls smooth and so close together the channel was barely large enough for Gale's diminutive frame. Sill had labeled the corridor Pygmy's Pass because even as a five-foot-five-inch teenager she had been forced to stoop to pass through. No one had an explanation for the alley's size. Nathan Glynn, the house's creator, had been a relatively large man, as evidenced by the Confederate uniform packed in the attic. By all indications he would have been forced to hunch his way down his own passage.

It wasn't until one entered the room at the end of the hall that Nathan Glynn hinted at his motivation. Despite her fatigue, Gale felt relief as she walked into the den and switched on the overhead light. A cordial glow fell over a worn houndstooth sofa and a blanket chest in the center of the room and extended to a knockabout writer's desk wedged against the wall. Since childhood this had been her retreat. In a house built from a returning warrior's anger, this room was an architectural joy. Six walls swung out in a hexagon from the doorway; at the ceiling, foot-tall etched glass panels depicting summer fruits made a milky band around the top of the room. Set in one wall were two massive exterior doors, gauzy curtains draping their glass fronts like fog.

Along the remaining five walls, Glynn had built bookcases, each packed so tightly that Gale was forced to store new books under the sofa. Potted grape ivy trailed from the bookcase tops. Dried and flattened snake skins like patterned saplings ran the length of the vertical boards separating the cases, so that every time she walked into the room, she felt as if she had wandered into an entire Forest of Knowledge—or at least the Garden of Eden as a folk artist might envision it. The effect was almost enough to make her overlook the mounted squirrel on the blanket chest or the row of sleek crows, suited and monocled, that perched on the carpet edge like accountants waiting for a meal.

"'Whosoever is delighted in solitude is either a wild beast or a god,'" she murmured. In her youth she had begun a needlepoint of the Francis Bacon quote but had deserted it in favor of the loom. The needlework had been too finger-dainty; the loom she could drive with her body.

Her eyes trailed over the books, some jammed cover to cover for so long that if extricated, they would split in half. Her husband Tom had scoffed when she told him about the room.

Barmy Americans. All that wide open space and they build little bitty rooms to separate themselves.

You should know about that, growing up in a village. Villages are terrible places to keep your own thoughts. Rooms give you space to breathe.

That's the female in you, luv. 'A room of her own' and all that jazz. Never understood it myself. How can you think with bric-a-brac cluttering your view? Better to have fields and paths.

Gale pressed warm fingers against her eyes. She had not seen Tom after he'd shot himself. She had heard descriptions—villages were terrible places to keep your innocence. But words weren't eyes, and despite the details, her picture of his death was clean. She imagined his body lying motionless on its side, back arched inward, hands nestled at his chin. In her vision there was a laxity to his lips, almost a pout, which of course wasn't possible. She had learned at the inquest that he had fired the bullet into his mouth.

She thought of the four women hearing the shot from Martin's rifle and finding his body. Several seconds must have passed before one of them screamed. She doubted she would have been able to suck in enough air.

She crammed her fists into her robe pockets and paced the room. At the desk she stopped. The lid was pulled down, making a table for her work. A notebook lay pressed open to her latest research.

The woman, a thirty-one-year old Morgan County resident, had written her diaries in pencil in a series of thin green booklets preserved in the University of Georgia's historical archives. Gale had copied them verbatim, using a pencil and paper as close to the originals' weight as she could find.

September 22, 1919
    Little Sam was up all night with fever. I got no sleep and I pray the ache in my legs is from fatigue and not the first signs of sickness. The Wilsons are coming in from Toccoa tomorrow, and I must wash the linens and put fresh meat to cook. But the baby won't stop crying, and he's so flushed. I'm tired, tired, and have sent Marcus for Dr. Allen. But it will take a day at least, and I fear I hurt past normal.

We all hurt past normal, she thought as she gently closed the notebook. Tom was wrong. A woman damn well does need a room of her own.

She threw herself against a pile of weary velvet pillows tossed into the corner of the sofa, only to recoil from a scratchiness at the back of her neck. She examined the pillows and found, peeking from beneath them, Linnie's coverlet, neatly folded into thirds. Like a shamefaced child Gale had hidden it there before leaving for the barbecue, and then like a child forgotten it. Ella would realize the coverlet was missing in either a second or a week: a perverse measure of a man's death.

She pressed her cheek into the woven cloth. The bleach smell was gone. The basis of the design was the classic bowknot with its loops so regimented they looked like hardened flames. This coverlet, however, gave a thumbed nose to vernacular. Gently Gale ran her finger over the indigo loops, marveling at their intricacy and ingenuity. Gale's loom work had been straight-forward, playing more with color than patterns. She had found the numbering of complex patterns too cumbersome, the counting too frustrating. And she had never contemplated an original design. For her, part of the joy had been in the repetition—the back and forth of the shuttle, the repeat of the line, the continuing of the tradition.

Linnie must have felt a different call. Gale spread the coverlet over her knees. The loops of the bowknots were almost the shape of paisleys, but their ends drifted off like vines and disappeared at the borders of the cloth. It was as if Linnie, frustrated by the geometric limits placed on her by her homebound shaft loom, had tried to mimic the fluency of the professional Jacquard. The work it must have taken was mind-boggling. And odd, too, since by the time Linnie reached adulthood in the 1920s, coverlets of both styles would have been outdated. No one but isolated Appalachian dwellers and artsy-fartsy commune types would have practiced either form.

From the other side of the house, the back porch door whacked shut. Gale dropped the coverlet across the sofa arm, crossed the room, and flicked off the light. It was still the dead of night—much too early for any serious questioning to have taken place.

She hurried down the gnomish passage and rounded the staircase. The kitchen door was closed, an infrequent event in the food-based culture of the Alden family. Puzzled, she walked to the door and pressed her hand against it, straining to hear any sounds. There were none. She slowly turned the knob and pushed the door open.

It took a moment for her to realize what was wrong. Ella, Cammy, and Sill sat at the kitchen table while Maralyn rummaged through the refrigerator. They must be hungry, she thought. She had read once that some people become ravenous in the face of death. They looked relaxed enough in their clean summer clothes. Then she saw it: Blood clotted their hair and blotched their faces.

"Sill," Ella said. "You use the bathroom first."

"All right, Mother," Maralyn said from behind the freezer door. "What have you done with the coffee?"

"Well, it's right . . ." Ella turned, saw Gale, and stopped short. "What are you doing here? The light in your room was off. I assumed you and Katie Pru were asleep."

Gale froze in the door frame. "Katie Pru is asleep. I was in the den."

Ella's glare was imperious. "Didn't you hear about your cousin Martin? Didn't you know he was shot?"

"Well, yes." Gale looked helplessly at the women, unsure. Cammy stared past the bowl of pink silk flowers in the middle of the table, her mouth slack as a rubber band. Sill's thumbs wrestled each other. "I was outside when it happened," Gale stammered. "I don't know what to say—I'm so sorry. But what in God's name . . . ?"

The freezer door popped shut. Maralyn kneaded the cold coffee grounds against her chest.

"Gale," she began.

Ella snapped her fingers at her eldest daughter. Gale had seen the gesture hundreds of times, a snap and a quick dash of her hand. It meant silence and automatic obedience. Maralyn closed her mouth. Gripping the edge of the table, Ella rose from her chair. She stalked to the doorway, the smell from her body making Gale gag.

"Go to bed, Gale," Ella said firmly. "You are not needed here. We can take care of Cammy and Sill."

"But Ella. For God's sakes . . ."

"Go on, Gale. You take care of Katie Pru. I have things under control here."

Ella's skin was almost translucent under the gore, her eyes hard enough to crack.

Gale stepped away from the portal as the door shut in her face. She stared at it, disbelieving, the stench of Martin's blood filling the hall.

Linnie Cane was a married woman.
Linnie Cane was a mother as well.
Linnie Cane took her life one summer.
Linnie Cane went straight to Hell.
      —Ballad sung by the Statlers Cross
        Methodist Church youth group
        during a cookout, 1949

 7

The jag-wire was having a grumpy morning. Katie Pru knew it as soon as she ran down the front steps of the house, her mother following behind with a cup of coffee in her hand and a satchel of papers flung over her back. It was early, so early, in fact, that the sky was the color of a quarter and the grass a funny shade of green.

"Mind the damp, K.P.," her mother said. "Don't sit on the ground. Don't step in the muddy parts. And eat your toast, please, ma'am."

Her mother didn't mind the damp—she sat down on the middle step in her blue jeans skirt, placed her coffee beside her, and rummaged through the satchel.

Katie Pru frowned and, clutching her wrapped-up toast, stepped onto a paving stone. Beside it was a patch of red mud. Glancing at her mother, she kicked her toe into it.

"Katie Pru." It was a warning. "If you want to play with the jaguar, either stay on the paving stones or on the grass. Otherwise we'll go back inside."

Katie Pru didn't believe it. She had awakened in the middle of the night, the bed so big and the furniture so strange she hollered. Her mother hurried to her, whispering and rubbing her back until Katie Pru grew drowsy. Then her mother turned away and began undoing the buttons on her blouse, slowly at first, then yanking at them until her elbows jerked up like chicken wings. When she finally stretched out on the bed, Katie Pru listed slightly toward her, rolling into a ball against her mother's stomach. She fell asleep smelling the vinegary warmth of her mother's skin.

This morning her mother had dressed them both before opening the bedroom door. The house was quiet and the door to Grandma Ella's room shut as they scurried downstairs and into the kitchen. A quick piece of toast and a cup of coffee from the microwave and they were out the door.

Katie Pru now walked up to the grumpy jag-wire, her toast soggy in its napkin. His mouth was open in a growl and his eyes—the only part of him that wasn't black—were yellow and peeling, so that it looked as if his eyeballs were busting out of their color. She held the toast out to him.

"Want some?"

He didn't answer. She stepped in front of him, where the ground was both grass and mud, and placed her hand in front of his mouth. His breath was cool.

"Okay," she said. "So what *do* you want?"

"Ketchup."

"What for?"

"It's good on girl toes."

"Stop it. Now you tell me, what do you want?"

"Move."

She stepped aside and, eying him warily, stooped and turned her head so that she could see where he was looking. There was the driveway, of course, and the leafy pecan tree with branches so big they wagged like dog tails when the wind blew. There was the thin road that passed in front of the house, and across it the mailbox with a plastic magnolia flapping from its post. Otherwise there was only the railroad track, long and tall and weedy.

She straightened and squinted at the jag-wire. "You looking at the railroad tracks?" she asked.

He didn't nod. His growl grew a teeny bit fierce and his voice gruff.

"The man's back. He's on the railroad tracks."

Katie Pru twisted around. Sure enough, the man was there, picking his way along the railroad tracks like a giant walking-stick bug. She glanced at her mother, but she was writing in her notebook, her coffee in her hand, and had not noticed.

"I don't like the man," Katie Pru whispered. "He tells scary stories."

"I don't like the man," the jag-wire snarled. "He spits at me."

The man walked in baby steps, his cane poking at the railroad track. Swinging from one hand was a white box tied with string. The man didn't come by every day—if he did, the jag-wire would have eaten him by now—but he came by more than Katie Pru liked. She crammed the toast and napkin into the jag-wire's mouth and scrambled onto his back, where she watched the man move into view between the animal's ears.

"Missy!" The old man raised his cane. Her mother jerked her head up, surprised. The old man jabbed the cane into the air, the white box banging against his wrist. "I thought I'd come by early today before the crowd!"

He said "early" funny—like "oily." Her mother

slowly set down her coffee and pushed her hair behind her ears.

"Well, Mr. Deak Motts," her mother shouted. "I'm afraid you're a bit too early. Ella's not up yet."

"Ella! Why'd you think I'd want to see Ella?" He came to the place in the railroad where cars passed over and started down the hill. "I don't want to see that old firebrand. Nossir!"

Her mother picked up her coffee cup and sipped, her eyes following the man as he reached the bottom of the hill, crossed the road, and started up the drive.

When he reached the jag-wire, he stopped. "Little miss," he said. "Why're you burying your head?"

Beneath Katie Pru's legs, the jag-wire moved. *Don't bite*, she warned. *Mama'll take you to the zoo if you bite.*

"I guess she's not in a talking mood, Deak," her mother said. "Why don't you come talk to me?"

He tapped the jag-wire's feet with his cane, then turned to her mother. "Sad about Martin. He was a good man."

From a space beneath her arm, Katie Pru saw her mother nod. "Thank you, Deak. I'll tell Cammy and Sill you said that."

"I was in the fish house, you know, when the gun went off. I knew right away it was wrong. There weren't no one around town that've been shooting a gun right then. Not for a legal reason."

Her mother closed her notebook. "I suspect you're right. It was certainly a shock."

"Here." He hobbled across the paving stones, his feet slipping into the red dirt, and set the box beside her mother. "My daughter-in-law made these for y'all. Zucchini muffins. I expect they're too gummy." He leaned on his cane. "I hope they keep doing the barbecue. I'd hate to see that quit."

"Oh, I'm sure someone will take it up again. Nobody's gonna let go of that kind of money."

"Don't be too sure. Something happens and then

people don't want to touch it again. Superstition, that's what that is. Like badness is a powder that comes off on your hands."

Her mother took so long to answer that Katie Pru lifted her head. Her mother sat silently on the steps, staring at the ground. Then she picked up her cup and tossed the coffee through the air like a flying snake.

"Tell me something, Deak," she said. "You were in the fish house when the gun went off—were you there when Sill introduced her friend to Martin?"

"The pretty dark-haired girl. I was there."

"Martin left the fish house angry. Do you know anything about that?"

"Well, Martin's bad with temper. Not that he means anything by it. Sill's just a girl who's always known how to set it off, that's all."

"Did you hear what their fight was about?"

Deak flicked a stone with his cane, sending it pinging against the jag-wire's foot. "He didn't want them there. Couldn't exactly tell why. The girl looked decent enough. They'd been in there for a bit, listening to us jabber. At first, when Martin came in, he seemed okay. But then he got that look. He could look downright mean when he got angry."

"So what did they say to each other?"

"Not much. Sill said something like 'I want you to meet . . .' and Martin said, 'I don't need to meet her, I've already talked to her.' And that was about it. He just blew up and stormed out."

"And Sill went after him."

"That's right."

Her mother looked at Katie Pru with eyes that gazed right through her. Katie Pru tightened her grip on the jag-wire. She hated it when her mother looked at her that way. It made her feel like she had disappeared.

"Tell me something else, Deak," her mother said at last. "That story you were telling. The one about the lynching. I remember you telling it when I was growing up. Is it true?"

"True?" Deak teetered over to Katie Pru. "Little miss, your mama thinks I been making up tales."

"I'm hoping you are," her mother said.

Deak cackled. He gripped the jag-wire's ear with a bumpy blue hand and leaned close to Katie Pru. Colors swam in his eyes.

"Know how old I am, little miss?" His voice was a whisper. "I'm eighty-eight. I used to build coffins as a trade. You build coffins, you hear stories. You ever hear the one about your great-aunt Linnie?"

Her mother was on her feet. "Deak!"

He tapped his cane at her in a way that looked both angry and silly. "Hush, missy. This one's all right for a child." He turned back to Katie Pru. "Your great-aunt Linnie—she'd be more than one great to you—she'd walk the railroad tracks, just like I do. There used to be a train come down that track, did you know that? It stopped right in front of the old mill. Brought in cotton and took out cloth, and it didn't go no further than here, 'cause this was the end of the line."

His fingers fluttered against the jag-wire's ear. His breath smelled of medicine. "Well, Linnie Glynn Cane, she didn't work in the mill. Nossiree, she was too fine for mill work. Wouldn't have no lint in her hair. She worked her own loom. She'd make a shawl and then she'd wrap it around her shoulders and walk up and down the road here like she was nobody's business. Sometimes she'd hike up onto the track and hop aboard the train when it left with the cloth. Only there weren't no train coming back, you see. The train only ran twice a week. So 'bout nightfall, she'd come walking down the tracks, shawl still on her shoulders, sashaying back the whole six miles from the station in Oaktree."

He grinned. His big teeth were yellow and lined in black. Katie Pru grabbed her mother's hand as she came up and hugged her.

"This ain't no scary story, little miss. Linnie's husband, Justin, was a friend of mine. For a while he believed she was stepping out, but you know what? She weren't. She just liked to ride away from town so she could parade back in."

"That's some story, Deak." Her mother's voice was flat. "You make it sound as if Linnie didn't do a serious day's work in her life. The truth is she had a choice—she could work on the farm or she could work at the mill. She chose her family's farm."

"Most folks didn't have a choice."

"Maybe. But that doesn't mean she wasn't out in those fields, hoeing and plowing with the rest of them. Land didn't mean leisure back then. And the Glynn farm supplied a fair amount of the cotton that kept the mill in business." She pulled gently on Katie Pru's hand. "Come on, baby. I feel like a change of scenery."

"She weren't working the fields when she was walking the tracks." The old man whacked his cane against the jag-wire's chest. "Some folks said there'd be a time when she walked too slow, and the next train would come up behind her and run her down. But that never happened. That was just folks bitching."

"Okay, ladybug." Her mother lifted her from the jag-wire's back. "Time to go."

"Hey, you see Miss Cammy, give her my condolences."

"I will, Deak. It's getting close to nine. Isn't it about time you got to church?"

The old man's eyes widened. "Church?" he said. "Ma'am, I got me a limited need for church." He turned to the jag-wire and spat.

The first five miles of the journey from the county seat of Praterton to Statlers Cross was over smooth, four-lane blacktop—a backroads I-75 with stunted signs lauding the sales of the tourist's trinity: peaches, peanuts, and pecans. Behind a line of roadside stands, a new Congregationalist church had taken root, a double-wide trailer with its bay window displaying a plastic rendition of Bible and cross. Past the church a side road emerged from a delta of gravel and dirt. Truitt bumped onto the rough two-lane and headed northwest.

The road started respectably, bordered on both sides by wire fences interlaced with honeysuckle and the sangria-colored flower of the trumpet vine. Piebald pastures unrolled around him, familiar fields studied in his youth from the cab of Martin's black pickup.

Now, when you shoot a buck, make sure you aim for a vital spot. Don't go messin' up the poor thing by aiming wild.

Their first hunting trip had been in the woods surrounding Stack Mountain in the northeastern corner of the county. They had been alone, Martin dressed in a worn hunting jacket with a patina of mud and old hairs, Alby scrawny under a bright orange vest, knife-new and smelling of polyester. At sixteen Alby was well past initiation age—the rifle in his hands felt as unfamiliar as a girl.

It was a chilly November morning, the sky layered in sheets of gray that plunged the pines into a military green and drank the definition from the needles beneath their feet. He followed Martin silently, hunching his shoulder and adjusting the vest that slipped uncomfortably down his arm. *Shit, it's cold,* he thought. *Where the hell's something for me to shoot?* Martin walked in front of him, his head turning from side to side.

"Whaddya looking for?" Alby asked.

Martin waved him quiet. "Hush, boy, just hush and pay attention. The stand's up ahead."

Alby matched Martin's glances, trying to discern what he might be seeking. To the left, to the right, nothing but pine and dead leaves. The bright orange vest rode backwards, rubbing Alby's armpits. He shrugged and hunched several more times, angry at his mother for not knowing what she was doing when she bought it. If his father were still around . . .

Martin stopped suddenly.

"Son," he said slowly. "What the hell are you doing?"

Alby looked up. The barrel of his gun rested against the center of Martin's back. He glanced down at his hand. His face began to burn. At some point, he didn't know when, he had slipped his finger around the trigger.

"God bless, Martin," he whispered. "Jesus."

"Put her down, Alby. Just go ahead and set her on the ground."

He flung the gun to earth, backing away from it and wringing his hand as if stung. Martin picked up the gun and without a word headed for the entrance to the woods. Unbelievably, Martin had taken him out again the next weekend, making him stay in the woods until he shot a deer. It wasn't big, merely a spike buck. But he had pointed the gun at something he meant to kill, and then determinedly, finally, done it.

A pothole the shape of Alaska materialized in the road. Truitt jerked the green Dodge right, then left.

Statlers Cross came upon him suddenly, as it always did, the railroad track an instant hill at his side. He slowed and puttered past the Statlers Cross Methodist Church. Its parking lot was jammed and its front doors were latched open. Inside the narthex a crowd of worshipers pressed to see the main event in the sanctuary. At nine-thirty it was too early for the regular service. No doubt Brother Teller, blocked in the night from comforting the family, in the morning had opted for some impromptu consolation of his flock.

Truitt pressed the accelerator. The half a dozen stores that lined Statlers Cross's commercial district had the spruced-up face of hopeful prosperity. Twenty years ago the shops had been slowly turning to rubble; now only the old photography studio remained permanently shuttered. He cruised by slowly, taking in the cherry dresser in the antique store window, the display of crocheted crosses and beribboned baskets marking a community gift shop, the windows of Greene's Hardware darkened since the proprietor's death. As he came to the end of the row, he noticed with surprise that, despite the Sunday morning hour, the fluorescent lights inside Langley Drugs were on.

Cool air nipped him as soon as he entered the store. Cooper Langley's customary business attire of jeans and plaids had been replaced by a baggy black suit. With his red hair slicked back and his skinny wrists jutting from his coat sleeves, he resembled a 1930s comics book villain. He was bent over the checkout counter quietly talking to a man Truitt didn't know. He glanced up as the sheriff approached.

"Alby. So how are you? Grab yourself a Coke."

"Thanks, Coop. And I haven't had breakfast yet, either. Ring me up some of those cheese crackers."

Langley punched the amount into the cash register. His elbow knocked a cardboard box sitting on the counter. "Bad business about Martin," he said. "We're just talking about how he was in perfect form yesterday."

"How's that?" Truitt asked, popping a cracker into his mouth. "Perfect form, I mean."

Langley picked up the change Truitt laid on the counter and dropped the coins into the cash drawer. "You know, everything up and running, going smooth. Something like that'll take months to plan, dozens of people, but it comes down to one man. I tell you, this town would've dried up and blown away years ago without Martin and that barbecue. Funny how one thing like that can put a place on the map."

The stranger shook his head. "It must be hard on the family. I guess you're back to see how they're doing?"

Truitt turned to the man. Tall, fiftyish, he was dressed in his church clothes. He looked oddly out of kilter from the people Truitt would expect to find hanging around Langley Drugs. His blue suit was too well cut, his shoes too spit-and-polish. Even his gray hair fluffed a tad too nicely around his tanned face for

Truitt to believe he was a native. Airline pilot, Truitt decided, one of the many who had moved to Calwyn County because it was far enough from Atlanta to be out of reach of most commuters, but not so far that the urban-inclined couldn't get back to civilization when they needed the fix.

Truitt cocked his head. "You know the Canes well?"

"Just some. My wife and I went to church with Martin and Cammy. I'm afraid that because of my work, our attendance is sporadic. Still, if you're a member of Statlers Cross Methodist, you knew Martin. He was involved in so many things. I had a lot of respect for him." He paused. "Martin was a true man of God."

The man had the accent of a citified Southerner, someone who had given up the dialect long ago and now used it uncomfortably. "I'm sorry," Truitt said. "I used to think I knew everyone in the county, but the darn place is getting so crowded. I'm Sheriff Alby Truitt."

The man took Truitt's extended hand. "Mal Robertson. I guess I'm a newcomer—we've been here for about a year now, although I have family ties that go way back. I'm a pilot for Delta."

Truitt smiled. "Pleased to meet you. I recognize your name from the statement my deputy took. Y'all were both in the group of men who went into the room, weren't you? Not in here this morning embellishing your stories, are you?"

"Good grief, no, Sheriff." Robertson said. "I'm flying tomorrow morning, and my wife wanted me to pick up some health care supplies before I leave." He pointed at the box. "She's doing a little nursing work these days. Cooper here was nice enough to open early for me."

"Hell, Mal, don't lie to the sheriff." Cooper bent over the counter and lowered his voice. "Truth was, Alby, we were both at church. But when Ryan Teller started going on about all the talk shows in Heaven booking Martin as a guest, we bolted. Can't stand tacky preaching."

Truitt chuckled. "Talk shows in Heaven?"

"Yeah, well, you'd have to know our preacher. Sometimes you wish God would call and find the line busy."

Robertson made a concurring grunt. "I was just telling Coop that I saw a woman taking pictures yesterday at the barbecue. Probably for some newspaper. Somebody ought to find out who she was and get some copies for the family. Like Coop said, Martin was in perfect form. It'd be a nice way to remember him."

"Do you know what paper she was from, Coop?" Truitt asked. "I can't recall there being any mention of a media person in the reports."

Langley shook his head. "I didn't see her. But I'd like to track her down. I wouldn't mind some copies myself." He swiped the countertop with his palm. "So, Alby, we were wondering when the funeral's going to be. I mean, don't y'all still have the body and all?"

"Just for another day or so. When the state crime lab has finished running its tests, we'll release it to the family. And then it'll be up to Cammy to make the arrangements."

Langley was silent. He quietly thumped the counter with his fist.

"It was an accident, right?" he asked. "Y'all aren't looking into anything else."

"You know how it is, Coop. Gotta get all the *i*'s dotted and *t*'s crossed."

"Shoot, I understand that. It's just . . . well, you know small towns. The quicker things're settled, the less likely people are to talk."

Truitt kept his smile polite. "Talk about what?"

"Oh, hell, you know, Alby." Langley's voice went falsetto. " 'Whuddya think them women were doin' in there, Mama? If they weren't doin' nuthin' wrong, why don't the sheriff just say it was an ax-see-dent.' You know how folks are."

Truitt extracted another cracker from its pack. "I'm surprised at you, Coop. You know I've got a procedure. You know I won't do anything out of line."

"I'm not saying you would. I'm just saying people'll talk. And Cammy, she's a good woman, but she's not the strongest thing in the world."

"I have to get my facts down, Coop."

"Oh, sure, Alby. I just hope folks understand that's all you're doing."

Robertson cleared his throat. "Look, Sheriff, Coop here is beating around the bush, but I think I can state his concern clearly, professional to professional. Sometimes good intentions can blur good judgment. Coop was just telling me how Martin took you under his wing when your father—"

Langley broke in. "I wasn't gossiping, Alby. It's just that I know how it is. My brother died in an automobile accident, and I spent two years trying to prove that the other guy was at fault. . . ."

Truitt felt the blood rush to his face. He stared from Langley to Robertson, angry enough to despise the one's weediness and the other's pomposity. "Thank you, Coop," he interrupted. "I'll try to follow my head and not my heart."

"Now, Alby . . ."

Truitt focused on Robertson. "With that in mind, sir, I'd like to go over your statement a bit."

"Sure. What do you want to know?"

"As I recall the report said you were looking for Martin when you heard the shot. Why?"

"Ryan asked me to find him. He needed to ask him a question."

"Did he say what?"

"No. I didn't ask."

"Where all did you look?"

Robertson shrugged. "In the yard, the fish house—I even went into the kitchen at one point, but Ella shooed

me away. She said she was fixing more iced tea and
didn't need some muddy-footed man getting in the
way."

"Anyone else in the kitchen with her?"

"Cammy. And the big woman someone told me
was Ella's daughter."

"Did you ask them if they had seen Martin?"

"Sure. Ella said he was out on the front porch, but
the only person out there was Zilah Greene, sitting on
the porch swing."

"How long did you look before you heard the
shot?"

"I dunno. Not more than fifteen minutes."

"And how long between the time you left the
women in the kitchen and the shot?"

Robertson raised his eyebrows. "Couldn't have
been more than five or ten. I was in the driveway when
I heard it. Took me less than a minute to get back to the
house. I nearly knocked Zilah over when I came running in."

"She was in the house?"

"No, on the porch. But I've never seen such fear on
a person's face. She had her skirt hiked up and was running down the steps like a bat out of hell."

"I wanna walk the tracks like Linnie." Katie Pru pulled
the back of her blue T-shirt up over her shoulders and
hopped onto the railroad tie. "I wanna wear a shawl
and sassy."

" 'Sashay,' " Gale corrected, "although it's very
nearly the same thing. At any rate, it's not something
four-year-olds do."

"You do it, then. You sassy and I'll watch."

"Oh, right, ma'am. I can see you now, swishing
your fanny up to Grandma Ella and telling her, 'See,
Mama taught me how to sassy!' " Gale swooped down
and tickled Katie Pru's belly. "You and I would be in
Southern lady classes by noon."

Katie Pru guffawed, her slim torso twisting in her mother's hands. Laughing, Gale swung her into the air and brought her down into a bear hug, burying her face against the tiny neck. God, she marveled at the physicality of her child: all implausible bones, pearly skin, and hair so fine she had to concentrate to feel it. Katie Pru was always changing, never the child she was. Gale felt a familiar ache as she planted a loud kiss on her daughter's cheek. Forget Linnie, she thought—children are their own apparitions.

After one more hug she gently lowered the squirming child to the ground. They stood atop the railroad tracks, Ella's house to the left, the mill ruins to the right. The last time Gale saw Deak, he was hobbling up the drive to the Greene house, the scratch of his cane on gravel audible from one hundred yards away. Now they were alone, and the only sound was the mournful chorus of "How Great Thou Art" rolling through the open doors of the church.

Katie Pru wrapped her arms around Gale's thighs and squeezed. "Let's go to the ruins, Mama," she whispered. "It's time to listen to the music."

They made their way down the southern slope and entered the mill's open space. The ritual had started the first Sunday in spring when Katie Pru heard the music from the open church windows and began running toward it. Gale had caught her, and they had ended up in the mill, where they sat on a large stone slab and listened to the voices float over the roofless walls. From there they could see the sky and the cluster of strangely shaped mill houses erected like squat telescopes on their plots.

The ground smelled moldy as they picked their way toward the stone slab. The congregation moaned the opening stanza of "Sweet Hour of Prayer." There would be no jaunty gospel music or high-church reverence today. Grief was sober and close. They will probably sing for Martin all morning, readying themselves to visit the family, Gale thought. And it should be so. Martin deserved no less.

They were ten yards from the stone slab when Gale stopped short. A woman huddled on the stone, her clothes the color of the rocks. She was so well camoflauged they easily could have sat down on top of her, Gale mused, had it not been for the slash of her red lips. Around her neck was the camera she had carried at the barbecue.

The woman looked up at them, startled, and buried her fist in the folds of her skirt. She was young, somewhere in her early twenties, and dressed in a long gray shift that fell straight from her shoulders. Had it been cut differently, it could have passed for one of the pricey country-girl frocks found on the racks at Macy's. As it was, the fabric was pressed but worn, the styling unconscious. Her oatmeal-colored hair was pulled back in a ponytail, and her blue eyes were little more than indentations beneath her naked lashed.

"Hello," Gale said. "We didn't mean to disturb. We just came to listen to the music."

"I know," the woman answered. "I see you here every Sunday. I just didn't think you'd be here today." Her clinched knuckles worked the thin fabric of her skirt. "I live there"—she pointed to a yellow house at the edge of the mill village—"and I can see the mill from my bedroom window."

Her voice was husky, at odds with both her artless appearance and her heavy Georgia Piedmont accent. Gale realized that the red she had assumed yesterday was lipstick was actually natural. She found herself staring at the woman's lips—they were extraordinary, so plump that when she spoke, the rest of her features receded away.

Gale's voice was light. "I hope we're not too boring to watch."

The young woman blushed, and her hands flitted in front of her. "It wasn't nothing like that, ma'am. I just looked out one morning and there y'all were. I thought you looked so pretty, a mother and child in the middle of all this mess." Her face crinkled with concern. "It's not like I was spying or anything."

"Despite the camera?"

The woman looked down at her camera in dismay. "Oh, no, ma'am, that's just for a class I'm taking over at the arts center in Praterton. It's nothing, honest."

Gale smiled and drew Katie Pru to her. "I'm just teasing you. I saw you yesterday at the barbecue and thought you were a journalist. Nicer to know you're an artist. I'm Gale. And this is my daughter, Katie Pru."

"My name is Nadianna Jesup. Nice to meet you, Katie Pru."

She stretched her hand out to Katie Pru, who looked at it shyly and began bumping her backside against her mother's legs. Nadianna tucked her long skirt under her thigh and patted the space on the rock next to her. "I have a secret to tell you, Katie Pru," she whispered. Cautiously, Katie Pru approached her. Nadianna continued. "You know that big cat in your yard? When I was a little girl, I had a make-believe tiger as a friend, and sometimes he'd run off and play with that cat. I'd look all over the house and couldn't find him, but if I'd crawl to the top of the tracks and look over, there he'd be, dancing in the yard with your cat."

Katie Pru pressed her palm to her mouth, muffling her words. "Where's your tiger now?"

Nadianna shook her head sorrowfully. "I haven't seen him in the longest time. If you find him, will you tell him to come home?"

Katie Pru nodded, her eyes wide. Gale regarded the woman quietly.

"You know a lot about us," she said.

Nadianna's gaze was clear as she looked at Gale. "Not really. At least, not any more than anybody else. I just grew up wishing I had a big iron tiger in my yard."

"Jag-wire," said Katie Pru.

"Jaguar. See? I'm not so smart after all." Nadianna put her hands on her hips. Humor tinged her voice. "Of course I know about you, Mrs. Grayson. This would be a pitiful excuse for a small town if I didn't. Trust me, though, there's nothing sinister in it. We just don't have cable yet."

Gale surprised herself by chuckling. "You're right. Let's begin again. It's nice to meet you. Out getting some early morning shots?"

"Uh-huh. I've got to change for church in a little bit, but I wanted to see the mill after last night's rain."

"You go to the Baptist church?"

"Pentecostal. Anyway, for my class, I'm supposed to take pictures that depict my culture. My grandparents worked at this mill. My grandmama used to say, 'So much hard work went on in that mill that the ground turned pretty with it.' " She suddenly thrust her hand out, palm up, and revealed a smooth fragment of green glass. "See? Pieces like this come up from the earth, pretty as a jewel. I keep running out here day and night trying to get the perfect photograph of light on the rubble."

Gale started to say "Nice concept," but stopped herself. She wasn't sure about this woman; she equally wasn't sure about her own response to her. There was something discordant in this stranger—what do you make of a person who looks like a Flannery O'Connor Southerner, yet takes photographs of her "culture"? You're being a bigot, Gale Grayson, she scolded. A pig-headed, big-city chauvinist.

"I know what you mean," she said. "I spent my summers in Ella's house, and to me it's always been the symbol of my own peculiar culture. I used to love looking at all the ways the sun could hit the roof." She grinned. "Of course, now that I'm a grown-up, I'd pay good money for the sun to be hitting my own roof."

Nadianna laughed. "Me, too. In fact, I'm looking for my own roof now. I used to work at the poultry plant before it closed down. Before that, I minded children. I'd like to do that again." She walked her fingers over Katie Pru's shoulder and gave the child's ear a wiggle. Katie Pru snickered, jumped away, then shyly stepped closer. Nadianna wiggled her ear again. "I'm good with children," she said. "And I have good references."

Gale nodded vacantly, anxious to get off the subject. "So how's your camera work? Did you get any good shots yesterday?"

It took Nadianna's harsh glance for Gale to realize what she had said. Heat rushed to her cheeks.

"I'm sorry," she mumbled. "That was horrible."

"Not as horrible as what happened." Nadianna pitched the green glass shard against the side of the wall, hard. "I should have had a movie camera with me. A thirty-five-millimeter wasn't enough."

Gale stared at her. "Why? Did you see something?"

Nadianna rose awkwardly. Her face looked pinched, the skin between her eyebrows puckered and white. The strains of "Nearer My God to Thee" filtered from the church.

"I didn't see anything, Mrs. Grayson. But I could feel the raunchiness. The ground was flat ugly with it."

*She was standing in the cow pasture, all in
white. Her fingernails were longer than claws,
and she reached out to the side of that bull and
dragged her nails along his hide. I could see the
blood spurt, but the bull didn't move. She must
have bedeviled him because he continued to
sleep, like he was already dead and waiting to
be gutted.*

—Deak Motts, at a VFW dinner, 1951

8

Sill awoke to the distant sound of a phone ringing. The
muffled trill sounded once, twice, and then was truncated in mid-ring. From the narrow bed, she could see
the room's only window, curtainless and severe against
the gray platen of sky. It was impossible to guess
the hour.

And then she remembered. Last night, how she had
run frantically around her parents' room, her mother
screaming on the floor beside her father's unyielding
bulk, Ella shouting questions. And Maralyn standing
stunned by the bedside table, her big hands open and
helpless.

The knock at the door was soft and rapid.

"Sill?" Gale's voice barely topped a whisper. "Are you awake?"

Sill pressed the heels of her hands to her eyes and, rubbing them briskly, slid from between the sheets. At the bottom of the bed lay a yellow chenille robe. Someone, probably Ella, hadn't neglected the niceties due unexpected guests, regardless of the circumstances.

"Come on in, Gale." Sill slid the robe over her head and zipped it to her neck. "I hope you have coffee."

The porcelain doorknob turned and Gale backed into the room carrying a large tin tray.

"Tea, actually," Gale said. "Ella assured me you'd had your fill of coffee last night." She was dressed casually in a chambray shirt and long denim skirt, more suited, Sill thought, for a brunch than a wake. She deposited the tray on a cobbler's bench angled against a threadbare green settee. Gently she pulled away a bright blue napkin, displaying the basket beneath it. "Zucchini muffins, courtesy of Myra Motts." She glanced at Sill. "Of course, you may not be hungry. If you'd prefer coffee, it'll only take a second to get you some. And I know there're two cups here, but if you don't want any company . . ."

Sill waved her cousin quiet and padded barefoot to the settee. "How's Mother?"

"She's asleep in Ella's bedroom—Ella and Maralyn have been in and out of there all morning, but I haven't seen her. It's quiet, though. Did she see a doctor last night?"

Sill nodded. "Dr. Bingham took a look at her. He said something about sedatives." She paused. "Who all's here?"

"Nobody—yet. Ella spent the morning on the phone to the relatives, telling them to stay home until the funeral. Of course, if there's someone you or Cammy would like . . ."

"No, there isn't." She mustered a weak smile. "I'm

in the Alden women's capable hands." She pulled the sides of the robe around her. "What time is it?"

Gale dragged a rocking chair from the corner of the room and plopped into it. "About ten. Ella says that if Ryan Teller follows tradition, church will be early this morning, and then everyone will head over here. That's why she suggested I come check on you."

Sill looked down at the dainty spread on the tray— a pot, a cream-and-sugar set, two cups and saucers, two spoons, and a pair of overly plump muffins. All beautifully laid out with the blue rose china and Francis I silver that had belonged to Ella's mother, Jessie. She smiled ruefully.

"My, but the women of this family have a stubborn sense of occasion. Do you know what this reminds me of?"

Gale nodded. "I thought of it while I was coming upstairs. Jessie and her hospitality story. Or 'Jessie Does the Preacher,' as you used to say."

"Let me see if I can remember it properly." Sill lowered her voice to a throaty Southern drawl. " 'It was during the Depression, and Jessie had her mother's exquisite crystal with which to entertain the new minister, but not so much as a cube of sugar or a pinch of tea to flavor the water. So she pulled the minister's chair next to the window where the mid-afternoon sun flooded his lap. On a tray she presented him a crystal glass filled with cool well water. He took the glass, and when the sunlight hit the facets, flashes of pink and blue leapt from the minister's hands. Afterwards, he claimed it was the best refreshment he had ever tasted. So from that day forward, Jessie always maintained that regardless of one's troubles . . .' "

Gale took a long breath. " '. . . it's the dishes that count.' Pretty good. I didn't detect a single mistake."

The back of the settee was stiff against Sill's spine; the stuffing cracked as she settled. "No," she said softly. "No mistakes. Ella trained us well."

Gale handed Sill a steaming cup of tea. "Faith's

called several times this morning," she said. "She wants to know if she should come over."

"What did you tell her?"

"That you were asleep. Someone would call her later."

"Would you do that?"

"And tell her what?"

"Not to come."

Gale's face was inscrutable. "All right," she said at last. "Will she need a reason?"

"No."

Gale rocked in silence, the chair runners droning on the flat wooden boards. It was always impossible to tell what Gale was thinking—Sill had often speculated that under different circumstances her cousin would have been a great business tycoon, or at the very minimum a hell of a card shark. Whatever her assumptions, she never let them show in her face. And when she did choose to reveal them, it was never directly. She always sidled up to her observations like a crab.

She did so now, running her finger around the rim of her cup.

"When I was in England," Gale said, "I usually only drank tea when other people fixed it for me, which wasn't that often. Funny, though, I wanted it so bad just now." She clasped her hands around the cup like a child, bringing it close to her face. "It's all those puddles outside. Tea is comforting."

"And that's why you brought some here for me? You thought I needed comforting?"

"Don't you?"

"No."

Sill stretched forward and heaped sugar into her cup. Jessie's sterling silver spoon was unexpectedly light in her hand. The silver, Sill knew, had actually belonged to her own great-grandmother Linnie, but in the aftermath of her suicide, all of the dead woman's belongings had gone to her sister Jessie instead of the young son Linnie had left behind. Sill had long ago accepted the fact that by killing herself, Linnie had diverted the family goods. So much of what should have been Sill's would eventually go to Katie Pru.

She glanced up at the wall over the bed. A black-framed collection of hair hung there like a beauty parlor advertisement for dyes. Light hair, dark hair, curly, straight—everyone on the 1925 Statlers Cross Methodist roll had their clipped remains preserved there. Except the dishonorable Mrs. Linnie Glynn Cane. The space where her lock had been was empty, the glue now darkened to a stain on the paper. Someone had even scratched away her name. Sill had always wondered who would have cared to the point of obliteration.

It was odd to see the fragile strands of people long dead. Almost paganish, this belief that preserving bits of their bodies would preserve their souls. Better to preserve dishes.

She saw Gale's eyes flicker from the reliquary down to her face.

"What are you thinking?" Sill asked.

Gale shook her head. "It's a powerful monument. We used to make such fun of it as children. We could be so cold."

"All children are."

"Maybe." The creaking under the runners stopped as Gale set her cup and saucer on the cobbler's bench. Selecting a muffin from the basket, she dug her fingertips into the moist bread and pulled off the top. She laughed softly. "You ever ask yourself how two white kids without a care in the world got to be so prickly?"

"How about the acorn never falls far from the tree."

Sill felt the blood rushing from her head. She didn't know why she had said it. It was simply a throwaway comment, but she should have known better than to throw it away on her cousin.

Gale sat perfectly still. She's thinking about Daddy, Sill thought. Panic rose in her chest. She wants to know about last night. She wants to know what everyone will want to know—why I think Daddy was cleaning his rifle.

Sill, too, sat motionless, holding her teacup, hoping Gale would let the moment pass. Perhaps her her sense of etiquette would win out, and she would concede to the Southern code that delicacy was more important than inquiry.

After a long moment Gale leaned back in the rocker and popped a bite of muffin in her mouth.

"I talked to Deak Motts this morning. God, he's a son of a bitch. Wonder what kind of secrets *he* has."

Anger seared Sill's chest like a hot blade. Goddammit, the bitch was circling her like a cat. Why didn't she just come out and ask? Why didn't she just say, "Tell me what happened in that room, Sill. You can trust me. I've a crime in my past, too." Suddenly she wanted nothing to do with her family. She wanted Faith.

She raised her teacup to her mouth. "So, tell me, cousin, how did you react when you learned that Tom was dead?"

Gale's face blanched. "I don't know. Stunned. Immobile."

"Do you know how I feel? I remember you telling me once what it was like right after Katie Pru was born. The birth had been difficult and you had been terrified and alone during the whole thing. When it was finally over, you said you were utterly exhausted. The nurse held the baby out for you to see and all you could think was, 'There. I birthed you. It's done.' Do you remember that? And you said that it was days before you had any more emotional attachment to the baby than you would have had to a room you'd just finished painting."

Gale's eyes were steady as she watched Sill. "The love came later," she said. "But you're right. It wasn't immediate. Coming on the heels of Tom's death the way it did, it was too much to feel all at once."

"Well, that's how I am right now," Sill said. "It's

all too much to feel. Maybe later I'll need to be comforted. I appreciate your gesture, but, to paraphrase Freud, sometimes tea is just tea."

From the kitchen window, Ella watched Zilah Greene walk across the side yard toward the house. She dipped her hands into the soapy water filling the sink and fished out a white ironstone bowl. Well, she thought, at least it doesn't look like Zilah's bringing food. If there was one thing she couldn't abide about death traditions, it was the ritual of feeding the family, as if stuffing the grieving with corn bread could somehow sop up the sorrow. Or that by eating in the face of death, one could absorb the lost soul. Ella wedged the bowl into the dish rack beside the sink. Martin might well have been lost, she thought, but she sure wasn't going to be eating for his soul. A body reaps what a body sows. And Martin Cane's body had darn well sown more than a bullet to the head.

She watched Zilah struggle with the wire that latched the gate in the fence separating the two properties. Ella's side hadn't put up the fence—had, in fact, never seen the need for one, her grandfather Nathan who built the place having gratefully died before Robert Frost's cynical pronouncement. It was Barry Greene who built the fence, concerned, he said, about the large dogs Ella's sister Nora had kept. Of course, everyone knew it wasn't dogs he was fencing out. It was Zilah he was fencing in. He had constructed for his wife a corral as neat and modest as the woman herself.

Ella yanked a dish towel from the drawer beside the sink, watching the sudden distress on Zilah's face as she jerked her hand away from the latch, shook it as if in pain, and stuck it under her arm. Then, her hurt hand clamped to her side, she reached out again and with an angry twisting motion wrenched the latch free.

Ella dropped the dish towel onto the counter and met Zilah at the back porch door.

"Well, come on in," she said, holding the screened door open. "Look how your feet are all wet from that grass. It rained up a storm last night—I declare we're going to be in for a rough summer."

Zilah picked her way up the stone steps and onto the porch. "Well, yes, it did rain badly last night," she said. "Barry used to say that every five years we'd have a really wet summer and then a really hot one. I bet if we counted back . . ."

"I've gotten too old to count back. Come on in the house, Zilah. This door's heavy."

Bits of brown grass cuttings clung to Zilah's black shoes and stockinged ankles as she stood in the middle of the kitchen, both arms wrapped around her middle. With the pointy blades of her shoulders and her skinny legs, Zilah Greene had reached the stage of elderliness that too closely resembled adolescence. People ought to die when they reach that point, Ella thought. Pulling out a chair from beneath the kitchen table, she motioned the other woman into it.

"I saw you hurt yourself out there," she said. "Want some first aid cream?"

"Law, no, Ella, I'm fine." She looked around the kitchen, her gaze trailing over the few foil-covered casseroles on the counter. "I didn't mean to bother you at such a bad time. I've got a seven-layer salad in the refrigerator—I'll bring it on later—but I just wanted to come over before church let out to see if Gale was here. I got a letter for her. Came to my house by accident."

Ella reached into the cabinet above the sink and pulled out a tube of antiseptic cream and a box of bandages. "So why aren't you in church yourself? I've never known Zilah Greene to miss a service."

"It was all too much last night, I guess. I didn't sleep well. I needed to deliver the letter."

"Gale's here. She was upstairs getting Sill dressed last time I saw her. You can just leave the letter with me. But you'll want to put something on that scrape,

Zilah. That latch is rusty. You'll be getting sick if you're not careful."

"No, I'm all right, really. And I want to talk to—"

"Don't be ridiculous. You don't go drawing blood on a rusty piece of wire and then ignore the thing." Ella sat in the chair next to Zilah and placed the first aid supplies in front of her. She leaned over and grabbed Zilah's arm. "Now then, let me see."

Zilah balled her hand into a fist. "No, Ella."

"Stop acting like a child. Give me your hand."

She tugged at the smaller woman's hand, pleased when it finally relaxed against her own chest. Reaching for the first aid cream, she turned Zilah's hand palm up and inhaled sharply.

Red, dragging rips, like those from fingernails, marked the tender underside of the wrist. Already, thin scabs covered the tears, but the skin at the edges was still pink. The scratches were new, made within the last day.

"My word," she breathed. "What have you been up to?"

Zilah tried to pull away, but Ella held her hand tightly. "Nothing," she murmured. "I need to talk to Gale. Isn't she here?"

Ella flipped open the cap on the first aid cream. "She's here. Of course, she's got things to do. I'll tell her you want to see her when she's got time."

She spread the cream on gently, sliding her pinky under the cuff of the woman's thin white sweater in an effort to see how far up the scratches continued. Zilah hunched in the chair, her eyes clamped tight. The blue-veined wrinkles of her lids jumped as Ella reached for her other hand.

"Do you want to talk to me, Zilah?" Ella whispered. "Do you want to tell me?"

Zilah didn't open her eyes. "I want to talk to Gale. I came to see Gale."

Ella held Zilah's hands for a long moment, studying her quivering face. The two families had lived next to each other for over seventy years. During that time, Ella had watched Zilah chase her children barefoot through the yard, whipping her apron at them as she would chickens, her warbled high voice stuttering at their insolent backs. She had watched from the porch the summer Barry installed the fence. She had draped damp linens over the porch's wicker furniture to dry, and watched him plunge the post-hole digger into the earth, yank apart its two handles and then haul the loosened dirt to the surface. *Trying to separate us?* she had thought. *As if it took a fence.*

"Go on home," she said, releasing Zilah's hands. "I'll tell Gale you were looking for her. And don't worry about bringing that salad over. Keep it for yourself. Honestly."

At the sound of crunching gravel, Gale hurried to Sill's bedroom window and pulled back the curtain. A caravan of rain-washed pickup trucks and aging sedans jostled over the railroad tracks and trudged up the drive.

Sill groaned behind her. "Don't tell me," she said. "The line's forming for the Mourn and Munch Buffet."

" 'Fraid so. Ella always said if we wanted to make a million on the stock market, invest in Pyrex and aluminum foil."

The sun was as hard and concentrated as a plate, creating a post-rain haze over the grounds. The yard was dotted with puddles, and as each car pulled into its slot along the wire fence, the wheels sagged into sopping clay. Doors popped open; thick, pantyhosed calves and baggy trouser legs extended from the floorboards and hesitantly probed the earth.

"Hope you're hungry," Gale said. "The magi come bearing spoonable gifts."

"Spoonable, hell. I hope someone brought vodka and a straw."

A blue sedan parted a clutch of visitors and pulled

to a stop beneath the pecan tree. Ryan Teller in khaki shirtsleeves and chinos climbed from the car. In the bright mugginess of the air he looked oddly naked—a feral preacherman loping through the water. No black threads echoed his purpose; no black on him at all save for the soft-bound Bible flopping in his large hands. He waved at the parishioners filing through the yard, but he didn't break his pace. He strode to the stoop and, smiling broadly, moved to the front of a small group gathered at the door.

"Ryan's here to do his ministerial duties," Gale said. "How would you like to handle all this?"

The faint trill of the doorbell sounded from downstairs, followed by firm footsteps in the hallway and the creak of the front door. Voices rushed in, a foggy mixture of urgency and condolence. The Lord's troops were here.

"So, Sill." Gale let the curtain fall. "Do you want to get dressed and go downstairs?"

When she turned around, Sill was huddled on the green settee, her legs and arms angled beneath her yellow bathrobe so that she resembled a broken kite in the grass. Her eyes were closed, her skin flushed. A filament of tears seeped through her eyelids.

Gale dropped onto her knees beside her. She tried to take her cousin's hand, but Sill kept her fists jammed beneath her armpits. She was breathing rapidly, forcing her bottom lip between her teeth, until Gale was afraid she would hyperventilate. She reached up to take Sill's face in her hands, but the touch must have startled her. Sill sat up abruptly. She pushed Gale aside and pressed her forehead to her knees.

"I'm all right," she gasped. "Just a second. I'll be all right."

She sat there with her arms clasped around her knees and her blond hair hanging in hanks down the sides of her legs. Every now and then she would jerk. Gale didn't try to touch her again.

When Sill finally lifted her head, a moist sheen covered her face. The tears had disappeared.

"I'm fine now," she said evenly. "I would like to get dressed."

"Look, why don't you just stay—"

"I'm fine." Sill's voice quivered but was firm. "Do you have anything I can wear?"

The line of her mouth was tight, her eyes stony. Some sort of resolution had set in, whether concerning her anguish or her hostess's responsibilities, Gale didn't know. And she wasn't about to second-guess grief.

Gale pushed herself to her feet. "Help yourself to my closet," she said. "And holler if you need me."

She left the room, pulling the door closed behind her. Ella's voice curled up the staircase. "Alma, why don't you take those beans and carry them right on into the kitchen. There's much more counter space in there than in the dining room, and this old table in here just doesn't do well with hot things on it—it'll have white circles in a flash. . . ."

Gale hurried down the stairs. Ella, dressed in a black linen suit, stood in front of the dining room door, barring entry like a girdled turnstile.

"Dot, why don't you go into the kitchen and organize it all, get everything lined up real nice. Y'all just help yourself to plates and cutlery. Now, you can come eat in the dining room, that's all right, just don't put any of those wonderful hot dishes on the table. BethAnn, . . ."

The roll call continued. As Gale reached the bottom of the stairs, Ella found a break in the line and crossed the hallway. Despite the carefully applied foundation and powder, her skin was pallid. Ella grasped her granddaughter by the elbow and pulled her to the far wall.

"How's Sill?"

Gale gently disengaged her arm from Ella's clamp. "Reasonably okay. She's getting dressed. She said she'll be down in a bit. Is Katie Pru still with Maralyn?"

Ella nodded toward the living room. "Maralyn just ran in there chasing her. It's good for Katie Pru to be here. She'll give people something else to talk about besides the obvious."

She pressed closer to Gale; her breath smelled of coffee. "Zilah was here a few minutes ago—she's got a letter for you—but, baby, first I need you to do something for me. Ryan Teller's in the den. He wants to 'meet with' Cammy and Sill. Meddle's more like it. I stuck him in the den because he wanted someplace quiet for prayer. Why don't you go sit with him?"

Gale winced. "Alone with Kid Pulpit? I'll go find Maralyn. She's better at things like this than me."

Ella's fingernails sank into Gale's elbow.

"Maralyn's busy," she said quietly. "Now you go in there and keep that man company. We don't need him roaming through the house."

She gave the skin between her nails a hard twist, then she was gone, sliding down the hall, her hand extended and her voice sweetened to a coo. "Dorothy, I didn't expect you to come, not with Joe being so sick. . . ."

Gale rubbed her elbow. Even for Ella, the behavior was strange. Throwing a last glance at her grandmother, she started down the small alleyway to the den. The weak morning light barely stained the gauze curtains and made no impression at all on the the etched glass circling the ceiling. Not that dimness seemed to be a problem. Ryan Teller sat slumped in an easy chair, his muddy loafers propped on her desk. Open in his lap was one of her research notebooks. Gale stood, her hand on the knob, and stared at him before shoving the door shut with her foot.

"Oh." Startled, Teller dropped his legs to the ground and tossed the notebook on the desk. "I didn't realize anyone was here." He unfolded himself, his khaki pants and skin pulling from the sage-green upholstery like a praying mantis departing a leaf. He palmed his Bible in his left hand and extended his right to her.

"Sorry." He nodded toward the notebook. "I saw it on the desk there and couldn't help myself." He lifted her hand and squeezed. "You must be Gale. I've seen you around. I've been wanting to talk with you."

"Really." His hand was moist. She flexed her fingers, a subtle request for release, but his grip tightened. "Yes, well, I knew you right away, too." She glanced at her notebook. "Good thing you're a preacher. If you were anything else, I might have to whack you. I'm a bit particular about who rummages through my papers."

"Papers?" He gave a soft laugh. "I hardly call one notebook papers. You want to see papers, you ought to come over to the parsonage sometime."

Her head reached the center of his chest. His top button was undone and little blond hairs curled over the cloth. He smelled sweet. His skin was unnaturally tanned, his hand uncomfortably hot over hers. His hazel eyes waited a fraction of a second before rounding in condolence.

"I'm so sorry, Gale. Martin was a truly unique and special man. I considered him my friend."

Gale reached up with her free hand, patted his, then gently shook loose from his grip. "Thank you, Ryan. It's good to hear that."

"You must be very grieved."

"It's hard on everyone."

He sighed. "You didn't like him, did you?"

His expression was almost friendly. He clutched the Bible to his chest, his fingers drumming a dulled rhythm on the black leather cover.

"Why would you say that?"

When he smiled, laugh lines surrounded his eyes, and a wrinkle spanned his nose like a gash. But his eyes showed no emotion as he watched her.

"Now, Gale, I know you're a sophisticated woman. Not like a lot of people out here. We can be candid. Martin once told me you were a big influence on Sill growing up, which was a pity because he didn't think you much cared for him. But I can understand how a woman like you might have a problem with someone like Martin."

Gale bit the corner of her mouth. "How's that?"

He lightly tapped his lips with a corner of his Bible. "While I was waiting, I read some of your comments in your notebook. I put you down as a historical revisionist."

"Interesting way to phrase it."

"Oh, I don't mean anything by it. But I notice you seem to take a revisionist approach to your work." He picked up her notebook. "Listen to this. 'Compare workday schedules of rural males, females at turn of century. Look into availability of doctors, dentists in Morgan County prior to 1930. Verify life expectancy of rural Southern women, 1900 to 1930.' " He poked a long finger at the middle of the page. " 'Reexamine long-held beliefs in the preeminence of the Southern matriarchy.' Now, to me that is very interesting."

Gale crossed her arms. "Why is that?"

Teller eased the notebook shut and sandwiched it between his hands. "Call me a male chauvinist, but I think the matriarchy is alive and well. It just has another name now: feminism."

Gale stared down at Teller's black tasseled loafers, splattered with red clay from the puddles outside. She shoved her fists into her skirt pockets and moved toward the door.

"You know what, Ryan? I really don't think this is the time to discuss this. We've had a tragedy in the family and—"

"Not your first tragedy, is it, Gale?"

She stopped and turned back to Teller. "Meaning?"

Ryan shrugged. "Just some gossip I've heard."

"Okay, you're right, Ryan. It's not my first tragedy. I know how facts can become distorted in a small town, so here is the story, short and plain. My husband murdered a barrister in England. The police believe he was also involved with a terrorist group. He killed himself before he could be arrested. That's all you need to know."

"And you knew nothing of it?" he asked softly.

"I knew nothing. But I have been well informed that ignorance is not absolution. That's all I intend to say about it."

"You should have taken the time to know Martin better."

"What are you getting at, Ryan?"

He hugged her notebook to his chest. "Martin was as straight an arrow as I ever met. He had a gift. Put a crowd of people in front of him and they'd be on their knees. He didn't see it, but I did. 'Let the Lord bring the people to you, Martin,' I told him, 'and you can lead them to the truth.' "

In an effort to cool the crowded house, Ella had turned the air conditioning on full blast. Gale could feel the cold air from the den floor-vent on her legs. But Teller's tanned face was dotted with sweat, the base of his blond curls greased with fervor.

"You should have spent more time with him, Gale," he said. "He could have shown you the way."

Gale punched at the insides of her skirt pocket. "All right, Ryan," she said. "I'm going to level with you. Martin was a certain kind of man I don't particularly care for. He hunted too much, talked too much, and prayed too much. He loved his family and did what he had to do to support them. But he was hard on Sill and Cammy. There's no doubt about that."

"Sometimes that's what God wants a father and husband to do."

"You don't really believe that."

He held his Bible out to her. "Gale, do you feel the need to pray?"

She looked at the black book, then lifted her eyes to his face.

"I don't know that you're a man I'd want to pray with."

Teller threw his head back and laughed. It was a

thick sound, made more clogged by the closeness of the room.

"Martin said you were a piece of work. Now I know what he was talking about." He lightly touched her upper arm. "Don't take anything I've said personally. A man dies, and it just gets you to thinking. Martin worried a lot about Sill—her friends, the people she listened to. He said she had turned away from the Word. I was just feeling you out." He gave a shamefaced smile. "I suppose I should have chosen a more tactful time. Your notebook stimulated my brain, that's all."

Gale crossed her arms. "Well, there's a house full of people out there, Ryan. I'm gonna let you stay here while I check on things."

"Of course. When Sill comes down . . ."

Gale walked to the desk, grabbed her notebook, and exited the den, not bothering to wait for his reaction. She emerged by the staircase. The hall was still choked with visitors. Clusters huddled on the staircase; others stood awkwardly, the jaws of fish not allowing them to lean against the walls. Across the hall a scratchy voice broke from the dining room.

"Linnie Cane was the orneriest woman in Calwyn County. She'd've sooner strangle the life out of herself than say good morning."

Gale peered between the open dining room doors. Deak Motts sat at the table, an empty plate in front of him, a half-dozen elderly women circled around him disinterestedly poking at their food. Deak jabbed his fork into the air as he spoke.

"That afternoon she washed her five-year-old son's hands and face, dressed him in his nicest clothes, and locked him in his room. She went out to the barn, found a strong rope, and took it and a little stool out to the biggest pecan tree. She slung that rope over the lowest branch, stepped up on that stool. . . ."

Gale grabbed the bottom of the banister and hiked

up the stairs. Mourners, their mouths full, made sympathetic noises as she passed.

Jesus God, she thought. In the Alden family, death had become a spectator sport.

"Come here to me, Katie Pru. I shut the door, see? All the noise is gone and now we can have some quiet. Your mama says you love this book. Climb up here beside me on the sofa and let me read it to you."

Katie Pru squinched her eyes shut and put her head down on top of the living room's glass coffee table. She didn't want to sit beside Aunt Maralyn. She didn't want to listen to the *skritch skritch* of Aunt Maralyn's yellow hair, all stiff and curly like a doll's, or get too close to her fingers, with their Band-Aid smell. And she didn't like the way Aunt Maralyn's powder made her nose tickle and her eyes water. But most of all, she didn't like the way Aunt Maralyn read.

"Now come on up here, Katie Pru. I know you like fairy tales. Your mama did when she was growing up. Come sit beside me and let's read about the funny little man.

Katie Pru lifted her head just enough to peek out at the copy of *Rumpelstiltskin* curling up from the sofa cushion. It was her favorite book. When her mother read it to her, they would snuggle together on the big bed, deep under the covers. And when her mother paused, Katie Pru would bellow out the names— *Marzipan! Geewhillackers!*—happy to be warm and brave at the same time.

She plopped her head back into her arms. "You can't read that book," she said. "Only my mama can read that book. She knows the words."

Aunt Maralyn laughed. Her hair skritched. "Oh, pooh," she said. "There's not a thing in this world your mama can read that I can't. Where'd you get such silly ideas? Now, come on up here, Katie Pru. You're smudging the glass on that table, and I can see your panties. I know you don't want to be a sulky child."

Katie Pru wriggled her bottom. She did too want to be a sulky child. With her head still down, she scooted around the edge of the table until her backside was away from her aunt. Then carefully, so Aunt Maralyn wouldn't see, she let her head slip from her arms until her nose squished flat against the table's glass top.

She stayed like that for a long time, knowing from experience that soon the grown-up would tire and she would win. With her head buried, she listened to Aunt Maralyn's hair and sighs and enjoyed the feel of the smooth glass against her nose. Sure enough, before long she heard the sofa creak and the sound of scratchy fabric. Aunt Maralyn had given up.

"All right, missy," she said. "I'm too tired to fight. You don't want to read a book, I don't want to read a book. I'm gonna go check on your cousin Cammy."

"Good," Katie Pru answered, her lips on the glass. "I wanna look at the pictures."

She heard the plonk of the book on the table beside her head. "Go ahead. I'll tell your mama you're in here."

Katie Pru waited until the room was quiet and then looked up. She was alone with the pictures, as she had wanted to be from the start. Putting her elbows on the table, she propped her chin up on her hand and idly pushed the book away.

It was the jag-wire who had first told her about the pictures, not long after she and her mother had moved here. Grandma Ella had put the living room strictly off-limits, but the jag-wire had said that didn't matter. Katie Pru had crept into the living room one morning while her mother was on the phone. She had walked into the room as silently as the jag-wire, turning her head from side to side as he would have done. At first she hadn't known what he wanted her to see. The room had just seemed cold and fancy, filled with curvy furniture covered in yellow. She brushed past the long peach curtains that reached the floor, smelled the lemony arms of the plump chair. And then she saw it—the round table in front of the sofa with the hundreds of faces, all black-and-white, gazing up at her from beneath the glass. Boys in overalls with dirty caps, girls with long, curly hair and big shoes. Some of the children looked like they had been caught outside playing—they grinned beside their bicycles or beneath big, leafy trees. Most, however, were dressed in Sunday clothes and stood unhappily in front of grown-ups, who stared back at her with stern faces.

Later she had asked her mother about the pictures, and they had gone into the room together.

"These people," her mother explained, "were Grandma Ella's family and friends from a long time ago. Some are even *her* mother's family. Grandma Ella put these photographs underneath the glass to save them."

Katie Pru pointed to a little girl playing at the beach. "Look! It's me!"

Her mother laughed softly. "No, baby. That's a picture of my mother when she was about your age. But she does look a lot like you, doesn't she?"

Katie Pru had drawn her fingernail around the little girl's face, down around the fancy bottom of her bathing suit, up around her short dark hair. "Where does she live now?" she asked.

Her mother, sitting on the sofa, crossed her arms in front of her chest and frowned. It wasn't an angry frown, but the kind she got when she was thinking. She rocked a little, quiet, and for a second Katie Pru thought she hadn't heard her.

"Does she live at the beach?"

Her mother shook her head. "She isn't alive anymore, Katie Pru," she said. "She died when I was very young. Grandma Ella took care of me when I was growing up."

Katie Pru had quickly pointed to another picture, not wanting to look at the little girl anymore. Now, however, she rubbed her finger across the glass, cleaning away the smudges that covered the picture of the girl. Many times, when her mother was busy, she would sneak into the living room and look at the little girl. She had never told anyone, but the picture worried her. Cemeteries were places for grown-ups who had been very sick or very old. She knew this because her mother had taken her once to her father's cemetery. The place wasn't scary, and it didn't hurt to think about her father because he died before she was born. But it hurt to think about this little girl who was her mother's mother. Mothers and little girls weren't allowed to die.

She covered the girl's face with her thumb. When she lifted it, a neat thumbprint showed on the glass. She had dirtied it; it would have to be cleaned. Rolling her tongue around in her mouth, she leaned close to the photograph and spat.

"What are you doing here?"

She jerked her head up. It was a man's voice, but there was no man in the room. She stared through the open door and into the hallway, but she couldn't see anyone.

"I'm supposed to be here. I'm the bereaved."

Aunt Maralyn's voice sounded strange, the way it did when Katie Pru painted her suitcase with peanut butter. Angry, but afraid to yell.

The man was afraid to yell, too.

"What's that supposed to mean?"

Aunt Maralyn's laugh was like a dog coughing.

"You didn't know? You mean to tell me that last night you didn't know who the hell I was? Well, Martin sure as shit kept a few things from you."

"You're a murderer."

"Oh no. I just keep garbage like you—"

"You're a murderer," the man repeated. "Do you feel the need to pray?"

The spit made little bubbles over the girl's face. Carefully, Katie Pru placed her finger in the middle of them and spread the liquid around in a circle.

"Pray with the likes of you? No, thank you. I wouldn't want God to think I was keeping bad company."

The wet circles got bigger and bigger until it covered the little girl's body. Katie Pru pressed her palm onto the table and hid the spot. She didn't understand why Aunt Maralyn was angry, but she figured she wouldn't think spit was any prettier than peanut butter.

No.

> — Malcolm Hinson's response when
> asked if he ever saw Linnie Cane
> hanging around his photography
> studio, 1955

9

Alby Truitt perched on Zilah Greene's brown flowered sofa, balancing a mound of seven-layer salad on his knee. Gingerly he stabbed his fork into the side of the construction and pulled loose a wedge of mayonnaise-coated lettuce. Johnny Bingham could say what he wanted about nobody loving a sheriff. In the past year Truitt had learned one thing about his office—in the eyes of little old ladies, sheriffs and preachers were always underfed.

On the other side of a maple coffee table, Zilah sat in a meagerly cushioned chair. As he ate, her eyes flitted from his hand to his mouth. She pressed her wrists into her lap and tore at a paper handkerchief. The shredded paper piled up like snowflakes on her cotton print skirt. Across her left palm was a fresh bandage.

He stabbed his fork into another chunk of lettuce and offered her a lopsided smile.

"This is real good, Mrs. Greene," he said. "I appreciate it. I didn't eat breakfast this morning."

She returned his smile. "Well, it wasn't hard to make," she said. "I meant to take it to the Aldens, but Ella said they wouldn't be needing it."

Truitt nodded and shoveled a clump of peas and cheese into his mouth. He had no doubt it was true. After leaving the drugstore, he had joined the caravan to the Aldens' house, parking his Dodge between a white Ford pickup and a scraggly pine. Within minutes an additional twenty cars had followed him up the drive and stopped along the wire fence. He had been forced to scramble over the fender of a beat-up minivan to reach the gate.

Truitt drew his napkin from beneath the plate and dabbed his mouth. "How'd you hurt yourself, Mrs. Greene?"

She glanced at her hand and tut-tutted. "Oh, law, it's nothing. I'd trouble getting the gate open, that's all. The latch is bad. Barry meant to fix it, but he never had time. Ella dressed the cut fine, though."

"Sad business over there," he said.

"Yes," she answered. "We owed Martin so much."

"How so?"

She looked at him in surprise. "Why, we never'd made it without him. I remember one year Barry coming home and saying, 'That's it, Zilah, I'm closing down the store, I can't make any money from it.' I said, 'You can't, we ain't got nothing else.' And he said, 'Well, we'll just have to sell the house and move to Atlanta.' I was so afraid. I couldn't leave my house. My daddy built this house."

Her eyes lit with remembered fear. Her hands, the

veins bright blue beneath the skin, trembled. Truitt carefully set his plate on the coffee table. He had never known the Greenes very well: The hardware store owner and his mousy wife were merely indistinct figures at the county fairs and church festivals. Very similar, Truitt thought, to what Martin and Cammy might have been had the barbecue not taken on its own spectacular life.

"It's a fine house, Mrs. Greene," he said softly. "I'm glad things worked out for you."

"They surely did. When people started coming to that barbecue, it was like the whole county woke up and remembered Statlers Cross. Folks from all over began bringing their business to the hardware store. I have a fine respect for Martin Cane."

"You were at the barbecue yesterday, weren't you, Mrs. Greene?"

Her fingers drifted to the pile of shredded paper in her lap.

"Of course I was. I always go, even last year when Barry was so sick. I tried to stay here with him, but he said, no, I had to go, just to show our thanks."

Truitt dragged his napkin across his mouth, folded it, and wedged it beneath his plate. "You know, Mrs. Greene, I have to look into Martin's death. The coroner's making a report, and I'll have to say what I think happened."

"I know that," she said.

"So I need to talk with you about it. I called my sergeant this morning and he couldn't find where any of my officers had talked with you."

She fingered the shredded paper. "I left before y'all got there."

Truitt feigned surprise. "Why?"

"I was tired. And I didn't need to be there. I didn't see anything."

"But you understand I need to ask you some questions anyway."

"Yes, sir."

He drew out his notepad. "This will only take a few minutes, Mrs. Greene. Can you tell me where you were when the gun went off?"

"The front porch. On the swing."

Truitt smiled. "I helped Martin hang that swing. It was a birthday present for Cammy. Had you been there long when you heard the shot?"

"I don't know. I wasn't real hungry—I'm not hungry a lot lately, and sometimes the sight of food doesn't do me well."

"So you were sitting on the swing until you felt better?"

"Yes."

"Do you remember if the front door was open?"

"I don't know. I don't think it was."

"Could you hear anything from inside the house—people talking, or moving around, maybe?"

She plucked a scrap of paper from the pile and pinched it flat against her thumb. "No. I don't think so."

Truitt ran his finger down the side of his cheek. "Now, let me think a minute. There's a window by that swing, isn't there? Do you remember if it was open?"

She hesitated. "I don't remember."

"Did anyone come onto the porch while you were there?"

"Yes, sir. That pilot—Mr. Robertson. He came out of the house and asked if I had seen Martin."

"Had you?"

For a long moment she didn't answer; she sat ramrod straight in the chair, eyes closed.

"Mrs. Greene," Truitt urged gently, "did you see Martin in the minutes before the rifle went off?"

Her eyes opened. "I told Mr. Robertson I didn't know where he was."

"That's not a straight answer, ma'am."

"No. I didn't see him."

"What about after the shot? What did you hear and see after the shot?"

She stood with an agility that surprised him. "I told you, Mr. Truitt, I came home. Quit thinking anything about it." She picked up his plate. The salad's fragile construction collapsed; pieces of lettuce scattered onto the table. "I'm going to get you some iced tea," she murmured. "You wait right here."

She disappeared through a doorway at the back of the house. Truitt stared after her, the notebook in his hand. Then he dropped it onto the sofa and, whistling tunelessly, began pushing the spilled salad together with his napkin. From the kitchen, he could hear the sound of a refrigerator door close, followed by the purr of a faucet and the crack of an ice tray.

He felt strangely relieved. Zilah didn't believe it was an accident. Whatever she had seen or heard from Martin's front porch, she was convinced it was significant.

A sharp rap rattled the front screen door. Truitt turned to see a nose push into the wire mesh about three feet from the bottom of the frame.

"If I were Play-Doh," the nose said, "I could squish through these holes and be spaghetti on the floor."

"If you were Play-Doh," Truitt countered, "I'd roll you into a ball and smack you against my forehead."

The nose giggled and a small pink tongue tried to push its way through the tiny holes. Smiling, Truitt strode to the screen door and popped it open. Katie Pru Grayson, a red cotton backpack strapped to her shoulder, jumped back and grinned at him from behind the screen.

"We came to get a letter," she announced.

At the bottom of the porch steps, Gale looked up at him in surprise. "I'm sorry, Alby. I didn't know Zilah had company."

The mid-morning sun had burned off the haze, and a rosy flush tinted Gale's face. Nevertheless, she managed to look cool; her hair, with its striking gray strips, was pushed casually behind her ears, and beneath her skirt her legs were bare except for a pair of anklet socks folded above white tennis shoes.

"No problem. I was getting ready to leave." He nodded at the Alden house and walked out onto the porch. "Good to see so many people paying their respects."

"With no sign of letting up." She squinted toward Katie Pru, who had jumped from the porch and was running circles in the tall grasses. "We needed a break. We're not used to hordes of people wanting to pinch our precious little cheeks."

"The best of us aren't. How are Cammy and Sill doing?"

At the sound of the screen door, he turned around to see Zilah backing onto the porch, a tray filled with glasses in her hands. He reached toward her. "Here, Mrs. Greene, let me . . ."

"You step away—I've got it." The ice in the amber liquid clinked as she hurried to the top of the steps. "Oh, Gale," she said, breathlessly. "I'm so glad you've come. Here, I brought you some tea. I saw y'all coming through the side yard. Please, sit down and visit a bit. I know both you and the sheriff could stand something to drink."

Truitt picked up a glass and held it out to Gale, intrigued at the change in Zilah. A few minutes earlier she had been fearful and hesitant; now she seemed nervous and—he tried to pin down the emotion—expectant.

"I can't stay long," Gale told her. "Any second I expect Ella's head to pop out the front door telling me to get myself home. Still, Alby, if you're smart you never turn down a glass of Zilah Greene's iced tea."

Truitt winked at her as he took a second glass for himself. "Make the gods weep, will it?"

"Just about."

Zilah set the tray down on the porch floor. "Listen to you. Go on, Gale, you two sit." In the yard, Katie

Pru did aborted cartwheels in the grass. "Think your little girl wants some?"

"She'll find us if she does." Gale arranged herself on the bottom step. "Zilah, so I won't forget, Ella said you have a letter for me."

"Ooh, it's right here." She reached into her dress pocket and pulled out a crumpled envelope. After carefully smoothing it out, she held it up for Truitt to see. "It's from England. You can tell from the stamp."

Across the lawn, Katie Pru stopped tumbling. "Is Space Lucy on it?" she yelled.

"Space Lucy was a stuffed dinosaur Katie Pru once had," Gale explained to Truitt. "We have a friend in England who draws him on his letters."

Zilah beamed. "Why, yes, Katie Pru, there is a dinosaur! I figured it was a secret message for you!"

Katie Pru ran toward the house, but Gale took the envelope from Zilah's hand and slid it into her own pocket. "We'll read it later, K.P. Go play a bit, and let me visit."

Katie Pru veered away as Zilah and Truitt sat down on the steps with their tea.

"I'm so glad you've come," Zilah repeated. "That's one of the worse things about widowhood. There's nobody around to keep you out of yourself. Your head can get up to all kinds of things. Which is why I needed to talk to you, Gale."

"Sure, Zilah. What is it?"

Zilah rested her hand on Gale's knee, leaning close to the younger woman. "Please don't think I'm crazy. You know, sometimes old people can say things, and people just figure they're crazy."

"I won't do that, Zilah. Now, tell me what's wrong."

"I want to talk with you about Linnie."

Gale's brow furrowed. "Linnie Cane?"

"Yes. Ella's Aunt Linnie. You know who I'm talking about?"

In the middle of the yard Katie Pru crouched down, so that only her red backpack was visible above the grass.

"Of course," said Gale. "Why do you want to talk about her?"

Zilah gave a strained laugh. "Well, believe it or not, I saw her last night—dreamed her up, anyway. Barry used to tell me dreams don't mean anything, but I think he was wrong. I think they mean a lot."

"Well, I think so, too," Gale said. "If nothing else, they can let us know what's bugging us." She paused and ran her finger down the condensation forming on her glass before giving Zilah a reassuring smile. "So, has Linnie been bugging you?"

Katie Pru stood up and struggled free from her backpack. Truitt could see her mouth moving but couldn't hear any sounds. She threw the backpack high over her head and took leaping giant steps toward the wire fence.

"Do you believe in visits from the dead?"

Zilah's voice was earnest, and as Truitt focused his attention on her, he kept his gaze noncommittal. Gale was less successful.

"Visits from the dead? Well, no, Zilah. I think the dead can get inside our heads so that we think . . ."

In the yard, the child had picked up the backpack again, and this time Truitt thought he could hear her singing, although the tune and words were indistinct. Again, she crouched down in the grasses, jumped up, threw the bag into the air, and ran in leaps for the fence. Truitt stood and stepped away from the porch, thinking his distance might free Zilah to speak openly with Gale. Haints. Christ, he hoped the old woman wasn't going senile. If she had indeed seen something at Martin's, he needed her to be competent.

"I suppose you're right," Zilah told Gale. "I've been thinking about her a lot lately, that's all. You know, she was a beautiful woman—tall, fine-boned. Real graceful when she moved."

"I've never seen a picture of her," Gale said. "You must have a good memory. You couldn't have been more than—what, when she died?"

"I was born in 1924."

"Zilah. Linnie died in 1925. You couldn't possibly have known her." Gale's voice was steady and soothing, as if she was speaking to a confused child.

Katie Pru was on her third cycle now, crouching into the grass. Truitt could hear the music more clearly. It was an odd tune, almost like a jig, and it ended in a grunt as Katie Pru flung the backpack into the air.

"You do think I'm old and crazy, don't you, Gale? I can see it by the way you're looking at me. You're trying to be sympathetic, but you're really laughing."

"Oh, no, Zilah. Honest, I wouldn't do that to you."

"You would. Just like people do to ghosts. They tell the stories to scare, but it's really just a laugh to them."

It was a warm spring day . . .

The story came to Truitt in one piece, like a memory.

. . . and everyone in Statlers Cross was getting ready for the debut performance of the town's first pageant. It was a big to-do—the play was original, written by a Northern playwright who'd come down here to get a taste of life. The Atlanta paper was going to cover it, folks were coming in from all over. And Linnie Glynn Cane had the lead female role. Well, Linnie Cane was the orneriest woman in Calwyn County. She'd sooner strangle the life out of herself than say good morning. About three in the afternoon, she dressed her five-year-old son in his nicest clothes and locked him in his room. She went out to the barn, found a rope and a stool, and took them over to the pecan tree at the side of the house. She slung that rope over a branch, stepped up on that little stool, and put the thing around her neck. Ever since she's haunted the town, regretful for the little boy she left behind.

Zilah's wrong, Truitt thought. He had never heard that ghost story and laughed.

He was far into the yard now. The little girl's song was strong and clear.

> " *'Hide in the house, miller's son, miller's son.*
> *Hide, all the angels sang.*
> *Run to the tracks, miller's son, miller's son.*
> *Go where your stocking hangs.'* "

On the word 'hangs,' Katie Pru hurled her backpack in the air and started leaping. With each step she counted, her voice loud enough to carry to the porch.

"One, two . . ." The backpack landed with a thud. Katie Pru pivoted toward her mother. "Only two, Mama."

"Keep trying." Gale shielded her eyes and chuckled at Truitt's perplexed look. "A game Sill and I used to play as children. Sort of like human jacks. Throw something up and see how far you can get before it hits the ground. All the while getting louder and louder with the song." She turned to Zilah. "You ever see us. . . ?"

She fell silent. Even from where he stood, Truitt could read the dismay in Zilah's features. Her lips pinched shut, her eyes widened.

Katie Pru's voice was near a yell. " 'HIDE IN THE HOUSE, MILLER'S SON, MILLER'S SON . . .' "

Zilah laid her hand on Gale's arm. "You let her sing that song?"

"Shouldn't I? You know that song, Zilah?"

"Sure I do. And you do too, Gale. You know where it's from."

"It's just something we sang when we were little. I don't even remember who taught it to us."

Zilah stared at Katie Pru. "She's got the words wrong. It's 'hide in the house, weaver's son, weaver's son.' "

Truitt fought a sudden shiver. Beside him, Gale

anxiously ran her hands down her bare legs. Zilah's gaze drifted to Gale.

"Folks used to do that long ago—make up songs so they wouldn't forget. I remember my mama passing them around like she did recipes. Mary Phagan, the *Titanic,* there were ballads for them all. And there was this one, set right here in Statlers Cross. But the child has all the words wrong."

A low warble started from the elderly woman's throat.

> " *'Hide in the house, weaver's son, weaver's son.*
> *Hide, all the angels sang.*
> *Run to the tracks, weaver's son, weaver's son,*
> *Far from where your mother hangs.'* "

"How terrible," Gale whispered.

Zilah nodded. "But it's more odd than terrible. Martin died last night and I see Miss Linnie. Your little girl comes over today midst all these mourners and sings a song I haven't thought of in fifty years." Her grip tightened on Gale's arm. Truitt could see the younger woman's skin turn white.

"You see it, don't you, Gale? Things don't just happen by chance. There's a reason. My daddy didn't believe it, but it's true. Ghosts step lightly because they have to trick us into listening."

Jeb said he saw her in the old schoolhouse, running from window to window as it burnt. That was going on fifteen years now, but to this day he swears it was her. The county closed the school down not long after we graduated because there were so few children. Jeb always figured Linnie started the fire because she was angry that everyone was moving away.

— Olive Pirtle to her friend Martha
Prescot during lunch in Atlanta, 1962

 10

Katie Pru in hand, Gale walked across Zilah's wilding yard toward the rusted wire gate. Behind them, Zilah stood next to Truitt on the porch, watching them pass through the long grasses. At the gate Gale tugged at the makeshift wire latch and ushered Katie Pru into Ella's yard. Only then did the screen door behind them bang shut. Gale scooted Katie Pru toward the back of Ella's house before turning to latch the gate shut. She didn't understand why Zilah had disturbed her so. She had long ago finessed the art of listening to—and then selectively discarding—the verbal ramblings of elderly women. It was a Southern girl's chinked but worthy armor. This time, however, her armor hadn't worked. She looked once more over the gate at the blue clapboard house, sitting in its collage of overgrown grass and neglected azaleas. She thought of the stories she used to tell Sill—Linnie devouring livestock, Linnie dancing on the rooftops of burning barns. Folktales, every one of them, passed down from one generation to the next with as much veracity as a blue ox or a cowboy riding a twister. And all fabricated about the tall, dark-haired woman who hunched over her loom clacking out cloth so fine she felt compelled to sashay down the railroad tracks, gossip be damned. Gale forced the latch into place and whirled around. Piss. Why did that loony woman bother her so much?

"Come on, Mama. The jag-wire says you're lolly-gagging."

Katie Pru looped her backpack over the jaguar's neck and placed her hands on her hips, as if she had just come across him feasting on a hiker. The sun was high in the sky, glinting off the few cars that remained in the gravel drive. With relief she noticed that Ryan Teller's blue sedan was gone. In its place sat a sleek black Jeep Cherokee with a Fulton County vanity tag that read TAXNSPND and a bumper sticker that said "Government-Employed and Proud." Gale raised her eyebrows as she passed. Some mighty brave city people were afoot.

"Come on, ladybug," she said to Katie Pru. "I'll race you to the back porch."

"Jag-wires don't like to race. They like to sneak."

"Okay, then. I'll sneak you to the back porch."

Katie Pru bared her teeth, stretched her hands into claws, and took slow giant steps toward her mother. Together they slunk past the pecan tree and headed for the rear of the house. Gale let Katie Pru creep by on her all fours, then tiptoed up the back porch stairs to join her outside the kitchen entry.

Sill's voice, tense and high, erupted from the house.

"I didn't want you to come. You coming here is just plain stupid."

"Stupid is me staying home. What did you expect me to do, just wait by the phone until you deemed fit to let me in on what the fuck was happening?"

A heavy object thunked into the sink. A stream of water blasted the basin and just as quickly cut off.

"I was going to call you when I had the chance," Sill said. "You should have known better than to come."

The second woman's voice was deep, a rich claret sound.

"Come on, Sill. I wanted to be here. Whatever it is, I'm with you. You know that."

Crouched at her mother's feet, Katie Pru suddenly growled and sprang, clawing at the kitchen door. Grimacing, Gale pushed the door open and let the child pounce into the room.

Sill stood at the sink, dismay on her face. Next to the kitchen table was the short, dark-haired woman Gale had seen at the barbecue.

Gale smiled apologetically as Katie Pru slinked into the room. "We can only be human so many hours a day. And today we've had to be even better behaved than usual." She shut the door behind her and walked toward the woman. "I'm Gale, Sill's cousin."

The woman's handshake was firm, her skin pleasantly dry despite the humidity. Even with the advantage of heeled sandals, she barely topped Gale by an inch. She wore a white oxford shirt, tail out, cinched around the waist by a black leather belt. Sharp creases stretched the length of her black linen pants. Behind blue-rimmed glasses her green eyes were clear and intelligent.

"I'm Faith Baskins," she said easily. "We talked over the phone this morning. If I hadn't recognized you from Sill's description, I certainly would have known you from your feline companion. Not every woman in these parts comes accompanied by a lion." She stooped down and gently scratched the top of Katie Pru's head. "Lions are my favorite."

Katie Pru poked out her lips. "I'm not a lion. I am a jag-wire. Lions have too much hair." She suspiciously contemplated Faith's tousle of iron and brown curls. "You're a lion," she said. "That's why you like them."

Faith straightened, laughing. "Well, there's probably more truth to that than I care to admit." She turned to Gale. "Sill was just telling me I should have stayed home. I hope I'm not going to put anyone in a difficult situation, but I felt I needed to be here."

Gale crossed the room and opened the refrigerator door. Glass bowls and casseroles, stacked on top of each other and held aloft by plastic wrap, filled the shelves. Reaching behind a bowl of fruit salad, she wriggled loose a grape juice box.

"I think that's between you and Sill," she said. "If she needs you with her, then you should be here."

"She needs me here."

"I just came back from Zilah's," Gale said. "Alby Truitt was there, and I think he's heading this way."

Sill whirled around. "What was he talking to Zilah for?"

"I don't know. Checking with everybody who was there, I suppose."

Faith looked up. "Who's Alby Truitt?"

"The sheriff." Gale pulled off the plastic packet containing the straw and ripped it open with her teeth. "Look, Sill," she said softly, "he's just doing his job. There has to be an investigation of some sort. He probably didn't get to question Zilah last night."

Faith began furiously cleaning her glasses on her shirttail. "That's right. He's probably going to want to talk to me, as well."

"What for? You left before . . ."

"Yeah, Sill, but I was there. And it's not as if nobody saw me."

"This has nothing to do with you, Faith." Sill

slapped the edge of the sink. "See, I said you should have waited until I called—"

"Sill!" Faith's voice was commanding. "Calm down," she said in a gentler tone. "There is nothing wrong here. You just need some rest."

Sill rested her head against Faith's shoulder for a moment, then lifted it. "You're right. I'm okay."

"Look, you're worried and tired. If it truly bothers you that I'm here, I'll get a motel room in Praterton. That way, I'll be close by—you can call me when you need me."

"That would make me feel better."

"It's done. Give me the phone book and I'm outta here."

Gale glanced at Katie Pru, who was crouching by the door, blowing small puffs at a roly-poly bug suspended in a spider's web. Holding the juice box away from her clothes, Gale jabbed the straw into the opening. Purple juice squirted down her fingers and onto the floor.

"Oh, shoot," she said. "Men invented these things. Nobody who ever had to wash a floor would design something like this."

With a yelp Katie Pru dove around her mother's legs and began lapping up the spill. Gale grabbed her around the waist and hauled her to her feet.

"Kathleen Prudence, you don't lick things off the floor. God knows every shoe in Statlers Cross has tracked through this room today."

"But I want the juice!"

"You can have the juice in the box."

"Jag-wires don't drink boxes—"

"Katie Pru—"

"I want the juice! Let me go!"

With her foot Gale dragged a chair away from the kitchen table and plopped Katie Pru down. She knelt in front of her and gripped the child's hands.

"You don't lick the floor. That's a rule. You're going to have a time-out."

Katie Pru slumped against the back of the chair and screwed up her face. "I hate time-outs," she said.

"You decide to have them. Now you have to sit there until the timer goes off. Sill, could you please set the oven timer for four minutes?"

Squinting her eyes closed, Katie Pru kicked at the rungs of the chair.

Sill twisted on the timer. "That reminds me, Gale. A woman came by today. Said she met you this morning. She left her number in case you ever need a babysitter."

The thumping on the chair legs grew louder. Katie Pru crossed her arms in front of her and panted through her nose.

"I'm going to blow boogers on you."

Gale took the note Sill held out and stuck it in her pocket. "If you hear from her again, tell her I appreciate it, but I don't need help. Regardless of how it looks, I can raise my own child, even if it does mean dodging nasal debris."

Truitt stamped his feet on the coir mat in front of Ella Alden's front door. The mat, a large semicircle on the brick stoop, was black, with a handpainted dogwood blossom in one corner whose leaves twined into the word *Welcome*. Beneath the flower, in choppy red lines, was a signature: *E. Alden 1988*. He gave a short sniff of satisfaction as he knocked on the door. The mat was incredibly pristine for its age. He had always suspected that Ella was a hermit at heart. How else to explain a woman who, with no obligations and only limited ties, had agreed to see an ailing invalid to her death?

When his mother had learned she was ill with hepatic cancer, she had made one request of him: that she die in the house in which she had raised him. Truitt had been mortified. Despite his profession, he was of a generation that believed natural death belonged in one place only—the cool, starched room of a hospital.

But she hadn't wanted it. She wanted to die in her own sheets with her own walls surrounding her. She called Ella.

Truitt never understood it—from either woman's perspective. There had been no special bond between his mother and Ella besides the few years Ella taught in the local high school where his mother was a student. And Ella had no medical training. Nevertheless, she was who his mother wanted. And Truitt, too weak to do the job himself, acquiesced.

At his mother's funeral he had asked Ella why.

"Death doesn't scare me like it does other people, Alby. I've seen death, been close to it, all my life. I've never made friends with it, but I won't let it scare me. Every living creature deserves a tended death. That's what your mother wanted. You'll want it, too, someday."

Perhaps he would. He wondered how many people actually got it.

The door opened abruptly. Maralyn Nash stood in the hallway, looking harried.

"Sorry, Alby," she said. "I was upstairs with Cammy. What can we do for you?"

"I have a few more things I need to go over, Maralyn." He looked past her at the broad staircase. "How's Cammy doing?"

"Under sedation, but restless. It's going to be hard on her. She built her life around that man." She peered at him, the muscle under her left eye jumping. "You need to come in?"

"I think so."

She stepped behind the door and waited for him to enter. He had been in the Alden house only once before when he had accompanied Martin to borrow a ladder, but now, as then, the house amazed him. Not so much for its grotesquery, although Lord knew it had that in abundance, but for its proof of a man's obsession. Driving away after that visit, he had asked Martin why Ella's husband had preserved all those fish. "Lust,"

Martin answered. "And power. I think that man mounted on the wall because of what he couldn't have in bed."

At the time, Truitt was on the fringes of understanding what Martin meant. Studying the fish now, he felt a slight bite of bile in the back of his throat.

"So, Alby, you have more questions?"

"Yes, I do. I can start with you, Maralyn. Is there a room that's empty?"

"That's just about all of them now. Mother told everyone to clear, and they did." She pointed to a room directly to his left. "Let's go into the living room."

He dropped himself into a peach overstuffed chair while Maralyn perched on the edge of a lemon-colored sofa.

"By the way, Alby," she said. "I need to go back to Cammy's house. She was asking for her purse this morning."

Truitt pulled his notebook from his suit coat pocket and rifled through the pages. "I can do that for you. Just tell me what it looks like and I'll have one of my men bring it over."

"I can't describe it. I'll know it when I see it."

"Well, the house is still sealed, Maralyn. I can't let you go in there unaccompanied. Maybe later today I can take you myself."

"Fine. On second thought, if she wants mascara, I'll let her use some of mine."

He looked up at her, stunned at the notion that Cammy was already contemplating her face. Or more to the point, Truitt thought, Maralyn was contemplating it for her. He had to hand it to her—the woman had poise. Last night he and his men had been voyeurs who had caught her in her most private moment with blood on her thighs and in her hair. Today, however, faced with her brassy coif and perfect makeup, he had the distinct impression of being received.

"Maralyn, I want to do Martin the justice of getting everything right about last night. Now, when was the last time you saw Martin before the gunshot?"

She pushed a tanned hand into the yellow sofa cushion. An ornate diamond wedding set glittered as she tapped her finger. "Well, it'd have to be when he and Sill had words. You've heard about that, I suppose."

"Yes, quite a few people told us about that. I understand there were some ill feelings between Martin and Sill. Can you help me there?"

"Ask Sill. None of my business."

She was dressed all in white—a cotton knit shirt tucked into a canvas skirt, thick crew socks folded down over her ankles, clean, laced tennis shoes. With her tan skin and muscular limbs, she could have been ready for an afternoon on the courts, except that no one, thought Truitt, but mad dogs and Republicans would be out in today's mugginess. Of course, she could be either one for all he knew; as Ella's oldest daughter, she was living in Atlanta by the time he met the family. To him she was always just one more of Martin's female relatives, widowed, stiff spined, and imperious.

"Maralyn, I'm gonna level with you. I'm at a loss here. I've talked with the coroner and he's hesitant to come right out and record Martin's death as an accident. Didn't Ella tell me you were a nurse? Well, you were in that room. Surely you realize how difficult it is for us to determine exactly what happened. As Martin's friend, I want to get all the facts straight, get his death recorded correctly, close the book on it and let all his family and friends get to the job of mourning him properly. I can't do that without knowing everything. Will you please help me?"

She relaxed into the sofa. "Sill and Martin had an argument at the barbecue. Sill had the uncommon bad sense to bring her lesbian girlfriend, and Martin was upset. I don't blame her and I don't blame him. It's her life, but it was his house and his church and he had every right to expect that to be respected."

"Did he know in advance that Sill's lover—Faith, I believe it is—was going to be there?"

"Yes. But all this is something you need to discuss with Sill."

"I will. Tell me exactly what you remember of the argument. Where were you?"

"In the kitchen by the window. I could see everything, although I couldn't hear. But I didn't need to hear the words, to know the sentiment."

"Really? Why's that?"

"I've known Martin all of my life—we grew up together, less than a mile apart—and I've never seen him so mad. He was angry and embarrassed. Martin wasn't exactly a liberal thinker. Sill flaunting her lifestyle wasn't something he would have accepted kindly."

Truitt gazed down at the coffee table. It was a little too bizarre for him, a bunch of dead people preserved under glass. He wondered which of the squinting children, apple healthy in their 1940s clothes, was Maralyn. He couldn't guess. Too many years and too much hardness had settled on this athletic older woman for him to detect the cherub within.

"So," he said mildly, "where precisely were you when the gun went off?"

"Still in the kitchen," she said. "With Mother, Cammy and Sill."

"Sill had joined you?"

"Yes. After the argument, Martin came inside the house—"

"Which door?"

"Back. He walked into the kitchen, mad as hell. He didn't even look at us. Just walked through and into the hall."

"When did Sill come in?"

"A few seconds later. She started after him, but Ella told her to let him be. That set Sill off. I've never seen her so upset—yelling at Ella, saying over and over that Martin *had* to accept her. I tried to calm her down, but she pushed me away. In the middle of the arguing we heard the shot."

"What was Cammy doing during all this?"

Maralyn grimaced. "Cammy's not going to get in the middle of her daughter and her husband. She'd be stomped to death from both sides if she did. She was over at the work table, messing with that fool wreath for the pig."

"Was anyone else in the house?"

"Not that I know of."

Truitt considered his opened notebook. "All right. So you hear the shot. Then what?"

"We run upstairs to the bedroom."

"Is the door open or closed?"

"Closed."

"Locked?"

"No."

"Then what?"

"Sill opens the door and we all go in."

Truitt settled back in his chair and took the pen from his shirt pocket.

"Tell me exactly what you saw."

She blinked behind her round wire glasses. "Martin on the floor beside the bed. Blood." She paused. "The walls, the floor, the lamp shade on the bedside table. Spatters of it, puddles of it. You know. You saw it."

"What I saw, Maralyn, was a room that had been the site of considerable activity. You women did a lot of disturbance in that room. Destroyed a lot of information."

"It was just so unbelievable." Her voice grew soft. "I'm a nurse—blood doesn't bother me. I deal with that and more every day at the clinic. But there was so much, and it was so unlikely." She focused her gaze on Truitt. "He didn't have a face, Alby. He was lying there on the floor, all curled up. I recognized the torso, the hands, the legs. Hell, I recognized those damn silly boots he insisted on wearing even in the summer. It was so unreal. I guess we went a little mad, figuring if we could just collect the pieces, we could put him back together. Of course, we couldn't. There were too many pieces. We wouldn't have known where to begin."

Truitt studied the point of his pen. "When my mother was sick, I'd go visit her and be just appalled by the smells. Bodies smell a certain way when they're dying. I couldn't face it. Yet your mother was there, nursing her, and she didn't have a problem with the odor. She had become adjusted to it, I think. I guess I'm a little surprised by your reaction to Martin's body. In my mind, I imagine nurses acting differently in a crisis. I suppose I feel you should have adjusted better to what was a basic medical situation."

Maralyn tugged the white skirt over her knees. "That's an interesting insinuation, Alby. But I did act as a nurse. My first instinct was to save Martin's life, not preserve the scene for you. If it got a little crazy in there, I'm sorry. But the truth was that man was the husband, father, and cousin to the four of us. We weren't in an examination room, but a bedroom. This wasn't blood rising in a vial, but blood out of control. If you want to question my professionalism, go ahead. I'll be the first to admit I wasn't being a professional at the time."

"What about blood-borne illnesses? Didn't your nurse's instinct tell you to at least protect the other women from all that blood?"

Her words were clipped. "Martin wasn't sick, Alby. He was dead."

Goddammit, Truitt thought. He shouldn't have let them go last night. Bingham had tried to warn him. *Consider the condition of that room, Alby. I'd take a good hard look at homicide.* But he had looked at Martin's widow and taken pity, confiscated their clothes, but left them free to talk. What had they had, fourteen, fifteen hours to sit down together and hash it out? He stared at Maralyn's strong hands, her muscular arms. *You're lying to me, lady,* he thought. *Sane people just don't do what you did.*

"Where was the gun before you picked it up?"

"I didn't. Mother did."

"Ella gave you the gun?"

"That's right."

"Did you see where it was before she handed it to you?"

"No."

"How was Martin lying?" he asked.

"On his side."

"How far from the bed?"

"Right up against it, as I recall."

"And how were his hands?"

Maralyn shrugged. "I don't remember."

"But when you were describing the body, you specifically mentioned the hands. Think back, Maralyn, where were his hands? Were they held close to his body? Were they close to each other? Was one flung over his head? Just how did they look?"

"I don't remember."

Truitt sighed and reclined into the chair. "According to the crime scene techs, the hands had been messed with, wiped clean. Do you know anything about that?"

"If by 'messed with' you mean did someone touch them, then yes. I recall Cammy holding them, maybe even stroking them a little, after we got him up on the bed."

He stared at her, incredulous. "And at no time did you think, 'We shouldn't be doing this,' or 'Let's just let him be until the sheriff arrives'? Not even in the back of your head, Maralyn, did you think, professional or not, that you might be 'messing' with the scene of a crime?"

Behind the wire-rimmed glasses, her eyes never wavered. "I think you forget yourself, Alby. First of all, this was no crime—it was an accident. And secondly, how in the world would you expect us to act?"

Her eyes held his until he broke his gaze. She's

thought all this through too carefully, he thought. She hasn't been grieving, she's been calculating. He tossed his pen on the table. "Where'd you get those clothes you have on? Did you make a trip into Atlanta this morning?"

"No, I'm here for the weekend—came in Friday night. I had these clothes with me in my suitcase."

"What do you think Martin was doing with the rifle out?"

He had timed the question to startle her, but it didn't work. "Cammy told your man last night. The gun was a stress reliever for him—whenever things got too bad, he'd take it out and clean and oil it."

"There were no oil and rods, Maralyn. What did y'all do, tidy them up while you were rearranging the body?"

The sarcasm didn't penetrate. She stuck one long finger into her nest of hair and lightly scratched.

"If you say there were no oil and rods," she said slowly, "then it must be true. Maybe the gun went off before he took them out, I don't know. But what's eating you is, you don't know either. And you're afraid as hell you're never going to find out."

Katie Pru stood on the bottom step of the staircase and grinned at her mother. "If you put me on your shoulders," she said, "I could see the fish."

"If I put you on my shoulders, I'd topple over."

"If you put me on your shoulders," Katie Pru said slyly, "I could be a grown-up."

Gale slapped her cheeks in horror. "I wouldn't want you to be a grown-up! You'd put me in the time-out chair."

Katie Pru collapsed into giggles and clamped her arms around Gale's neck. Gale gave in to the hug, enfolded her daughter and swayed back and forth.

Faith walked down the hall and halted by the front

door. "See, this is what I like about kids," she said. "You make them sit in a chair and they love you for it."

Gale looked over the mess of brown hair and tried to blow errant wisps from her mouth. "Oh, they may love you," she said, "but they still plot."

The living room door opened, and Maralyn emerged.

"Sheriff's here," she said blithely. "I have been duly questioned and released. He wants to talk to Mother now. I didn't volunteer to get her."

She stepped past them and sauntered down the hall. Gale glanced at Faith, who raised her eyebrows and shrugged.

"Gale."

She started. Truitt stood in the living room doorway, studying the disappearing figure of her aunt.

"Gale," he repeated, directing his attention on her. "Have you got a minute? I'd like to talk to you."

Gale looked at Faith, who nodded in comprehension. "I don't mind watching her," she said. "I'll even let her get up on my shoulders."

Truitt had turned to retreat into the living room when he stopped. "Excuse me, ma'am," he said. He extended his hand to Faith. "I'm Sheriff Alby Truitt. And you are . . ."

Faith's smile was friendly. "Faith Baskins. I'm a friend of Sill's."

"Ah, yes. I heard mention of you. You were at the barbecue last night, weren't you?"

"Yes, I was. Briefly."

Truitt nodded. "I don't think we had a chance to talk with you."

"I must've left right before it happened."

"Later on today, or tomorrow, perhaps . . ."

"No problem. I'm staying at the Creely House Inn in Praterton."

"That your Cherokee out there?"

"Yes, sir, it is."

"Interesting license plate."

"My personal philosophy. We don't pay nearly enough taxes in this country for what we get."

Truitt grinned. "You must be great at a dinner party."

"Things get lively."

"You washed your car."

Faith's mouth dropped open for only a moment before her tone grew teasing.

"Gee, Sheriff, I tend to do that sometimes," she said.

"Pretty recently."

"This morning."

"Before you came over here?"

"That's right."

"Why's that?"

"It was a dump. I wanted to be of help here, and I thought if I was going to chauffeur people around, they'd prefer a modicum of cleanliness."

Truitt's eyes traveled down Faith's clothes, taking in, Gale was certain, the woman's cinched black belt and ironed linen pants. This was surely not a woman who drove around in a dirty car. He traced the line of his cheek with his finger, a skeptical smile on his features.

"Mind telling me where?"

"No problem. At Kennedy's Car Wash on LaVista. That's in Atlanta."

He nodded. "I know LaVista. Thank you."

Still smiling, he motioned Gale inside the room and shut the door. As she settled into the yellow sofa, he took a seat across from her in Ella's peach-colored wing chair. The chair sagged as he collapsed into it.

"Bet there's horsehair in here." He pounded the arm gently. "You can always tell a good piece of horsehair furniture. It looks so stiff you think you'll crack your spine on it, but it's really unbelievably giving."

"It's well broken-in. Growing up, if I wasn't jumping on it, I was curled up in it reading."

"Is that right? Somehow I can't see any child

reading in here." He indicated the glass table. "However did you concentrate with all those people watching you?"

Gale smiled. "And which room do you think didn't have people watching me? This wasn't an easy house to concentrate in, Alby."

"Don't imagine it was. Everybody knew your business." He continued to gaze at the table. "Speaking of, tell me about this Space Lucy. Wouldn't be a secret code or anything?"

Gale laughed. "You'd have to ask Katie Pru about that."

Truitt shifted forward. "You're going to get testy about this next question, but don't. I just need to cover all the bases. You got a history to you, Gale. I'm not suggesting anything—I just need to know. Who's the letter from?"

Gale waited, letting her irritation rise, then dissipate. "No testiness here," she said breezily. "If you're looking for a connection between Martin's death and international terrorism, you won't find it in my letter, Alby. It's from a detective. One of your kind. I suspect when I read it, it'll be about the weather and how much he enjoyed my latest Katie Pru story."

"Huh. Damnedest thing. You know, when I was a teenager, I wanted to move to England and join Scotland Yard. Or failing that, MI5. Too much James Bond and *The Man from U.N.C.L.E.*, I guess. It seemed so exotic."

"It's more entertaining left on the screen."

"I don't doubt it." He pushed his forefinger back until it cracked. "It can't have been easy, coming back. I know a little about the limited tolerance of a small town."

"It wasn't easy staying there, either."

"No, I don't suppose it was." He moved to his middle finger. "The coroner's not ready to call Martin's death an accident."

Gale, feeling a familiar sickness in her stomach, nodded wordlessly.

"He doesn't like the idea that guns go off by themselves," Truitt continued. "I don't like the idea that Martin was upstairs in his bedroom with a loaded rifle while outside half of the county ate his barbecue."

He stopped. Gale studied her tennis shoe. He was waiting for her to say it, waiting for her to be the one to acknowledge what really happened in that room. Well, why not, she thought bitterly. When you have a problem, call in an expert.

"You think it was a suicide." Even to herself, her voice sounded flat.

Truitt frowned. "Suicide? With no note? No planning? Just run upstairs and bam, it's over? Hell, no, Gale. I don't buy suicide."

From above, Gale could hear the creak of assured footfalls. Ella was in her bedroom, treading on the floorboards, stressing the joists.

"So what else?" Her voice was hoarse.

"Tell me what you think."

She bit down on the inside of her cheek until a saltiness stung her tongue.

"It was an accident. Or it was suicide. If you're thinking anything else, you're dead wrong. Men commit suicide, Alby. They put guns in their mouths and don't give a damn about who finds them or how."

"He didn't put the gun in his mouth. I know that much. The gunshot was at close range—very close, I'll give you that. But this wasn't a suicide. I've known the man for over twenty-five years. Martin had a problem, he solved it. He wasn't the suicidal type."

"The suicidal type." Her hands were cold. The fingers felt thin and dry, and her wedding ring dropped easily to her knuckle.

Truitt walked to the window. "I've got half a dozen witnesses, Gale, who say no more than sixty seconds passed between the time the gun went off and they found the bedroom door locked and those women locked behind it. Several minutes—maybe as long as ten—went by before Ella let everyone in, and by that time, the crime scene had been demolished. Now, I'm sorry, there's too much television, movies, and books out there for those women to think it was okay to ransack the scene of a violent death that way. It flat-out, plain wouldn't happen, Gale."

"You don't know. You've never been in that situation."

He spread his arms wide. "I've been in law enforcement long enough to know when something isn't right. They would've had to go crazy—"

"And you think that's unreasonable? Put yourself in their position, Alby. You wouldn't scream? You wouldn't . . . ?"

"Scoop up brain pulp and slap it on a dead man's head? No, Gale, I don't think I would. Not unless . . ."

"Not unless what? I can't imagine doing anything else. If I had found Tom, I would've done anything. God, Alby, how can you not see that?"

"And how can *you* not see? How the hell can you stand . . . ?"

Truitt dropped back into his chair, bringing his hands to his face and rubbing hard enough so that his eyes moistened. "Dammit," he said quietly. "I'm sorry," he said. "I keep forgetting these are your people. I keep thinking you're . . . Goddammit, Gale . . ."

He leaned forward and clumsily knocked his knee against the beveled edge of the table. The glass moved, exposing the corner of a photo. He stared at the white triangle, flicking it with his thumbnail.

"I'm trying to be objective." He sounded tired. "You know about my father. His body was found in a burning house, tied to a chair. Cocaine smuggler—nice little sideline for a country boy out in the middle of nowhere. I was fifteen, bad age to be a pariah. And I would've been, except for Martin. He took me under his wing and told everybody, 'See here. This boy's all right.' "

He brought his eyes to her face. "He made me his son, Gale. And when I didn't need him anymore, I let him go. I was a hot young sheriff and there he was with his tacky barbecue, tapped into the good-ol'-boy network. I didn't want people saying, 'See? Alby Truitt's one of the courthouse gang. Just a more palatable version of his old man.' I had contacts with the state and at the universities and in Atlanta, and I didn't want those folks thinking I was just one more ignorant, redneck, backwater sheriff. Truth is, Gale, Martin was an embarrassment to me."

Gale turned her hands up helplessly in her lap. "He would have understood, Alby," she murmured. "He wouldn't have blamed you."

Truitt glared at her. "Yes, he would have. He would've read me for the piece of shit I am. Then he would have stood by me. He was a better human being than me. And I owe him."

Ella stood at the window, looking out on the back fields and absently running her finger along the waistband of her black skirt. At one point she thought she heard thunder, far off and grumbling, but she couldn't be sure. All her attention had been focused on the heating grate at her feet and the voices in the living room rising from it.

Behind her, Cammy rustled in the bed.

"Sill?" A half whisper, half moan. "Baby?"

Ella turned to her. "It's Ella, Cammy. Are you waking up?"

No answer. Cammy's hand slid under the pillow, bunching the fabric beneath her cheek. In the curtained dimness of the room, she resembled a pouting child—mouth puckered, eyes squinched tightly. Ella walked to the bedside and gently rested her palm on Cammy's head. A strange singing sound, like a high note on a violin, came from the younger woman's mouth.

"Hush, now," Ella cooed. "You go back to sleep.

There's not anything for you to wake up for. You just go on back to sleep."

The singing sound stopped and Cammy's closed eyes relaxed. Ella waited for her breathing to grow regular once again, and then stepped back to the grate. She strained to hear the voices, but they were silent.

Outside, the sky had turned a vibrant purple. A storm was coming. The weather had settled into one of those alarming summer patterns of hot, heavy days and violent, storm-filled nights. She and Nora used to huddle by the window on those nights and watch lightning slash the sky and the wind twist the limbs of the pecan trees. Once, a branch finally cracked, leaving a sudden white tear where the limb hung from the trunk. That was the most terrifying part to her, not the flash of the lightning or the crack of thunder, but the raw white of that torn wood, as shocking as blood against the gray patina of the bark.

Before her the acres of Alden land stretched in yellow fields, broken by mounds of kudzu, hillocks, and the occasional stand of pine. In total her father had left her and Nora 326 acres, much of it parceled out to longtime cattle farmers. No chump change, not by today's standards. A lot of land for a storm to cover.

Cammy mumbled, and once more Ella stepped to her side. A drop of perspiration rolled from the sleeping woman's forehead and darkened the mauve pillowcase beneath her head. Ella felt a surge of pity as she put her finger to the spreading damp circle. You've entered a deep hole, Cammy, she thought. It's a well with a stone cover. What you emerge as is God's own guess.

She turned and faced the grate. Gale and Alby would take some thinking about.

*I've seen ghosts in girdles throw better pitches
than us.*
        —Bob Hinson, after coaching a losing
        church softball game, 1964

 11

Zilah Greene had an uncommon memory. She could
remember the sound of the gourd rattle her father made
her, and the taste of the rungs on her baby crib as she
tried to chew them apart. She remembered the rawness
of her bottom when her mother took too long to change
her, and the smell of grease on her daddy's hands when
he lifted her into the air. Barry would shake his head
and mutter. *It's not normal for a person to recall like
that. Nobody remembers when they were a year old.*
But Zilah did.

    Across the yard, she could see the Alden house, red
angles against the stormy purple of the sky. Behind it

the massive pecan trees shimmied in the wind like huge, aging belly dancers with leaves instead of bangles on their veils. She stood silently and watched them move, their arms corpulent and hips heavy. The sensation of her stomach falling swept over her. She pulled out a chair from the kitchen table and eased herself down.

Her mother liked to sit and watch the trees. She would drag the rocker to the window and lift Zilah into her lap, where they would wait for the coming storms and watch the big trees sway. More often than not, she'd fall asleep, a victim of the rocker's soothing rhythm and her mother's soft singing. *Zilah, Zilah, Zilah. Zilah, Zilah, love.*

Her parents never had much, not the way she and Barry did when the hardware store began to flourish after the war. Her daddy worked next door for Mr. Steve Alden, tending to the cotton crops and minding the machinery. Before that, he'd done the same for Mr. Justin Cane, whose wife, Miss Linnie, had inherited the house from her father. *I work for no man, Zilah. I belong to the house.* Barry used to say that was foolish—a man belonged to himself. But the longer she lived, the more she understood what her father had meant. You see something long enough, it becomes yours; you live in its shadow, you become its part. That's how she felt about the red house outside her kitchen window. The people who lived there died, moved, came back—it didn't matter. *She* was the constant.

The thunder erupted like a yawn, loud at first and then softer as it rumbled in the distance. She pushed herself from the table and walked to the sink. The light beneath the pecan trees was meaty, shadows and storm combining to make darkened hollows below the branches. Nevertheless, it was adequate. She didn't need light to see the brown cloth dangling from the big pecan tree closest to the Alden house.

Hush, baby, hush. Mama'll make it go away.

Nothin' happened to scare my baby girl. And then her mother's song. *Zilah, Zilah, Zilah. Zilah, Zilah, love.*

Her mother's chin had trembled as she sang. The rest of her face was smooth, like a sock doll before its features were sewn on. It was the only thing she couldn't figure out: Why, if she remembered so much, couldn't she remember her mother's eyes?

"Nap time."

"I don't want a nap."

"You'll be cranky if you don't have one."

"*You'll* be cranky if I don't have one."

Gale plucked at the nubby cotton spread covering her bed and pulled it free from beneath the pillow. If Katie Pru's logic is this unimpeachable at four, she thought, what do the teenage years threaten to bring? She looked at her daughter, arms folded across her white T-shirt, a gaggle of honking geese running along the hem of her shorts. She patted the cool white sheet underneath the spread.

"I gave birth to a wise women, K.P.," she said. "All right, we'll both be cranky if you don't have a nap. Besides, it's gray and gloomy outside. When I was a little girl, there was nothing I liked better than to climb under the covers on a rainy day with my socks on and go to sleep. So kick off your shoes and come on up here."

Katie Pru plopped down on the floor and tugged off her blue tennis shoes. Frowning, she first peered skeptically at the creased socks flopping over her toes, then at the plump white expanse of the bed. Finally she looked at her mother.

"Snuggle with me," she said.

Gale sighed. "All right. I'll snuggle for just a bit. But you have to go to sleep. I've got work to do, Katie Pru. I'll stay and do it in the room, but only if you're fast asleep. Any problems and I'll have to go downstairs. Deal?"

"Deal."

Humming, Katie Pru hiked into the bed. Gale waited until all four of her daughter's limbs were flat on the mattress before bringing the covers up and tucking them under her chin. Katie Pru smiled and rolled over to face the wall as Gale climbed into the bed beside her.

Katie Pru wriggled her rear end until it fit in the curve of Gale's stomach. "I'm not going to close my eyes," she said.

"That's fine. You can sleep with them open."

Gale crooked one arm over the nestled child and slipped the other one under the pillow. The murmur of women's voices filtered in from the hallway. Although the words were unintelligible, there was no mistaking Ella's voice, reedy and sharp through the wood. She wondered how much the four of them knew, and if Alby had been as candid with Maralyn as he had been with her. Not likely. She knew enough about hunting to know a good hunter didn't shout at the deer before pulling the trigger. So how good a hunter was Alby? And what did it say about them both that he had momentarily forgotten she was one of the herd?

She tilted her head closer to Katie Pru's. The child's hair held a strong, earthy odor, as if she had been playing hard outside. Gently, Gale laid her forefinger in Katie Pru's palm and dragged her fingertip across it. The small paunches of flesh were dry.

And inert. Gale ran her finger across Katie Pru's hand again, wanting, as with a Venus's-flytrap, the stimulation to enclose her daughter's fingers around her own. It didn't happen. The reflex hand grip, so strong in the infant, had long since matured into a deliberate grasp. Gale closed her eyes. It was such a simple thing to be such a deep loss.

She forced her thoughts back to the women. So Alby Truitt suspected them of murder. Or, more accurately, he suspected one of them of murder and the other three of conspiracy. Somehow, in his Southern sheriff's thinking, blood on a woman's hands meant bloodletting. He didn't understand that a woman's hands were made to carry blood, that over her palms passed the blood of children, parents, strangers, and spouses. And sometimes, in dark basins and empty rooms, they even carried their own.

She loosened her grip around Katie Pru. Under the white bedspread the child's little body was no more than a hump. Gale and Ella had lain in this bed once in just this way—the day of her mother's funeral. Ella had hurried her away to the family house in Statlers Cross before the funeral tent was down. No technicalities like fatherhood or the law were going to deprive Ella Alden the right to raise her dead daughter's child. So the night of the funeral she had slept with Gale in the guest room's mahogany bed, ignoring the incessant ringing of the phone.

In the middle of the night, Gale had awoken. Her first thought was for her mother, Kathleen, snuggled against her in the shadowed room. She turned to hug her, intending to slip her hand up to her mother's face and maybe crook one finger over her lip. But when she rolled over, the light from the hallway struck the sleeping figure next to her. Gale screamed. The woman who rose up from the bed was ancient. The skin hung from her face, and her gums, spread apart in surprise, gleamed in a toothless O. She reached out to Gale, but the child fell from the bed, swiping frantically at the blankets. Now, whenever she thought of her mother, she remembered Ella and the shiny black gap in her face.

Outside, the wind knocked the limbs of the pecan tree against the side of the house. Carefully, Gale pushed herself away from Katie Pru and climbed from the bed. The window flashed with the green of whipped leaves. The storm was building. She walked to the window and peered outside. She could see nothing of the sky. While the other windows in the rear of the house looked out over the grasslands, here the pecan tree was so close that the room seemed wedged in the leaves.

Pressing her face against the pane, she strained to see the ground below. The base of the tree was massive, the root system spreading out at least fifty feet from the five-foot-wide trunk. She wondered how fast pecan trees grew. This one had always seemed mammoth to her, but then, how could it appear as anything else? It was Linnie's tree. It had been her weapon.

As she turned away, the envelope in her skirt pocket knocked against her leg. She pulled the letter out and immediately felt her chest tighten. Usually Daniel Halford's missives were long and rambling. This letter was one page, front and back.

Gale,

Had Saturday luncheon at Maura's and Jeffrey's today. They are, it seems, as happy as ever, the sergeant having elevated "pluckiness" to a mission statement. I gave her the drawing Katie Pru sent. Be sure to tell her Maura was thrilled. A barefoot little girl pulling worms from the ground and placing them on her head—we surmised it was autobiographical. You must have had a fun day.

Glad to hear your work is going well. "The domestic writings of Southern rural women from 1900 to 1929." A little esoteric for me, but then I'm just a simple British copper who still thinks history means Robin Hood vs. the Sheriff of Nottingham. I do know enough about the history of the American South to ask one question, however: Between poverty and the boll weevil, when the hell did these women have time to write?

I visited a used-book shop near Victoria Station yesterday. You would like it: cosy— pools of light around overstuffed chairs—a proprietor who knows everything but has the

*sixth sense to understand when to let you be. I
came across a copy of your book. It was there
in the shelves, blue spine, gold letters. I believe
you once said discovering writings from
someone gone from you was like coming across
ghosts. You were right.*

Call.

There was no signature; there never had been, not
since she and Halford had begun corresponding a
month after her arrival in Statlers Cross. For the most
part their letters were general communications—how
Katie Pru was adjusting, whether it was better to be
soaked in London or sweltering in Georgia. This letter,
however, had a different tone to it. She reread the last
paragraph, her eyes tumbling past the words. *Someone
gone from you.* A plank of guilt moved down her
throat. She hadn't felt gone from him, not really; she
had felt they were the appropriate distance apart.

She tiptoed to the bed and tucked the envelope
under Katie Pru's pillow so that the corner with Space
Lucy peeked out. *Call.* She had never wanted to call
him. There was more distance in writing. More control.

In the corner of the room was an antique rosewood
chair, upholstered in an outdated mustard velveteen.
On the chair lay a pen and one of her research notebooks, opened to a page covered in her own neat handwriting. The hard-boiled paragraphs of mothers and
wives: mothers whose children died at birth, wives
whose men—sons and husbands—walked out the front
door and never returned, wives who weren't wives at all
but misled lovers in an age when neither credit cards
nor telephones could leave a trail.

The page held the transcription of a woman from
Walton County, Georgia, in 1919:

*I stayed up last night crying, for my fingers
hurt so from the needle. I stitched for nine
straight hours, stopping only to feed the*

*children and bathe Mama, who has in truth
become my seventh child. Last week I told the
minister of my crying times, they grow so
frightful to me, and he said I should be joyful
for my life which I truly am, for in God's love I
have abundance.*

Abundance. It was hard to tell, approaching a century later, whether sincerity or cynicism fed the word. If
there was one thing that had surprised her in her
research it was the shock these young brides experi-
enced once they understood the full breadth of their lot.
Such anticipation during the courtship, such concern
over their parents' approval, and then stunned amazement over the physical work of keeping house and
raising children—as if their own mothers had worked
behind curtains.

*. . . she washed her five-year-old son's hands and
face, dressed him in the nicest clothes she had made for
him, and locked him in his room . . .*

Gale knew all the Linnie stories by heart. Everyone
did. It had always amazed her how consistent the local
storytelling was. Even hand gestures, facial expressions,
all the accompanying dramatics, seemed to have been
passed down from one generation to the next.

*She went out to the barn, found the strongest rope
she could, and took it and a little stool she used to pick
plums to the biggest pecan tree. . . .*

Here the speaker usually slowed, knowing what
was coming and figuring the listener did as well. Put a
rope and a tree together in the same story and there's
always a hanging. Westerns were built on it—so was
the South.

*She slung that rope over the lowest branch, stepped
up on that stool . . .*

And left a five-year-old child. Gale looked up at the
window and the tossing branches. Linnie had left a five-
year-old child, dressed in his Sunday best, locked in a
room. Which room? This one, disconnected from every-

thing with only its view of the tree? Surely not. So one of the others, with their windows opening onto infinite grasses.

Gale shivered. Did Linnie's son go through his life remembering that day? Did he remember the concern with his clothes, a kiss, an admonition to be good and wait for his daddy to come home? Was there a promise? *Be good and we'll have cake tonight.* And when his mother didn't return, did he stumble from window to door, trying to get out, trying to find someone to help him?

Gently she flipped through the pages of the notebook. Words from women who were tired, frustrated, lonely. But they found time to write. They made sure they left some sort of record, like a message in a bottle, tossed out to sea for someone to find and decipher. Linnie, on the other hand, had left nothing, just a coverlet on a wall and a self-destruction that spawned a hundred tales.

Behind her, Gale could hear Katie Pru breathing regularly. There had been times, after Tom had killed himself, when she had thought her pain was endless. But she had always known she would never kill herself for one simple reason—she had a child.

So the question was, why hadn't Linnie made the same investment?

She was the orneriest woman in Calwyn County. She'd've sooner choked the life out of herself than say good morning. Gale picked up the black pen and turned the notebook to the back page.

She had Katie Pru. There was no doubt in her mind that her chances of surviving Tom's death would have been much less had she been childless. A mother will go through a great deal for the sake of a child's clasp.

The night of her mother's funeral Gale had lain on the bed and listened to the phone ring for what seemed like hours. She had known then, with the mysterious instinct of a child, that the caller was her father, trying to get her back, trying to take her home. In the ensuing years Ella would allow little contact. She would raise her granddaughter, men and their laws be damned.

It took a cold heart to lock out a father. Perhaps Sill had been right. Perhaps as children they all had to be cold.

She started writing. Names. Approximate dates. Places of birth, family friends, long-forgotten ministers and doctors. When she finished, the page was full.

The acorn doesn't fall far from the tree. Sill had tossed it off as a trite end to a conversation, but neither one of them had accepted it as that. Gale stared at the paper. Linnie didn't have to leave a written record. Her family was record enough.

Slowly she drew a box around one name: Jules Samuel Cane. The five-year-old little boy Linnie left behind. Ella's first cousin. Martin's father. Linnie Cane, suicide and ghost, was Martin's grandmother. Gale shook her head in wonder. Zilah had been right. Gale had to be tricked into listening.

I can't tell you how horrible it is here—the smell, noise, napalm. Sometimes I just close my eyes and dream of the days we thought frightening was sitting around the fireplace telling ghost stories.

— Jason Stone in a letter to his brother Butch, posted from Da Nang, 1967

 12

Ella Alden's choice of her austere dining room for her interview didn't surprise Truitt—and he supposed that her sense of the cinematic shouldn't have surprised him either.

Ella sat with her hands folded on top of the mahogany table, lipstick even, white hair neatly poofed. On the plaster wall behind her arched a fully grown swordfish, an easy seven feet from the tip of the bill to the tail. The fish's one gray eye stared at Truitt, and its lower jaw displayed a row of sharp teeth caked with dust. The body gleamed with shellac, and it curved above Ella's head like a taxidermic rainbow.

Truitt tried not to laugh. "Goodness, Miss Ella," he said. "I guess I've never been in your dining room before. Where in the world did you get that fish?"

Her smile skirted a simper. "Oh, that. My husband, Gerry, caught that off the coast of Florida, oh, must have been in 1953. He was a great sportsman, Alby. He died in 1965. He was born near here, but he much preferred city life, except when it came to hunting. That's why we moved the family to Atlanta in the '50s. Do you remember anything of him?"

"No, ma'am." The fact was, Martin's family was notable for its women, not its men. Martin used to grouse about it. Both his father and his grandfather had sired only one child each, both boys. The remainder of the family sprouted from Linnie's sister Jessie, and there were nothing but girls. They married, of course, but nobody of note. Or, in Gale's case, possibly of note, but not of longevity.

"I'm afraid he didn't leave much of an impression around here," Ella said. "He was always off somewhere, hunting, fishing, bringing back all these carcasses and having them stuffed and mounted. If it breathed, it was huntable. Not so many laws back then, you know. If Hemingway hadn't already invented himself, Gerry would have taken the role."

Truitt lightly pressed his fingertips onto the table top. "Let's see . . . 1965. About how old was Gale when your husband died?"

"Gale?" Ella cocked her head in mild surprise. "She wasn't born yet. Why?"

"I don't know. Just trying to get a handle on things. Martin talked about his family, and growing up near here, I always felt I knew everybody. It turns out I've got a pretty weak grasp. I'm just trying to fit it all together. Now, how did Gale's mother die?"

"Automobile accident. You don't think Gale . . ."

"No, no. I've got several witnesses who said they saw her and Katie Pru at the moment of the shooting.

In fact, Miss Ella, Gale's the only woman in this house who doesn't really concern me."

"Gracious, Alby. You make it sound as if something sinister has happened." The smile on Ella's face was benign. "It hasn't, you know. Tragic, of course. But tragedy we can deal with. We'll pray, we'll help Cammy and Sill, and we'll get through it."

Ella adjusted the gold bangle on her arm, pulling at the safety chain until it swung untangled from the bracelet. She wore an amber knit shell, topped with a short-sleeved black linen jacket. Above her left breast was a gold pin in the shape of a tree, with tiny seed pearls serving as leaves. She patiently waited for him to speak, her face calm but her eyes sharp. She was, as Martin would have said, a piece of work.

"You know, Miss Ella, you remind me so much of my grandmother. Nothing bad could happen to our family that she couldn't fix. After my father died, I remember one of my great-aunts sitting in the kitchen, whispering about how shameful it was, how would we ever hold our heads up. And my grandmother, she just raised her hand and said, 'That's it. We don't talk about it anymore. It's the Lord's place to judge because He knows judgment'll just eat us humans up alive.' And it was never spoken of in the family again."

"That's what families are for. They keep us safe from the gossip outside."

She said it slyly, a woman, Truitt thought, too taken with herself for subtlety. He grinned at her.

"Two points for you, Miss Ella. There was a lot of gossip outside, wasn't there? A fifteen-year-old boy needed some special protection against it."

"And he got it, didn't he, Alby?" Ella's dark eyes were raven sharp. "I knew your grandmother Tannie some. We were in high school at the same time." She paused. "So what do you think she would tell you now, Alby?"

"About what?"

"About Martin."

"Hmm. That's a question. What would Tannie tell me now?" He began drawing circles on the cover of the notepad before him. "Well, Tannie was a firm believer in intuition. I suppose in today's lexicon, you'd say she was a right-brain thinker."

Ella grunted. "I've never trusted heart-oriented people. Intuition sounds too much like intellectual laziness to me. Tannie wasn't much of a reader, as I recall."

"No, ma'am, I can't say she was. She wouldn't have been likely to compare my grandfather to Hemingway. But that doesn't mean she was stupid. In fact, when I said you reminded me of her, I didn't mean in a superficial way. She didn't wear clothes like yours. The only piece of jewelry she owned was her wedding ring, and her house certainly wasn't anything like this one. But there are other things about you that make me think you and she were of the same breed."

"Such as?"

Truitt flipped open the notebook and began drawing his circles on a blank sheet of paper. He glanced at Ella. Her expression was still pleasant, but her eyes darted from his face to his hands.

"Well, for starters, you were both born between the World Wars and raised, I'm willing to bet, at the knees of grandmothers who could still recall the Civil War. I'd ask Tannie about the stories her grandmother used to tell about the Civil War, and she'd say, 'There were no stories, Alby. Just clenched jaws and dirty hands.' "

"So what's your point, Alby?" Ella's voice was almost lilting.

"Well," he said, "I suppose I'm thinking that behind all the fine decorum of this family, there's a hell of a lot of clenched jaws and dirty hands."

Her face hardened. "What happened in that room, Ella?" he asked softly.

"I told your officer last night."

"You told him a version last night."

"It was the truth. We were in the kitchen and heard

a gunshot. We went flying upstairs and all ran into the room together."

"According to Maralyn, Sill was pretty upset in the kitchen. You and she had an argument after Martin went into the house."

"That's right. She wanted to talk to him further, and I told her it wasn't the time. Sill can be highly emotional. She had what I'd call one of her classic fits."

"What's that exactly?"

"Oh, you know—blind anger, tears, stomping, theatrics. When Sill gets mad like that, she repeats the same words over and over, as if her brain gets stuck. Yesterday it was 'He can't walk away from me.' There's nothing to do when she gets that way except batten down the hatches and stay in control."

"Would you say she was out of control?"

"Sure she was, but if you're trying to suggest anything, Alby, you can forget it. Sill was in that kitchen with me and Maralyn and Cammy when the gun went off. I'll swear to it."

Truitt flipped to a clean sheet of paper and slid the notebook across the table to her. "Could you sketch where you found Martin's body when you went into the room? And note where the rifle was located, please."

Ella took the pen from him and drew a few lines across the paper. She turned the notebook to face him.

"This is the bed. This is Martin. And this," she said, pointing with the pen, "is the gun."

He stared at the page. "Ella, you've drawn the rifle clear across the room."

"That's where it was, by the dresser."

"You sure?"

"Quite sure. I picked it up."

"Why?"

"To get it out of the way. So no one else would get hurt."

"Why did you give it to Maralyn?"

"I had other things to attend to."

"So you handed the gun to the only medical professional in the room." He paused, waiting for her to reply. She said nothing. "Who else's fingerprints am I going to find on that gun, Ella?"

Her bracelet clanked against the table. "Oh, for pity's sakes, Alby, I have no idea who handled that gun. And what does it matter? We were all lucky that no one else got hurt, considering the thing was faulty."

Truitt leaned back in his chair and scratched his chin. "Why do you think Martin had his gun out?"

"I don't know. Cammy says he often took it out when he was anxious. She says he cleaned it the way she cleans the kitchen sink."

"To relieve stress."

"That's right."

"But there was no oil or rods."

She looked at him in surprise. "Well, yes, there were. I saw them myself."

"Where?"

"On the nightstand. Right beside the bed. Rags, too. Martin cut his own patches."

He studied her face. She was a generation or two past the period when Southern ladies eschewed the sun. Although her skin was pale beneath the powder, it was evident that at one point freckles had dotted her face. They didn't look like freckles now. Time had alligatored her cheeks. The freckles had folded in on themselves so that her face appeared covered with splinters.

"The only thing on the nightstand, Ella, was an alarm clock and a lamp. I looked."

"Well, Alby, that just can't be. They were right there, on top of the table handkerchief."

"What did the handkerchief look like?"

"Oh, I don't know. Square. Lacy border, embroidery in the middle. The oil and rods were right on top of it."

"The only thing on the nightstand," he repeated, "was an alarm clock and a lamp."

Her voice rose. "Well, then one of your men must have moved them. I . . ."

She stopped and dropped the pen on the table.

"You what, Ella?"

"They were right there. I saw them myself."

He flipped through his notebook until he came to his notes on the murder scene. "No, ma'am," he said. "My men wouldn't have moved them. And we looked all over the room. If we'd found something to indicate Martin was actually cleaning his gun . . ."

"But he was, Alby. I'm telling you."

She stared at him, her faded brown eyes as fixed as the swordfish's above her head.

"Well, I'm sorry, Ella. You telling me isn't enough." Truitt rapped his pen on the table. "I realize you're used to being the final word, but with all due respect, it just don't work that way."

Sill stood outside Ella's closed bedroom door, listening for any sound within. At four o'clock in the afternoon and after a ceaseless drone of voices, the house was finally silent.

Along the upstairs hallway the doors to the four bedrooms were shut. Earlier, from her own room, she had heard Gale and Katie Pru enter theirs, the soft murmurs of mother and child preceding a long period of inactivity. She imagined them in there now, both lying on the old mahogany double bed, Gale's arm tucked protectively around her sleeping daughter. A sudden burn caught at Sill's throat. Grasping the knob to Ella's door, she turned it and walked into the room.

Inside, it was curtained and cool. As she closed the door behind her, the air conditioner leapt into action. The cloaked light was furry, and Sill had to open her eyes wide to make out the form beneath the covers in Ella's massive carved bed.

"Mother?" Sill whispered. "Mother, are you awake?"

There was no reply. Beneath the tangle of blankets, her mother slept with knees to chest, her fist clasping a wad of dark sheeting to her cheek. Her breathing was deep and slow. Sill crouched beside the bed and touched her mother's hand.

"Mother?" she repeated. "Please wake up. I need to talk to you. I couldn't go downstairs today. I stayed up in my room. I couldn't face everyone." She paused. "Ryan Teller was here."

Nothing. She stared at the sleeping face, its features made malleable by the dimness. Had her mother's hair not gleamed gray against the pillow, she could have been any age—the certain mother of Sill's childhood, the sturdy one of her adolescence. Tears gathered on Sill's lashes and spilled down her cheeks. It isn't fair, she thought. I don't need you like this. I need you in the past. When you wanted to take care of me.

In the hallway a door closed and footsteps headed down the stairs. Sill stood and wiped her palm across her face. Gale must have left Katie Pru asleep in their room, bundled in the bed's light covers just as Cammy was. No doubt she fell asleep knowing her mother was with her, comforted by the warmth of her body, the tight clasp of her arm. Tears burned hot in Sill's eyes again. How is it children ever sleep, knowing that when they awake they will be alone?

Blinking the tears away, she eased herself onto the mattress and quietly kicked off her shoes. Then, gently picking up the covers, she slid into bed next to her mother.

It was strange at first, the warmth of this aging skin against her own. She tried to think back to the last time she had fallen asleep with her mother. It had to have been in early childhood, when she was still small enough to rest on Cammy's stomach. She closed her eyes and inched closer, wrapping her arms around her mother's waist. She remembered the smell of freshly laundered cotton, the expanse of a white shirt, the silky blue of a tie. . . .

The pain was so sudden it strangled her—the image of her father, holding her to his chest as she listened to his heart and tried to match the in-and-out of his breathing.

She buried her face in her mother's hair. Sobs wracked her body. *Help me, help me, help me.* Then, *Stop me, God, Mother, stop me.*

It don't mean nothing to me. A woman who can't take care of her child got no business claiming to be a human at all.

—Jules Cane, Linnie's son, answering a question about stories of his mother's ghost, 1969

 13

Gale paused outside the closed dining room doors and checked her watch. Two forty-five. Alby and Ella had been secluded in the dining room for at least forty minutes. From behind the closed door, the sheriff's voice rumbled briefly, serving as a prelude to Ella's monosyllabic response. She's either being a study in brevity or she's antagonizing the hell out of him, Gale thought. Stepping quickly across the hallway, she tilted her head toward the door.

"So, do you want to change anything you've told me?"

"No."

"Now, stop and think about it. . . ."

"If you keep badgering me—"

"I'm not badgering you, Ella. But we've got some discrepancies here, and I've got to get the answers to make some sense."

Silence. Gale thought she detected a sigh, followed by the scrape of a chair against the wooden floor. She stepped back as the door opened and Truitt stalked into the hall. Behind him Ella was still seated, her back board-straight and her hands folded on the dining room table. She didn't move while Truitt closed the doors behind him.

He rested against the doors, his hands on the knobs, and looked at Gale.

"You know what Martin used to tell me, Gale? He said Mother Nature planned it so that nothing happened that didn't move the whole world. When I was younger, I didn't understand that—bugs die, leaves fall, so what? I'd bring that up, and he'd say, 'That's right. They sure do.' Like my pointing it out was proof enough."

Gale slouched against the wall and felt the tip of a fin snag her hair. She reached up and disentangled herself. "It seems a bit tree-huggish to have come from a hunter like Martin."

Truitt shook his head. "You're wrong. That's one of the things he taught me. Hunting is a connective act."

Gale lifted her eyebrows. "He used that word, did he?"

Truitt smiled. "Maybe not. But you're a historian. You know what he meant. You ever done something just to see how your ancestors lived? Dipped candles? Cooked sweet potatoes in the hearth ashes? Anything like that?"

She hesitated. "I used to weave."

"Well, then you know. Martin told me hunting helped him to keep touch. He felt his father and his grandfather were in the woods pulling that trigger with him." He waved his arm toward the dining room. "Hell, Gale, have you ever really studied that swordfish? It's an incredible creature. Ella seems to think your grandfather hunted to emulate Hemingway. I don't believe it. I think every time he reeled in a fish or recoiled from a blast, he felt his father in his arms."

Gale thought of the crows in the den, dressed in their stiff red vests and yellow shoes. She was damned if she could find any nobility in them, nor did she want to contemplate what sort of paternal connection drove the man who created them.

"I don't know, Alby," she said. "I think you may be giving my male relatives more credit than they deserve."

He smiled at her, a lopsided grin that could have passed for chauvinistic if it hadn't been for the seriousness in his eyes. "I'm just trying to figure out the gun, Gale," he said softly. "I know how seriously Martin took those church barbecues. What was he doing in the house with a loaded gun with all those people outside?"

"Goodness, Alby." Gale laughed more from surprise than amusement. "You make Martin sound like Oswald."

"Oswald? No, I didn't mean that. I meant, from all accounts, everything's going fine, people are just starting to get their plates and are sitting down to eat. Martin goes in the house, and minutes later he's dead. Now, the obvious thing that happened was the fight with Sill. But according to Maralyn, he knew they were going to be there. He had time to contemplate his reaction, judge how to handle it."

"Maybe he had a stronger reaction than he'd figured."

"So strong that he ran in and grabbed his gun? And then what? This stress-relieving explanation is bizarre. I can't believe Martin Cane ran into his bedroom and started cleaning his loaded gun during a church function because his nerves got a little frayed."

A chair creaked behind the closed dining room

door. Truitt stood motionless, his eyes focused on a point near the hem of her skirt. He knows Ella is listening, Gale thought. He damn well intended her to. Gale felt a familiar pang of disgust. She liked Truitt. And she knew he was genuinely perplexed by the death of a man he had respected—maybe, on some level, even loved. But she wasn't going to help him. Not in the way he wanted.

She stood up from the wall. "Well, Alby, I have some work to do. And since Katie Pru's asleep, if it's all right . . ."

"Oh, sure." He frowned, plainly reluctant to end the conversation. "I was just thinking out loud. I won't keep you."

She nodded briefly and walked down the hall. Someone had left the front door open; the gunmetal sky made a greige wash over the foyer. In the living room it was dark enough that Gale switched on the overhead light before sitting on the sofa.

She had grown up calling the glass coffee table "the people bench" for its collection of photographs and oblong shape. She knew the story behind every photograph in the table, and if during childhood she sometimes had been forced to elaborate for the sake of drama, she hadn't been above doing it. Now her eyes went to one photograph in particular, a woman with three children standing in front of a painted backdrop of the Parthenon. The woman was dressed in a lace and satiny dress that reached her midcalf. In front of her stood two young girls, the smallest reaching up to hold the woman's hand. To the right of them, slightly apart, was a boy in white shorts and an oversized white shirt.

She looked up as Truitt stepped into the doorway. "By the way, Gale, I have two quick questions. Do you know what Cammy's purse looks like? Maralyn says Cammy was asking about it this morning. I was going to run over to the house and get it."

It was doubtful Cammy was asking for anything this morning, Sheriff, Gale thought, but she said nothing. Instead, she shrugged. "I honestly don't know, Alby. I don't pay attention to other women's purses."

"Oh. And did you see a female photographer taking pictures at the barbecue?"

"Yes," Gale replied. "I ran into her this morning. Her name is Nadianna Jesup. She lives in the old mill village."

"Mill village? Is she a reporter?"

"No. Just an amateur photographer. Taking pictures for a class."

"Huh. Thanks." He entered the room and looked inquisitively at the table. "Part of your research?"

The question hadn't sounded antagonistic, but Gale found herself coloring.

"Well, yes . . . no. My book is about women in the first quarter century, which includes Linnie Cane. I realized after my chat with Zilah today that I've never seen a picture of her. I'm wondering if one exists."

"Hmm." Truitt sank into the horsehair chair and let his eyes roam over the photographs.

"So what are you looking for—just any woman from that period so you can try to identify her as Linnie?"

"Not exactly. I know the identities of all the people here, or at least their family name and who they're related to. Actually, I was looking for something a little less direct."

"Like what?"

Gale tucked her hair behind her ears and sighed. "There's a frame—a picture frame—in Katie Pru's room containing a lock of hair from every person who was a member of the Statlers Cross Methodist Church in 1925."

"Lovely."

"Yeah, well, the interesting part is that Linnie's hair used to be there, but somewhere along the line someone removed it and scratched out her name. Whether out of anger or superstition, I don't know. I was just thinking perhaps . . ."

"Someone cut her out of all the family photos as well?"

"It just seems so odd. I mean, look at this photograph here. The woman is Jessie, Linnie's sister, and the two girls are Jessie's daughters—Ella and Nora. But see this little boy standing next to Nora? What does he look like to you—two or three? That's Jules, Linnie's son."

Truitt peered closely at the picture beneath Gale's finger. "Martin's father," he said.

"Right. But no Linnie. And she didn't die until he was five."

"So the story goes."

"So the family Bible goes. The women in my family did a pretty good job keeping up with all the births and deaths through the years. Both Jules and Ella were born in 1920. Linnie died in 1925. If you'll look at this photograph, Alby, you'll see it was taken in a studio— it's got a canvas background of the temples of Greece. Why would Jules be in a studio photograph with only his aunt and cousins if his mother was still alive?"

Truitt shrugged. "Jessie was babysitting that day."

"I don't think so. Studio photography was a big deal back in the early 1920s. Families made an appointment, got dressed up. The photographs were literally poor men's portraits. Now, if the two sisters, Jessie and Linnie, had gotten together and decided they wanted a picture of just them and the children, then that might make sense. But for Jessie to have her picture taken with her sister's child? I don't get it."

She tapped the glass. "I'd be willing to bet that most of the formal portraits in here were taken at the photography studio across the road. I wonder if any records are sitting around in someone's barn."

"Ask Deak. If anyone knows what's in folk's barns around here, it'd be him."

"Most likely you're right." She stared at the photograph. The boy stood next to a pedestal in the shape of an Ionic column, his back straight, his feet pointed forward. But his left hand was a blur, as if at the last second he couldn't resist reaching out and touching the pedestal's ornate papier-mâché. Gale felt a surge of affection for the child. Katie Pru would have touched the pedestal, too.

Truitt broke into her thoughts. "So what, you were looking for a disembodied hand on his shoulder, or the tip of a foot sticking in from off camera?"

Gale laughed sheepishly. "Yeah. That's exactly what I was looking for. But there's nothing here. Still doesn't make any sense."

Truitt kneaded the bulb of flesh between his eyebrows. "So," he said casually. "What do you think this has to do with Martin's death?"

Gale looked at him, surprised. "Nothing. Zilah just piqued my interest, that's all. And I figured it might help with the research on my book."

"Bullshit. Martin was killed yesterday and you're back to work today? With his widow and daughter in the house and me stomping around asking questions? You'd have to be a pretty cold customer to be so nonchalant."

"I've got a deadline."

"That's a most remarkable statement."

A lock of hair flopped into his eyes, and he impatiently pushed it away. He fixed his eyes on Gale, but when she didn't respond, he hunched over the tabletop.

"I've never seen photographs handled like this," he said. "But it's a good way of keeping the oral record alive. I mean, you don't have to pull out an album to look at the family pictures. You just sit down with a cup of coffee and voilà, you're face-to-face with Aunt Bitsy."

Gale watched Truitt's finger trail along the glass.

He chuckled softly. "Look, here, Gale. This young lady looks just like Katie Pru."

"That's my mother, Kathleen. She died in a car accident when I was around Katie Pru's age," she said.

"Pretty. How old is she in this photo?"

"Thirteen, fourteen, I think. That picture was taken when she was a bridesmaid in Martin and Maralyn's wedding."

"Cammy's," Truitt corrected.

He looked at her, but Gale couldn't stop the flush that covered her face.

"Cammy." His voice was firm.

"No, it's Maralyn's wedding." Gale closed her eyes and breathed deeply. She hated lawmen. "Maralyn's and Martin's. They were married briefly as teenagers. Cammy is Martin's second wife."

I swear to God, man, I come upstairs and there she is, in my bed, the motherfucker. I don't touch her, don't know what to do. I think, there's a damn ghost in my bed, and I'm thinking, what a joke, when all the sudden she sits up and rats run out of her chest and I think, Jesus, she looks just like my ex-wife.

— Tim Falcon to his buddies at the plastics factory, 1971

 14

Nadianna Jesup knew the man was coming to speak with her as soon as he rounded the cotton mill and started down the dirt path that led to the village. She knew he was coming to speak with her because Gale Grayson had seen her taking pictures at the barbecue.

Her sister had pointed it out yesterday, after Nadianna had come running into the house and shut herself in her room. "Just go on and call the sheriff and tell him you got some pictures," Ivy had said. "Someone's gonna tell him and you'll have to give them up anyway."

"But I don't want to," Nadianna had protested. There's nothing on them. And it's nobody's business."

"It don't matter, Nadi. A man was killed over there today. You think the sheriff ain't gonna want to see what's in that camera? And besides, how do you know you didn't get a picture of something? Those lawmen are trained. They can see things you can't."

Nadianna had rolled onto her bed, her pillow crushed to her belly. Her pulse was racing so fast her skin pounded. She tried to think—what did she have on the film? Some elderly women sitting in the fish house, a man carrying chairs, a bird. And then the pictures of him—preaching, bending over and whispering in a woman's ear . . .

She started shaking violently. Ivy sat down on the bed and hugged her, telling her to calm down, it was all right, this kind of thing was a shock but God in His mercy . . .

Nadianna stuffed the pillow in her mouth and bit down hard. She wouldn't scream. She wouldn't yell at Ivy. Ivy didn't know. Ivy hadn't been there.

During the night, Nadianna had slept fitfully. The grit that scratched her eyes scratched her dreams as well. Scenes from the barbecue flickered yellow and gravelly. *Now, many of you know me. . . . You know me as a citizen of this town, as someone who loves this little community. . . . But those are all earthly things. I now want you to see me as I truly am, a humble member of God's flock. . . .*

And then the shot, cracking, piercing. She had heard animals being shot—squirrels, birds—but never a man. It sounded different. There was no likening the voice of a bullet taking a human life.

The man now knocked on the front door. Nadianna smoothed down her dress before she reached for the knob. In her palm was the roll of film.

She held it out to him before he could speak. He looked down at her open hand in surprise.

"This is what you came for, isn't it?" she asked.

"Well, take it, sir. I hope it does you some good, but I don't think it will."

He took it from her, studying her face as he slipped it into an envelope. "I'll write out a receipt for it. Nadianna Jesup, is that right?"

"Don't bother. I've thought about it a lot. There's nothing on there I want. Why would I? It's all just badness."

The man pulled back his coat to show the badge on his belt. "I'm Sheriff Truitt," he said. "Could I come in? I just want to talk to you a bit about yesterday."

She shook her head firmly. "No, sir," she said. "My father and sister are gone across county to visit relatives, and I'd just as soon stand here with you, if you don't mind."

"That's fine. I appreciate you giving me this film, Miss Jesup. It might help me place people—where they were with who at what time. We're just trying to figure out exactly what happened yesterday."

"I don't know anything. I was just there with my camera."

Truitt looked around the small wooden porch, then leaned against the narrow railing. The branch from a flowering quince scraped his back, its pink blossoms tousled by the breeze.

"I need to ask you some questions, Miss Jesup. Why were you taking these pictures?"

"For a class. I'm trying to find things that depict my culture. That barbecue's been part of my culture for as long as I can remember. Even when I was little and my parents wouldn't let me go, I'd stand outside and smell the air." She hesitated, not sure what this man wanted from her. "It smelled of cars and meat."

He smiled. "I can imagine that. Where are you taking your class?"

"The arts center in Praterton."

"Really? That's a far piece from here. You drive all that way for a photography class?"

The question made her angry. She could understand Mrs. Grayson getting a bit uppity—after all, she was an Alden, and besides, considering what she'd been through, Nadianna couldn't help having pity on her—but for this public servant . . . She answered with an icy smile.

"That's right, Sheriff. I drive the thirty minutes to Praterton once a week to an arts class. I even saved my money and bought a real camera. And guess what else, I've won awards in competitions so I'm even applying for a grant. . . ."

He held his hands up, laughing. "Whoa, there, Miss Nadianna. I didn't mean nothing by it." He stopped, his smile fading as he studied her. "No, that's not true. You're exactly right to call me on it. I was being condescending. I apologize."

She crossed her arms and rubbed the sleeves of her blouse. "Okay," she said. "People just think . . ." She didn't finish. He knew what people thought. Little Pentecostal mill village girl. Even if the mill was gone and the village just a bunch of houses, the label stuck.

He looked grim. "I know what you're talking about," he said. "People think all kinds of things without knowing anything about you. Again, I'm sorry. It's a mistake I won't repeat with you. Now, about the barbecue, did you see anything during your picture taking that might have something to do with Mr. Cane's death?"

She bent down and picked up a petal beside the door. She rolled it between her fingers until the juice seeped out. "Nothing," she said.

"Nadianna if you saw something, you need to tell me. It might help me find out what happened to Mr. Cane."

She lifted her chin. Her father called it her proud look, and he hated it.

"There's a difference between praying and politicking, Mr. Truitt. Leastways, there ought to be. If you find anything in my photographs, you'll find that

Martin Cane wasn't nearly as good at dividing the two as he thought."

Cammy's bones were sodden, like cotton left to the rain. Once, when Martin tried to stop smoking, he had taken to sucking lollipops. Only he wouldn't stop at the candy; when he reached the stick, he kept on sucking, the stick going further into his mouth until it was bent and pulpy. She'd find them in the ashtrays, crotch-shaped with the paper turned to sludge around the core. Her limbs felt like those lollipop sticks. If she moved, her bones would bend.

She tried to open her mouth, but there was glue on her lips. Her eyelids were sewn shut. Everything was heavy—even her hair bore into her skull until it hurt. She started shivering. She wanted a blanket but was afraid that if she reached for one, her knuckles would collapse and her wrists would sag useless to the floor.

Martin? There was no answer as there had been no sound. Her whole body jangled. *Martin, I need a blanket.*

Ella had wanted a blanket. Ella and Maralyn had wanted a blanket to put on the floor. But she wouldn't let them tear up her bed. She had put too much work into making it that morning for the barbecue, and if Martin found it messed up, he'd raise hell. Besides, there was one right in front of them on the floor, rolled up and bulky. But it was heavy. They couldn't lift it by themselves. Sill had to help them lift it, and Sill had argued the whole time.

Silly Sill. The children had called her that at school. *Silly Sill. What a pill.* But Sill was far from that. She was a good daughter, so pretty, so smart. Cammy was proud of her. She and Martin had their arguments, but that was normal for fathers and daughters. Fathers and daughters couldn't get too close, so they sometimes had to fight.

Grab it here, Sill. Grab it right here and we'll lift it

to the bed. Ella had been so bossy, but Sill had helped, even though she hadn't wanted to. Cammy hadn't understood why Sill was so reluctant. It had seemed a simple enough request: Take that end and lift the blanket onto the bed. But after it was done, Cammy had looked at Sill's hands and understood. The blanket had come apart. The fabric had stuck to Sill's hands like paint.

Her teeth were clacking. They broke into her lips as her jaw jumped. She was cold. She needed something to get her warm.

Beside her in bed Martin moved.

"Oh, God, Mother, are you awake? You're shivering! Let me warm you up."

Sill pulled something heavy over Cammy's body. She tucked it around her, leaving her own hand wedged beneath Cammy's stomach.

"There, now, Mother, you'll be warm. Everything's all right."

Sill, not Martin, was in the bed. Not Martin for the longest time.

Cammy's belly grew warm where Sill touched it. Warm as water. Warm as the scraps of blanket dripping red from Sill's hand.

Cammy sat up and screamed.

I wonder if ghostiness runs in families.
    —Gale to her cousin Sill following the
    death of their aunt Nora, 1973

 15

Deak Motts hobbled to the screen of his son's front porch and lifted his critical eyes to the sky. He could remember a time when he didn't give a damn about the weather, when he would walk anywhere, anytime and defy a lightning bolt as quick as he'd defy the law. Lightning hit mild men with nothing to pay for— golfers, boaters, lone readers in aluminum lawn chairs. Both Deak Motts and his God had known he was not a mild man.

Now he scanned the sky for evidence of a heavenly sharpshooter. Age had done that to him—he wasn't afraid of death, he just wanted to set the terms. If someone had asked him at twenty how he would view death at eighty-six, he would have scoffed and said for him to reach that age, God would have to die intestate. He had since learned not to be so flip. God could take a man out in a flash, and there was nothing glorious about being charred like a hog when they dropped you in your casket.

The sky was heavy, but it hadn't quite reached the storming color. He had fifteen minutes, maybe twenty. He shuffled to a bench pushed against the clapboard wall and picked up his bucket and trowel.

"I'm going out to the cemetery," he called over his shoulder. "I'll be back later for my shower."

No one answered. He had often wondered what would happen if he was hit out there on that flat land. They probably wouldn't look for him for hours, and when they finally found him, he'd be this poor burnt lump among the graves. He had no doubt he would be mourned properly. But after that, then what? How long before the memories died and he became just one more headstone? Better to be a ghost, he thought ruefully as he undid the hook on the screened door. There's never been a bad ghost story. Once a body gets conjured up, there's no death to it.

He let the door whack shut behind him and picked his way along the short grassy path to the cemetery, as he did every Sunday evening at precisely five P.M. The division between his son Miles's property and the church cemetery was demarcated by a series of granite blocks, set like bread loaves in a north-south line running from the road to a distant stand of pines. When he reached the line, he slapped his foot once on the top of a block and then gently pressed his toe into the damp ground on the other side before shifting his weight and crossing over.

He moved toward the center of the cemetery, pausing to note that his wife's grave was still clean and neat. Good. He didn't want to worry with Bethie right now. Martin Cane was due to be buried in the next few days, and the monument had to be ready.

In the dead center of the cemetery he stopped. The monument's marble point glinted beneath the clogged evening sky. As a child he had envied other cities that built their Confederate memorials after the turn of the century, when the vogue had become the lone soldier resting upon his rifle. This simple white obelisk, constructed in the decade following the war, had seemed colorless in comparison—his own great-grandson had grown up calling it Apollo 11. He used to be afraid that one day everyone who knew about the monument would be dead, and no one would understand what the inscription 'We shall mourn and remember' meant. It didn't bother him anymore. He had learned a long time ago that voices, not stones, were the best conveyors of memory.

He dropped his bucket and trowel onto the ground and slowly lowered himself to his knees. The weeds around the monument were new, and they gave in easily. He pulled deftly, his thick fingers grabbing the green tips and flicking them into the bucket.

"I got Band-Aids on my knees, but you can't touch them."

He lifted his head. The little Alden girl—he couldn't remember her name—stood about three feet away from him, scrawny legs sticking out from beneath a pair of shorts. He waved his finger at her.

"What you got Band-Aids on for, little miss? You skin yourself or something?"

She shook her head. "I drew hurts on my knees with my markers. They won't come off, so Grandma Ella put Band-Aids on them."

From behind him he heard a woman clear her throat. "Ella didn't think it was proper for little girls to run around with bloody-looking knees. Better to waste a couple of bandages."

He twisted his head until his neck hurt. The other

Alden girl—Lord, he couldn't remember her name either—quickly stepped into his line of vision.

He turned back to the chickweed. "Well, that's Ella for you," he answered. "During the Second World War she'd walk around with her stockings painted on. Used to burn Bethie up. Ella always did think she was better than she really was. Atlanta'll do that to you."

She laughed softly—a good laugh, not the kind that was forced or polite. She knelt on the ground beside him and began pulling the tiny shoots on the monument's left side.

"Come over here and help me, Katie Pru," she said. "Let's see how many of these weeds you can throw in Mr. Deak's pail."

Katie Pru jogged to her mother and crouched between them.

"I'll watch," she announced. "You throw the weeds into the pail."

Deak chuckled at her mother's frown. Gale—her name was Gale. "Well, I never knowed a child that didn't want to get her fingers dirty," he said.

"Oh, she likes to get dirty, no problem. She just likes to pick her own time."

"I understand that rightly enough."

The sky was getting close. The tiny weeds began to shiver in the wind. He'd say seven to ten minutes at the most.

"Deak," Gale said, "I wanted to ask you something. I'm trying to find some photographs of the people who lived in Statlers Cross in the earlier part of the century. I was wondering about that old photographer's studio in the middle of town."

"Malcolm Hinson's place?"

"Was he the last one to own it?"

Deak pinched a weed at the root and pulled it from the earth. He dropped it on the growing mound inside the bucket.

"He was the only one to own it. It shut down when

he quit taking his pictures. I guess that'd have been after World War Two sometime."

"He closed it down because of the war?"

"The Depression, really. Couldn't nobody afford no pictures then, and he never did catch up. Later, after the war, folks started getting their own cameras. And if you wanted a fancy picture taken, you made a day of it and went to Athens."

She dropped a handful of small stems into his bucket.

"Whatever happened to him?"

He shrugged. "Well, for a while he talked of moving back north, but he'd married himself a wife—the Butcher girl—and she didn't want to go. So him and that other Yankee fellow, Parrish Singleton, they went to work as hands for this big farmer over in Walton County."

"Parrish Singleton. The playwright, wasn't he?"

"That's right. He married Lucy Stone. Now, I thought for sure Parrish was a man who would hightail it out of here. New York City—that's where he came from and that's where I thought he'd go back. But he never did. He stayed, grew some vegetables, became a truck farmer for a bit. Never heard much from him. Died way back."

Gale ran her hand over her newly weeded patch of grass. "He wrote that town pageant, the one that never got performed." She paused. "He and Malcolm Hinson came down here during the early 1920s as artists to preserve the Southern culture. Sort of a precursor to the Federal Art Project, I guess."

Deak snorted. "Meddlesome Yankee SOBs, if you ask me. Making us like the rest of the country, that's what folks like them were really up to. I never took cotton to them. Malcolm walked around with that camera equipment of his, asking if he could set up in the fields while we were planting, in the church while we were praying. The preacher asked us men what we thought and we said hell no. We weren't no natives for him to be snapping pictures of—we weren't no cover for the *National Geographic*. Now, his gallery was different. Then we could come to him, as we wanted to. But that taking pictures of us as we minded our business—I wouldn't have nothing to do with that."

Katie Pru stuck her hand into the bucket and lifted a fistful of plants. Holding them tightly, she stood and began lining them up on the narrow ledge of the monument's base.

"What are you doing there, missy?" he asked.

"I'm decorating the castle."

Deak sighed and glanced at the sky again. Three minutes. He'd just make it back to the house as the first drops fell.

He placed the trowel in the bucket and lumbered to his feet. "Well, Miss Gale, we gotta get out of here if we're going to beat the rain. Did you walk? I didn't hear a car."

"I parked at the Methodist church. Just one more question, Deak. Do you know who has the key to the studio?"

He settled his eyes on her. "Why do you want to go in there?"

"There might still be some photographs. They could give me a better feel of the county during those years."

He shook his head. "I doubt it. Malcolm's been gone for at least forty years. I'm sure someone cleaned it out a long time ago."

"You're probably right. I just wanted to check."

"I wouldn't bother. There's nothing but rats and roaches in there now." He picked up his bucket and moved away from them. "If there ever was anything, it'd be eaten." In the gathering darkness he could just make out the lines of granite blocks past Bethie's grave. Clutching his bucket tightly, he headed toward them.

Behind him the grass rustled. "One more thing, Deak. You were eighteen when Linnie Cane died, weren't you?"

His foot was up, preparing for another step, and for a wild second he thought he might never move again. Then he brought it down slowly and turned toward her, swinging the bucket out for balance.

"Yes."

"She was only twenty-five. You must have known her some."

"Small place. Knew everybody."

"I'd like to sit down and talk about her. Soon."

"What for?"

"I want to know why she did it."

"You think she told me?"

"Maybe you have some thoughts on it."

"You've heard all my stories."

"What about the parts that didn't make it into the stories?"

"Weren't none, missy."

The smell of thunder filled his nostrils. It would be a bad storm. Lots of bolts starting in Heaven and scorching the earth. He had lived in Statlers Cross all his days—it was going to break his heart to watch it die. But Martin's death would be its end. He could see that now.

His chest hurt suddenly, and he wondered if it would help to sob. But in the end he started walking. He had seen too much lightning to stand around and gawk. Even if he was the one about to lob the bolts.

"Missy?" he yelled. "I hear Malcolm's got a grandson come back to Calwyn County. A pilot. He might know something about that old photography place."

A full streak of lightning spit in the southern sky as Truitt climbed into his truck and started down the drive. In his rearview mirror he could see the Alden house jostle behind him like a flashlight, beams pouring from the windows. He reached over, picked up his cellular phone, and punched the button for the sheriff's office. Haskell answered in one ring.

"Has the rain hit you there yet, Alby? It's coming down pretty good here, and it's heading north. You should run into it coming home."

"Tell you what, why don't you bring it on up here?" Truitt said. "We need to go over the Cane house again."

"Did you get to talk to all of them?"

"No. Just two. The wife woke up hysterical and had to be tended to." He grimaced. It sounded lame to him, and he knew that to Haskell, born one decade later and two counties over, it sounded positively limp. "I'll see the two of them tomorrow. I did decide one thing. We need to take another look at the crime scene."

"Give me about thirty minutes."

"Fine."

He slipped the phone back in its berth. The first heavy plops of water hit his windshield as another bolt crackled to the south. He turned on the wipers and watched the large raindrops spatter to the margins of the window. Enclosed in the truck, he could nevertheless smell the loamy odor of the outside air, a close-packed mixture rising from dampened clay and tar. Usually such smells comforted him, assuring him that his feet were on the proper piece of earth. Now, however, he felt depressed. Whichever way this case blew— and blow it would—nothing would ever be settled. When he'd shot his first buck, the animal's legs had buckled beneath him, as if an invisible stick had whacked the deer's limbs. It's going to be that way with this case, he thought. When it's all said and done, it's going to be the invisible stick in my own hand, and not Martin's bullet, that will do the most damage.

It took no more than two or three minutes for him to pull up to the Cane house. Yellow crime scene tape, pummeled to the ground by the previous night's rain, made a limp circle around the tents and tables. The food and garbage, he knew, would be bagged but not disposed of. He wrinkled his nose at the prospect of having to sift though it, but if his suspicions were right, that's precisely how his crew would be spending their evening.

He parked the truck on the side of the road and walked up to the officer sitting in his car. "Anything happen today?" he asked.

"No, sir." Ruch hastily put his styrofoam cup on the seat beside him. "It's been pretty quiet. Several sightseers just driving by, a couple of people who wanted to see the family. I directed them down to the Aldens like you said. The only person who wanted to get into the house was the reverend. Said he wanted to go inside and pray for the deceased."

"What? Is he nuts?"

Ruch grinned. "I didn't ask him that directly, sir. He also said Mrs. Cane asked him to bring her Bible to her."

"Mrs. Cane has been under sedation all day. I hope to Jesus you didn't let him in."

"No, sir. I told him he could pray outside the yellow tape all he wanted, but he couldn't go inside the house unless he was escorted by someone from the sheriff's department."

"What did he say?"

"Something about not being allowed to do his pastoral duty. I told him we'd be more than willing to accommodate him, but he'd have to have permission and an escort, and, well, he just sort of pouted and left. Other than that, nothing much."

"Okay. I'm going to go on into the house. I'm expecting a search team. When they get here, tell them I'm already inside."

"Yes, sir."

Truitt nodded a farewell and stepped over the crime scene tape. The sky was slate gray, and the rain had begun to fall steadily. Another lightning slash sent him jogging through the grass, the immediate clap of thunder spurring him to sprint beneath the canopy of oak trees that sheltered the front yard. On the wooden stoop he paused with the knob cupped in his left hand and the key at the latch. Rain slopped onto his bared head. The house was still an active investigation scene. Had the death already been determined an accident, someone would have arranged for a thorough cleaning. As it was, the day's heat and humidity had been given ample time to work their effects on the contents of the house. Truitt stamped his feet. The contents of the house. He was a shitassed SOB. Clutching the knob tightly, he jammed in the key and threw open the door.

A meager yellow glow tinted the walls as he flicked on the overhead light. He reached into his back pocket, pulled out a pair of plastic gloves, and tugged them on.

Truitt switched on the light in the den. Plastic sheeting still covered the smudges of blood on the carpet; stepping over it, he made his way to Martin's gun cabinet. He stared at the guns inside, standing nozzle down on a piece of white felt. Crouching down, he pulled out the drawer at the bottom of the cabinet. Inside lay boxes of bullets and a few old copies of *Guns and Ammo* magazine. Taking a pen from his pocket, Truitt lifted up the magazines, examined their covers, and then turned his attention to the floor of the drawer. He bent down and smelled. If the subtle odor of gun oil was present, he couldn't detect it above the sharp smell of solvent and the mustiness of aging paper and cardboard. No signs of oil stains on the bottom of the drawer or on the magazines themselves.

He slid the drawer shut, walked to the staircase, and lurching side to side to avoid the footprints, hiked up the stairs two at a time. The door to Martin and Cammy's room was shut, and he let it remain so. His team had searched there yesterday, and he would ask

Haskell to do it again before he left tonight, but Truitt was confident he would find nothing.

The master bathroom was a small space that opened both into the bedroom and the hallway. One bulb from the double lamp over the mirror was burned out, and in the dimness the entire room, decorated in yellow, took on the look of old transparent tape. Truitt ran his finger along the sink and dipped his head under the faucet to smell. He checked the toilet bowl and tub as well, examining the porcelain for any globules or beading. Nothing. The cubicle, for all its dingy coloring, was immaculate.

He opened the narrow linen closet hidden behind the bathroom door, releasing the aroma of fabric softener and soaps. Yellow and brown towels and washclothes were folded and neatly stacked on two of the three shelves. The third shelf was evidently the repository of unwanted clutter—a bar of soap decorated to resemble a swan, an extra roll of toilet paper covered by a crocheted doll, loose soaps in the shapes of fish and shells. These had been pushed to one side to make room for a pile of paper. Careful not to dislodge the knickknacks, Truitt pulled the papers from the closet.

A pamphlet from the top of the stack fluttered to the floor. Truitt stooped to pick it up, then sat on the edge of the tub.

The front of the pamphlet showed an old photograph of a dead child, a Star of David prominent on his coat. Above the photograph were the words "Nazis killed children." Truitt turned the page. "And so does the United States government." A bloody fetus, the umbilical cord still dangling from its belly, took up the entirety of the two-page spread. "Is any price too high to pay for her life?" On the back cover was a list of clinics throughout the Southeast, along with the attending doctors' home addresses and phone numbers.

Truitt thumbed through the stack of papers— solicitations from prolife groups, some with which he was familiar, others with names he had never heard of.

One sheet looked like a rough layout of the pamphlet, with penciled notes in the margins. "Make photo bigger." "Double-check these addresses." "Consider adding names of abortionists' wives and children." He studied the handwriting. It was strong and slanted forward. He couldn't say for sure if it was Martin's or not.

"Martin," he said. He repeated the name, louder. "Martin. What in the hell have you gotten into?"

MISS LINNIE CHEESE GRITS

1 cup of hominy grits
1 teaspoon salt
1 cup water
1/2 cup of Monterey jack cheese, shredded

Add grits and salt to boiling water. Cook for 20 minutes. Stir in cheese. Serve with dash of paprika.

So good it doesn't stand a ghost of a chance.

— The Statlers Cross Cookbook, 1975

16

Zilah switched off the kitchen light and leaned across the sink to look out the window. Outside, the rain fell steadily, the drops so big that even in the night she could see the blades of grass flatten beneath them. Her own little house was darkened; she peered out over the side yard where her plot of land stretched in sooty lengths to the fence. This was her favorite time, when the sun had finally fallen and she could stand in darkness. No one could see her. At night she and her little bungalow were nothing but the blackest part of the shadow cast by the Alden house.

Two beams suddenly played across her yard, illuminating the fence as they swung into the driveway next door. They danced for several seconds along the trunk of the pecan tree, lighting the lower branches and the necklaces of rain.

The engine fell silent as the headlights went out. The driver's door swung open and a figure climbed out, bent over from the rain. While Zilah watched, the figure reached back into the car and pulled an umbrella from the floorboard. The interior light bathed Gale's face.

Katie Pru sat in the passenger seat, her dark hair barely visible over the bottom of the window. Gale's head bobbed as she talked. She was evidently trying, without success, to coax her daughter from the car. Katie Pru's hand shot up, and the ice cream cone she held swayed dangerously in the air. Gale lurched forward and took the cone from the child's grasp. Twisting away from her mother, Katie Pru sat up and pressed her nose against the car door's wet glass.

Zilah, come away from that window. There ain't nothing to see. There ain't never been nothing to see.

Her mother had sounded frightened. *There ain't nothing to see out windows. Come over here and rock with me. Come over here this instant.*

She had rocked long hours in her mother's arms. Rocked in the chair, just like she had rocked in Martin Cane's porch swing. And she had seen things she wasn't supposed to see. But then she had been a child. It was her mother who had no eyes.

She stared into the darkness, the mother and daughter on the other side of the fence suddenly blurred. She hadn't been the only child to see, all those years ago. Another child had watched, looking down from on high from the red brick house, like an angel hidden among the leaves.

And that child had eyes.

Outside, rain pelted the den's long French doors, and sporadic flashes of lightning illuminated the etched glass around the ceiling until the room's bookshelves looked as though they wore a halo with an electrical short. Gale sat on the sage green sofa and smoothed the sheet over Katie Pru's shoulder. Sleep hadn't come easily to the child. The sounds from upstairs—muffled sobs, abrupt keening, all gratefully absent the night before—had left her wide-eyed and worried in Gale's bedroom. After a few minutes Gale had pulled linens from the closet and tried to settle Katie Pru into the seclusion of the den. Even here sleep was difficult. Dead crows and snakeskins might be a kick for a four-year-old during the day. At night they were simply carcasses.

"Put them outside, Mama. I can't sleep with those birds in here."

Gale had complied, moving the entire flock down the narrow hallway and into the kitchen, where they perched in the flashing light amid covered plates of brownies and biscuits. After several lullabies and a throaty rendition of "Hi-Lili, Hi-Lo," Katie Pru had finally mumbled herself to sleep, her last plea of "Snuggle with me, Mama" satisfied by Gale leaning over and rubbing her back.

The etched glass lit up, followed by a clap of thunder. In the dark Gale strained to see Katie Pru's shoulder rise and fall. Assured she was asleep, Gale eased herself from the cushions and walked to the French doors. The soft light from the back porch light shone through the gauzy curtains and fell upon her wristwatch. It was eleven forty-five.

She ought to go to sleep. She looked at the neat pallet of blankets and pillows she had made on the floor in front of the sofa. Perhaps once she placed her head on those pillows, she would drift instantly to sleep, but she doubted it. She had too much to think about—too much to sort out.

She plopped down in the overstuffed chair by the door and pulled her legs up under her skirt. Leaning her head against the upholstered back, she breathed deeply. Linnie had been wiped from the factual record. It had been accomplished with the effectiveness of a town council decree—get rid of her pictures, get rid of her hair, eliminate her entirely except for a coverlet. Recreate her as a goblin, someone controlled by oral history and folklore. Gale turned her head away as lightning flashed behind the French doors. Was suicide that much of a taboo? Did taking one's life in the 1920s warrant such total manipulation?

And what about the child the suicide left behind? Gale's eyes shot open. Katie Pru's leg slipped from beneath the white sheet and slid over the side of the sofa. A hot ball formed in Gale's chest.

She pushed herself from the chair and walked once more to the French doors. Her watch read 11:50. It was a little before five in the morning in England.

Odd how she had never called, but she knew the number. She picked up the phone from the trunk in front of the sofa and punched the buttons.

It rang once. The voice was sharp.

"Halford."

"Daniel?" She faltered, not sure what to say.

"Gale? Is that you?"

"It's me."

"Are you all right? Is Katie Pru all right?"

Despite her anxiety she smiled. He sounded the same, his voice a mix of control and concern. He's a bloody British bobby to the core, she thought. He has to check the parameters before venturing in. Grabbing a pillow from her pallet, she sank to the floor and leaned against the trunk.

"I'm fine. We're fine. I didn't know when you had to get up to go to work. Is this a bad time?"

For one horrified second she realized how presumptive it had been of her to assume he was alone. The question stammered from her mouth before she had time to second-guess herself.

Halford grunted in answer. "Of course I'm alone. I'm a ruddy copper on a Sunday night. Excuse me,

Monday morning. What the hell time is it over there, anyway?"

"Way past my bedtime. Listen, I wanted to talk to you about something. Have you got a minute?"

"Sure. Hold a sec." She heard a rustling sound and the creak of box springs. "There. I'm set. You're positive Katie Pru's all right."

"Positive."

"Good. Now, in a little bit I'm going to tell you it's bloody terrific to hear from you. But right now tell me what's wrong."

She didn't know where the tears came from, and she felt it was to her credit that they were fine ones, relegated to the corner of her eyes. It was good to talk to him, good to hear his voice.

She attempted to tell him the story chronologically, starting from Martin's death and the events of the last thirty-six hours. But she soon found herself weaving back and forth, interlacing Martin's life with Linnie's suicide and seventy years of community nurturance and malice. Halford let her ramble, interrupting only to clarify genealogy and background. Finally she sagged against the trunk.

"God," she said. "What time is it? Don't you have to go to work?"

"Don't worry about it."

"Daniel, I don't know what to do about Alby. He's convinced someone killed Martin."

"That's because he's a smart man, Gale. Look what he has to work with—a dead body, a locked door, and the evidence disturbed beyond usefulness. Under the circumstances I'd pursue the same line." He paused. "Why do you think your grandmother and the others acted the way they did?"

"Shock.'

"Come on, Gale. Do you really believe that?"

She felt a surge of anger. Outside, the thunder was a slow grumble in the distance. "I don't know, Daniel.

I've never come across the body of my slain husband. I have no idea on earth how I'd react."

There was silence on the other end of the line. The tears sprang to her eyes again, but this time she impatiently blinked them away. When Halford spoke, his voice was soft.

"I'll tell you how I think you would react, Gale. Something would fall over you, like a shield or a glass box. It would make you safe and numb, at least for the moment. And you would do as you thought you ought to do—you'd feel for a pulse, you'd speak consolingly in case he could hear you, and you'd immediately find help."

Her tongue was thick. "You don't know that, Daniel."

"Yes, I do. I know that because I was there when you found out Tom was dead. I know how you reacted."

"But I didn't find his body,"

"True. But then only one of those women was Martin's wife. Only one was his daughter. And the fact is that all of those women are claiming some sort of hysteria took over the room. I don't believe it, Gale. And neither does Alby. And neither, for that matter, do you."

Katie Pru kicked at the sheet, forcing it off her. Gale pulled it from the sofa and gathered it to her chest.

"No," she whispered. "No, I don't."

"Do you believe he could have been murdered?"

"Are you asking me if one of my relatives killed him?"

"I'm asking you, based on your knowledge of those four women, if he could have been murdered."

The rain had stopped—she strained to hear it against the French door panes, but all she could detect was the occasional click of water hitting a leaf on the lower branches of the trees.

"Yes. He could have been murdered."

Halford's voice was steady. "Then you need to tell

Alby that. You need to tell him what you know about those women that leads you to think it possible someone killed him."

"I said it was possible. I don't believe one of them did."

"Gale." He sounded ragged. "You have no expertise here. Let Alby handle it."

"But Alby—and you—you're both thinking A leads to B. That's not the case here. I just spent twenty minutes telling you the bare bones about Martin, and I must have backtracked and sidetracked fifty times." She stopped, aware that Halford, for all his patience, was probably reaching the end of his rope. "It goes back to Linnie somehow, Daniel. I'm certain of it."

Over the line Halford sighed heavily.

"Don't be meddlesome, Gale. You're a historian. Read, take notes, postulate, do whatever it is you want to do, but don't get in Truitt's way. I won't be a character witness when he arrests you for interference."

"Fair-weather friend, that's wot you are, guv-nor."

Halford laughed. "Horrible cockney. You've been away too long." His voice grew suddenly tender. "I've tried to talk you out of things before, Mrs. Grayson. I've had damned rotten luck."

Well, I double-dog dare you. They say you can't tell if what you hear is your own teeth chattering or the cow's milk hitting her jawbone.

—Tommy Falcon, daring his friend, Greg Dawson, to spend the night in a pasture where it is said a ghost drinks milk from the cows' udders, 1977

17

Gale knew Mal Robertson's house, although she only vaguely recognized the steel-haired and blue-jeaned man polishing an ecru Volvo in the yard. The house was situated at the corner of two dirt lanes, both turned muddy by rain during the night. As the crow flies, it was probably no more than a mile northeast of Ella's, but the way the country roads meandered, the odometer tallied 3.2 miles as Gale pulled the gray Chevrolet into the clay patch that passed for a driveway. The last time she had been to the house was the August she was thirteen, when she and Sill, bored to delinquency, had roamed through Ella's back fields and come across the place abandoned. For a week they had carried picnic lunches to the dogtrot house, where they clattered through the open central passageway and fed rich chicken salad to a family of feral cats living beneath the makeshift front porch. Each day before they left, they gave benediction by hurling chunks of granite through the windows.

She cringed now at the thought of those aged windows, reduced to shards by that week's end. Not that anyone would miss them, she thought as she stepped from the car. Either Malcolm Hinson's grandson was one hell of a handyman, or the good descendant believed in putting his money where his ancestry was. From the outside the house appeared to have been totally renovated. The central passage had been enclosed, connecting the two symmetrical pens. A glossy coat of ivory paint covered what she remembered as virgin pine boards, complemented by a pale taupe on the shutters and trim. The door was a robin's egg blue with pink dashes like a whipstitch outlining the knob and knocker. A brass pineapple, the colonial symbol of hospitality, was bolted to the clapboard underneath a glistening brass porch light.

"It's gorgeous," she yelled, motioning Katie Pru from the car. "The last time I was here, it looked like something out of *God's Little Acre*."

The man straightened and palmed his chamois cloth. "My wife said the same thing. Especially after she found a snake in the toilet. After that there was no holding her back on the renovations." He took one last swipe at the hood of the Volvo and then turned to them. "I'm Mal Robertson."

"Gale Grayson. And this is Katie Pru." Gale nodded toward the house. "I would have thought this house was too far gone."

"If the truth be known, it probably was. But it was in the family. And when my wife gets a bee in her bonnet . . ." Robertson picked up a clean cloth from the grass and pulled his fingers through it as he winked at

Katie Pru. "Sorry I made y'all get up so early. But I've got to be at the Atlanta airport by eleven. . . ."

"No problem. Katie Pru and I were up anyway. Things aren't exactly calm at the house right now. It was good for us to get out."

He balled up the cloth and tossed it into the grass next to an open can of polish. "I'm sorry as hell about Martin." His eyes darted to Katie Pru, who was studying the car care kit. "I didn't know him extremely well, but I knew him enough to understand that he was a man of principle. You don't find that a whole lot—certainly not in Atlanta, and after being a part of Great Rural America for a while, I can tell you, not out here either."

"You sound like Diogenes looking for an honest man."

His laugh was short and loud. "Yeah, well, you fly all over the world, sometimes you feel like you're carrying a lamp in the daylight. But Martin—Martin was somebody I had a lot of respect for. He had a . . . moral core."

Gale gazed at the house. She thought she caught a flicker of movement in a window, but it was lost behind the mirror effect of the morning light.

"It's funny how people lose their subtleties when they die," she said. "Martin was a very moral man. But he had so many other facets to him. I don't think most people picked up on them all." She glanced at Katie Pru, who was still entranced by the can of polish. "When I die, I hope Katie Pru has the gumption to eulogize me in all my grouchy glory."

He smiled. "I hope you've warned all your elderly relatives that you like the idea of laying dirty linens on their caskets."

"Shoot, I fully expect my 'elderly relatives' to lay the dirty linens out on their beds before they go. That's one thing we've all learned by now—rattle your own skeletons before someone else has a chance to rattle them for you."

The morning air had moved from being merely hot to heavy, and Gale felt the first beads of perspiration on her forehead.

"Mal, as I explained on the phone last night, I'm interested in your grandfather's photography studio. Or rather, the photographs that were taken there."

"Want to rattle some of my family's skeletons?"

She grinned. "Actually, I need help with my research. I'm writing a book on Southern rural women in the early part of the century, and I have names and words, but I'd like some faces as well."

"I don't know that the studio is going to help you much. I went inside about a year ago—not much there but some old props and a whole lot of dust."

"No old files or discarded photographs?"

He took a handkerchief from his shorts and wiped his wet forehead. "Well, I can't say categorically 'no.' The building inspector checked it out, but I didn't go with him into the attic. My sinuses were acting up from all the dust. There were some tarpaulins tossed about— old backdrops, mostly."

"Inspector?"

He folded his arms. "Yeah. That's one of the reasons my wife and I moved out here, if you want to know the truth. She's interested in opening up a little restaurant—a tearoom, actually—and, well, we had this property out here, so I said let's see what we can do. Of course, we got here and the house was such a mess . . . But the studio is structurally sound. Once we can find someone to take over her job, she's going to start working on the tearoom."

A tearoom in Statlers Cross. Gale kicked at the clipped grass beneath her feet.

"What's your wife's job?"

"A little practical nursing. Eldercare, I think the current word is. But she's not happy with it." He gazed thoughtfully at the house. "It's been a hard year for her. Planning the tearoom has really changed her attitude about a lot of things."

"So you'd have to clean out the studio soon anyway."

"Yeah, that's what I'm thinking. My father used it mainly as storage, and after he died, my mother took out everything she wanted. So you'll find a few pieces of old furniture, maybe a box or two—nothing valuable. If you want to go in there and get a head start on my cleaning for me, great." He walked over to the porch and picked up a key lying on the step. "Of course, I'm trusting you in this. I have a friend who's a history professor at Georgia State. After you called last night, I talked with him. He's familiar with your book—says you're legit."

"I'll be very careful."

"I'm sure. I would like to get back whatever you find. I'm not a professional historian, and all that genealogy stuff leaves mc cold. Still, I'd like to see what all my grandfather did. I have a few of his photographs framed in the house. I think had circumstances been different, he could have made a name for himself." He looked at his watch. "Next time you're over, I'll invite you in. I'd do it now, but I've got to get . . ."

"Surely. Listen, I really appreciate it. By the way, when exactly did your grandfather pass on?"

From the other side of the Volvo, Katie Pru started singing "The Wheels on the Bus." Gale glanced down at the ground. The can of polish and both cloths were gone.

"Katie Pru! What are you doing?"

"I'm a window wiper."

Gale hurried around the car. Katie Pru sat on the ground beside the car's back door. She looked at her mother and grinned.

"This is a bus. The wipes are making a mess."

Gale stared at the side of the blue Volvo, recently gleaming in the morning sun. Globs of polish hung off the door. Katie Pru stuck all five fingers into the can and scooped out a huge dollop. "Look, Mama," she laughed, holding her fingers aloft. "I can eat the peanut butter all in one bite."

Gale dived for her daughter, grabbing her hand before the polish entered her mouth.

"No, ma'am!"

Katie Pru flinched at the harsh sound of Gale's voice. Her chin dimpled as she tried to hold back her tears.

Gale gripped Katie Pru by the wrist and led her roughly around the car. Robertson held a clean cloth out to her.

She bent down and furiously wiped her daughter's hands. "Kathleen Prudence, you don't ever put something like that in your mouth. You could get sick. Your stomach could hurt very bad. Katie Pru, you've got to learn to think."

"For what it's worth," Robertson said, "I don't think it's poisonous"

"She doesn't know that. God, Katie Pru. You've got to learn not to do these things."

Katie Pru closed her eyes and turned her head away from Gale. "Go away," she said. "Go away and don't yell at me. Mamas shouldn't yell at little girls."

Gale sat back on her haunches, a sense of helplessness flooding her chest. "I know, baby. Mamas shouldn't yell. But what if . . ."

Gale's throat ached. *What if you hadn't started singing? What if I hadn't noticed the can gone? What if you'd eaten the goddamn stuff and I'd found you . . .* She closed her eyes, fighting the burn behind them. I can't do it, she thought. I can't do my work, live my life, and keep this child safe. Not by myself.

Two days ago she would have trusted her daughter with the women in her family. Two days ago she would have sworn they were, for all their peculiarities, the salt of the earth.

She pulled Katie Pru to her and buried her face in her hair. "Please learn to be safe," she murmured. "You've got to learn to keep yourself safe."

"Okay, Mama." Katie Pru pushed herself away from Gale and then laid her hands on both sides of her mother's face. She leaned forward until her forehead rested against Gale's. "I can be safe," she whispered.

Truitt slipped the receiver to his desk phone back into its base and stared at it dolefully. An abandoned house outside the south Georgia town of Hahira had burned to the ground Friday night—only it hadn't been abandoned. By Saturday morning firefighters had pulled six bodies from the char, all prospective murder victims because the sheriff there suspected arson. The state crime lab was now conducting tests. Martin was having to wait his turn.

"Not until this afternoon," Truitt shouted to Haskell. "Maybe they'll get around to having some verbal results from the tests by then."

Haskell popped his head into Truitt's office. "So what do you want to do till then?"

"I want you to go out and see our Reverend Teller today. Find out why he was trying to get into the Cane house last night."

"Will do." Haskell drummed his fingers on the door frame once before disappearing back into the hall.

Truitt pushed his chair back and stood. Lined up across his desk were the six photographs developed from Nadianna Jesup's roll of film. He knew nothing of art, but he could tell these pictures were more than the typical Kodak moments—a side shot of a man with metal chairs hiked under his arms like crutches, *SC Methodist* plainly stenciled across the back of one chair; a pigeon pecking at a melting ice cube, by a woman's open-toed sandal; three elderly women seated side by sid. in the fish house, plates piled high with food. And then there was Martin. Truitt thought of old photographs he had seen of Huey Long in the 1930s. Eliminate the color and these photographs could have been of him. Truitt scooted a picture of Martin—arm raised, perspiration pouring, microphone pressed to his lips—across the desk, then reached over and picked it up. *There's a difference between praying and politicking, Mr. Truitt. If you find anything in my photographs, you'll find that Martin Cane wasn't nearly as good at dividing the two as he thought.* Damned if the girl wasn't right.

He put the photograph down and picked up another. This one was a bit artier. Nadianna had evidently been standing in the fish house door, the edge of it barely visible on the right. Inside the shack, Martin leaned over a seated woman. It was impossible to see his face in detail, but his slouch suggested a casual, almost friendly, interest. Nadianna probably didn't know who the woman was, but Truitt did. Even with her back to the camera, he recognized the brown curls and narrow shoulders as Faith Baskins's.

In the photograph Martin leaned toward and over Faith until she reared slightly back—the stance of a man intrigued, not one about to banish his daughter and her lover.

But it was the final photograph on the roll that interested Truitt the most. Martin was under the food tent, the contents of the table visible at the base of the photo. His jaw hung loose and his eyes looked frozen in an expression of utter shock, and something else Truitt couldn't discern. *What were you looking at, friend? What did you see in the lens of that camera?*

Sitting next to the phone was a cold cup of coffee. Truitt picked it up and drained it. "I'm no damn good, Martin," he murmured. "I think I am, but I'm just shit with feet."

Last night's search had not fared well. They had found the place in Martin's closet where in all probability he had kept the gun oil, but no bottle or rags or rods. Today a team would continue sifting through the garbage bags. He set the cup on the desk and gathered up the photos. *What were those women playing at?*

"Haskell!" he shouted, sliding the photographs

into an envelope. "You still there? On second thought, give me five minutes and I'll go with you to Teller's. I have a feeling we're going to make another day of it over at Statlers Cross."

Haskell didn't reply. Frowning, Truitt stepped out of his office and headed down the hall. He leaned into the doorway of Haskell's adjacent office and, finding it empty, peered out into the reception area.

Haskell had his back to Truitt, but it was clear from the way his hands were jammed into the pockets of his uniform that he was not a happy man. He seemed to be talking with someone—or rather, someone was talking with him—but the speaker was shielded by Haskell's hulking body. The sergeant removed one hand from his pocket and held it up in a pleading gesture. When he did, a white-trousered leg and a clean, laced tennis shoe broke out of Haskell's frame. His frown deepening, Truitt wrenched open the door and walked up to Maralyn Nash.

"Maralyn," he said. "What can I do for you?"

Her glasses flashed as she settled her hard brown eyes on him. "I've been trying to explain to the good deputy here that I need to go into Cammy's house and get her some items she wants. Your man guarding the place said I couldn't go in without an escort and he doesn't have the authority. Well, I'll be damned if I'm going to be told by some boy scout that I can't go into my own family's house. . . ."

Truitt reached out his hand and gently took Maralyn by the elbow. He looked up at Haskell. "Craig, go find someone who can take Mrs. Nash out to her cousin's house. Maralyn, you come on in my office while he does that."

He held the door open and directed Maralyn to his office.

"Take a seat right there," he said. He picked up his empty coffee cup from his desk. "I was just about to get a refill. What do you take in yours?"

"Milk. Not much."

Nodding, he exited the office. He slipped into the evidence room, signed out a manila envelope, and quickly filled the coffee cups before entering his office again. He handed one of the cups to Maralyn and sat down behind his desk.

"So," he said, blowing the steam from his cup, "I guess y'all decided a secular person was better for the job."

Her look was blank. "What?"

"Bringing Cammy her Bible. I guess you figured Ryan Teller wasn't the person to go into the house and get it."

Behind her glasses her eyes were steady. He waited patiently.

"Oh," she said. "Well, Cammy has more tolerance for Ryan than I do." She paused. "Did you let him into the house?"

"Of course not. We didn't let you in, did we? No, he'll have to get an escort like everyone else. Provided, of course, that Cammy actually requested him to enter."

"I don't know when she would have. She's been under sedation." She sniffed. "I know he and Martin were close. He probably thinks he has some sort of holy privilege to be in their house. I know men like him."

Truitt looked at her over his cup. "So, how's Cammy doing this morning?"

Maralyn took a sizable gulp of coffee. "Not too well. Some women handle situations like this better than others."

"It's tough. I don't know how anybody handles it."

"I guess it's in the upbringing. When my father died, my mother didn't cry for a month. She couldn't— she had four daughters to worry about."

"Grown daughters."

Maralyn stared at him. "Yes, grown daughters, although my youngest sister, Victory, was only twenty. What did you mean by that?"

He shook his head. "Nothing. Just trying to keep

everything straight. I knew Martin practically all my life, but still, there're things about his family I didn't know. Your family tree's a bit confusing. There were four of you, right? Let's see—you, Kathleen, who's deceased, Victory, and . . ."

"Ginnie. She's a year younger than me. She lives over near Lake Lanier in Gainesville."

"I haven't seen her here."

Maralyn brought her elbows down onto the arms of the chair, and held the cup at breast level. "No. Mother called both her and Vic and told them not to bother coming until the funeral. With Gale and Katie Pru living with her, there's not enough room in the house for two more people."

"Ah. I imagine it was quite a boisterous upbringing you had. Now let's see, y'all left Statlers Cross and moved to Atlanta . . ."

"When I was fourteen."

"Spent summers in Statlers Cross?"

"Summers, weekends, whenever."

Truitt sipped his coffee. "Huh. Four girls. And in the summer you throw the cousins in on top of that . . . I guess it was no wonder you and Martin grew close."

There was a slight setting of the muscles around her mouth. She had been expecting this, he thought.

"Martin and I didn't grow close, Alby. We grew together."

He scrutinized her, taking in the leathery folds of her cheeks and the brashness of her bleached hair. Her fingers were large but bony, and sinews rippled the skin on the back of her hands. He thought of Cammy, scurrying upstairs to hide in the bedroom while her husband and his hunting buddy devoured fresh sticky buns in the kitchen. He couldn't imagine this woman scurrying anywhere.

"How long did the marriage last?" he asked.

She didn't move, the coffee cup held immobile in front of her chest. "A year. Thirteen months to be exact."

"Irreconcilable differences?"

"You could say that. I didn't like being hit."

He looked down at his cup. He believed her. One of the paradoxes he had learned to handle as a sheriff was the fact that decent men could do indecent things.

"How often did he hit you?"

"Once, and I said we would work it out. After all, his father had been an abuser. He struck me a second time, and I walked out the door. I didn't give him a third chance."

"Did he ever hit Cammy?"

"I don't know. She never told me if he did. I have my own theory, of course."

"What's that?"

"Men like that don't reform."

"Sill?"

"I don't know. He'd spank her, too hard in my opinion."

"What did you ever do about it?"

"What can you do? He was her father."

"Does your clinic perform abortions?"

Coffee slopped onto her hand. She yelped and dropped the cup on Truitt's desk. The liquid rolled toward his papers. Quickly he picked them up and, reaching into his desk drawer, pulled out several tissues.

He handed one to her. "I'm sorry, Maralyn," he said, wiping the desk office. "Didn't mean to surprise you like that."

She pressed the tissue to her hand. "The hell you didn't, Alby. I don't know why you want to know, but yes, we handle all manner of women's health care."

"Did Martin ever come to your clinic?"

"Well, no. Why should he?"

He opened the manila envelope and took out the anti-abortion pamphlet, now unfolded and sealed in a plastic bag. Avoiding the wet areas, he pushed it across the desk to her.

"I found this in his house. Have you ever seen it before?"

She gingerly picked up the pamphlet and read it slowly before laying it back down.

"Not that particular one, no. But others like it. There are a lot of people out there who don't understand what we do."

"Look on the back, please," he instructed. "Recognize anything?"

She flipped the pamphlet on its back. "My clinic's listed here."

"Right. Do you know any of the others?"

"Most of them. We're becoming a fairly select group, you know."

If she was attempting sarcasm, it failed. Beneath her tan, her face had paled.

"Any idea why Martin would have it?"

"Who knows? He was very involved with religious activities—perhaps he got onto some mailing list."

"It strikes me as strong stuff. Not your mainstream prolife approach, I would think."

"If every group was mainstream, doctors and nurses wouldn't be getting killed."

"So it would surprise you if Martin was involved with this type of group?"

"It would be out of the question. I'm very much aware of Martin's stand on the issue. He didn't condone, but he wouldn't try to stop a woman from choosing. And he certainly took his religion seriously enough not to be involved in any fascist propaganda."

Truitt pulled out the bagged mock-up with its penciled remarks and placed it in front of her.

"We found this in his house, too. Are you familiar enough with Martin's handwriting to identify the writing on this page as his?"

She stared at the pamphlet, her hands in her lap.

"Maralyn, does this strike you as reflecting what you knew Martin's opinion on abortion to be?"

She was silent. Light blinked on her glasses.

"Maralyn." His voice was stern. "Was Martin part of a group harassing abortion clinics?"

She stared at the mock-up, then her eyes darted from it to the finished piece. She shook her head.

"He couldn't have been. How could he?" She placed her sinewy hands on her cheeks and pushed her skin upward. Her voice broke. "He knew what I went through. He knew the goddamned results."

"What results, Maralyn?" Truitt asked gently. "Tell me what happened to you."

The phone buzzed. Irritated, Truitt answered.

"Not now."

"The crew's back from the Cane house, Sheriff. You need to see this."

Truitt hung up the phone and looked at Maralyn. Her eyes were riveted to the mock-up. Standing, Truitt slid it and the pamphlet into the envelope.

"Give me two minutes, Maralyn," he said. "Then we can talk some more."

He met Haskell in the hall. Ruch stood beside him. He held out a closed grocery bag.

"You might want to put gloves on," Haskell said.

Truitt pulled on a pair of gloves. "Both of y'all are going to be cleaning my yard if this isn't good."

The officers were silent as Truitt opened the bag. At first Truitt thought it contained a towel. The cloth was worn looking with blue stripes. But as he pulled it out of the bag, he saw that it was a droopy woman's purse.

"You're not going to believe where I found it, sir," Ruch said. "In the living room, crammed down the back of the sofa."

The exterior of the purse bore large red-brown smudges. Inside, among the jumble of female paraphernalia, were a small can of gun oil, a disassembled rod, and a wad of rags.

I don't know why that Foxfire fella doesn't come interview us. My grandmother still churns her own butter, my grandfather's got haint stories that would put those mountain people to shame, and we'd know what to do with the publicity.

— Randy Motts, talking to a customer at his car dealership in the Calwyn County seat of Praterton, 1979

18

Ella noticed the crows on the kitchen counter the exact moment the phone rang. For a frantic second she stared at their beaks, trying to figure out which one had squawked. But then the ring sounded again. She moved past the covey to the phone on the wall.

She waited until the third ring to lift the receiver. The voice on the line was level and held an anyplace urban quality. She knew immediately who it was.

"I'd like to speak with Sill, please. This is Faith."

Ella dropped her own voice to a Southern purr. "Faith, this is Mrs. Alden. I'm sorry, but Sill's upstairs with her mother right now. It was a rough night. I'll tell her you called."

"Mrs. Alden, I was at your house yesterday. I'm sorry. I didn't get to meet you. But I'm coming over again this morning. I just wanted to check and see if I should bring anything."

"Oh, goodness, there's really no point in you coming, Faith. Sill needs to concentrate on her family right now. I'll tell her you called, though. I'm sure she'll get in touch with you when she's ready."

"Mrs.—"

"We really can't have company right now, dear. Good-bye now."

Ella hung up before Faith could wedge in more pleas. She picked up the sponge from the sink and ran it under cold water. It was so difficult to deal with family add-ons. Strangers always felt they should be able to step easily into the clan, like blue cards shuffled into a red deck. Sometimes it took decades for the new-comers—as well as the family members to which they attached themselves—to comprehend that it simply wasn't possible.

She dabbed the sponge at one of the birds. "You'd think people would understand that," she said. "You would think they could look at their own families and see that the wires were too finely woven to let anybody through. Yet they keep yammering to get in, don't they?"

She began to wipe down the counters. She hadn't lied to the girl. It had been a rough night. Whatever drug Johnny Bingham had given Cammy had worn off suddenly. Ella had been standing at the dining room window, watching Gale and Katie Pru climb into the Buick and drive off, when she heard the scream.

She didn't know what time Gale and Katie Pru returned home. It was well after dark, because when she left Cammy's side briefly to get a cold rag, she hadn't seen the Buick in the yard. She didn't check again, consumed as she and Maralyn were with the grieving mother and child. By morning they all four were exhausted, and blessedly so. The initial stage was passing. Soon it would be evident what kind of widow Cammy Cane would be.

Ella squeezed out the sponge and ran it under the faucet again. What could that woman with the Jane Doe voice know about grief?

From the hall behind her she heard her granddaughter's quick footsteps. "Excuse me a second, Ella. I'd like you to meet someone."

Gale stepped through the doorway, a young woman behind her. "Nadianna, this is Katie Pru's great-grandmother, Ella Alden. Ella, this is Nadianna Jesup. She's agreed to keep Katie Pru today. Sort of a trial. If it works, she'll become Katie Pru's child care provider."

Ella couldn't place the name, although Jesups grew in clumps throughout Calwyn County. And the face, with its washed-out eyes, was unusual enough that had she seen it before, she felt certain she would have recognized it. But there was something about the clothes, the long beige shift, the worn but polished loafers. The form she was familiar with. She had seen this figure before.

The girl chewed awkwardly on her lips. Ella held out her hand. "Well, Nadianna, I hope you know what you're getting yourself into. Katie Pru is a mess. A wonderful mess, mind you, but a mess all the same. I've always said children like her are the reason women shouldn't bear offspring once they're past thirty-five. It takes too much energy. More importantly, it takes too much thought."

The girl stopped biting her lips. Her face suddenly receded behind their fullness. "I'm sure it'll be all right, Mrs. Alden. I've been talking to Katie Pru and I'm sure we'll be friends. I have a couple of nieces her age."

Ella stared at the remarkable crimson lips. Where on earth have I seen her? she thought. Somewhere, sometime recently. She smiled.

"Which Jesups are you?"

Nadianna pointed toward the front of the house. "We live over by the mill. My granddaddy was Howard Jesup."

"Uh-huh." Ella didn't know any Howard Jesup. The truth was, she didn't know any of the Jesups by their first names.

"Well, I hope everything works out," she said. "So, you're going to start today?"

"I'm gonna do a trial today. Give me and Katie Pru a chance to get to know each other."

"Good idea." Ella turned to her granddaughter. "Which reminds me, Gale, I need to talk to you. Perhaps we could get Nadianna and Katie Pru set up with something to do."

"All right," Gale answered. "We left Katie Pru reading a book in the living room. Nadianna, why don't you ask her to take you into the den? She loves to talk about the beasties there."

Nadianna raised her eyebrows but said nothing as she left the kitchen. Gale pulled out a chair from the table and sat down. "Okay," she said. "What did you want to talk about?"

"Alby."

"What about Alby?"

Ella picked up the sponge and with her back to Gale began scrubbing the Formica.

"I know he formally interrogated you yesterday," she said.

"It wasn't what I'm familiar with as an interrogation."

"And I know he informally interrogated you as well."

Silence. Ella tilted her chin and examined her granddaughter over her shoulder.

"I want to know what he said to you."

Gale shrugged. "I think he was getting at family dynamics, but I'm not sure. He wanted to know what it was like spending my childhood in this house."

"You didn't spend your childhood in this house."

"My childhood summers, then. Near enough."

"No, it's not. I spent my childhood here. So did your mother. Even Sill spent more time in this house growing up than you did."

Gale's face reddened, whether from embarrassment or the first flush of anger Ella couldn't tell.

"What point are you trying to make, Ella?"

Ella turned on the faucet and held her hands under the stream of water. "There's a lot about this family you don't know, Gale, whether you like it or not. I raised you in Atlanta. Spending a couple of months here every summer, knowing you were leaving, knowing you *could* leave—that doesn't carry a whole lot of weight around here. I'm not blaming you for anything, I'm just telling you. Before you go spouting off about this family's dynamics to the sheriff, just remember you're not of this place. You've no authority to talk about it."

Behind her she heard the chair scrape across the floor. "Is that all you felt you needed to say?" Gale's voice was quiet.

Ella continued rinsing her hands. "I believe so. Don't go thinking you know more about us than you do. Alby Truitt is not a simple man."

"I didn't think he was." Gale's voice wobbled with anger. "And I know a damn sight more about this family than I care to admit."

Ella knew Gale had left the room by the way the air sounded. Her mother had once told her that if she listened closely enough to silence, the air would crackle, as if fire had rushed into the void. It wasn't fire she felt right now. It was ice.

She grabbed a towel and patted her hands dry. Oh well, she thought, sometimes things just had to be done. And she was the one to do them.

Maralyn's voice was hoarse. She sat in front of Truitt's desk, tears streaming from behind the severe wire glasses, impervious to the closed grocery bag he set next to the phone. He opened the drawer and handed her a box of tissues.

"I had an abortion before Martin and I were married," she blurted. "He went with me. I hurt for the longest time afterwards. He came by the house every day to check on me."

"You were at Statlers Cross?"

She nodded. "It was during the summer. We found a doctor in Athens. It was horrible. I came home and could barely move. I think Mother suspected, but she never said anything. She's never said anything to this day. It was back in the bad, old illegal days. It left me sterile."

The muscles in her arms worked—she must have been squeezing her hands, although he could not see them below the line of the desk. He looked down at his own hands and discovered he was doing the same. "Do you think it contributed to your divorce later?"

"No," she said. "He was wonderful about it. Blamed himself, actually. Said that first of all, he should never have talked me into having sex, and that second of all, once I became pregnant, he should have married me right away. I never told him, but that was all hogwash. I wanted to have sex with him, and I didn't want that baby."

"I'm not real clear on this, Maralyn. Are you thinking it wasn't in Martin's character to have become politically active in the prolife movement?"

The light from the window behind him flashed in her glasses. "It's just not possible. He and I had an understanding. It was a horrible thing we went through. When I decided to go into women's health—to aid women in their abortions—I talked it over with him, even though he and Cammy had been married for several years. He was so supportive. It reminded me of the part of him that I had loved—the reason I had married him."

"Had you discussed the issue with him recently?"

She brushed her nose with a tissue. "No. All these years we had an understanding. It was the secret we kept. It was the part of him I could continue to hold."

She sobbed. Truitt walked to his office door and motioned Haskell inside. The investigator took a seat by the wall and pulled out his notepad.

Truitt gripped the back of his desk chair and leaned forward. "Maralyn," he said quietly. "I'm going to ask you a question, and I want you to think before you answer it. When you went into the room immediately following the shot, did you see any gun-cleaning supplies?"

She blew her nose. "No."

"A bottle of oil?"

"No."

"Brushes? Rods? Rags?"

"You've already asked me this."

"You never answered. I want you to be sure of what you're saying."

"I make it a habit to be sure of what I say, Alby. I saw none of that."

"Ella did."

"Mother was mistaken."

"Helluva a thing to be mistaken about."

Maralyn flung her hand into the air, the tissue flapping. "Listen, Alby, my mother is in her seventies. No telling what you've gotten her confused about during all your interrogation."

Truitt laid his hand on the closed grocery sack but didn't open it. "We found Cammy's purse."

She gaped at him.

"You wanted me to get Cammy's purse, right?"

"Where. . . ?"

Truitt ignored the question. "Interesting contents, Maralyn. Wanna tell me about them?"

Her mouth clamped shut. For a long moment she stared at him. "I need to talk with Mother. I may want a lawyer," she said.

Whatever sorrow had been in her voice, it was gone. Her voice was hard, her mouth taut.

Truitt slapped the back of his chair and pushed the grocery sack in Haskell's direction. "Fine," he said. "You two can discuss it at Ella's house. We'll follow you out there."

The reason Jimmy Carter lost the election was because too many damn Yankees think we're quirky and quaint with our "Aw, Andy" shuffling and our possum-eating grins and our won't-stay-dead relatives who keep popping out of the closets and scaring the dogs. The frustrating part is, we like it that way.

—Calwyn County newspaper editor
  Brad Stone, in a January 1981 column

19

The jag-wire yawned. "It's so hot I can drink the air," he said.

Katie Pru watched as her mother, carrying a heavy bag and wearing her walking shoes, waved at her from the top of the railroad tracks and disappeared over the other side. "Nu-uh," she said. "You can't drink air. You can only drink rain and Cokes."

"I can drink the air. In the mornings there's drops on my tummy. It's the air dripping through my skin."

"Stop it. You're teasing."

"I'm not. You look tomorrow morning. You'll see."

Katie Pru wanted to reach up and pinch the jag-wire on the ear, the way she had seen grown-ups do children in movies, but she stopped herself. If she did it, the jag-wire might yowl and then Nadianna, who was watching her from the pecan tree, would run over and grab her away. Nadianna might even go into the house, get a rope, and sling it around the jag-wire's neck. Then she'd drag the jag-wire away and put him in the pen with the angry dogs and the pig. The jag-wire would hate that. He wouldn't want to share the pig with anybody.

"Pigs are good to eat," the jag-wire had said when she told him what she had seen in the pen at Cammy's house. "They make good sandwiches."

She hadn't been able to play with the jag-wire much because of the weather, so during the storms she pulled aside the peach curtains in the living room and leaned against the window to talk with him. From there she could look out at him as he got pelted with rain. He didn't mind the rain—he loved it, in fact, because it made his black coat shiny and changed the dirt below his feet to mud. During the thunderstorms he would stand in the front yard with his mouth open and the water dripping from his teeth and tongue. Sometimes he would roar, and lights would flash in the sky. She knew he could drink the rain. But no jag-wire could drink the air.

"Trains drink air."

She poked him on the head. "No, they don't."

"You watch. They drink the air and spit out the hot."

She didn't say anything. He knew there were no more trains. He knew that no matter how long she stared out at the railroad tracks, no trains would pass by for her to watch. And no Linnies either. Linnies didn't sassy along the tracks anymore.

She heard the creak of the front door and, from the corner of her eye, saw Grandma Ella come onto the stoop.

"Katie Pru!" Grandmama Ella hollered. "You doing all right? Where's Nadianna?"

"I'm right here, Mrs. Alden." Nadianna hurried to the front of the house. "I'm not far away. I can see her fine."

"Just checking. You need to be on your toes with that child. Y'all come in when you need something to drink."

The door slammed behind her. Katie Pru looked quickly over at Nadianna, but she was already walking back to the pecan tree. Katie Pru stared at her long dress, wondering how, with each step, it always missed the mud. Even with shorts on, Katie Pru never wore clothes that missed the mud.

At the tree Nadianna ran her finger along the chain buried in the trunk. She pressed one finger, then all five, against the links. With one arm, she leaned into the tree like she was trying to push it over, and then slowly pushed herself back again.

Katie Pru hopped off the jag-wire's back and ran over to her.

"What are you doing?"

Nadianna blinked. Two tears fell on her cheeks. Nadianna wiped them away and folded her arms. She nodded at the chain. "I was just looking at this."

"It's iron. It makes the tree strong," Katie Pru said. "That's what Grandma Ella says."

Katie Pru tried to reach up and to grab one of the links, but instead her fingers scraped the bark. Stepping onto the roots at the base of the tree, she stood on her tiptoes and scratched at the trunk, but all she got was crumbs of lichen under her nails. She folded her arms like Nadianna and stared at the chain.

"Why are you crying?" she asked.

A hum like an airplane whined past them. Nadianna brushed at the mosquito that landed on Katie Pru's leg. "I've heard about this chain," Nadianna said. "My grandmother used to tell me a story about it."

"I want to hear the story."

"I don't know, Katie Pru. It's very sad."

"My mama tells me stories."

"Does she tell you sad stories?"

"The Little Mermaid doesn't really marry the prince," Katie Pru said. "She turns into sea foam. And the Walrus eats all the baby oysters."

Nadianna smiled. "Those are sad stories. Well, all right." She leaned against the tree trunk, so that her head touched the chain. "Once there was a very beautiful woman who was also very sad. The man who loved her, he tried to make her laugh. He'd wear funny clothes, and she'd giggle, but she'd go to being sad again. He'd sing her funny songs, and that would make her laugh, but as soon as he finished, she'd get so melancholy."

"What's that mean?"

"Blue. She'd get blue. And he'd even tell her jokes and tickle her and chase her through the fields, but as soon as she calmed down and stopped laughing, she'd be sad all over again. One day, Sadness himself came knocking on the door. He had long legs and he wore a big hat. And he said, 'Lady, it's time to put away your things and come with me.' So she washed her little boy's face and hands and dressed him in the nicest clothes she had made for him, and then she stepped through the door to Sadness and went away with him. And the man who loved her, he saw how clean and neat she had made the little boy, and he took it for a sign that she was finally happy. And to show his love, he put this chain around her favorite tree so that as long as the tree grew big and strong, their love would, too."

Katie Pru glanced at the chain and wrinkled her nose. "What happened to the little boy?"

"He was just fine, 'cause when Sadness went away with his mother, that old goat never came back. So the little boy was happy for the rest of his days."

"Oh." Katie Pru picked the lichen out of her fingernails.

"And see how the tree has grown around the chain?

That's because the tree wants to hold on with all its might. It loved that woman, too."

"Okay."

Katie Pru stepped over the roots of the pecan tree, ran to the jag-wire, and climbed onto his back. She rolled over and lay on top of him with her eyes shut and her mouth wide open.

"What are you doing?" the jag-wire finally asked.

"I'm drinking air," she said. "I'm drinking air and not thinking about the Blue Lady."

It was a slow-moving caravan—first Maralyn Nash in her black Mercedes, then Truitt in his Dodge, with Ruch in the brown sheriff's patrol car bringing up the tail. Truitt kept precisely two car lengths behind Maralyn. She responded by driving no faster than 35 miles per hour.

From the Dodge passenger seat, Haskell nodded at the lead car. "Pretty icy, don't you think? One minute she's crying buckets and the next she's calmly talking about a lawyer."

Truitt pulled his sunglasses from his pocket and slid them on. During the fifteen minutes they had been driving, the silhouette of the driver in front of them never moved, not even a tilt to glance in the rearview mirror. Icy is right, he thought. He watched the speedometer needle quiver to 36, then immediately drop to 33. Icy and damned nervy.

"So what do you think, Craig? Give me your ideas."

Haskell stretched his considerable legs and rested against the door. "Well, I've been thinking, and it doesn't make a whole lot of sense to me. If you want to kill someone and get away with it, wouldn't you leave the primary evidence that suggests it was an accident? And if it was an accident, why screw with the scene? And if it was a suicide, why would the gun-cleaning supplies be out in the first place?"

"Unless Martin wanted it to look like an accident."

"Why would he? I checked with his insurance agent this morning. He's had his life policy for five years—way past the suicide clause time limit. So what's the incentive for mucking with the scene?"

"Because you're hysterical? Because dear Daddy—or husband, or cousin, whatever—is lying there in bits and pieces and you just go wacky and destroy all the evidence you can?"

Haskell snorted. "If that's their defense, they better hope the Dithery Simpering Belle Club is the jury. And another thing—how do you explain the gun being across the room? And why would Mrs. Alden say it if it wasn't true?"

"Now, I've actually heard of that happening before. The death was ruled an accident even though the rifle was found nine feet away from the body. The investigators figured it had something to do with the reflex of muscles as the gun went off. So, it's possible."

"But likely?"

Truitt pushed the air conditioner to high. "When we get back, I want you to call Dr. Blair at the University of Georgia. Ask him if we can come up and talk to him tomorrow morning."

"What are you thinking?"

Truitt drummed his thumbs on the wheel. "What about this: A teenager gets an abortion back in the 1950s and becomes sterile. Nobody but she and the boy know about it—no family support, no counseling. She marries the boy, they divorce, she remarries, is widowed. Goes to work in an abortion clinic. I'd like to know what kind of profile he can do on a person like that."

"So, what, you're thinking she finds out he's a radical right-to-lifer, feels betrayed, and goes berserk?"

Ahead of them the silhouette remained frozen. "Something caused at least one of those women to go berserk. But I'd bet everything I own that Maralyn Nash didn't know of Martin's abortion activities until I plopped that brochure down in front of her. Now, what I want to know is, who did?"

Gale stood on the sidewalk in front of Malcolm Hinson's photography studio and swore. A small shingled overhang jutted out above her, shielding her from the blistering noonday heat, and on either side the boarded-up display windows recessed the door into a drab alcove. Nevertheless, she felt exposed and block-headed as she tried to jam the key Mal Robertson had given her into the uncooperative lock.

"Shit," she whispered. "Damn, damn, shit and hell."

The satchel she had flung behind her back fell forward and tilted her off balance. The key in her hand was obviously a new copy of something, although not of the implement that could unlock the studio's front door. She moved out of the alcove's protection and started down the sidewalk in front of Greene's Hardware. Once past Langley Drugs she eased down the two stone steps that connected the sidewalk to the street, and skirted the side of the building to the rear.

A garbage Dumpster stood directly to her left. Black flies swarmed around the open container. Past that were a stack of wooden pallets and a pickup truck. A white van, the words *Piedmont Antiques* scripted in gold and black on its sides, was parked farther down the narrow back lot. With Barry Greene's death, Statlers Cross's mercantile section once again looked paltry.

She picked her way over a stack of cardboard boxes next to the drugstore wall and stopped at the rear of the studio. So this is what will soon be Statlers Cross's gen-teel tearoom, she thought. Two large windows, each measuring about eight feet high by ten feet across, bordered the back door. Many of the panes were broken; at some point, boards had been hammered on the inside of the window frames, and only a few fragments of glass could be found in the gravel at the base of the building. Gale studied the locked door. If this was the entrance Mal Robertson and his inspector had used a year ago, the spiders had effectively reclaimed their property. Cobwebs feathered the corners of the door and draped around the knob. Among the large strands, dead insects lay, suspended and dry. Brushing them aside, Gale gripped the knob and tried the key.

It took two shoves with her shoulder to get the door open. After the bright light of the sun, she could see nothing inside the building. She blocked the door frame with her satchel and began searching the parking lot for an appropriate doorstop. In a patch of weeds near the dumpster, she found a broken chunk of asphalt. Pushing the door against the exterior wall of the structure, she wedged the chunk in place. She dusted her hands and looked around the deserted parking lot. The last thing she wanted was to find herself playing Nancy Drew, locked in an abandoned building with nothing but a flashlight and toothy perkiness to save her.

One foot over the threshold and she stopped. Unlike Nancy Drew, she didn't have to worry about a villain conking her on the head and leaving her for the rats and dehydration. She did, however, need to worry about law-abiding shop owners who loaded with buckshot first and asked questions later. She quickly walked over to the rear door of the drugstore and knocked.

The cool air that blew from the store was worth the de-evolutionary scowl Cooper Langley directed at her as he opened the door. A couple of slow beats, however, and he recognized her.

"Oh, Gale," he said, smiling. "I didn't know it was you. I was expecting it to be one of the boys from the mill village. It's summer, and they can't think of anything more fun than riding their bicycles over here and banging on my door for the hell of it." His scarecrow arm waved at the coil of bungalows. "I swear I'm thinking of calling Alby and telling him to come round those boys up and send them to a work camp."

"They're no worse than kids ever were." Gale smiled. "I was just thinking today of all the trouble Sill and I used to get into during the summers."

"Well, y'all didn't go around making a mess of noise. The difference was, y'all weren't hoodlums."

No, Gale thought, the difference was we were Aldens. She glanced over at the bungalows, most of them neatly kept with pruned bushes and parti-colored flowerbeds. The only flowers on the Alden property were the dogwood on the doormat and the tangle of honeysuckle that grew unattended along the fence lines. For Ella lawn decor was reduced to a black painted jaguar and the clothes on whoever happened to be in the yard. But it didn't matter. When one could point with equal certainty to lineage and eccentricity, pride of place was evidently not demanded.

Langley shoved his hands in his pockets. "Gale, I'm real sorry about Martin. You know I thought the world of him."

"Thank you. Folks have been so supportive. It really does help."

"It's an awful shame, a man like that who's done so much. And he never asked anything in return. Always quiet about it. You be sure to tell Cammy if there's anything I can do . . ."

"I sure will. Listen, Cooper, I'm going to be working next door in the photography studio. I have Mal Robertson's permission—he gave me the key. I just wanted to warn you in case you heard any strange noises."

Langley raised his skinny black eyebrows. "What you working in there for?"

"It's a long shot, but I'm hoping to find some old photographs. I'm researching a book about rural life in the 1920s, and I understand Malcolm Hinson did quite a bit of documentary work during that decade."

"Huh. I remember my grandfather talking about it.

He didn't have a whole lot of good things to say. 'Prying' is what he called it."

"That's what Deak said. Anyway, I thought if I could track down some of his photos . . ."

"Hmm, 1920s. Boll weevil years." Langley ran his thumb across his chin. "Ate up families as well as cotton crops around here. Probably wasn't a good time to be shining a camera in a man's face."

"That's probably true. Still, it could be handy for me that he did."

"Nice to be able to look back at it, isn't it. To hear my grandfather tell it, that was a time to batten down the hatches, stand your ground, and know the Good Book."

"I'm sure. Well, I'm going to see what I can find. If you hear me screaming . . ."

"I'll come running with my shotgun in one hand and my broom in another." He grinned at her quizzical expression. "Shotgun for rats—broom for snakes. It's illegal to kill a nonpoisonous snake in the state of Georgia."

"Fine. If I see a snake, I'll be sure to ask its intentions."

Snickering, he nodded good-bye and closed the door. Gale walked back to the photography studio door. Roaches, rats, and snakes. Wonderful. She knelt beside her satchel and fumbled with the latches. Well, she wouldn't go down without a fight. She reached into the satchel and pulled out a pair of gardening gloves, a flashlight, and a hammer. If nothing else, she'd beat the damn things to death.

She stepped inside the room and stamped twice. Nothing skittered, nothing hissed. She scooted farther into the space, letting her shoes slide noisily across the floor. Silence. Flicking on the flashlight, she swung the beam around the room. Satisfied that nothing carapaced or squiggly was going to fall into her hair, she eased the satchel off her shoulder, set the hammer on the floor, and began a more serious examination.

The space wasn't large for a commercial property—probably no more than thirty feet wide. A wall separated the back room from the front of the studio, but gauging the depth, she calculated this rear section took up the bulk of the structure with the anterior serving as little more than a display area. The floor was wood plank, held up, she surmised, only by the floor joists. As she walked, the boards moaned.

If there was ever a smell of chemicals in the studio, it had long since given way to the odors of stale air and dust. A few pieces of furniture sat around the room—a gentleman's dresser, its drawers missing; a metal table of the type found in kitchens during the 1940s; a china cabinet with curved sides empty of glass. Interspersed with these were starched waves of canvas. Gale passed the beam over them. At some places the canvases jutted up into pyramids; in others they collapsed into limp rolls on the floor.

Despite the intensity of the flashlight and the illumination from the open door, the room was still too dim for detail. Gale couldn't make out the colors, much less the forms, on the exposed painted sides. Frustrated, she looked around the room. It was too much to hope the studio still had electricity, and indeed, she couldn't find so much as a switch or a fuse box.

She walked over to the large window on the right side of the door. The boards covering the panes were thin, little more than cut plywood, and they appeared to have been hammered in haphazardly. Gale reached out and grasped one of the nails. It came out easily. Well, hell, she thought. I'll offer my apologies to the Robertsons later.

She picked up the hammer and pulled from her satchel the largest screwdriver of a seven-piece set. With each board that came down, visibility increased. By the time she had removed all within reach, a clean, slanted light flooded the room.

She stood panting and covered with sweat and dirt.

Grimacing, she dropped her tools into the open satchel and surveyed the studio.

The canvases could have been a painter's cloth or dust covers, they were tossed about so casually. Gale walked to the nearest one and gingerly lifted its corner. She slowly pulled the canvas back on top of itself until she could make out the image. The pigment had cracked. Hairline fissures snaked across the fabric; nevertheless the composition held. The peaks of snow-capped mountains appeared first, then the tops of pine trees, then a lake. Gale spread the canvas out as well as she could and gazed down at the artwork. It could have been the Alps, it could have been the Rockies. One thing was definite: It had nothing to do with Statlers Cross or any other part of Georgia.

She examined the bottom of the backdrop, looking for a signature, but there was none. Little wonder. The artistry respected here was in the technology of lens and chemicals, not the archaic play of woven cloth and colored oils. She went through the other backdrops—a ship at dock, a fancy parlor, a sweeping staircase with ornate iron grillwork. She wondered if these fantasies were region specific; if, going through an abandoned photo studio in Chicago, she would find the same painted scenery. Or more to the point, she thought, perhaps these subjects were precisely what would be found in Chicago, translated here by the Northern Malcolm Hinson. She suddenly remembered something Zilah had said about widowhood: *There's nobody around to keep you out of yourself.* There must have been some of that in what Malcolm Hinson did for the impoverished natives who resented his intrusion into their workaday lives but welcomed it for a pose. He lifted them out of their poor Southern selves.

She reached forward and picked up the corner of the last backdrop. A pale blue background, a rocky ground, then three stone steps topped by a line of Doric columns—she had found the backdrop of the

Parthenon used for the photograph of Jessie and the three children.

For no logical reason she felt a frisson of excitement. It wasn't a major discovery; certainly if other backdrops were still in the studio, the chances were this one would be as well. The thrill was of recognition, and the memory of the woman who had not stood before this canvas with her sister and child.

Gale pulled gently at the backdrop, trying to smooth it out on the floor. A mound formed in the center, forcing the Parthenon into a bulge. Frowning, she lifted the backdrop above her head and carefully dragged it to the side of the room. As she let it fall to the ground, dirt and dust billowed from a large pile of rags that had lain underneath.

She sneezed twice before nudging the pile with her foot. When nothing scampered out, she knelt beside the rags and began studying them. Bits of paper mingled with shredded fabric in the heart of the pile. A rat's nest. She fought the impulse to run for her hammer. It was evident by the flatness of the cloth that nothing living had occupied it for a while. Cautiously she pinched the edge of a piece of fabric that had not been pulverized and shook it loose from the pile. Despite the dirt and age, she could tell it was a burgundy sateen, the seam of a bodice still visible along the neck and sides.

Piece by piece, she went through the intact contents of the pile—the severed skirt that had once attached to the bodice, a pair of men's trousers made of a rough brown material, a yellow cotton bonnet, a grimy frilled petticoat, a crumpled and tattered fichu. Her hand knocked something hard, and she pulled from the mound a woman's black boot, twisted laces swaying from the eyes. At the bottom of the pile, beneath a pair of butternut wool pants, she found a Confederate infantryman's kepi, the sloping crown of the cap creased with age.

Gale straightened the kepi's brim. A strange collection to be found in a Yankee's workshop, she thought.

She picked up the burgundy bodice again and slid her fingers over the fabric. It was cheap, like Christmas ribbon. Turning up the edge, she examined the area where stitching at one time would have bound the skirt to the bodice. The holes left by the needle were readily evident in the slick material—and much too widely spaced for a respectable seamstress. She studied the skirt. A length of thread still hung from the waistline. When she pulled it, two stitches slipped free.

"Hello? Gale? I'd knock but I'm afraid of what I'd dislodge."

Faith, dressed in jeans and a polo shirt, stood in the studio doorway. She took a hesitant step into the room and then paused, swiping at a column of dust motes. "Jesus, Gale. Sill said you were looking to move out of Ella's house, but you think this is the answer?"

"There are days . . ." She dropped the skirt into her lap. "So, let me guess. Ella threw you out."

"Ella? Oh, she'd never be so bold. She just very nicely explained that 'Faith, dear, it's so nice of you to come, but Sill's resting and only *family* can see her.' " Faith cautiously made her way into the room. "Of course, I suppose if Sill really had wanted me, she would have made it clear."

"Wouldn't have meant anything if she had. Ella abides by her own wishes."

"You're right. At any rate, Katie Pru saved me. She said you were at the picture store and would I please tell you to bring her a picture for the jag-wire? Working on the theory, I suppose, that one should always give an adult something to do. Nadianna told me where this place was." She looked around with a moue of distaste. "I'm so grateful."

Gale laughed. "Hey, I've made it presentable."

"Don't give up your day job." She stopped beside the pile of clothes and hooked her thumbs into her belt loops. "One of the reasons I came over was to tell Sill that I talked to Sergeant Haskell this morning."

Gale picked up the bodice and fluffed it in front of

her. A puff of dust billowed forward. "And?" she asked.

"Nothing really. He just wanted to know what time we got there, what time I left, had I ever met Mr. Cane before, et cetera. Pretty dry stuff. But Sill was so worried yesterday about me getting involved, I wanted to assure her it was okay." She slid the toe of her shoe beneath the pile of clothes and lifted up the fichu. "So what are you doing in here?"

Gale sighed. "Chasing geese." She held up the ragged bodice for Faith to see. "What do you think this is?"

"A whorehouse for rats?" Faith took the cloth and walked to the window. She rubbed the fabric between her fingers. "Kind of chintzy, isn't it? Like it's not a real piece of clothing at all."

"That's what I'm thinking. More of a costume, maybe."

Faith brought the bodice back to Gale and knelt beside her, picking up the Confederate kepi. "Do you think this is authentic?"

"Seems unlikely. It's in better shape than I'd expect for a hat 130 years old."

Faith lightly touched the seam at the brim. "I know someone over at the High Museum in Atlanta who would probably be able to tell you."

"Right now," Gale said, "I'm more interested in why it's here than if it's authentic or not."

Faith laid down the cap. "Why's that?"

Gale picked up the woman's boot. "Well, I have two theories. This was a photography studio until the 1940s. All those canvases over there are painted backdrops—a fancy parlor, mountains, the Parthenon. Now, it's conceivable that these costumes were for customers who wanted to dress up for their pictures. . . ."

Faith wrinkled her nose. "A bit tacky."

"Right. And why, if they were going to put on long dresses and look like Aunt Pittypat, would they worry about their feet?" Gale balanced the boot on the palm of her hand. "But you might worry about your feet if you were in a play ... the debut production of a Northern playwright ... in front of hundreds of people and the big city newspapers. Then you just might want to be sure that even if your dress was cheap, your shoes didn't look like you'd been out picking cotton in them."

"Theater costumes?"

"Could be. In 1925 a playwright named Parrish Singleton wrote a pageant for Statlers Cross. It was supposed to be a big to-do—culture-in-the-hinterlands type of stuff—but it was never produced. The female lead killed herself hours before the first performance."

Faith shivered and then laughed. "Jesus, Gale. Sill warned me about you and your stories. She said you were the reason she took up smoking—had to be tough for her scary-mouthed city cousin."

Gale brought the shoe to her lap and rolled the boot's twisted shoestring between her fingers.

"So Sill never told you this story?"

"You'd be surprised how little she talks about her family."

"So she never told you that the woman who killed herself was her great-grandmother? She never told you about all the ghost stories? She never discussed with you how hard it was to grow up in a small town where your legacy was a crazy haint with sharp teeth who devoured livestock and chased old men down the outhouse path?"

Faith laughed, but her eyes looked horrified. "No," she said. "Was it really like that? I thought the Canes were a respected family."

"Martin was respected. Martin was also mean as a snake. I think he beat Sill. I didn't understand it at the time. Everyone just talked about how Sill had an iron deficiency and bruised so easy."

Faith's face grew hard with anger. "No one stopped him?"

"Martin was a man of God, Faith," Gale said quietly. "Martin turned this whole damn town around.

Who would care if he disciplined his child every now and then?"

"Jesus. So why did she want me to meet him? Why was it so important to her?"

Gale didn't say anything. The slant of the sun had changed—the light on the floor seemed deeper and broader. She checked her watch. A little past one. She needed to get back to Katie Pru.

"You'll have to ask her, Faith," she replied, hauling herself to her feet. "You want my opinion? You gave her a little power. It's a victory to be able to go back to someone who has abused you and say, 'See, I can walk away if I want to.'" She bent to dash the dirt from her jeans, not wanting Faith to see the set in her jaw. "I've got one more quick thing to do, and then I've got to relieve Nadianna. If you'll wait a minute . . ."

She left Faith huddled on the floor and headed for the plaster wall that separated the rear part of the building from the anteroom. In the center was a thick milled door. Gale looked mournfully at the black iron knob. Gritting her teeth, she grasped the knob in both hands and jerked it to the left. The door swung open without so much as a creak.

The anteroom was black—even the light from the rear windows shining through the ingress was not sufficient to light this cramped chamber. She played the flashlight beam across the space. It danced over the black satin drapes covering the windows, the locked front door. She settled the beam on the wooden counter and the brass cash register that took up all of one end. She walked over and punched a button on the register. The drawer sprang open. Empty.

"Nothing," she muttered. "Deak Motts certainly knows his roach dwellings." Flicking off the flashlight, she slipped through the doorway and went back to the main room.

Faith stood in front of the Parthenon canvas, arms folded. "Bizarre," she said as Gale approached. "What was going on in those people's heads?"

Gale smiled. "Remember the drape we all wore for our senior pictures? Like we were debutantes with our off-the-shoulder gowns? Damn thing barely covered my breasts."

Faith laughed. "All right, I'll give you that. But the Parthenon?" She turned around, arms extended. "And besides, doesn't photography take light? Did he have electricity in here?"

"That's a good question. I don't think the town got electricity until the 1930s. Maybe flash powder. Or maybe the light from the windows was enough."

Faith looked at the windows skeptically. "I don't know . . ."

Gale gathered up her satchel and slung it over her shoulder. "Or maybe he had a generator. On the other hand, I think a long time ago photo studios had roof windows. Maybe . . ."

She jerked her head up. The ceiling boards ran east to west, each stretching the entire thirty-foot width of the room. Exposed joists ran the length, disappearing behind the wall and into the anteroom.

"There's an attic up there," she said softly. "Robertson said the building inspector went into the attic."

She flung open the anteroom door and shone the flashlight beam over the ceiling. The boards continued evenly—no openings, no hinged hatchway covered with off-color wood. The beam of light bobbed over the walls, down behind the counter. She could find no means of entry. She went back into the main room.

"I gotta run next door a second," she told Faith. "I'll be right back."

Cooper Langley was alone in his store, reading a sports magazine. Gale picked two Cokes from the cooler and placed them on the counter.

"Coop," she said, "Mal told me I could go into the attic, but I can't seem to find the entrance. Can you help me?"

Langley crossed his arms, his sharp elbows poking the cloth of his plaid shirt. "Well, the short answer is you can't get there from here. When this row of stores was first built, those next two were all a dry goods store, owned by Calvin Falcon. He eventually decided he didn't need that much space, so he put up a wall and sold half to Hinson. The dry goods business he held on to until he retired and then sold that part to Barry Greene. So the photography studio does have a separate attic, but old Hinson never bothered to cut through his own door to it."

Gale impatiently scooped her damp hair behind her ears. She kept her voice genial. "So how do I get to it?"

Langley swatted at a fly that buzzed past his face. "I'm guessing you're going to have to ask Zilah if she'd mind opening up the hardware store."

Every woman's a ghost, and every man a medium.

> —Jasper Singleton to his son Darcy
> after the latter's breakup with his
> girlfriend, 1983

20

The first thing Truitt noticed about Sill Cane as she entered Ella's living room was how tiny she had become. She had been a toddler when he first met Martin, and throughout the course of their friendship he had been aware of her on the fringes, a wheat-haired girl-child with stubby legs and a moon face. Cammy had kept the child's blond hair tied up on both sides of her head in puppy dog ears, and when he and Martin returned from a hunt, Sill would come running through the front yard to greet them, wrapping frantic arms around Martin's torso and pressing her happy mouth to his shirt.

The smile she gave him now as she sat on the sofa was wan, the color of her lips as blanched as her skin. Instead of puppy dog ears, her hair was pulled back in a loose knot. The outfit she wore—a simple white T-shirt beneath a pink denim jumper—hid the shape of her body, but Truitt could tell from her arms and face that the sturdy child was at present a gaunt and tired young woman.

A ladderback chair behind Truitt creaked as Haskell lowered his large frame into it. Beyond the closed door Truitt could hear Ruch's amiable tone. "Honest, Mrs. Alden, I've never seen so many fish. . . ."

Truitt dropped into the horsehair chair and placed his notebook and the manila envelope on the coffee table. He smiled sympathetically at Sill.

"Gale told me you had a rough night. How is your mother?"

"Not very well. Ella's losing patience with her." Sill crossed her arms and rested them on her knees. "According to the Good Book of Ella, women are supposed to be stoic at times like this. Mother's not measuring up."

"I want to talk to you again about what happened Saturday night, Sill. I've gone over your statement, of course, but I wanted to see if you can remember anything else."

"Is this an official murder investigation?"

He brought his eyes up to hers. "Has somebody told you it was?"

"If it's an official murder investigation, I think it's time this family called in a lawyer. You've been asking questions of us for two days. I would think it's illegal for you to keep hounding us without letting us know where we stand."

Her tone was belligerent, her square jaw lifted and defiant.

"If you would feel more comfortable with a lawyer, Sill, then I'll let you go do that. The situation that we face here is a violent death, and until we can determine what happened, we have to treat this as a homicide investigation. We have to collect the data, conduct the interviews, just like we would in a ruled homicide case. To be honest, Sill, I simply don't have a handle on it yet. And that's why I need to get a clear picture from everyone involved." He scooted the envelope back and forth beneath his fingers. "I'm sorry if I appear to be hounding you."

"You talked to us all Saturday night. You were back over here yesterday. Now today. We've all told you what happened. If that's not hounding, what would you call it?"

"I call it taking care of a friend, Sill."

"Which friend would that be, Alby? Daddy wrote you off long ago."

"I think what you mean," he said softly, "is Martin wrote you off long ago."

It was cruel, and he regretted saying it. She lowered her head a fraction. Tears dropped, missing the sunken line of her cheek and falling directly to her lap. He made no move to help her, no sounds to comfort her.

She placed her hands beside her on the cushion, as if she intended to get up. "By the way," Truitt said. "We interviewed Faith Baskins this morning."

Her mouth drooped. "Why did you need to talk to Faith? She has nothing to do with this."

"She came with you to the barbecue. According to witnesses, that act caused an argument between you and your father. Minutes later he's dead. I think Faith's an important person to talk to, don't you?"

"She has nothing to do with this," Sill repeated. "I've kept her out of it."

"When did she leave the barbecue?"

"When I told her to."

"And that was . . . ?"

She shook her head, agitated. "Right after the argument. Before Daddy went into the house."

"How long before?"

"Right before. As he was going inside."

"And you stayed with Faith until she got into her car and drove off?"

"No, of course not. I followed Daddy inside the house."

"So you never saw Faith leave?"

She exploded. "What the hell are you saying? Faith left! I told her to leave and she did. Now, leave her alone."

Her voice rose to a shrill pitch. She closed her hands into fists and pressed them against her knees.

"I'm just saying that Faith witnessed the argument, Sill." He spoke quietly. "And we need to talk with everyone."

"Keep her out of this. She's not part of this family. She's not part of the problem."

"What problem is that?"

Her jaw fluttered. "Daddy's death," she managed. "Daddy's death is the problem."

He picked up the envelope and removed the two plastic bags from inside. He dropped the finished brochure on the table and twisted it around until the aborted fetus faced her.

"What's your stand on abortion?" he asked.

The impact would have been the same if he had taken his fist and slammed it into her forehead. She stared at the brochure for a second. Then her head reared back, and a mottled wash sluiced over her face.

"You shit! What the fuck are you doing? You goddamn redneck thug!"

She was off the sofa, her knees knocking the coffee table and pushing the glass top off-kilter. A couple of the photographs beneath it drifted to the floor.

The intensity of her reaction surprised him. He leapt to his feet, but the coffee table was too close to his legs for him to maneuver. She shot her hands out at him—claws, not fists—and he had to knock them away twice before Haskell grabbed her from behind and forced her to the sofa.

He heard the door open behind him and Ella's stunned voice.

"What on earth . . . ? You let her go this instant!"

Haskell held Sill by the arms as he pressed her into the sofa. "Calm down, Sill," he said firmly. "I want to let you go. But you've got to show me that you've calmed down."

Her arms flexed beneath his, then she slumped into the cushions. The color had drained from her face again, and the front locks of her hair had come free. Truitt watched as Cammy brushed past Ella, Maralyn, and Ruch and hurried into the room.

"Sill, baby, are you all right?" Cammy slid onto the sofa next to her daughter. "I shouldn't have let you come down alone. I'm sorry. I wasn't thinking."

She looked much as he had seen other newly bereaved women look—graying hair combed, but not recently; face pulpy; a pair of sloppy, oversized jeans and a loose cotton shirt covering her body. She pressed her hand against Sill's cheek. Straightening into a sitting position, Sill laced her fingers between Cammy's and drew her mother's hand to her lap.

Maralyn followed Ella into the room. "Mother," she said. "It's time to call a lawyer."

Ella shooed her hands at her. "Don't be ridiculous. Nobody in this family needs a lawyer. We can take care of this on our own." She turned to Truitt. "Alby," she said, "there's no call for this. You knew and respected Martin and therefore we're cooperating with you. But you've got no business coming around here and treating us this way."

Truitt sighed and raked his fingers through his hair. He dropped back into the chair and leaned forward.

"I'm sorry, Ella, Cammy," he said quietly. "I didn't realize I was going to hit such a sensitive nerve. If I had, I would have handled it differently." He looked at Sill, her eyes still pinched close. "Sill, I apologize. But I have some questions that need answering, and I keep getting these strange reactions to them."

He picked up the bagged brochure, careful to keep it out of Sill's line of vision, and handed both it and the mock-up to Ella.

"I found these in Martin's house," he said. "Now, I was admittedly surprised by them—not exactly what I would have expected from Martin, but then, I haven't been as close to him in the past few years as I might have been. But what really has me curious, Ella, is the way y'all have responded to them."

Ella handed the two bags back to Truitt. "I don't need to see them, Alby. You may put them away."

He carefully slid the bags into the manila envelope and wrapped the string around the closure. Placing the envelope on his lap, he settled back in the chair and raised his palms in a questioning gesture.

"Well?" he said softly.

The four women gathered on the sofa, as silent and still as pegs. He wondered what would happen if he suddenly moved. He didn't have an opportunity to test it. Cammy moved first. She pushed a lock of cottony gray hair away from her face.

"Leave it be, Alby," she said. Her eyes were closed and her voice sounded oddly muffled. "Martin would have wanted you to leave it be."

"I can't do that, Cammy."

"You can. You have the authority. Martin gave you a lot, Alby, and he never asked much of you. But he would have asked this. He would have told you that some things can't be made still again once they are disturbed. So please, stop this. Martin's death was an accident. Accept it, and let us get on."

She faced him as if she were blind, her eyes permanently shuttered. Several necklaces of fine wrinkles circled her throat. His mother had once told him that, like a tree, a woman revealed her age by the number of those natural strands woven around her neck. Ridiculously, he counted Cammy's. Five. She was in her fifties, the same age as his mother when she died.

"If it was an accident, Cammy," he said, "what was Martin doing with his gun out?"

"Those guns were his arms, Alby. They were his body. When he needed comfort, he went to them."

"And why did he need comfort at that particular moment?"

Phlegm caught in Sill's throat. "You've already determined that it was my fault. I shouldn't have brought Faith."

"I keep hearing that, but I'm not sure I buy it, Sill. Granted, I can understand how a man with Martin's point of view would have a difficult time accepting your lifestyle, but it's not like he didn't know about it. You didn't drop a bomb on him in the middle of a public function—you merely introduced him to someone he already knew about."

"But that was the problem." Sill wrenched her hand from her mother's and pounded her fists against her knees. "I did it in front of everybody. I humiliated him."

"But he knew she was coming."

"So what if he did?" Ella asked. "That's not the same as meeting someone face to face. Cammy tried to talk Sill out of bringing her to the barbecue, but Sill insisted. It was a foolish decision, Alby, but then both those girls are young and didn't understand what it would mean to someone like Martin."

Truitt let his eyes roam over Ella's face as he reached for his notebook and opened it. "One of my investigators talked with Faith this morning. She said that she called Martin herself Saturday morning. She had hoped that talking with him in advance would take the edge off the encounter."

He waited for a reaction from one of the women, but he could discern none. He looked down at his notes and continued.

"Furthermore, she described the conversation as cordial. He asked that she not come, but she said Sill was intent on it. He then said he would do nothing to stop them from coming, but that they shouldn't expect much of a polite welcome. He had, quote, social responsibilities to think of, unquote." Truitt stood, stepping sideways to free himself from the table. "Doesn't sound to me like a man who would be shocked to find his daughter's lover in his yard."

"We had an argument in the fish house," Sill said feebly, pulling the rubber band from her hair. "It was terrible. That's what he was upset about."

Truitt waved his arm toward the open notebook on the table. "According to Faith, you provoked that argument, Sill. There were a couple of elderly people in the tent, and he kept motioning you outside so that no one could hear. But you insisted on referring to Faith as your lover in front of these people. Faith says that's what he blew a fuse about. Up until you used that word, Martin was being more civil than Faith had expected."

"He had to," Sill countered. "He was in public."

"Look, Sill, I'm not blaming you for the argument. I know what's it's like to feel rejected by your father, believe me. But I just don't buy that Martin was so upset with that exchange that he went into the house and pulled out a loaded gun."

He moved to the table and picked up the manila envelope. "And another thing. I want someone in this room to tell me about this. I want someone to explain to me why I get tears when I wave this thing around?"

He looked at each one in turn. They all averted their eyes, with the exception of Maralyn, who met his gaze calmly.

From his left came a rustling sound. Cammy eased from the sofa and smoothed out the wrinkles from her loose cotton shirt.

"I think you're right, Alby," she said. "Sill's lifestyle was a big deal to Martin, but maybe not big enough. I'd like to talk to you in private, if I could."

• • •

From her kitchen window, Zilah couldn't see the shed behind her house, but then she would have been disappointed all these years if she could have. The shed, with its streaked plank walls and carroty tin roof, would have looked shabby within view of the Alden house. It would have plunked her down in reality, much as the fence had done when Barry had taken his comealong into the side yard and tacked a roll of hog wire onto the line of posts. For days afterward she had been miserable, feeling like she was penned. But she soon learned to look past the fence. As the weeds grew and began to bend into the square holes, she even developed a fondness for it, seeing it as a sturdy perch and the Alden house a rare, crimson bird with its open beak pushing toward the sky.

She waited several minutes in front of the window, warm water from the sink faucet running over the jelly glass in her hand. Maybe they can't find it, she thought. Maybe it isn't in the shed at all. Maybe Barry left it in the hardware store, or gave it to the Langley boy, or carried it into the yard for a chore and then forgot it. She was about to go to the back door and holler *I'm sorry, I'm an old fool. It isn't there at all,* when she heard something knock against the rear of her house, and around the corner they came, Barry's wooden ladder jostling between them.

They weren't in enough of a hurry. She had wanted them to go quickly, to run across the railroad tracks and dash into the hardware store. Instead, they leaned the ladder against the side of a black vehicle and held a discussion before opening the back door and sliding the ladder toward the front. It stuck out, so after a little more talk, Gale climbed into the back and held the back door down while the curly-headed girl got into the driver's seat and started the engine.

They waved at her and started down the drive. "Hurry, hurry, hurry," she whispered.

She realized her sense of haste was unwarranted.

She knew what Barry would say: *Hell, woman, what's taken seventy years can wait another two minutes.* But sometimes she felt as though her whole life had been lived in periods of two minutes, always waiting for the next moment when it might all make sense and she could quit worrying. It was the worrying that was getting to her. She was half convinced it was the worrying that was making her so sick. And here were these young people thinking they had all the time in the world. Well, they don't. That was one thing she learned as a child. People were forever dividing time into right or wrong, good or bad, but time itself didn't work that way. It had no use for morality. It flickered and went out with as much sense as a blink.

She looked toward the Alden house. Four cars sat side by side along the fence. The light around them was low, as if the hazy sky was pressing against the earth and trying to flatten the sunlight beneath it. Storm clouds were gathering once again—she could see it in the dead green of the pecan tree leaves and the quake of the grass below her window.

"Maybe the storm'll push out the bad air," she said aloud. "I've been feeling like the air has gone bad lately."

It ain't bad air, Zilah. Barry's voice sounded so close that she clutched at her chest and jerked around. *Bad air comes from caves and ditches. This is a good place, Zilah. This is a very good place.*

Entering Greene's Hardware store was like walking into an iron blanket. Barry had been dead only a couple of months, but in the pyrexic weather of the South, two months was enough time to parboil any space. Behind the heat rolled out the smell of metal—tenpenny nails baking in their bin, lengths of double-loop chain wound around cylinders, empty mailboxes, reams of hardware cloth. Gale reached her arm through the back door portal, felt for the electrical switch, and flicked it on.

"I guess Zilah hasn't thought to turn the electricity off," she said.

Faith shifted the end of the ladder onto her shoulder. "Think we might be so lucky as to discover the air conditioner in working order?"

"What a lovely thought. Wait here."

It took her only seconds to find the thermostat on the south wall. She pushed aside a stand of rakes that had tilted forward in their barrel and clicked the adjuster to Cool. Instantly the hum of forced air filled the store.

She hurried toward the entrance, anxious to get on with her task. At Zilah's she had noticed Truitt's Dodge and the sheriff's patrol car on the other side of the fence. Her first impulse had been to run to Ella's house, to offer some sort of protection. But then she had looked at the upstairs bedroom and seen Katie Pru waving from the window, all smiles. *My child is fine,* she had assured herself. *And the adults can fend for themselves.* The guilt, however, remained. She could not get past the thought that she should be with her family and not here clambering over galvanized tubs and plastic garbage cans to satisfy what was little more than a hunch fed by a daffy old lady.

She picked up the rear end of the ladder, and together she and Faith carried it through the store.

"Watch out," Faith said. "Bags of cement to your right."

Gale sidestepped and held the ladder out in front of her to allow Faith room to turn. *But this is darker than a hunch,* she thought. A tightness pinched her chest. *Linnie committed suicide and now her grandson was dead. Tom committed suicide. . . . So many things get passed down.* She had to be here.

"I've found it," Faith announced. "Hole in the ceiling, middle of the west wall—just like the lady said." She set her end of the ladder on the floor. "Hopefully he ran the electricity up here, although you never know. Some of these Depression babies are so damn cheap."

Gale rested the ladder on the floor and moved down the aisle to the wall. The attic entrance was a three-foot-square opening in the ceiling with two medium-sized hooks extending over the lip of the hole. Peering into the opening, she could discern the outline of rafters beneath the roof, overlaid with lengths of board.

"All right," Faith said. She bent down for the ladder. "This is why we've gathered here today."

Together they lifted the ladder above their heads and angled it so that the two eyebolts screwed into its ends slid easily over the hooks. Faith jostled the ladder to check its stability.

"I'll go first," she said.

"No, I'll go."

"Listen," Faith said. "My father was a builder. I grew up on rickety boards. Wait just a second."

She disappeared around an aisle but was back in less than a minute, a nail apron with heavy pockets tied around her waist. A hammer hung from her hip. She smiled grimly and started up the ladder. As her head crested the top, she paused and extended her arm into the space. "Light switch on the floor."

Gale heard a click. Above her the attic space glowed yellow.

"What do you see?"

"Hard to say." Faith reached into the apron, pulled out a nail and hurled it into the room. It clattered across the floor. "Don't seem to be any rats."

She pulled herself into a sitting position on the attic floor and stuck out her hand to help Gale up. It was evident to Gale as soon as she topped the opening that while Barry didn't scrimp on the electricity in his storage area, his largesse hadn't extended to cool air. She made a face as she stood up.

"What kind of effect do you think the heat would have on whatever you think you're going to find?" Faith asked.

"I don't know. They say dry heat is good for preservation."

"There's no such thing as dry heat in Georgia."

Gale edged past several wheelbarrows and drop spreaders until she came to the wall that divided the hardware store from the photography studio. It was of a simple board construction, but the majority of it was hidden behind stacks of hardware supplies. Gale moved in and around cartons of fertilizer and cleaner. Behind a tower of peat moss bags, she found the door.

At first she was amazed at how easily the door gave, as if the years of disuse had had no effect. But once in the room, it was evident that disuse had not been a problem. Barry Greene may have been a decent man and a damn good storekeeper, but he wasn't above stealing a little space from an absent neighbor. The caged bulb of a reel light, its cord snaking from a small hole in the dividing wall, hung from a hook near the door. The weak light barely lit the runover from the hardware store. Gale picked her way past unopened cartons of Miracle-Gro and stacks of packaged saw blades, taking stock. "Lightbulbs. Hornet Killer. Magnetic Stud Finder."

Faith rustled through boxes behind her. "Doesn't look like much here."

The light grew more anemic the further from the door Gale moved, causing her to regret her decision to leave her satchel—and flashlight—in the car. She found herself unable to read the names on the boxes, relegated to simply identifying the indistinct pictures.

"Some sort of plumbing fixture. A fan. Something that looks like screws."

She was along the northern wall now, virtually working blind. The light had dwindled to extinction, submerging this corner of the room into blackness. She held her hands out, her eyes straining in the dark.

She stumbled. Her hands shot out and slammed against the wall. Splinters dug into her palms as her hands slid down the rough wood. Her knee hit a metal tube.

"Gale!" Faith sounded frantic. "Where the hell are you?"

The beam from the reel light swung in her direction. It made huge arching movements over the corner where she lay.

"Keep the beam there, Faith. Don't move it. Hold the beam steady right where you have it."

It's not a big cache, she thought. But then, maybe some caches don't have to be big. Under her throbbing knee was the leg of a tripod. Next to it, placed carefully one after the other, were four old cameras and a mechanical apparatus she couldn't identify. She dragged a nearby box toward her.

"What the hell are you doing? Are you all right?"

"I'm fine," she answered. "Just don't move the light."

The box was filled with cardboard rectangles of different sizes, all either bone white or a curious purplish black. She gingerly lifted one from the top. It was blank, with the exception of a fancy border embossed around its edges, and the words *Malcolm Hinson, Photographer, Statlers Cross, Georgia* printed in gold script in the lower right-hand corner. She began taking out the pieces in handfuls. All were blank.

The cardboard matts spilled from her lap and onto the floor. She continued to dig, piling more matts onto the mound in front of her. When her fingers touched the small stack of paper at the bottom of the box, she swept the cardboard from her lap to make a space, and gently lifted it to her.

Rats had gnawed off the lower outside corner, but the type was still legible. The name of the pageant was *In the Footsteps of Glory*. She had never known what it was called—the title had been lost in the aftermath of notoriety. The play wasn't very long, a mere fifty pages of dialogue. She ran her finger over the name scrawled along the upper margin of the title page. Justin Cane— Linnie's husband.

Gale smiled as she turned the first page. "Faith," she said softly, "you're not going to believe what I've found."

"Well, okay, you found something. But can you walk? Have you been amputated below the knee?"

"Wait a second. I'm coming. Just don't move the light."

She turned several of the pages, skimming through the notes Justin had jotted in the margins. His character had been named Clarence Walker, and from a quick perusal, it appeared to have been the male lead. "Move stage left." "Make a disgruntled noise." "Take her in your arms."

The latter was written during a scene between Clarence and Megan Dempsey, "a young lady." Linnie's part. Linnie and her husband, Justin, had been cast to play opposite each other.

"Gale . . ."

"All right. I'm coming."

She lifted the script up by its tied spine. When she did, an uncreased letter, writing crammed from corner to corner on the front and back, fluttered to the floor.

There was no date. There was no formal salutation or signature. It started simply.

Darling.

You can't realize what it means to see you every day and not be able to touch you. I'll be sitting in the church, practicing my lines, all proper and good, but really I'm thinking about your mouth and your tongue and the sweet smell of your hair when we lay in the grass at night.

The light went out and Gale found herself in darkness again. She sat motionless on the floor, not remembering how to move.

"That's it," Faith said. "I'm coming in after you."

Gale was silent. There was no date, and there was no signature, but she recognized the large flowing "L" carefully scripted in the corner.

21

Widowhood had always been an enigma to Truitt. He was never sure where the starting gate was located. His aunt had become a widow upon divorce, his sister through night rages against napalm and Agent Orange. He suspected it was one of the reasons he had not yet married—he didn't want to look at his wife and understand that part of her had already given him up, her sight focused on a future bullet ripping through his chest.

Sitting next to her on the den sofa, he couldn't tell at what point Cammy Cane had begun widowhood. Her face was blotchy from crying, and the muscles around her mouth had loosened until her lips seemed dragged apart in shock. She refused to open her eyes.

Two bed pillows and some folded sheets took up one end of the sage sofa, and he found himself almost wallowing on them as he shifted to face her. He pushed the pillows aside roughly and took his notepad from his pocket. "What did you want to tell me, Cammy?"

She twisted Sill's rubber band around her fingers furiously, belying the calmness in her voice.

"Sill wasn't responsible for Martin's death," she said. "Ella thinks it's simpler if we let it go at that, but it'll eat Sill up someday. I won't permit it."

"I understand that."

"No, you don't. Not really. But what I want you to do, Alby, is to believe me. I want you to listen to me and understand that what I'm telling you is the truth."

In the distance Truitt heard thunder. "I'm listening, Cammy."

The rubber band made a fat orange ring around Cammy's finger. "Do you know what Martin used to say about you?" she asked. "He said you weren't born with the hunting instinct, just like some women weren't born with the maternal instinct. He figured you chose law enforcement because it gave you some order to go by. You rejected hunting, but what you never understood was that the hunter lives by order. In the woods everything has a place and a cause. He'd come in from taking you out and he'd say, 'He just don't see it. That boy just don't see it.'"

Truitt smiled. "The lesson wasn't totally lost. Martin was a very good teacher."

"Not as good as he wanted to be. There were a lot of things that he wasn't as good at as he wanted to be."

"You could probably say that about any man."

"But not every man is haunted."

Truitt took a deep breath. "Haunted by what, Cammy?"

The rubber band wove in and out of her fingers. "There's an order in what I'm about to tell you, Alby. You have to try and see it."

The gauzy curtains over the French doors had been pushed to one side. The rain began to pelt the glass spasmodically, a dollop here, a trickle there.

"I'm listening to you, Cammy," he repeated softly. "What was Martin haunted by?"

She pulled at the rubber band until he was afraid it would pop against her hand. "You've found out about Maralyn's abortion."

"Yes."

"That was an uneasy thing with Martin. I think they honestly believed at the time it was the only thing they could do—small town, prominent family, the whole nine yards. But when the doctors told Maralyn she'd never have children, well, Martin came to see it as the work of God. They had sinned—they had been punished. Or rather, she had been. That was Martin's view. Her body. Her sin."

"He had no responsibility?"

"He wasn't the mother."

"But Maralyn seemed to feel they had an understanding."

"Maralyn wanted understanding."

"So Martin was involved in an antiabortion group. What, as penance? Revenge?"

Cammy shook her head. "No, Alby. I know this is going to sound strange, but I think he did it as a pinch, a jab in order to wake himself up."

"Why would you say that?"

She spoke carefully. "I heard it once said that young women who undergo abuse sleepwalk through their lives. That's what Martin did. I think there were only two times when Martin ever felt happy—when he was working for the church or carrying a gun. And I think in his mind the two were alike."

"You mean they gave him power."

"No, they gave him salvation."

On the bookcases the dried snakeskins seemed poised to slither to the ground. The natural light through the windows had dimmed. He rapped his pencil on the wire binding of the notepad and studied Cammy closely.

"Has Sill had an abortion?"

Cammy's eyes finally opened. They wandered around the room for a moment, then settled on the mounted squirrels posing on the trunk in front of the sofa. "No," she said flatly. "Sill's never had an abortion."

"Then why did she react the way she did when I showed her the pamphlet?"

"She had a miscarriage."

"When?"

"About a year ago." Cammy inhaled deeply. "She's never told us who the boy was. We didn't even know she was pregnant. She went straight to Maralyn's clinic. Not for an abortion, mind you. She wanted the baby. She was just trying to figure out a way to tell us."

"What happened?"

"One day she went to the clinic for a prenatal visit. There was a protest going on outside. Faith was an escort—they hadn't met before. Faith and several other volunteers tried to get her into the building, but it got ugly. They were knocked down. There Sill was, lying on the sidewalk, with people standing over her, yelling at her, shoving pictures into her face. The police were there—it lasted probably less than a minute. But a minute was enough. She claims someone kicked her. A week later she lost the baby."

"Did Sill tell you all this?"

"No." Her voice was a whisper. "I was there. I was

a protester. I tried to get to Sill—she was on the ground and I could hear her screaming." Tears welled in her eyes. "I could hear my baby screaming—a mother can always tell when it's her own child crying—and I couldn't get to her."

"Did she see you?"

"Yes. She said she forgave me. But Faith came to visit her when she was healing from the miscarriage; it was Faith who took care of her. She didn't want me around." She ignored the tears inching down her cheeks and into her mouth. "We've agreed not to talk about it."

Truitt gazed up at the halo of windows. "So, was Martin with you that day?"

Her smile was weak. "Usually he was, but not that day. He was hunting."

"What did he say when you told him?"

"We didn't. Sill didn't want him to know. Martin could get so . . . angry, Alby. It was best that he just not know."

"Not know that someone in a group he supported kicked his daughter and possibly caused her to lose his grandchild?"

"Best he not know she was ever pregnant."

Truitt walked to the writer's desk and switched on the lamp. Above him rain beat against the etched glass panes. He felt bewildered, as he had the weeks following his father's death. He hadn't known either man.

"You say Sill was lying on the sidewalk. Did she see who kicked her?"

Cammy's shoulders sagged. She covered her eyes with her hands. "Yes. There'd been an article on him in *Atlanta* magazine the week before, so she recognized his face. She was lying half on her side, half on her back, and she says he leaned over and spat on her. Then he reared back his leg and kicked her in the stomach."

"Who was it, Cammy?"

When she removed her hands from her face, they were wet. She stared at them before wiping them on her pants.

"A prominent advertising executive who heard the call of God, Alby. He got a lot of mileage out of that— a lot of new members to the cause."

Truitt searched his memory. "Ryan Teller?"

She nodded, then turned to him, almost pleadingly. "But, honestly, Alby, there's no way of knowing if he caused her to miscarry. I mean, no matter what she says, there were so many people—it could have been anybody. And it was a week before she lost that baby. The doctor told her there was no way of knowing the reason."

Truitt was silent a moment. "So, Cammy, did Martin get Teller his job?"

When Cammy finally spoke, she sounded tired. "The Methodist Church doesn't work that way. But Martin called a few people. Maybe it helped." She looked at Truitt. "He was so impressed with Ryan. He said the man could see clear to his soul. I think Martin believed Ryan could help him—that Ryan could find him that salvation."

"And did he?"

Her voice was bitter. "No. That's obvious, isn't it? And now I have to look out for Sill. I can't let her take the blame for this, Alby. She's not responsible for Martin's death. I don't want her haunted like her father."

The thunder was still distant. The rain on the French doors had slackened.

"So who is responsible for Martin's death, Cammy?"

Her eyes grew hard. At that moment Truitt knew precisely when her widowhood had begun.

"Why don't you find the slut who's been sleeping with him?"

• • •

Gale sat in the Cherokee with her legs drawn up under her. The afternoon sky had split into tables, a thin band of yellow light topping a blackened base. The rain had let up, but only temporarily. Out the car window she could still see dribbles of water disappear into the photography studio's broken glass panes.

Faith appeared at the studio's left window. She grinned as she stretched a length of duct tape in front of her face, clipped it, and stuck it across the holes left by their inexpert replacement of the boards. She repeated the process, covering every gap to protect the canvases inside.

The canvases were little more than a curiosity to Gale now. She balanced the pageant script in her lap. In her hands she held Linnie's letter. Gently, she turned it to the light.

I did something for you yesterday. No, that is wrong. I did it for me. It was a small thing, but I felt so much excitement that afterwards, I ran all the way home, closed the door to my room, and just laughed. I was at the parsonage, picking up the preacher's shirts for cleaning. He wasn't at home, and something made me bold. I went to that picture hanging over the desk and took it right off the wall. I had the pin you gave me hidden on the inside of my skirt. I took hold of the lock of my hair that was on that picture and yanked it off. Then I picked, picked, picked with the pin until my name was gone. "Linnie Glynn Cane don't belong to you anymore," I said. Then I put the picture back together best I could, hung it on the wall, and walked out of that house like nobody's business. I ran all the way home, laughing so loud I know people heard me and wondered. It wasn't until supper that I remembered I had forgotten the preacher's shirts.

I put that lock of hair in my pocket for you. Sometimes I forget how black the days were. My thoughts had grown so small. It was much easier to be angry than to think. But then, you would say I was being too harsh—"You can't grow, Linnie, what you can't water." I imagine there are some places where thoughts spring out of the ground like dandelions, not needing the least bit of feeding. But not here in Statlers Cross. You knew that when you came, didn't you? You can't heal yourself here because no one will allow that you're ailing. It's all a matter of God's will and woman's duty. Did I mention that I never did go back to get the preacher's shirts?

J. is getting more difficult. He doesn't like it when I tell him no. He wants more babies. I tried to make him understand. "Babies are a blessing," I says to him. "I love little Jules. But babies sap you, Justin. They take your breath and sometimes it feels like your life is going with it." He hit me again last night. I started to hit back, I was so mad, but then I remembered what you said. It is better if I just bide my time until we leave. I've been making clothes for Jules on the sly. When it's time, he'll be the nicest looking boy in New York.

The letter ended there, the last line barely fitting on the page. Gale gazed out the car window at the strips of duct tape crisscrossing the broken glass. Her chest hurt. All she could think of was getting home to Katie Pru.

A rumble of thunder hastened Faith to the car. She wrenched open the car door and climbed in.

"Done," she said. "What do we do now?"

"I've got to get back and let Nadianna go home. I think she's had enough of a trial period for one day."

"But I thought you were on the trail, in hot pursuit, or whatever the metaphor is."

Gale opened the script and placed the letter in the middle. She carefully slid both into her satchel. "I've got to get these documents under some sort of protection. They've been through enough."

Faith started the engine. She nodded toward the script. "So, have you found anything interesting there?"

"I don't know," Gale said honestly. "I need to think about it some more." She buckled the satchel and draped her arms over it. "Do you know anything about practical nurses?"

"Not much. I know they don't have to meet the same requirements as registered nurses. My grandmother had one."

"At a nursing home?"

"Oh, no. She lived in the house with her. Why?"

Gale sighed. "I don't know. Let's get home."

Faith pulled away from the building slowly, careful to avoid the potholes in the asphalt. The Cherokee crept past the drugstore, past the wooden pallets next to Langley's pickup, and turned left at the Dumpster.

Surprisingly, all the parking places along the main street were filled; the grassy verge at the base of the railroad track was hidden by a string of parked cars.

And then they saw the sign. A woman in a white dress suit and jogging shoes walked by the Cherokee, a poster flapping in hand. The picture on it was in color—a mess of reds and browns. Then Gale recognized with shock the shape of a dismembered leg, a tiny bloodied skull. Across the top, in bold black letters, were the words *Baby Killer*.

Beside her Faith let out a sharp hiss of air. "Jesus Christ," she murmured. "What the hell is going on?"

Dozens of people strolled along the main street, all well dressed, all with signs. Several women, young children clinging to their arms, pushed baby strollers across the road, while the men gathered in a loose pack at the base of the tracks. There were at least fifty people. A beat-up white sedan pulled past the Cherokee and double-parked along the side of the road. A man with a camera and a woman with a reporter's pad jumped out. As they hurried toward the men, the pack broke open, and Ryan Teller started briskly up the ledge to the railroad track.

At the top he stopped and faced the crowd. Gale quickly rolled down her window as he lifted his arms.

"People, listen to me here a minute." He waited, face grim, while the crowd gathered at the base of the hill. When it had quieted, he continued. "I want to thank y'all for coming today. It's a far drive for most of you, and it was short notice. But we were thwarted from doing our work Saturday. Let us commence today. Everyone join me atop this hill, please."

The crowd started up the incline, parents carrying the strollers stretcher-style. Faith leaned over and looked out Gale's window.

"What the hell is going on?" she repeated.

"I think we're about to witness a protest," Gale answered. She watched as Teller pointed up and down the tracks. The crowd began to drift into a line. Gale glanced nervously at the crossing. "I hate to sound melodramatic, but if they're going to stage a protest on the railroad tracks, I'd just as soon be on the other side. If they can block a clinic, they can certainly block a ramp."

Faith sped up. As they passed the mill village, a group of children ran shouting across the mill grounds, followed more cautiously by several adults. The protestors drifted toward the crossing, their graphic red signs high in the air.

Faith put on the blinker and crossed over the hump. As they pulled into Ella's driveway, the front door of the house blew open and Alby Truitt emerged.

He was halfway to the road when Gale stepped

from the car. The protestors were lined up along the tracks, positioned roughly six feet apart. They held their signs above their heads, facing not the shops and any passersby, but the row of sparse houses on the track's northern side.

Teller walked up and down the ranks. "We do not speak. We do not have to speak. Hold your signs high. Let the dead speak!"

The signs thrust into the air; the cardboard bowed, making swift whipping sounds. Far down the track a baby wailed. The photographer stood halfway up the ledge, his camera clicking. Leaving Faith at the car, Gale slung her satchel over her shoulder and followed Truitt to the street.

"Reverend Teller," Truitt yelled. "I need to talk with you a minute."

Teller slid down the incline, joining Truitt in the middle of the street. The photographer and reporter stationed themselves at the bottom of the ledge, well within hearing distance.

"What's going on here, Reverend?" Truitt asked.

Teller smiled. "Just some prayer, Sheriff."

Truitt glanced at Gale standing by the roadside, then turned and looked at the protestors. "Prayer? I must have missed the amen."

"No amen in this prayer, Sheriff. It'll go on until we've changed a few things."

"Were you planning to change a few things on Saturday?"

The two men were less than ten feet from Gale, their voices lowered but still audible. Behind them the signs made blood-colored splotches against the stores' roofline.

"What are you talking about, Mr. Truitt?" Teller's smile locked.

"My deputy heard you say you couldn't do your work on Saturday. Why's that?"

Teller scanned the sheriff's face. "You've got an abortionist in that house."

"Answer my quest—"

"You've got a baby killer in there. She actually aids in the killing of babies. I know this for a fact. I've met her before."

"Mr. Teller, what were you—"

"Have you asked her about Martin? If you can kill a baby, what kind of moral quandary would you have about killing a man?" He turned to the protesters and raised his voice. "Isn't that right, people? Once God's ultimate law is broken, all other laws fall away. Once it is acceptable to rip a baby from its mother's womb, then society is lost."

The shutter clicked; the signs whipped in the air. Truitt gazed steadily at the minister. "I tell you what, Mr. Teller," he said. "I am going to give you one more chance. I am in the middle of an active investigation, and I've just received information that suggests you might know more than you've been letting on. Now, you can either cooperate now or you can go to the station."

Teller's smile widened just a fraction, and his voice dropped even lower.

"I think, sir, if you want to hold me for questioning, it'll have to be at the station." He glanced at the line of people standing on the tracks. "Others will carry on my work. They might even feel a bit more passionate about it once they see me carted off by the county sheriff."

Truitt shrugged, his jaw set. "I ain't doing the carting, preacher. I've got more important things to do." He whirled away and stalked back to the house. As he reached the jaguar, he hollered. "Ruch! Take this penny-ante preacher to the station. Find out what he knows about Saturday. And get somebody over here to take these folks' names."

Truitt sprinted up the stairs and disappeared inside as Ruch headed across the yard. A murmur went up from the crowd. Teller turned and motioned them to silence.

"Stay here and continue with the job, people. I won't be long. We've broken no laws, and even if we have, there are no laws stronger than the death of a child. Now, let us sing to the Lord."

Strains of "Amazing Grace" rolled dolefully from the tracks. Gale searched the figures for a familiar face. There were none. At the end of the track the people from the mill village eyed the strangers with suspicion.

"Mama."

Katie Pru and Nadianna stood hand in hand next to the pecan tree, staring transfixed at the protesters. They had both been running—their breath came quickly and their faces were bright red. In her hand Katie Pru held a strand of honeysuckle. It fell to the ground as she turned to Nadianna, her arms outstretched, begging to be picked up.

Shit. Gale ran through the yard and grabbed her daughter into a hug. She turned to Nadianna.

"I'm sorry I was so long. Here." She fumbled in her satchel and pulled out a twenty-dollar bill. "Let's talk about it later, okay? If you don't mind, I'd just like to get Katie Pru out of here."

Nadianna took the money wordlessly. She continued to stare at the protesters. Gale reached out and touched her arm.

"Are you okay, Nadianna?"

She nodded her head. "I'm fine, Mrs. Grayson. It's just so shocking, isn't it? But then, I suppose that's their point. It's so awful we'd just rather not see it."

Gale hiked Katie Pru onto her hip. "It's awful, all right. But the alternative is awful as well." She picked up the satchel and tried to sling it over her shoulder. It fell. Nadianna reached out and gently adjusted it into place.

"Ask Katie Pru how it went, Mrs. Grayson," she said. "Then call me when you like. I think I better get home."

Gale turned and headed toward the back fields, looking for the bundle of blackberry vines that signaled the mouth of the path. She hadn't walked the path in seventeen years, but it was still there, used annually by hunters chasing wounded deer onto Ella's property. After a short way she set Katie Pru onto the ground and pointed to a break in the grasses.

"Come on, K.P.," she said. "We're going on a hunt."

We create ghosts to warn ourselves that the world isn't forgiving.
  —Mason Jacks, writer, during a lecture at the Praterton Book Club, 1987

22

Faith Baskins stood next to the living room coffee table, hands in pockets, smudges on her face and glasses. From outside the Alden house Truitt could hear the distant wail of a gospel song. Faith shot him a wry smile.

"So you haven't finished with me. More questions about my washed car?"

Truitt shook his head. "Nope. We called the car wash. Seems you're a regular. They said they didn't find anything out of the ordinary in your car. Besides, I've already found what I was looking for."

She raised her eyebrows. "Really?"

"Yeah. But that's not what I wanted to ask you

about." He laid three photographs on the table. "Take a look at these for me, please, Ms. Baskins."

She picked them up and leaned against the sofa arm, chewing the inside of her lip thoughtfully. "The last of Martin," she said. "God, life is something, isn't it?"

Truitt waited a moment. "Tell me about the one with you in it."

She studied the photo, her finger tapping its edge. "Sly photographer, I'll tell you that much. I didn't even know I was being photographed."

"A problem for you?"

She shrugged. "No. Sill probably wouldn't care for it much. She's not exactly enamored of her dad, you know." She looked at him, her eyes angry behind her glasses. "Gale told me he beat Sill. Did you know that?"

"No." Even if he had, he wouldn't have believed it. His wife, perhaps. But his child? How could Martin take in another man's child while beating his own? How could he be so loving of a dishonored fifteen-year-old, yet so terrifying that his daughter wouldn't tell him the circumstances of her miscarriage?

"If I had known," he said wearily, "I would have tried to stop him." He sank into the horsehair chair. "About the photo . . ."

Faith placed the photographs on the table. "It was before he knew who I was, I can tell you that. He was actually quite friendly up until Sill introduced us. And even then, he tried. Sill kept prodding him, like she wanted him to blow up."

"And he did."

"That's right."

"How many times had you met him before Saturday?"

"None. I'd never laid eyes on him. I'd talked to him on the phone the one time, but that's all."

"You're quite sure."

"Believe me, I'd remember." She lightly thumped

one photo with her nail. "This one's interesting, isn't it? What a peculiar expression on his face."

"That's the last picture of him."

Her brow crinkled. "Jesus. Wouldn't you like to know what he was looking at? Isn't there some process where you guys can blow up the picture and see what's reflected in his pupils?"

Truitt scooped the photographs up and slid them into an envelope. "To tell you the truth, I don't think it's going to be necessary. Okay, Ms. Baskins. Thank you very much."

Gale and Katie Pru emerged in the Robertsons' backyard as lightning slashed the sky. The storm was moving in quicker than Gale had anticipated. The front door opened as they rounded the corner of the house.

"Goodness gracious, get yourselves in here. Y'all look like wet rabbits running out of that brush!"

"I almost misjudged that one," Gale said, guiding Katie Pru into the house. "I thought surely we had more time before the rain hit."

"Sometimes there's no judging. Y'all come on in."

The woman looked to be in her early thirties, with coppery hair clipped just below the ear. She wore a well-cut pair of navy walking shorts and a silky white top. And she was draped in gold, from the beaded earrings that danced beside her cheek to the dainty gold bracelet that encircled her ankle. Gale suppressed a smile. She could damn well imagine what came out of this sorority sister's mouth when she found a snake in the toilet.

"Mrs. Robertson," Gale said. "I'm Gale Grayson, and this is Katie Pru. We were here earlier this morning to borrow a key from your husband."

The woman's porcelain face broke into a grin. "Oh, I knew that," she said. "I saw you out the window when I got up this morning. I don't think Mal expected you to be so efficient. Did you find anything?"

"Well, I didn't find any photographs, which is what I was looking for. But it wasn't a wasted trip. I just wanted to return the key and talk to your husband."

"He's not here, and he won't be until the weekend." Her blue eyes widened. She clutched Gale's arm with bright red nails. "I mean, goodness, I hope you didn't make a special trip."

Gale laughed, surprised to find this well-dressed young thing so infectious. "Well, I'd hate to present false pretenses, but I didn't make the trip just to return the key." She paused. "I'm sorry, Mrs. Robertson, I don't know your name."

"Jen. And it's not Robertson. I still go by Butler. It took a lot of talking to Mal, but I convinced him I didn't feel like a Jen Robertson and I wasn't going to be one."

Gale smiled, thinking of Ella setting her jawbone onto that morsel. "Well, Jen, I didn't find any photographs in the studio, but Mal was telling me that y'all had found a few and framed them. I was wondering if they were hung where I could take a look?"

"Sure. They're in the living room. Don't mind the mess. I just let the place go when Mal's not here."

Gale took Katie Pru's hand and followed Jen into the room to the right of the central door, doubting she would find a mess. The wooden floors glowed with polyurethane, and the log walls were covered with scores of framed paintings and contemporary photographs—all, Gale noted, selected with some taste. The paintings were predominantly watercolors: light, airy flowers and liquid cityscapes. The photographs were black-and-white and showed a similar style.

"It's Mal's hobby," Jen said. "I say he inherited it from his grandfather, but he just shrugs it off."

She led them past an expensive pastel vegetable-print sofa to an English oak cupboard. The cupboard doors were open, displaying a sizable selection of pewter and Roseville pottery.

Jen stopped and closed one of the cupboard doors.

"Here they are," she said. "You can take them down if you like."

There were two pictures, both mounted on pieces of the purplish cardboard backing she had found in the studio attic. *Malcolm Hinson, Photographer, Statlers Cross, Georgia* was scrolled in the corner of each one.

The one on the bottom was of three girls dressed in their Sunday best, holding what looked like hymnals. Their mouths were open in song. Gale recognized all three from photographs on the living room coffee table—two of them were Stone girls, and the third was a Falcon. The composition was good, but it held Gale's attention for only a second. She stared at the photograph above it.

Gale had seen only one photograph of Parrish Singleton, in the Calwyn County Historical Society's single published book. That picture had been taken in the 1950s near the end of his life, when his role in the history of the county had been nothing more than a caption. Even at fifty he had been an elderly man— hollow-eyed with a pulled-putty face and a slack mouth. As a cruel teenager, she had studied the picture and wondered how he could have ever had the imagination to come south with no other aim than to write and produce a play. It had seemed such an utterly preposterous ideal. And one that was simply out of the range of this rot-toothed coot grasping a cigarette in bulbous fingers.

That teenager should have seen the photograph she was looking at now, she thought. Malcolm Hinson had caught him in action, with shirtsleeves rolled up against the Georgia sun. He was standing with an open script in his hand, and he was gesturing—the light accentuated the long sinews of his bare arm. With his dark hair slicked back with sweat, his jaw jutted slightly forward, he could have passed for an expert country preacher. He must have seen the irony in the photo as well, for scrawled across the bottom of the photograph were the words *Great shot, Malcolm. Jesus Saves. Brother Parrish.*

In the upper corner of the picture, pressed flat by the glass, was a lock of dark brown hair.

"We didn't have to get this one framed—we found it this way. Mal says it's one of the best photographs from that era he's ever seen. We don't know who Brother Parrish is, but Mal keeps saying he's going to take it around town and ask people if they know anything about him."

Gale felt her heart sink. "Sounds like he and I are on similar missions." She mustered a weak smile. "You know, I was half hoping . . . well, when Mal said you were doing eldercare, I started thinking maybe Malcolm Hinson was still alive."

Jen's jewelry jingled as she put her hands on her hips. "Well, he is. It's just that he's so darn stubborn sometimes. He won't say a word about the man in the photo. In fact, I keep it hidden behind the door here because he gets so mad when he sees it." She grinned. "I'm really fond of him, actually, although there are days I don't think we're both going to make it. He owned this house—and some other property—and agreed to deed it all to us if we'd take him out of the nursing home and look after him. So I grandfather sit. And 'sit' is an accurate word. That man rarely leaves his room. Of course, at ninety-eight, who could blame him? He just prefers to stay there in the back bedroom with our cats and his grumpiness."

The protestors were still singing as Truitt crossed the railroad tracks and headed for the mill village. The sky was dangerously black; a few parents had already broken ranks and were inching their baby strollers down the grassy bank. The small crowd that had gathered on the mill grounds and along the storefronts was dispersing, too, the threat of weather evidently stronger than the treat of spectacle. As he neared the crowd, he noticed people looking his way, quizzical expressions on their faces. Christ, he thought, I don't have time for public relations right now. Nodding with what he hoped was a reassuring grin, he changed course and hurried through the old mill entrance.

The first thing that struck him was the separateness. Ahead of him were woods, above him the sky, yet the two remaining walls were enough to divide him from the outside world. He could still hear the protesters' song, but it was dwindling; he could hear the slice of the grass as the townspeople ambled away, but it was faint and could have been mistaken for the sighs of millworkers a century gone.

A chill swept over him, and he quickened his pace. In his hand was the envelope of photographs.

If she hadn't sobbed, he would have walked right past her. She huddled on a slab of stone, the bottom of her beige shift slick with mud. She didn't look at him as he approached.

"Nadianna," he said softly. "It's about to storm. What are you doing out here?"

She rocked forward slightly and grasped her elbows. "Nothing. Just didn't want to go inside, that's all. Cooler out here."

"Not by much, I'll tell you that. Come on. Let me walk you to your house and you can tell me what's wrong.'

"No, sir. I'm fine where I am."

She wiped her nose with the shoulder of her dress. Truitt pulled a handkerchief from his pocket. "Well, I've got something I want to talk to you about, Nadianna," he said, handing her the handkerchief. "Something's been bothering me ever since I got your photographs developed. Excellent work, by the way. No wonder you've won awards."

She blotted her eyes with the linen square and carefully folded it in quarters. "What's been bothering you?"

Truitt flipped open the envelope. "I want you to

take a look at this photo. It was the last picture on the roll. I want you to tell me about it."

Wordlessly, she took it. Her gasp was audible, followed by a sob so sharp Truitt felt the pain in his chest.

"It's Mr. Cane," she whispered.

"I know. I want you to tell me what was happening when you took it."

The picture trembled in her hand. "He had just come from the fish house. He was angry at his daughter. He was on his way to the kitchen."

"And where were you?"

"In the food tent."

"And you just stepped up and shot the picture?"

"Yes."

"I see." Truitt leaned over her. "What's been bothering me, Nadianna, is the expression on his face. Look at it for a second, would you? How would you describe it?"

Her chin puckered and her tears fell freely. She held the picture tightly between her fingers and said nothing.

"Well, I've been studying it and studying it," he said, "and I'll tell you what I think it is. Shock mixed with fear, but there's something else. Don't you see it? Don't you see something else in his face?"

When she didn't answer, he straightened and shook his head. "I've been trying to figure it out, and it occurred to me that it might have to do with what he was looking at. At first I thought maybe he was looking at Sill, but that was wrong. She was behind him. And then I thought he might be looking toward the house, or at the crowd under the tent, but then I realized the angle of his face was all wrong for that. He wasn't looking away from or past the camera, Nadianna. He was looking *directly* at it."

Her head fell forward. Truitt reached down and grabbed the photograph before she could crumple it in her hand.

"He was looking at you, Nadianna, wasn't he?"

Her sobs racked her body. Truitt crouched beside her and waited until she quieted.

"Where did you meet him, Nadianna?" he asked gently. "How did it start?"

It was a minute before she answered. When she did, the words came out as smoothly as if rehearsed, a fact he didn't doubt—how else would this young woman have spent the past two days?

"I met him at the poultry plant about a year ago. He had come to give a talk. I knew he was married. My mother used to work for Mrs. Cane and when I was little, I'd go over there on days when she had to iron. I always thought Mrs. Cane was the quietest woman in the world. Not quiet in a good way, but in a sad way. So when he came to the plant and everyone said he was Martin Cane from Statlers Cross, I knew right away who he was. He was the man who had made that woman so quiet."

She looked at Truitt and lifted her chin slightly. "She was sad before I started with her husband, Sheriff Truitt. And he was also. It had nothing to do with me. It was before me and bigger than me, too."

"Statlers Cross is a small town. How did you manage an affair?"

"We never met here. We always met in Praterton, on the night I'd have classes at the art center." She pointed out an indentation in the soil beneath the stone slab. "We had a signal. On the mornings of my class, he would leave a piece of old glass in this hole—green he'd make it; brown he couldn't."

She looked at him defiantly. "I never meant him to leave his wife," she said. "But a man's got responsibilities, and Martin Cane didn't want any."

"What kind of responsibilities, Nadianna?"

"A month ago, I found out I was pregnant. I didn't want him to divorce Cammy—I'd made my decision, and I wasn't about to break up a marriage because of a choice I made. You know what he told me? He said he had a cousin who was an abortion nurse. He said I should see her about taking care of the problem—he'd pay for it. Well, how was I suppose to react to that? I knew he was in one of those groups. He'd told me about it. And here he goes wanting to kill our baby. I got mad, Sheriff, there's no other word for it. I called him Saturday afternoon and told him I was coming to the barbecue, and I was talking to his family—to the whole county, if I had to—and I'd make sure he supported his child." The tears spilled down her face. "Do you know what he told me? He said I'd better stay away—that he'd kill either me or himself before he'd let me tell the world about our baby. I didn't believe him. I didn't believe he wanted me to abort our baby, really. It wasn't until I heard the shot and I knew what he had done that I understood he had meant all of it."

"Where were you when you heard the shot, Nadianna?"

"Outside. In the parking lot."

"You were leaving? Why?"

She took a deep breath. "After I took his picture, I ran around to the front of the house. I could hear yelling in the kitchen. But I snuck into the house and found him in the den."

"Were the two of you alone?"

"Yes. I told Martin I was sorry, but I had to do it. I had to do it for the baby."

"What did he say?"

He accused me of killing him. He pulled away and ran upstairs. I got angry and left. Then I heard it. Not more than a few minutes later, I heard the shot."

"And what did you do after that?"

"I ran to my car and went home. And it took me exactly half an hour to figure out that this baby was all there is. Martin didn't understand that. He was a poor soul drowned in sadness. I didn't see it until it was too late. If I had, I'd have never been with him."

Truitt ran his hands over his face, trying to rub feeling back into it. "You're the second person today who's told me how sad Martin was. I never saw it,

Nadianna. I've know suicides before. He didn't fit the profile."

"Martin didn't come off as sad." Her narrow eyes widened, so that for the first time he could see the pure clarity in their blueness. "He came off as strong. That's why I loved him."

Truitt stood. "Nadianna," he said. "I need you to think carefully. Did anyone see you leave the house? Can anyone confirm that you were out of the house when that shot went off?"

She looked at him, confused. "I don't know. I don't remember seeing anyone."

Truitt instinctively glanced in the direction of Zilah Greene's house, but it was blocked from view by the stone wall. From his billfold he pulled out a business card.

"I'm gonna have one of my men take you down for a formal statement, but here, Nadianna, take this. She's a good lady. I want you to give her a call. She works for the state and will be able to help you get over Martin's death."

Nadianna looked at him with a wonder that left him feeling ashamed.

"Get over his death," she whispered. "I don't need no lady to get me over his death. I need my baby. And I need to make my way."

The "back bedroom" of the Robertson house ended up being an oblong space carved out of the right-hand pen and what used to be the tail end of the central dogtrot. The only way into the room was through what Jen Butler called the library, a small but richly finished room with more game boards than books. Jen knocked on the bedroom door and, without waiting for an answer, poked her head into the room.

"Grandpa," she said. "There's a lady here who'd like to see you. She lives over in Statlers Cross and she's writing a book. You feel up to it?"

Gale heard a grumble, but she couldn't discern any words. Jen wrinkled her nose.

"It's okay," she said. "He's always like that. You go on in. I'll just ask that you be aware of how he feels. If he seems tired . . ."

Gale nodded. "I won't stay long. I only have a few questions." She put the satchel on the floor and knelt beside Katie Pru. "Now listen, ladybug. We're going to go in to see a man who may not be used to children. I want you to—"

"Oh, you don't need to do that," Jen said. "Why don't you let her stay with me?"

Gale looked uncertain. "I didn't come over here to take advantage . . ."

Jen waved her hand. "Don't be silly. Before I got married I was a kindergarten teacher. Four-year-olds are my specialty." She knelt beside Gale and took Katie Pru's hand. "In fact," she said, "I've had a hankering to make Play-Doh cookies, Katie Pru. Would you like to help me make some?" When Katie Pru nodded, Jen stood up and started leading her away from Gale. "Great. Then you come on with me to the kitchen and let's let your mommy get some work done."

Gale waited until the other woman's peppy chatter dwindled to a muffle. Then she picked up her satchel and pushed open the bedroom door.

"Mr. Hinson?"

The room had two windows, one on the narrow west wall and a second set at a close angle to it on the long wall that was the rear of the house. Both of these were curtained with a heavy print material. Spanning the corner between these two windows was a plump armchair, its leaf pattern barely recognizable in the gloom. The room was darkly paneled, giving the space the feel of dusk. Gale could make out the footboard of a bed and the dim gleam of sheets, but beyond that detail was lost. She heard a faint sough, like a wave rolling over pebbles. She moved further into the room.

"Mr. Hinson? Are you awake?"

She jumped as a loud clap cracked the hush. A small lamp beside the bed switched on. An ancient figure was propped up against the pillows, a cat slumped over his chest. The soughing sound came from the cat—unlike Gale, it seemed unperturbed by the sudden noise.

A wheezy crackle broke from Hinson's mouth.

"Scared you? Jen bought me the damn thing."

He clapped again and the room descended once more into darkness. Gale pointed her hands toward the lamp and smacked them together. The light turned on.

The old man laughed again. "Not bad," he said. "Gotta have a good clap." The chuckle sighed into a growl. "I told Jen I didn't want any visitors. That girl doesn't pay attention."

"I think she probably does," Gale said. "She just feels confident in her ability to judge a visitor's worth to you."

Hinson was silent a second. "You're right," he said. "And you're a bold thing to say it."

"If you'd really rather not have any visitors, Mr. Hinson, I'll leave. But I have a problem and you're the only person who can help me." She paused. "My name is Gale Grayson. I'm Ella Alden's granddaughter."

"I don't know an Ella Alden."

"You knew a Linnie Cane. Ella is her niece."

The glow from the lamp wasn't substantial, but she thought he sunk further into his pillows. He lay inert except for his finger which scratched nervously at the sheets.

"The light's shitty in this room," he said. "Come over here where I can see you."

There was another clap, this time of thunder. After the lull a sudden rain clacked against the windows. Gale walked to the bedside and stood awkwardly, wondering why Jen had not bothered to put a chair on this side of the room for visitors. Because there were no visitors, she answered herself. For thirty years she had moved in and out of Statlers Cross, and she had never heard Malcolm Hinson's name mentioned in anything but the past tense. In a town the size of Statlers Cross, it seemed inconceivable that someone could just disappear. But then, Malcolm Hinson was an intruder, and a bothersome one at that. Perhaps he found the blithe Jen and his cat better company than the resentful Southerners of his earlier years.

"My God."

His hand had fallen on the cat, who purred roughly. He lifted a crooked finger of his other hand and waved it toward her.

"You look just like her," he breathed. "Maybe shorter. And a touch older. But other than that . . . my God."

"I look like who, Mr. Hinson?" Gale asked gently.

He dropped his hand back to the sheet. "You damn well know who. Don't turn stupid on me. You're not that damn Jen."

"You're right. I'm sorry." She looked at the chair on the other side of the room. "Are you agreeing to talk with me, then? Because if you are, I'm going to pull that chair over here so I can sit down."

"All right. Just don't think that means I have a lot of time. I don't. And I may not answer what you ask."

"That's fine." Gale slid the satchel out of the way beneath the bed and, lifting the chair off the floor to protect the boards, hauled it across the room. She angled it so that the light shone equally on them both and then plopped down into the cushions.

When she looked back up at him, he was staring at her face. "Same eyes. Same chin," he said. "A few more years and she might have had that same strange light and dark hair. What a peculiar way to gray. Makes me wonder what's in your past."

"It's not my past that's bothering me, Mr. Hinson. I want to talk about Linnie."

"If you think Linnie's not your past," he answered softly, "then you're lost indeed."

"What can you tell me about her?"

"Nothing."

She ran her finger over the outline of a leaf in the fabric of the chair. "I have a coverlet she made. It's extraordinary, really. The skill it took to produce it—I weave and I can't even comprehend it."

His hand slid over the cat's back. "You weave?"

"I used to. But I look at Linnie's coverlet and it's like nothing I've ever seen. Her talent was immense, Mr. Hinson. You knew that at the time, didn't you."

"I knew shit at the time."

She looked him full in the eye. "Linnie committed suicide, Mr. Hinson. My husband did as well, and it's taken me a long time to . . . well, I still don't understand it. But something about Linnie's suicide disturbs me."

"All suicides disturb."

"No, not like this. First there was the timing—the afternoon before she was to play the lead in the town pageant. And there was her son. She washed his hands and face. Why? Why would that be the thing you do before killing yourself?"

"Why couldn't a mother choose to say good-bye to her child with a motherly act?"

She drew her finger along the leaf's stem and followed the curve of its line to its point. "It's possible," she said. "Do you happen to know which room she locked him in?"

His eyes didn't waver from her face. "Why else do you doubt her suicide?"

"I found something in the attic of your photography studio."

She reached under the bed and dragged the satchel out. Carefully she lifted the gnawed script into her lap.

"You saved this on purpose, didn't you?" she asked softly.

The cat yowled. Hinson had dug his fingers harshly into her fur. The animal flipped back and forth before scratching the old man's hand and running from the room.

"Did you find anything else?" he whispered.

Gale gently rifled through the pages until she came to the letter. She held it up to him.

"Linnie didn't commit suicide, did she, Mr. Hinson? Her husband murdered her. My question is, why on earth didn't you tell someone?"

"What the hell does it matter now?"

Gale flashed with rage. "It matters, Malcolm. Introducing suicide into a family opens a door. Damn it all, it opens a door and if it doesn't get shut, children, grandchildren, great-grandchildren—they can all fall through it."

Zilah pulled her kitchen chair over to the counter, sat down, and rested her head against the cool stainless steel of the sink. There had been a knock at the door, but she had ignored it. Let them think she had gone to bed. She was tired. She felt as though the air had been taken out of her, as if the voices she had heard two days before had stolen all her breath.

"Martin," the girl had said. "Sit down with me. Let's sit down and think this out."

"I can't believe you're going to do it, Nadianna. I love you. How can you do it?"

The windows had been open, an electrical cord running over the sill, across the porch, and through the grass to the side of the house. Zilah sat in the swing, her shoes making padded thumps on the planks as she slowly rocked back and forth. Inside the Canes' den, the girl stood up from the sofa, her long, strange clothes brushing her ankles. When she spoke, her words were hushed and hurried.

"Listen to me, Martin," the girl said. "I love you, but I love this baby, too. And you will have to take care of it and be a daddy to it. That's all there is to it."

"Bitch. Why don't I just give you the gun now and let you finish me off?"

"Martin." The girl reached out to him, clutching

his shirtsleeve. He jerked free of her and raised his hand abruptly to strike. The girl recoiled, fear on her face. From around the side of the house came the rumbling chords of the choir like a hundred feet on the earth. Martin stopped and turned toward the sound. And then he was gone, the thud of his footsteps running up the stairs. The girl stood in the den, hands to her face, looking around the room in confusion. Zilah gripped the swing chain, and willed it to stop. The girl was suddenly in front of her, rushing down the porch stairs, disappearing in the field among the cars. Zilah sat in silence, an uneasiness rankling her chest. And then the gunshot, so loud and near that the wood above her head rattled.

She was tired now. Outside, the storm tossed the top of the trees and spiked the sky with fierce bolts. The thunder was immediate. Light. Crack. The pattern played over and over through her house until she closed her eyes and let her forehead loll back and forth across the metal.

Flowers at the sill—big blue flowers she could reach out and touch. There were no screens, and black bugs crawled over the sill and down the wall, sometimes running over her feet as she stood. The air at the window was cool, and when her mother worked in the room, Zilah liked to hold on to the frame and let the wind blow in her face.

She liked to watch the house next door. A boy lived there, and he played under the tree. Sometimes he would see her in the window and run across the yard to give her a present—a twig, a rock, a long blade of grass. When he was in his house, he would run to a room upstairs and pull back the curtains and wave at her. She would wave back. The boy was her friend.

The boy didn't wave today. He stood at the window, but he was very still. He pressed his face against the glass. She didn't like the look on his face. It made her sick.

*She could hear yelling from inside the house. The
boy's mother was yelling.*

*Her own mother called to her from the other side
of the room. "Come away from the window, Zilah. It's
not our business."*

*But the boy didn't leave his window, and Zilah
held on to the sill, even though there was no wind to
blow in her face.*

*The yelling stopped and the back door swung open.
The boy's father came out of the house. He had the
mother by the hair. Around her mouth was a piece of
cloth.*

"The first person you need to understand is Parrish. I've
never known a man so vital. It was his upbringing. He
was raised in New York City, his father a painter and
his mother an activist. He claimed his grandmother was
at Seneca Falls, but who knows? All I knew was that he
was the most energetic, most robust man I'd ever met.
He talked me into coming down here—said I needed to
head south and put my talent to some use. He fired me
up. I went. And once I was down here I wrote him and
said, 'All right, you son of a bitch, you talked me into it.
Now you come.'

"And he did. I don't know what he thought he'd
do—get material, I suppose, and go back north with a
story that no one could surpass. And he sure got one.
But he never went back home, and believe me, he never
told the story. He didn't have the heart. All the heart
had been bled out of him by this godforsaken place.

"I never figured out why he got married except that
men get horny far from home. I don't believe he loved
his wife. And I think that even back then he would have
divorced her if things had been different. But they
weren't.

"He saw Linnie as a challenge. She was so angry.
People used to talk about it. 'Stay clear of Linnie. She'll
bite your head off.' She wasn't a particularly beautiful

woman—like you, she was pretty, but Parrish had had prettier women in New York. But one thing no one ever disputed was the fact that she was smart. Smart as a whip. Her anger was smart. You could look in her eyes and know a million thoughts were going through her head and she was livid—livid at you, at the world, at God Almighty for not letting her get them out.

"I don't know when they fell in love. It had been going on a couple of months before Parrish told me. I told him he was an idiot. I said, 'Men down here will get a rope and put it around your neck for being such a fool.' But I was wrong. Parrish wasn't the one who had to worry."

The boy's mother fought. She broke free and ran for the railroad tracks, but the father caught her. She tried to pull the cloth from her mouth. But the father grabbed her arms and held them behind her back. He pushed her with his stomach toward the tree.

"Zilah, come over here. Whatever's going on out there is Alden business. It's nothing to do with us. We work for food to put in our mouths. That's all we need to do. They want to fight, let them fight."

The boy in the window was watching. He could see past the branches of the tree. His hands came up to the glass. He hit and hit and hit the window.

"He was going to take her to New York. I told him he was crazy. What would little country Linnie Cane do in New York City? He said his mother would adore her, that she would take her and educate her and then there would be nothing stopping her. I said, 'God, Parrish, you're treating her like a circus act.' And he said, 'Malcolm, you don't see her, do you? You can't see beyond the clothes and the dialect and the manner.' And I said, 'You think she's going to like you changing her?' But he never answered. It was like they had both gotten caught up and couldn't see the consequences.

"They were going to take Linnie's five-year-old son with them. Like Justin Cane was going to let them just walk out the door. It was like they were both demented—deluded with possibility. They had it planned. The day after the pageant, I was going to the mill to take photos. Parrish was to act as my assistant. When the train pulled up, Linnie and the boy were to walk over, and just as it was about to leave, the three of them were going to jump aboard. I kept telling him, 'Life isn't that forgiving. The payment will be enormous.' But he wouldn't listen. He was eaten up with her."

The rope was around the mother's neck before Zilah saw it. The look on the mother's face changed. It was just like the look on the little boy's. He pounded on the window, and his mouth opened and shut. Zilah couldn't hear what he said.

A man came running into the yard and tried to grab the rope. But the father pushed him down.

"Get away, Deak! They was planning on stealing my boy!"

The man sat in the grass, his hands on his face. The father took the other end of the rope and draped it over the limb of the tree. Then he pulled it and pulled it until the mother's feet left the ground. She kicked and tried to take the rope from her neck, but he grabbed her hands and held them behind her back. She twisted so much Zilah thought she was going to break the branch, but she didn't. Soon the twisting slowed. And then it stopped.

"Zilah, why are you crying? Come over here to me. Zilah, Zilah, Zilah. Zilah, Zilah, love."

"Parrish knew. He came to me, crying. But by then his wife was pregnant. He had to make a choice. He could tell everyone what he knew and maybe be lynched. Or he could swallow it. He swallowed it. But it didn't go down.

"He found the letter in the script—Justin must have left it during rehearsal and forgotten where it was. Parrish, of course, had never received the letter. We never knew how Justin got ahold of it. I said, 'Keep it. It's proof. You may decide to use it someday.' But he didn't. He raised his child, provided for his wife.

"He told me once he wished he'd gone ahead and let them lynch him. 'It would have been a quicker strangulation,' he said. And I couldn't argue."

Light. Crack. The metal beneath Zilah's head had grown hot. She tried to lift her hands to the sink to push herself away, but they wouldn't move. They were heavy, much too heavy to hold.

Leave her alone, Zilah. She's evil. Ghosts are evil. But her daddy didn't know. And her mother didn't see. It was left to Zilah to remember, and she had done well. *Haven't I, Miss Linnie? Haven't I done well?*

Zilah's chest began to hurt. She felt it tightening, tightening. It was splitting, like the ribs were breaking one by one and stabbing it like a knife. She tried to catch her breath, but she couldn't.

Her head, then her body slumped to the floor. Light. Crack.

Nobody ever thinks about the family of a ghost.
—Victory Alden to her sister Maralyn
   Nash while visiting their mother Ella
   in the hospital, 1989

23

From the dry safety of the Ella's back porch, Truitt watched the Greene house, its darkened windows obscured by the pitching limbs of the pecan tree. For a split second the sky was noonday-bright, and then came the clap—loud, terrifying, sharp as a bullet. Something close had been hit. But it hadn't been the Greene house. It sat undisturbed on the other side of the fence, still and disquieting.

Truitt had been knocking on Zilah's door when Haskell came running from the Aldens'. The state crime lab had finished the autopsy; the medical examiner had some points to discuss with Truitt and Bingham. In his hand now were the notes from their conversations. He felt sick. Damned if Nadianna wasn't correct. He wouldn't have figured it—after what he'd heard in the past two days about Martin's violence toward others, he wouldn't have banked on the man turning his violence on himself. All it took now was for Zilah to say she had seen Nadianna leave the house before the gunshot, and he could close the case.

"They're in the living room, sir," Haskell said. "All but Mrs. Cane. Mrs. Alden says she took some more tranquilizers and she's too drowsy to come down."

It didn't matter. What Truitt had to tell the women could just as well be done individually. Not that they didn't already know. They had known the instant the rifle went off. As they lifted Martin's corpse on the bed, fumbled with his hands, touched the gun, smeared blood around the room—they knew. It was fantastic, really. Ella Alden's gut must be made of granite.

"Craig," he told Haskell. "I'll handle this. You try and get Mrs. Greene to answer her phone. If she doesn't, run over and see if her car is in the garage. I don't like how she's got no lights on during a storm like this."

Haskell was already dialing as Truitt walked through the kitchen and down the hall. The rain had given the house a peculiar smell, as if the dust on the fish, always old, was now damp. He didn't want to do this. He pitied these women. And he was mad enough at them all to spit.

At the living room door he stopped. Inside, Ella and Maralyn sat on the sofa.

"Where's Sill?" he asked.

Ella answered. "I sent her up to sit with her mother. She doesn't need to be here. Whatever you have to say, it will be to me and Maralyn. We'll tell the others."

Truitt sucked in a deep breath as he took his seat in the peach chair. "I don't think so, Ella, but we'll deal with that later. I've talked with the medical examiner.

He's found physical evidence to suggest Martin committed suicide. And I have a witness who corroborates it."

Ella's question was harsh. "What physical evidence?"

Truitt ignored her and instead looked at Maralyn. She held his gaze. "It's fascinating what y'all did," he said. "I'm still trying to figure it out. It took incredible concentration—you couldn't get flustered, you had to make every second count. But what I don't understand is *why*."

"It was an accident, Alby," Ella insisted. "If you have physical evidence to prove otherwise, it's wrong."

His eyes were still locked on Maralyn's. "Somebody in that room knew enough about forensics—or at least had an uncanny amount of common sense—to figure that with a high-velocity rifle wound, we'd have a near impossible job of proving the circumstances of death except by focusing on the scene. So what did you do? You wrecked the scene, disturbed the body so there was no way to reconstruct the event, and did it all in a manner that could, on the fringes of reason, have been a natural reaction. Haven't women in these parts always laid out the body? So what if there was a little craziness—you were just doing what came naturally. But I still don't know why, Maralyn. It would help me—and yourselves—if you would at least explain to me why."

"You don't know what you're talking about, Alby," Ella insisted. "I want to know what physical evidence you have."

"His arms," Truitt said baldly. "The M.E. said that in all the years he's done autopsies on suicides who used rifles, there is usually very little blood on the arms. They're stretched out below their heads when they pull the trigger, you see. There was blood on Martin's arms, Ella, but somebody put it there."

" 'Usually' doesn't sound incontrovertible to me, Alby. We'll fight it."

Truitt smiled. "I know, Ella. But I also have a witness—perhaps two. One of them spoke with Martin right before the gunshot. She says he told her he was going to commit suicide."

For the first time Maralyn spoke. "Who?"

Truitt shook his head. "I'm not ready to say, yet. But she's made a very compelling statement. Given Martin's personality, his stake in the community, the time and place—all those people, all those eyes on him—it makes sense to me. And unwittingly, Ryan Teller had upped the stakes. What I want from you now is the truth about what you did."

"We've told you, Alby," Ella said. "We were in the kitchen when the gun went off. We ran upstairs and found him dead in the bedroom. Gun-cleaning supplies were on the bedside table. Maybe we lost control a little bit. But anything we did would be understandable—to any person with feeling."

"A person with feeling." Truitt rubbed his eyes. "Ella, I called a buddy of mine in the Walton County sheriff's department and told him about this case. Know what he said to me? He'd have arrested all of you the first night. I screwed up. I'm just damned lucky you were covering up a suicide and not a murder."

"How dare you accuse us of a cover . . ."

Truitt's temper flared. "Oh, come on, Ella. Your own daughter's admitted that much to my deputy. She told him that you instructed the oil and rags be put on the bedside table, but that she hid them in Cammy's bag at the last minute."

Ella glared at Maralyn. "You said that?"

"We didn't need to be messed up in insurance fraud, Mother. I took the purse down the stairs with me and hid it in the sofa cushions. If Martin's insurance company could prove fraud, we'd all be in jail. Besides, the oil and rags don't have . . ."

Ella turned back to Truitt. "Money had nothing to do with it. If fraud is what you're concerned about, Alby, I'll sign a statement right now saying we won't accept a dime in insurance money."

"Pretty cool, Ella, but I figured money had nothing

to do with it. So why don't you tell me what *was* behind it?"

Silence. Truitt reached into his pocket and pulled out Nadianna's photographs. Martin's face stared out over the food table. Truitt thought he now understood the expression in his old friend's eyes—shock, alarm and an overlying resignation. The truth was Martin had committed suicide the millisecond the shutter clicked; the decision had been made. Truitt was willing to bet he wore the same expression the instant the bullet entered his skull. Truitt's throat burned as he laid the photo on the coffee table. He wouldn't have thought it of Martin. It just didn't seem in his character.

"This man was my friend, Ella," he said quietly. "I abandoned him. The least I owe him is the truth about his death."

It was Maralyn who finally spoke. She reached over and clasped Ella's hand.

"Mother," she said wearily. "This isn't getting us what we wanted. I'm going to tell him."

"But Sill—"

"Sill's going to have to deal with it her own way."

Maralyn stuck her hand into her pants pocket and pulled out a tissue. She carefully wiped her mouth.

"You're right, Alby. We knew as soon as we heard the rifle go off. Maybe we had known all day. Martin had been in a mood—nervous, angry and, yes, I'd say depressed. Sill should have known better than to do what she did, but recently she'd grown more and more combative toward Martin. I'm not blaming her, I'm just saying this time she went too far. I don't think he could take it. It was humiliating for him, for his own daughter to defy him in that manner in front of everyone. I think he decided, 'Hell, I'll just show everybody.' Some people commit suicide out of anger, you know. And Martin's always been angry."

Truitt stared down at the photograph. She was right—there was anger there, too. "Go on."

"What I'm going to tell you now might be difficult

to understand, Alby. There's probably only a handful of people who can relate to it. I sincerely hope so."

"Maralyn, please . . ." Ella's voice was an entreaty.

Maralyn laced her mother's arm through her own and continued. "Any family who endures a suicide is scarred, Alby. One suicide makes another more likely. But imagine what it's like when the suicide becomes part of the town lore, the local entertainment. Imagine what it's like to have your family's tragedy as everyone else's campfire story. It's worse than gossip or whispers. When I was growing up, teenage boys used to come by on Halloween with dresses on and ropes around their necks. I would laugh, but it scared me, Alby. In my heart I always knew if Linnie could do it, I could do it, too."

Truitt realized with a shock that she was crying.

"One suicide makes another more likely," Ella repeated hoarsely. "Are you hearing that, Alby? Are you listening to what we're saying?"

Outside, thunder slapped against the side of the house, vibrating the walls. *My mother died in an automobile accident . . .* Gale's voice had been so matter-of-fact, as he would have expected from someone raised by a grandmother who distanced her from her mother's death.

Jesus Christ. He looked down at the coffee table, searching for the smiling little girl in her bathing suit. "Ella, are you telling me your daughter Kathleen . . . ?"

Maralyn interrupted. "We don't know, Alby. She and Gale's father were on the verge of a divorce. Her car hit the base of an overpass on I-75 late one night. The police said she must have fallen asleep at the wheel. But we don't know. And it terrified us."

"Does Gale know?"

"No. And please don't tell her."

"I watched Linnie's son grow into a bitter, mean man who abused Martin," Ella said. "My mother and sister struggled with what Linnie left us, and I watched my own daughters struggle, too. I tried my best to keep

Gale separated from it. But I couldn't do anything to help Sill. Until now, Alby. Don't make her live with a suicide as a father."

"But she knows, Ella. She was in the room when you covered it up."

Ella's eyes shone as she leaned toward him. "But she doesn't know for sure. If you and Johnny Bingham rule it an accident, she'll believe you. She can get on with her life."

"But she'll still think her argument caused Martin to take out his gun . . ."

"But we can deal with that, Alby. Being responsible for an accident isn't the same as dealing with a suicide. Please, Alby. You admitted you owed Martin. Pay him back with this."

He did owe Martin. Gently, he picked up the final photograph. He had always been so intent on the face that he had merely scanned the rest of the photo—the stretched skin around Martin's knuckles as his hand curled into a fist, the sweat around the belly of his shirt, the head of the roasted pig just visible at the bottom, a woven vine circling its neck.

Truitt's throat went dry.

"Maralyn," he said softly. "Tell me again what the four of you were doing when the gun went off."

At first he thought the noise was thunder, strange and strangled. Then he recognized it—the grind of an engine. He rose from his chair as Sill walked into the room, her face pale and confused.

"Mother's left," she stammered. "We could hear you through the vent. She took the keys from your purse, Ella . . ."

Truitt ran from the room, shouting for Haskell. There was no answer. He yanked open the front door and raced through the yard. Rain slashed at his face. He climbed into his car and turned the ignition as Ella's Buick bumped over the railroad tracks.

He wheeled around the gravel drive and lurched across the tracks. The sky was dark; the Buick had vanished in the murk ahead of him. Gathering speed, he passed the stores, thankful that the rain and early shop hours had vacated the street. He passed the cemetery, the churches, straining to catch a glimpse of the car in front of him. Nothing. In the distance he thought he heard sirens, but he wasn't certain. He was reaching for his phone when suddenly the Buick was there, less than ten yards away, its turn signal politely flashing. As he slammed on his brakes, the Buick crossed back over the tracks.

He followed cautiously. At the top of the tracks he watched the Buick ease up the Canes' driveway and disappear behind the house. His deputy stationed outside the house got out of his car; Truitt flashed his lights, waved him back inside, and slowly started down the drive.

The Buick was parked beside the fish house. At the barbecue pit Truitt braked. With his car door as a shield, he slid from his car.

"Cammy!" he yelled. "Can you hear me?"

Silence from the fish house. The space between the shack and the barbecue pit was not more than twenty yards, but it was open ground. He pulled his revolver from his shoulder holster. He had no way of knowing if she had a gun. But he was pretty damn sure she knew how to use one.

"Cammy," he repeated. "It's Alby. Let me come in and talk to you."

More silence. He twisted around to see if his deputy had followed him into the yard. He had; the brown-clad figure crouched at the side of the main house.

Then he heard a scraping sound from the shack, like a chair dragged across cement. A few seconds later she called out to him.

"Alby? I need a couple of minutes. Can you give me that?"

"Sure, Cammy, I can do that. But I'd like it better if you'd let me sit with you."

For a long moment she didn't answer. "You know what, Alby? I think I'd like that."

"Have you got a gun, Cammy?"

Her laugh was faint; he could barely hear it above the rain. 'No, I don't have a gun. I hate the things, don't you know that?"

He looked over at his deputy, who pulled out his revolver and aimed it at the fish house. His own gun extended in front of him, Truitt dashed to the shack and peered inside through the screen.

She sat on a picnic bench, her hands folded on the table in front of her. She gave him a sad smile as he returned his gun to his holster and entered the shack.

"I was hoping to have enough time to think about how I wanted to tell you, but I guess you would prefer I not do that. I've had two days to come up with the right words, but I thought Ella would be able to pull it off. I never thought Ella would fail at anything."

He took a folded aluminum chair from against the wall and placed it near her. "What did she fail at, Cammy?"

"The cover-up. That's what you called it, isn't it? It's the funniest thing, Alby. It just fell in my lap. It would never occur to me to lie—at least, not at the time. But there they all were, in the room, Ella saying do this and do that, and I thought, 'God's going to save me. He's going to save me after all.' "

"Cammy, I need to tell you about your rights . . ."

She waved her hand at him. "Don't be silly, Alby."

"You need to talk to a lawyer . . ."

"I don't need a lawyer. I killed my husband. It was a mistake. I'm very sorry."

"Cammy, come with me. Let me take you to my office so you can call someone to help you."

"No, Alby." Her voice was soft and a little patronizing. "You wanted to come in and sit with me. Now sit. I thought I could lie. I thought, well, if all these other women are lying, I can do it, too. But I can't. And after I heard what Ella was planning to do to Sill, I won't. Sill's not responsible for her daddy's death and I won't have her thinking she was."

She picked at a hole in the red-checked tablecloth, making it large enough to stick the length of her finger underneath the plastic. "You know what, Alby? There must be something about me and kitchens. You remember those mornings you'd come over to the house to hunt? You and Martin would sit down at the table and eat like I wasn't even there, like I'd gone invisible or something. The same thing happened Saturday evening. I had gone out to put the wreath on the pig when Martin and Sill had their argument. I was standing at the back door, about to go back inside. Martin walked right past me. I followed him in, then Sill came into the house. She and Ella started having a fight, and I went into the hall to find Martin. I wanted to talk with him. I thought that maybe if he knew about Sill's baby, about all the stress she's been under, he'd be kinder to her."

She pushed her finger against the plastic. It held firm. "When I got to the hallway, I could hear voices. Martin and a woman. Thing was, nothing she said surprised me. I think if I had been surprised I wouldn't have killed him. But I knew Martin had been cheating on me. You know how they say something snaps in you? Well, that's exactly what it's like. I could hear the snapping sound in my head. So when the woman left, I followed him up the stairs. He was in the bedroom, sitting on the bed. He didn't even look up until I had the gun pointing at him. And then he didn't say anything. He just gave me this blank stare, like he didn't even know who I was.

"After I did it, I ran into the bathroom. Then all of a sudden Ella and them were in the bedroom. I didn't know what they were doing at first—messing things up, moving Martin to the bed. And then I understood. They thought it was suicide. I just started praying. I went into the room, and the craziness just took me over. They never doubted I had come up the stairs with them. Later that night at Ella's house, we talked about what we were going to tell you. Ella wanted us to say exactly what we were doing when the gun went off so we wouldn't be caught in a lie. I told them I was in the kitchen corner, working on the wreath. They believed me. They didn't even know I had left."

The plastic strained against her finger, the red stretching to white. Abruptly, her finger burst through. She withdrew her hand and gave him a weak smile.

"There was only one thing I could do, Alby. Sleep. I figured if I fell asleep Ella would take care of things. But I couldn't let her blame Sill. I had to protect my baby."

Truitt stood and walked to the fish house door. Outside two department cars had pulled up beside the pit.

"What about Nadianna's baby?" he asked heavily. "You knew she was pregnant, yet you tried to implicate her in the murder."

She stared at him, astonished. "Well, she *is* guilty, isn't she, Alby? She decided to have an affair with my husband. If it hadn't been for her, I'd have never shot him. Did they think they could just mess around and take everything away from me? I'm a good woman, Alby. I've made it my life to be good."

I dunno—some old ghost story. Or shit like it.
> —Charlie Perkins, when asked by his
> social studies teacher if he had ever
> heard of a local character named
> Linnie Cane, 1993

Epilogue

Gale was in a dead sleep when the phone rang. The fear was sharp and instant—it was still dark outside, no one should be calling, where the hell was Katie Pru? She struggled to a sitting position from her pallet on the floor and fumbled for the phone.

"Gale? Just thought I'd call and check on you."

She slumped against the side of the den sofa and stretched her arm up to feel for her daughter. She was there, breathing steadily under the sheets.

"Daniel? Are you all right?"

"Fine." He sounded ... flat. She searched for a better word. He sounded deadpan.

"Why are you calling? What time is it anyway?"

"I don't know about there. Here it's ten A.M. Let's see that would make it about . . ."

"Five in the morning. You're such a turd." She could almost hear him grinning. Policemen, she thought, have such futile senses of humor. She positioned herself more comfortably against the sofa.

"Okay, turnabout's fair play. Although it was rather brave of you. How did you know I wouldn't be in a house full of sleeping women?"

"You said as much in your fax. . . . I didn't know there was a fax machine in Bump-Yer-Arse, Georgia."

"Only one, but you have to keep shooing chickens off it."

"Ah, that indomitable Grayson spirit." He grew sober. "I spent some time trying to read between the lines of your message, Gale. Couldn't quite figure the tone. How are you doing?"

She pulled Linnie's coverlet from the arm of the sofa, draped it over her knees. "It's hard to say. Sad. Not grief-stricken exactly. More resigned. I mean, it happens. Spouses sometimes kill each other. It's a very old story."

There was silence on the other end of the line. "But there is more here," he finally said.

"Yes." There was more, but she didn't want to think about it. "We had back-to-back funerals yesterday. First Martin, then Zilah Greene. Ryan tried to talk Zilah's daughters into delaying the funeral a day, but they insisted. It was poignant, actually. I don't know how many people in this town ever gave Zilah more than two seconds' thought, but they were all there, along with half the county."

"You went to the services?" he asked gently.

"I went." She rubbed the coarse fabric of the coverlet against her cheek. She didn't tell him she had quietly cried during both services, something she had never done before. And she didn't like to admit even to herself that her tears were more for Linnie than Martin.

"Cammy's stuck by her story, which has had an interesting effect on Ella. She was so certain Martin killed himself." Gale took a deep breath. "I was, too," she said softly. "It just seemed so likely to me. Anyway, Ella's lawyer's confident no judge in these parts is going to be tough on her destroying the crime scene, but she's irritated as hell that she was wrong about something. She's spending a couple of days with Sill and Faith in Atlanta, making sure Sill's okay. Not that I'm worried about Sill. Faith is such a strong woman. . . ."

She was rambling. She had heard women ramble in the face of grief—she had memories of Ella, so bereaved after Nora's death that she sat with her guests at the dining room table, droning on, unaware she was stirring her hot tea with a chicken bone. The difference was Gale's rambling sprang not from sorrow but fear. She looked at her daughter, still asleep under the sheets. Tears filled her eyes.

"Gale . . ."

"The door's been opened for Katie Pru, Daniel." Her voice was a whisper. "Ella was right. My family grew up thinking Linnie committed suicide, and it directed everything they did. Tom opened the door for Katie Pru and I don't think I'm going to be able to shut it."

"You shut it for yourself. It wasn't easy dealing with Tom's death, but you did. You can shut the door for her."

"But I shut it for myself because of her. It won't be as simple for her."

"It'll be simpler. She won't be doing it alone. She'll have a damn good mother to help her."

The light through the ceiling windows had turned white by the time she hung up the phone. She leaned her head against Katie Pru's arm and closed her eyes. The house was silent around her—the peculiar silence of an unfamiliar space. Perhaps Ella had it right. She wasn't of this place after all.

Beneath her arm, Katie Pru stirred. She opened her eyes, looked at Gale, and smiled.

"Good morning, Mama. You're not the Blue Lady. The jag-wire told me so."

Gale gently tickled her daughter's chin. "And who, please, ma'am, is the Blue Lady?"

Katie Pru squirmed as she giggled. "The Blue Lady's sad. Nadianna knows all about the Blue Lady. She'll tell you the story. She's coming over today. You said so."

"You know what Nadianna told me the other day? She was looking at this coverlet and she said she'd like to learn to weave."

"I remember you weaving," Katie Pru said. "It sounded like sticks whispering."

Gale laughed. "You're right, baby. That's exactly what it sounds like. Nadianna said she'd come tell you stories and help look after you if I'd teach her to weave. What do you think about that?"

Katie Pru thought a second. "It's good," she decided. "But no more Blue Lady stories."

"No more Blue Lady stories. We'll tell her those are done."

ABOUT THE AUTHOR

Teri Holbrook is a former journalist who lives in Atlanta with her cartoonist husband and their two children.

BANTAM OFFERS THE FINEST IN CLASSIC AND MODERN BRITISH MURDER MYSTERIES

C. C. BENISON

Her Majesty Investigates

____57476-0 DEATH AT BUCKINGHAM PALACE $5.50/$7.50
____57477-9 DEATH AT SANDRINGHAM HOUSE $5.50/$7.50

TERI HOLBROOK

____56859-0 A FAR AND DEADLY CRY $5.50/$7.50
____56860-4 THE GRASS WIDOW $5.50/$7.50

DOROTHY CANNELL

____56951-1 HOW TO MURDER YOUR
         MOTHER-IN-LAW $5.50/$7.50
____29195-5 THE THIN WOMAN $5.50/$7.50
____27794-4 THE WIDOWS CLUB $5.50/$7.50
____29684-1 FEMMES FATAL $5.50/$7.50
____28686-2 MUM'S THE WORD $4.99/$5.99
____57360-8 HOW TO MURDER
         THE MAN OF YOUR DREAMS $5.50/$7.50

Ask for these books at your local bookstore or use this page to order.

Please send me the books I have checked above. I am enclosing $_____ (add $2.50 to cover postage and handling). Send check or money order, no cash or C.O.D.'s, please.

Name _____

Address _____

City/State/Zip _____

Send order to: Bantam Books, Dept. MC 6, 2451 S. Wolf Rd., Des Plaines, IL 60018
Allow four to six weeks for delivery.
Prices and availability subject to change without notice.   MC 6 12/96

ELIZABETH GEORGE

> "George is a master . . . an outstanding practitioner of the modern English mystery."—*Chicago Tribune*

A GREAT DELIVERANCE _____ 27802-9 $6.50/$8.99 in Canada

Winner of the 1988 Anthony and Agatha Awards for Best First Novel.
"Spellbinding . . . A truly fascinating story that is part psychological suspense and part detective story."—*Chicago Sun-Times*

PAYMENT IN BLOOD _____ 28436-3 $6.50/$8.99

"Satisfying indeed. George has another hit on her hands."—*The Washington Post*

WELL-SCHOOLED IN MURDER _____ 28734-6 $6.50/$8.99

"[This book] puts the author in the running with the genre's masters."—*People*

A SUITABLE VENGEANCE _____ 29560-8 $6.50/$8.99

"Both unusual and extremely satisfying ."—*The Toronto Sun*

FOR THE SAKE OF ELENA _____ 56127-8 $6.50/$7.99

"George is . . . a born storyteller who spins a web of enchantment that captures the reader and will not let him go."—*The San Diego Union*

MISSING JOSEPH _____ 56604-0 $5.99/$7.99

"A totally satisfying mystery experience."—*The Denver Post*

PLAYING FOR THE ASHES _____ 57251-2 $6.50/$8.99

"Compelling...infinitely engrossing..."—*People*

Ask for these books at your local bookstore or use this page to order.

Please send me the books I have checked above. I am enclosing $_____ (add $2.50 to cover postage and handling). Send check or money order, no cash or C.O.D.'s, please.

Name _____

Address _____

City/State/Zip _____

Send order to: Bantam Books, Dept. EG, 2451 S. Wolf Rd., Des Plaines, IL 60018
Allow four to six weeks for delivery.
Prices and availability subject to change without notice.   EG 11/95

Edgar Award Winner!

LAURIE R. KING

Kate Martinelli Mysteries

A Grave Talent

THE UNTHINKABLE has happened in a small community outside of San Francisco. A series of shocking murders has occurred, each victim a child. And to bring the murderer to justice, Detective Kate Martinelli must delve into a dark past—even if it means losing everything she holds dear. . . . ___57399-3 $5.50/$6.99 in Canada

To Play the Fool

WHEN A BAND of homeless people cremate a beloved dog in San Francisco's Golden Gate Park, the authorities are willing to overlook a few broken regulations. But three weeks later, when the dog's owner gets the same fiery send-off, the SFPD has a real headache on its hands. The autopsy suggests homicide, but to prove it Inspector Kate Martinelli will find herself thrust along a twisting road to a disbanded cult, long-buried secrets, and the hunger for bloody vengeance. ___57455-8 $5.50/$7.50 in Canada

Ask for these books at your local bookstore or use this page to order.

Please send me the books I have checked above. I am enclosing $___ (add $2.50 to cover postage and handling). Send check or money order, no cash or C.O.D.'s please.

Name _____

Address _____

City/State/Zip _____

Send order to: Bantam Books, Dept. MC 12, 2451 S. Wolf Rd., Des Plaines, IL 60018
Allow four to six weeks for delivery.
Prices and availability subject to change without notice.   MC 12 6/96